Draft Pick Season One: Carver

DRAFT PICK

DARIE MCCOY

Edited by: All That's Wright

Cover Art/Design: A.S. McCoy

For the nerdy girls. I see you. Also, for all of the readers who loved and cheered for Carver and Alyssa just as hard as I did.

Prologue

Everyone's eyes were glued to the television as they listened to the commentators reviewing player stats. They waited anxiously for the actual draft to begin. Finally, the commissioner took the stage and Carver asked his girlfriend, Mary Beth to move to allow his mother to sit beside him. His dad stood behind him with his hands on Carver's shoulders.

Unlike most players being considered for the NFL draft, Carver had chosen to have a gathering to watch the televised broadcast rather than attend the event in person. His agent was noticeably unhappy about the decision, but he appeared to have resigned himself to the current arrangement. Sitting in an armchair near Carver's position, he intermittently called out instructions to the small camera crew.

Alyssa watched the scene play out between Carver and Mary Beth as her friend poked her bottom lip out, pouting prettily. A brief scowl flit across Carver's face. It only lasted a few seconds, but it was enough to get Mary Beth moving. Although, she didn't go far. She perched her narrow behind on the arm of the sofa, sliding in as closely as she could in order to stay in the frame of at least one of the cameras operated by the small crew.

Alyssa didn't consider herself a part of that inner circle. So, she sat off to the side sipping her fruity drink. Her thoughts regarding the interaction between Carver and Mary Beth would stay firmly locked inside her brain unless she was asked about it specifically.

Her gaze returned to the large, wall-mounted, flat screen TV just as the commissioner announced the first pick of the 2005 draft. As the analysts predicted, it was him, Tech's starting quarterback—Carver Wyatt Jamieson.

The room erupted in celebration. Camera flashes brightened the room as the video crew documented it all. No doubt it would be replayed on a loop during the endless cycle of sports shows that discussed the NFL draft for days to come. Carver smiled so big; she thought his face might split in two. His parents were alternately hugging him and each other.

Looking up from their embrace, his gaze swept the room as if he were looking for something. Feeling confident in her position on the periphery, she wondered what it could be, but didn't look around to track his stare. When his eyes landed on her, his face splitting smile brightened even more. His excitement was contagious. So, she returned the smile without hesitation. She was genuinely happy for him.

A tug on his arm broke their connection and Alyssa observed Mary Beth trying her best to insert herself into the middle of the circle his parents created. Tossing an arm around her shoulders, Carver pulled her into his side as he answered his cellphone. His mother fanned her hands and used shushing motions to quiet the room as Carver spoke with the owner of the team to which he'd just been drafted.

He was the number one draft pick of a team in the midst of rebuilding. If the sports experts were correct, the team was going to pay him a shit-ton of money to pull the franchise back to greatness. Alyssa was confident he'd do just that.

Her certainty wasn't misplaced. Carver was more than an impressive athlete. He was the total package. A true student of the game, he spent hours weekly pouring over old footage and scouting videos. In addition to his knowledge of the game, he was intelligent, considerate of his teammates, and kind to everyone he met while maintaining the ability to be ferocious when necessary.

Although she knew how he and Mary Beth met, she often

wondered what kept them together. Mary Beth didn't quite match him in more than one of those areas. For all intents and purposes, her friend was in college to find a husband. Actual course study came in at a distant second. She'd never be accused of overtaxing her brain or spending too much time on her lessons, not leaving enough time for him.

She wondered at the tie binding them together, but Alyssa felt it wasn't her place to question their relationship. It wasn't like she wanted to date Mary Beth. Nor had Carver or anyone similar to him ever looked twice at her with more than a passing interest. Not that she lacked male attention. She just wasn't very interested in most of the guys who approached her.

As she watched the room, Carver's cousin slid into the seat next to her. She'd taken up residence at the high-top café style table slightly away from the festivities. Lord...She hoped he wasn't seriously there to hit on her. He was a nice-looking guy, but something about him didn't sit well with her.

"Hey there, beautiful. Why are you sitting over here all alone?"

Working to keep her internal eye roll from becoming an actual eye roll, Alyssa gestured around the room.

"These are the only available seats left." She was polite, but decidedly standoffish.

"Ah... I guess you're right. I hadn't noticed."

His chuckle at her response, came off as disingenuous since not only was her statement not funny, but she hadn't attempted to couch it as a joke. His smile appeared pasted on an otherwise placid looking face.

Studying the contents of her cup as if it held the secrets to deciphering the complex algorithm she had programmed for the final project in her Python class, she mentally wished him away. When she looked up from her cup, he was still there.

His stare tracked her movements as she placed the straw between her lips and drew deeply on the drink. *That's not creepy at all.* The thought crossed her mind accompanied by another internal eyeroll. The slurping noises of the empty cup were a welcome sound.

"Excuse me, I'm going to go get a refill." She scooted forward to step down from the tall chair.

"What are you drinking? I'll get it for you." He offered.

I think the fuck not. The words blared across Alyssa's mind, but instead of giving them voice, she politely declined.

"I appreciate the offer, but I can get it."

Thankfully, he got the hint and slinked away. Relieved that there wouldn't be a scene which turned into a thing to create awkwardness, she left the table and moved into the kitchen.

She was the designated driver, so she restricted herself to mocktails and sodas. Both Mary Beth and Carver had asked her to come tonight, although she couldn't figure out why. One-on-one interactions with Carver were few and far between, even though she never missed a game. Each Saturday, she was right beside her friend cheering him on—no matter what the weather.

At the start of the evening, Alyssa fully expected to drive back to the apartment she shared with Mary Beth alone. She figured her friend would stay with Carver either at the suite or at his apartment. Now, as Mary Beth entered the kitchen with her face pinched in displeasure, Alyssa wasn't so sure.

"Can you believe what just happened!?"

Mary Beth's face flushed and her cheeks pinkened under her peachy complexion. Her fists clenched at her sides as she strode to stand next to Alyssa at the kitchen island.

"What do you mean? Everyone knew Carver would go number one. Why is that a surprise? He's a great quarterback."

Alyssa refilled the ice in her cup before looking over the beverage selection trying to decide if she wanted to continue with the alcohol-free daiquiri mix.

"Not that. We all knew that." Flipping her long straw-colored hair over her shoulder she moved in closer to Alyssa. Glancing over her shoulder before she lowered her voice to continue. "Can you believe he asked me to move so his **mother** could sit beside him? That was supposed to be my spot! I've been his girlfriend for two years now."

She whisper-hissed when she said the word mother, and stopped just shy of stomping her foot with the last sentence. The whine in Mary Beth's voice annoyed her, but Alyssa kept her face neutral. She didn't personally have an issue with Carver wanting his mom beside him at such a crucial moment in his career. She actually expected it. *Why hadn't Mary Beth?*

"Mary Beth, why wouldn't he want his mother beside him?"

"Because! I'm going to be his wife. It should've been me holding his hand while they made the announcement. The same way it's been me for the past two years cheering for him and traveling to support him."

"Wait! Carver asked you to marry him?" Alyssa's eyes widened in excitement.

"Not yet, but I know he will." Mary Beth tipped her chin up as if her words were a foregone conclusion.

Alyssa's surprise melted into confusion. Her brow pinched as she regarded her friend. "How do you know that? Have you guys talked about it? You're still a month out from graduation."

Both Carver and Mary Beth were two years older than Alyssa. Because of the program she enrolled in, she wouldn't graduate until the following spring. When she did, she'd receive her bachelor's and master's degrees on the same day. It was a grueling program, but Alyssa felt it was worth it.

"Oh Alyssa... When you have someone that is into you the way Carver is into me, you'll understand. I'll be his wife. The rest is just minor details."

"Oh. Okay then. If you say so." Far be it for her to tell Mary Beth what could or couldn't happen in her own relationship.

"I do, which is why I'm pissed that I had to perch on the arm of the sofa like some hanger-on instead of being in my rightful place beside him."

"I think you're over-reacting."

"What?! Why?"

"That's his mother, Mary Beth." Alyssa struggled to keep her frustration from showing.

"And?"

Mary Beth's flip reply rubbed Alyssa the wrong way. So much so that she allowed the bridle, she usually kept on herself, to loosen when she responded.

"She's the woman who gave birth to him. The one who wiped his runny nose, patched his boo-boos and did any number of things to get him to this point in his life."

"I nursed him when he was sick and rubbed him down when he was sore, so what's your point?"

Not bothering to correct Mary Beth's statement regarding rubbing him down and nursing him through sickness, Alyssa took a calming breath. Her friend had selective memory. When Carver had soreness in his throwing arm and shoulder, it was Alyssa who rubbed him down—at Mary Beth's insistence. It was also the soup Alyssa made which Mary Beth fed Carver when he was sick.

Maybe merely asking Alyssa to physically do those things was what Mary Beth considered doing it herself. Like hiring staff. Alyssa didn't care for the image that evoked. Mentally, she shook herself and marveled at her friend's ability to hear what Alyssa said while missing the entire point.

"Mary Beth, you've done those things for roughly two years. His mother's been there for him for all twenty-two years of his life. She's the one who trekked all over the city then the country taking him first to practice, then games and God knows what else after that.

She's the one who sacrificed so he could have the opportunity to even be considered for the NFL draft. Her. Not you. Why would you expect to have more importance than her in his life right now?"

"Because! I'm going to be his wife! I should be more important. Aren't you always saying a husband should put his wife first?"

"Yes, but you aren't his wife. Going to be and being are not the same thing. Right now, you're his girlfriend. Girlfriend doesn't come before mother."

"I should have known you'd take his side." Mary Beth crossed her arms over her chest and angled her body away from Alyssa.

Sighing in irritation, Alyssa attempted to speak reasonably to her friend. "I'm not taking sides. I'm just pointing out some things you're over-looking."

"Well, it sounds like you're taking his side."

"Mary Beth, there are no sides here and if you want to know what I really think, I'll tell you."

"Don't stop now. This is apparently dump on Mary Beth night."

Shutting her lids against the wave of annoyance, Alyssa ignored the attempt to manipulate her into feeling guilty. Occasionally, Mary Beth could be self-absorbed. This wasn't the time or the place for her antics.

"I think you should pick your lip up off the floor and go back in that room and support your man. It's not about you right now. This is his moment. Acting this way, trying to make him choose between you and his mother, it won't end well for you. If you can't see that, I don't know what else to tell you."

Lifting her drink from the counter, Alyssa moved around Mary Beth and exited the kitchen. As she crossed the threshold, she almost ran smack into Carver's mother. Mumbling quick apologies, she stepped aside. Walking double-time, she went back to reclaim her seat at the high-top table.

Her cheeks heated with embarrassment as she considered the possibility that Carver's mother overheard them. If she heard even a portion of it, it was a bad look for Mary Beth. For her friend's sake, she hoped Mrs. Jamieson hadn't heard anything. However, Alyssa's gut told her that hope was wishful thinking.

Chapter One

IS THIS SOME KIND OF TEST?

Fifteen years later

"Hey, Mama. I can't talk long. I'm getting ready to go out." Alyssa rushed the words out as soon as she answered the insistently ringing phone.

"You're actually going out?" Surprise, along with disbelief laced her mother's voice.

Alyssa's eyes rolled in exasperation. So what if she didn't like going out all the time or taking the thirty minute drive into Vegas to live it up in the bright lights of Sin City. It didn't mean she was a complete hermit as her mother's question implied.

"Yes, Mama. I'm going out. I have a date with Torrence." Putting the call on speaker, she went back to the task of preparing for her date.

"Oh. Okay. Well, I won't hold you long." The line went silent as Alyssa waited for her mother to get to the point of her call.

She didn't miss the flat tone of her mother's speech when she heard *'going out'* included Torrence. It was no secret that Anna Ripley didn't think Torrence was worth Alyssa's time.

"What's up, Mama?" Alyssa attempted to keep her impatience from carrying over into her words, but her mama's version of not long usually meant at least twenty minutes. She didn't have twenty minutes to dawdle catching up on family gossip—which was usually why her mother called.

"Huh? Oh, sorry. Right. Your father and I were watching one of those sports reporting shows he likes earlier today and I saw your friend Carver. They said he has a new job as the Quarterback Coach with the Las Vegas Ravagers.

I thought to myself, I need to call Alyssa and see why she didn't tell me about it. So...Why didn't you tell me your friend from college was moving out there? You know how we worry about you being in Vegas all by yourself."

Alyssa's lids dropped over her eyes and her head tilted back on her shoulders. "Mama...First of all, Carver Jamieson and I aren't friends. We weren't friends in college. He dated my roommate Mary Beth and was friendly towards me. We weren't friends. Second, I don't follow football like that."

Even as she spoke the words, she knew her assertion of not following football was a blatant lie. She'd been known to rattle off stats better than both of her brothers and her father. Whether her mother would call her on it was the question.

"I had no idea he'd been hired by the Ravagers."

Another lie. She didn't live directly in Vegas, but she was close enough that her local news carried the story of the hotshot former pro-bowler who'd been hired by the Ravagers to spread his quarterback magic onto the struggling offense.

"And Third, I'm not out here by myself. Did you forget that Ulysses and Braxton live in Vegas?"

"Pssh! You know I don't count Ulysses and Braxton. You probably don't even hear from those two until it's close to a holiday and they want you to cook."

Alyssa couldn't dispute her statement since that's exactly when she heard from her two older cousins. Perpetual daters, neither was married and when the holidays rolled around, they either flew back to Georgia or called her to see what her plans were.

"Since when don't you follow football? I had as much trouble prying you away from the television for Sunday dinner as I did your father and the boys."

"I haven't been that into it in a while, Ma." *Why did she keep piling on the lies?* Alyssa had no answer for her sudden aversion to the truth.

"Mhmm. If you say so." It didn't sound as if her mother was buying it. "Back to Carver, I don't think we're remembering the same thing. He was always so nice to you. He talked like y'all were friends whenever we came up to see you at school."

"Mama, that was almost fifteen years ago. A lot can change in that time. Besides, I haven't seen him in a really long time. Why would you think we were friends?"

"Whenever your father brings him up, you always seem to know what's going on. I figured the two of you stayed in touch even after you and Mary Beth fell out. You know, I never liked that girl."

"Mama..."

Alyssa had no desire to go down memory lane about her former friend. Not simply because she didn't have the time, but her mother couldn't seem to stop once she got going on all the ways Mary Beth let Alyssa know they weren't really friends long before Alyssa cut her off.

"Don't Mama me."

"Mama, remember you said you weren't going to hold me long? I need to finish getting dressed." Attempting to thwart a possible lecture, Alyssa reminded her mother about the earlier promise.

"Mhmm. Fine. I'll just tell your daddy you didn't know about Carver, and that's why you didn't say anything." Once again, her mother spoke with the tone of disbelief.

"Okay, Mama. You have a good night. I'll call you in a few days." Relief washed over Alyssa when she realized she'd secured a slight victory. This time.

"Okay, baby. Love you."

"Love you too, Mama. Tell Daddy, I said hey and I love him."

Sighing at her good fortune, Alyssa finished with her date prep. She and Torrence were meeting at one of the casino restaurants at the edge of the Vegas strip. If she didn't get a move on, she'd be late.

She'd never tell her mother, but her level of affection toward Torrence was mediocre. While they had stimulating conversations, there was something holding her back from really seeing things with him moving beyond where they were.

It wasn't physical even though he wasn't the body type she normally went for. Since she found intelligence sexy, she didn't hold his slighter, lanky form against him. When they were together, they were a walking stereotype as one of her thighs was easily larger than both of his put together.

The thing about skinny men being attracted to plus sized women was in full effect. Putting the optics aside, he simply didn't make her stomach flip nor her nethers clench. Like ever. The few times they'd been together sexually had been pleasant but nothing to write home about.

Truth be told, she knew her days of entertaining Torrence were numbered. They'd refrained from saying what they had was an exclusive relationship, but they were approaching the six-month mark. It was time to step up or move on. Sadly, she didn't think it would hurt her feelings a bit if he were to break things off.

Apathy was never a good sign when considering a relationship with someone. Alyssa honestly wasn't sure if she was continuing to see him to prove something to herself or not. Most of her dating eligible life, she seemed to find herself enamored with someone who either didn't acknowledge her existence or only wanted to be friends with benefits. Both situations stung and didn't make the practice very appealing.

With Torrence, they seemed compatible in so many other ways. So what if he didn't make her heart race or her skin tingle. That type of passion fades over time. If she was to be with someone, it shouldn't be based solely on physical attraction.

Still, she knew the lack of passion wasn't an attractive prospect when considering tethering oneself to another person. Heaving a resigned sigh, she gathered her purse and keys before walking out of her townhouse.

Alyssa walked through the archway past the bistro tables sitting just outside the entrance to Wolfgang Puck's Lupo restaurant in the

Mandalay Bay Casino. As far as casino restaurants went, she enjoyed eating here. The prices weren't so outrageous that she'd only delegate it for special occasions. Still, she wasn't inclined to shell out a hundred bucks on one meal very often. So, her visits weren't frequent.

After giving the hostess her name, she was led to a table just off the bar area where Torrence was already seated. Standing as she approached, he pressed a kiss to her cheek and pulled out her chair. While she didn't shrink away from his touch, she didn't lean in to it either.

"You look nice."

His eyes swept over her, examining her from her feet clad in peep toe pumps to the modest vee neck of her dress showing off the tops of her cleavage. She looked better than nice. The dress hugged her curves in all the best ways. Rather than correct him, she replied with a soft thank you as she took a seat in the chair he held out for her. Say what you will about Torrence, he played the gentleman thing to a T. *Most of the time.*

As she picked up the menu, he informed her that he'd already taken the liberty of ordering an appetizer.

"I didn't order your meal though. I know how you like do that yourself."

On the surface, his words appeared polite, but there was an edge to his tone as if he took offense to her having her own mind and ordering what she'd like to eat and not always yielding to what he wanted.

"Thank you." Alyssa replied as she opened the menu perusing it even though she was almost certain she would have the salmon. The question was really if she would pair it with the suggested wine or stick with water.

Their server approached the table just as she opted to forego the wine. Placing the Ciabatta bread appetizer at the center of the table, he pulled out the small folio flipping it open.

"Good evening. Have we decided what we're having tonight?"

"I have. Are you ready, Alyssa?"

Torrence hadn't even opened the menu before him. She figured he'd gotten there far ahead of their agreed upon time if he'd already made his selection. She hadn't arrived early, but she wasn't late either.

"I'm ready." Both men looked at her expectantly, so she lifted the menu once again. "I'll have the Scottish Salmon cooked medium please."

"Yes, ma'am. Would you care for a glass of wine with that? We have an excellent Cabernet Sauvignon that pairs quite well with the Salmon."

Torrence shifted in his seat and cleared his throat at the waiter's suggestion to add wine. He wasn't a fan of wine, but she didn't think his shifting was related to the drink itself. Thinking of the drive home and her potentially full stomach, Alyssa declined the offer with a smile.

"No, thank you. I'll stick with water for the time being."

"Yes, ma'am. And you, sir?"

"I'll have the ravioli. No wine for me either."

"Very good. I'll get this order in for you. Again, my name is Adrian. Please let me know if you need anything."

"Thank you, Adrian." Alyssa murmured as she passed him the menu.

After dating for the past few months, she'd noticed a pattern with Torrence. She really wished she hadn't but, it came with the territory of how her brain worked. Especially considering some life lessons she'd learned the hard way.

They went to nice places when they ate out. However, he tended to order the least expensive item on the menu. From everything he'd told her, he earned an excellent living at the accounting firm where he worked. He'd even mentioned that he was in consideration for partner. Which was admirable since he hadn't reached forty and had only been with the firm for five years.

She tried to shrug it off as him being frugal. Given his profession, that wasn't too far-fetched. Although she couldn't quite balance that against the times she invited him out and his tastes leaned toward more expensive menu items. His selections didn't bother her in regards to her ability to pay. Paying wasn't an issue.

The pattern was even more apparent tonight for some reason. Maybe it was because she was already on the verge of telling him to kick rocks. Considering the dating horror stories she heard from her girl-friends, her experiences with Torrence weren't anything to complain about. Still....

Their conversation over dinner was polite, but not overly stimulating. Movement at the bar caught Alyssa's attention, but she quickly returned her focus to what Torrence was saying.

"I can't find my wallet." His hands roamed his slender frame patting the pockets of his pants then reaching into the inner pocket of his jacket.

"Oh. Do you think you dropped it, or left it at home?" Concern wrinkled Alyssa's brow.

"No, I don't think I left it home, maybe I dropped it. But, I don't remember pulling it out since I've been here."

"Okay. Where's the last place you remember having it?"

Essentially done with her meal, Alyssa placed her knife and fork on her plate. Pushing it away, she gave him her full attention.

"I remember picking it up as I walked out of my apartment. I could have sworn I put it in my back pocket, but it's not there."

"Oh. Well maybe it fell out in your car. We can get the check and go look." Alyssa suggested.

"Get the check? Didn't I just say I couldn't find my wallet? How do you expect me to pay with no wallet? You know I don't trust those apps on the cellphone."

His voice was harsh and his dusky brown skin held a reddish undertone that hadn't been present moments before. He was freaking out, but that was no excuse for him to take it out on her.

Before she could respond to his outburst he sat back in his seat. His body language in complete contrast to what it was only seconds before. *What in the entire hell?*

"What am I worried about? You've got me right? You shouldn't have any trouble forking over a hundred bucks on one meal. I do it every time I take you out. It won't hurt you to do it for a change."

Sitting there in his chair, his entire body relaxed. The smile on his face could only be described as smug. His demeanor set off warning bells in Alyssa's head. If she was reading the situation correctly, and she was positive she was, this was a test of some sort.

This was the part of dating she hated. The need some people had to test their potential mate, instead of coming straight out and communicating about what was bugging them, irked her. Heaven forbid they behave like adults and discuss the issues that bothered them.

Warmth crept up Alyssa's neck once the realization set in. They didn't even have a real relationship and he had the audacity to try to test her. To what end? To see if she was a Gold-digger? Refusing to play his game, she asked him.

"Torrence, did you really lose your wallet, or is this some type of test?"

"Why would you say something like that? Because I asked you to pay for a change?" Far from trying to keep their conversation between the two of them, he raised his voice above the conversational hum of the restaurant.

"First of all, there's no reason for you to get loud with me. It was a simple question. I told you in the beginning, I don't do games. I'm not about that life. Secondly, if you're nothing else, you're meticulous. There's no way you would be here without your wallet, unless you planned to put on an act to see if I'm only interested in you for your money."

"Well, are you?" He shot back immediately. Leaning forward, he put his elbows on the table.

"The fuck?" Alyssa's brow crinkled. Keeping her voice even, she decided to enlighten him on a few things.

"Torrence, I'm not sure what gave you the impression that I need your little check from being a drone at an accounting firm. I don't. Just because I don't brag about my ability to provide the way you do, doesn't mean I can't provide. It simply means I don't feel the need to broadcast it. I have nothing to prove to you or anyone else."

"I didn't say you had anything to prove. All I said was I pay all the time. I don't see why you can't pay this time."

"You asked me out. I didn't ask you. When I ask you, I pay. If you had a problem with that set up, you could've said something instead of pretending to lose your wallet to see what I would do. And in case you didn't notice, I *was* offering to pay. Then, I was going to help you look for the wallet that's probably in your damn pocket."

Pushing back from the table, Alyssa tossed the cloth napkin on her empty plate and swept her gaze over the room looking for their server. Catching Adrian's eye, she lifted a hand to call him over.

"What are you doing?" Torrence asked as if it weren't obvious. Ignoring him, she waited until Adrian stood next to the table.

"Yes, ma'am. Would you care for dessert or an after-dinner drink?"

"No. Thank you. Could you bring the check for the meal I ordered?"

If Adrian was shocked by her request, he covered it well as he immediately walked away.

"What the hell do you think you're doing?" Now, it seemed Torrence had learned volume control as he lowly growled his question.

"I'm giving you what you want. I'm paying for *my* meal, so you don't have to." Cool, dark amber, eyes regarded him as understanding filtered into his mind. He'd gambled. And lost.

"I didn't say you had to pay. Stop being a bitch."

Adrian chose that moment to reappear. Having already removed her wallet, Alyssa barely glanced at the receipt in the folio before placing three crisp twenty-dollar bills inside and passing it back.

"Keep the change."

"Thank you, ma'am." Adrian accepted payment and placed another folio in front of Torrence. "Whenever you're ready, sir." With that said, he quietly backed away.

Before he made it more than three steps, Alyssa was on her feet slinging her purse on her shoulder. Pushing her vacated chair to the table she glared at Torrence.

"I think it goes without saying, but I'll say it anyway. We're done."

"Done? You're acting like you were doing me some type of favor. You're lucky I even bothered."

Torrence was spoiling for a fight. Alyssa didn't care enough about him to give him any more of her energy. Shooting him a withering glance, she spun on her heel to leave and ran smack into a wall of man.

Chapter Two

GET OUT OF THE CAR ALYSSA

Carver's arms wrapped around Alyssa's soft body to steady her when she literally bounced off his chest. Assessing her strained visage, he reluctantly put some space between them.

"Are you okay? Is this guy bothering you?"

He wouldn't pretend he hadn't overheard the conversation between her and the guy she was intent on walking away from. He'd only caught a few words, but they were enough.

"I'm fine, Carver." If she was surprised to see him, she didn't let on. Pushing at his chest, she silently requested more room. As much as he wanted to deny her wish, he allowed it.

"Holy shit! You're Carver Jamieson."

No matter how many times it happened, he'd never understand why people felt the need to tell him who he was. He knew his own name. Years of experience allowed him to squash the outward appearance of annoyance.

Flicking his eyes to the obnoxious man behaving as if he wasn't being a complete ass to Alyssa just moments before, Carver blatantly disregarded his statement. Ducking his head, he peered into her face trying to capture her eyes.

"Are you sure you're okay?"

Rubbing her bare arms, she looked over her shoulder at her date. *Or whoever he was.* Tipping her chin up, she gifted Carver with a slight smile.

"Yeah. I'm good. Thank you."

"If you're good, why does your face look the way it did that time Professor Thigpen accused you of cheating?"

"It's nothing, Carver. Don't worry about it."

Her soft hand landed on his bare forearm sending a jolt to his system. He hadn't felt those hands on any part of his body in at least ten years.

"Don't lie to me, Bit." Slipping easily into the nickname he'd given her all those years ago, his gaze left her face to stare at her companion who now stood directly behind her.

"Yo, man. I've watched you play for years. Since your days at Tech. You're a living legend. Would you be cool with snapping a pic with me? My dad will never believe I met you not two days after they announced you'd joined the Ravagers. This is so cool."

The guy's lanky body practically vibrated with excitement. Had Carver not heard him being a such an asshole to Alyssa, he might have taken the pic and possibly even told him to call his dad on video chat. The problem is, he'd heard every venomous word the otherwise mild-mannered looking guy had said to her.

Heard it and didn't appreciate it. Moving Alyssa until she stood behind him, he ignored the pleading in her dark amber stare. He wasn't going to let it go. She should know that. He hadn't changed that much over the years.

"What's your name?" Carver asked, lulling the star-struck man into believing he would get exactly what he'd asked for. And he would. Just not the part where Carver would take a picture. The request his behavior and treatment of Alyssa made on his behalf.

"Torrence. Torrence Phillips."

Carver looked down at the hand extended to him, but didn't make a move to shake it. Instead, he folded his arms across his chest. While the move probably made him appear imposing, it was the only way he could keep himself from smacking the guy's hand away. Dude was either so star-struck that he couldn't pick up context clues, completely oblivious or such an asshole that he considered what Carver witnessed to be something easily brushed to the side.

"Torrence, I'm normally happy to accommodate a fan when I'm not in a rush."

"If you don't have time, I understand. I was just hoping to surprise my Pops."

"Oh, I have time. But I don't want to." The shocked expression on Torrence's face was priceless. Carver could tell he wanted to ask why, and before Torrence could jump to any conclusions, he told him.

"Why would I smile for the camera with a guy who's comfortable trying to embarrass a woman and refusing to pay for a date that *he* asked *her* on? Hard pass."

"What? That's why you're turning me down?" He held up a hand like he was being sworn in to testify. "I didn't say I wouldn't pay. She got all in her feelings and jumped to conclusions. Come on man. You of all people should know what it's like."

"Know what what's like?"

Carver inclined his head as if he actually wanted to know the answer and wasn't just letting Torrence talk himself into a hole.

"These women. They're always looking for a man to spend money, but they never think about reciprocating. I'm sure you've come across your share of Gold-diggers. You know what I mean."

"You know...You look like a smart man, but your elevator doesn't go all the way to the top floor does it?"

"I don't know what you mean."

Carver wondered if Torrence was aware he'd poked his lip out like a petulant child when he said that.

"Yes you do. You know exactly what I mean. Let me put it to you plain. I came over here because I heard you trying to shame this beautiful lady. Before I said a word to you, I checked on her. What kind of idiot would then think I'd take *his* side in that scenario?"

Understanding morphed Torrence's expression into anger coupled with embarrassment.

"Whatever man. I don't need a stupid picture with some washed up jock. If you're so concerned about a random fat black chick, you're welcome to feed her from now on. I warn you though. It ain't cheap. She likes food. Expensive food."

That's it. He'd had it. Lighting quick, Carver's arm shot out grabbing the slighter man by the front of the shirt. His fingers wrapped around the expensive tie and edges of his collar at the same time, lifting his thin body from the floor. A choked gasp pushed past Torrence's lips as he struggled to adjust to the sudden loss of air. Ineffective slaps rained against Carver's forearm as he tried to free himself.

"Who the fuck do you think you are to talk about her that way?" Carver's question was answered in another series of sputtering gasps because he'd literally cut off the other man's air supply. *If the only reason he used air was to insult Bit, he didn't need it.*

"Excuse me, Mr. Jamieson. I'm Mr. Hollister. Is there a problem?"

Carver cut his eyes to the white-haired man who appeared on his left side. "Nope. No problem."

Adjusting his tie against his crisp white shirt, the man spoke again. "Sir. I'm sure if you release the gentleman, we can discuss this and come to a positive resolution."

Returning his stare to the man flailing at the end of his wrist, Carver considered the words. The fingers of his other hand formed a fist as he contemplated knocking the douche out with a punch or letting oxygen deprivation do it for him.

He felt Alyssa's fingers wrap around his other arm, thereby taking the punching option off the table temporarily.

"Please, Carver." Her whispered plea reached his ears easily. "Please stop. People are looking." Pressing closer to him, she tugged at his arm. "They have their cameras out recording. Please stop."

Despite his desire to drive his fist into that asshole's disrespectful mouth, he listened to Bit and released his hold. The other man collapsed to the floor holding on to the edge of a chair to remain upright, desperately trying to refill the air in his lungs.

Under normal circumstances, Carver didn't get physical with men much smaller than him. It gave off bully vibes. These weren't normal circumstances and he'd be damned if he did nothing while the prick tossed insults at her.

"Thank you Mr. Jamieson. Now, if you could tell me what happened, I'm sure we can fix this."

Carver had almost forgotten the white-haired man was there. He must be the restaurant manager or somehow affiliated with the casino because the staff standing at his back deferred to him.

"He just choked me for no reason and you're trying to fix things with *him*?" From his position on the floor, Torrence's hoarse voice entered the conversation.

Alyssa's fingers tightened around Carver's forearm. Placing his right hand on top of both of hers, he squeezed her fingers in reassurance. He loved the feeling of her touching him and loathed the motivation behind it.

"Mr. Hollister, is it?"

"Yes, sir."

"I appreciate your attention to the matter, but I'm certain Mr. Phillips here understands my point and is going to make amends. Aren't you, Mr. Fredericks?"

Carver gave Torrence a pointed look as he watched him pick himself up from the floor and straighten his clothing.

"What?"

Carver inhaled deeply before releasing the breath. He understood the optics. As repugnant as he found the man, he was clear headed enough to understand how it could be interpreted with him as a well-known white man being in a confrontation with an African-American man.

"You were just telling me how you weren't going to allow Ms Ripley to pay for her own meal seeing as *you* asked *her* out. Right?"

The last word came from behind gritted teeth as his eyes shot daggers at the smaller man. "Right?"

"Uh... Yeah."

Maybe the man wasn't as dumb as Carver thought. Reaching into the inner pocket of his jacket, he pulled out his wallet. Picking up the black folio from the table, he slipped a credit card inside before handing it to the server standing nearby.

"Can you make sure to put the entire bill on this card and give the lady back her cash?"

"Don't bother." Alyssa spoke up. "I don't want it. I don't want another red cent from you."

Unsure of who to listen to, the server stood transfixed. Finally, Mr. Hollister intervened instructing the young man to run the card and retrieve the cash. He returned in an astoundingly short amount of time.

One of the perks of being well-known. People in certain places tended to bend over backwards to be accommodating. Carver rarely took advantage of it, but he silently encouraged it in this instance.

"Here you are, ma'am. My apologies for the inconvenience." The young man held three twenty-dollar bills out to Alyssa. Folding her arms, she refused it.

"You keep it. Consider it a tip." Her face was set in stubborn refusal, Carver didn't press it.

"Thank you, ma'am!" The server made a hasty exit.

Tossing Alyssa's date one final look of disgust with a tinge of a threat to beat his ass, Carver slipped an arm around Alyssa's waist.

"Thank you for your assistance, Mr. Hollister. We'll get out of your hair now." If no one had seen him nearly strangle a man in the middle of a crowded restaurant, they wouldn't guess he'd been furious only moments prior.

Using his fingertips, Carver guided Alyssa from the restaurant by applying pressure to her lower back. Ignoring the blatant stares from around the restaurant, he escorted her through the faux outdoor seating, automatically leading them to the right.

Alyssa's steps faltered when they reached the corner at Citizen's Kitchen and Bar. His brow furrowed as he looked down at her questioning gaze.

"What's wrong, Bit?"

"Where are we going? I'm parked that way." Hitching a finger over her shoulder, she indicated the glass doors behind them which led to the outdoor parking area.

Should he tell her that his first instinct was to take her to his suite? He hadn't purchased a place yet, so he was renting one of the Presidential suites in the hotel. When he'd looked up from signing the check for the meal he'd eaten at the bar of the Lupo and seen her, his breath caught in his throat. It had been ten years, but when he saw her profile, it felt like just this morning that he'd awakened to an empty bed in Chicago.

"I was just thinking about getting you somewhere safe and away from prying eyes. So, I was heading to my suite. Besides, it's been a while, I figured we can catch up." *And talk about why you ghosted me.*

The last part he was smart enough not to say out loud, but the way she planted her feet said she heard it anyway.

"Oh, this is where you're staying?"

"Yeah. I haven't found a place, so I'm renting a spot here until I do. I have an appointment with a realtor to look at some places next week."

"Oh. Ok. Well, I appreciate you looking out for me, but I'm okay. I'm just going to head home now. It was good to see you though."

Carver's eyes said the words before he spoke them aloud. There was no way in hell he was allowing her to simply walk away. Even if he didn't want answers, he wouldn't simply let her go out into the night alone when she'd just had a verbal altercation with a disgruntled date.

"You know I'm not letting you go out there on your own, Bit. It's dark and you and your boyfriend just had a fight."

"He's not my boyfriend."

"Good to know." Using the hand he still had on her waist, he turned her until they were facing each other. "I'm still not comfortable with you driving off alone, but I'm willing to compromise."

"Carver, even if I were inclined to join you in your suite, I'm not up for walking all the way through a casino in these heels. These are for short distances and sitting." Lifting one foot, she rotated her ankle to display the four-inch heels which increased her height enough to put the top of her head close to his chin.

"Like I said, Bit. I'm willing to compromise. I'll walk you to your car. Then, you can drive us around to the hotel side. We can leave your vehicle with the valet and have a quick night cap. That way, I can feel sure you aren't out there alone just in case your little friend decides he wants revenge for being embarrassed."

Shaking her head and waving a dismissive hand, she refuted his assessment. "Torrence wouldn't do anything like that."

"How do you know? Did you ever think he'd do the things he did tonight?"

"No..." She dragged the word out, obviously not wanting to admit she may not know the guy as well as she thought.

Using the pressure of his fingertips, he rotated them both until they faced the doors leading to the parking lot. Without any further urging on his part, she started walking towards the doors. It didn't take them long to reach her SUV. Carver visually inspected the slate grey Lexus RX and gave a silent nod of approval at her choice.

Just as she started the vehicle, she gasped lightly. Had he not been so focused on her, he would have missed it.

"What is it?" Looking from her face, he followed her gaze out of the front window.

"It's nothing. I thought I saw something."

"Something like what?"

"Nothing. I'm sure it was just my imagination."

"Bit..." Placing a hand on her thigh, he gave it a squeeze. "If the thought was enough to cause you alarm. You need to tell me."

Biting her lower lip, Alyssa looked at Carver before returning her eyes to the well-lit parking lot. "I thought I saw Torrence's car drive by."

"Ok. So, he parked in the same lot and he's leaving. Good." As he said it, he knew if seeing Torrence leave was all there was to it, she probably wouldn't have acknowledged it.

"The car was going the wrong direction to leave the lot and it was moving really slow."

"What kind of car is it?"

"I don't know." At his expression, she explained more. "I don't pay much attention to cars to know the names of them."

"Ok...What does it look like?" Even though her lack of knowledge about the actual name of the vehicle didn't mesh with the detail-oriented person that she was, he tried to keep his voice neutral.

"It's red and low to the ground. I know it a sports car and it's supposedly really expensive."

"Ok. Do you still see it?" Scanning the area, he didn't see a vehicle matching the description she'd given.

"No." Pointing to the left, she continued. "I saw it between those two cars one aisle over. It could have just been my imagination overreacting to what you said earlier."

"Maybe." He said in a non-committal tone as he continued to study the cars and people in the parking area.

He remained quiet and observant as she maneuvered through the lot and traffic on the road to ferry them around to the hotel entrance. When she pulled into line behind the other cars, she turned to him and did exactly what he expected.

"Carver, I don't think I should come up. It's still relatively early in the evening, I should head home before it gets late."

Shaking his head, he pierced her with a knowing gaze. "That's not what we agreed to, Bit. Besides, if that guy really is riding around hoping to see you, I don't want you on the road alone."

"Carver, it's not your job to look out for me."

"Says who?" His brows dipped so low, his eyes became slits.

"Me. I'm an adult. I'll be fine. He doesn't know exactly where I live. We always met up. I never had him over."

"Bit, this isn't up for discussion." Pointing to the valet now standing at her door, he instructed, "Give the man your key and let's go upstairs."

Pressing the unlock button on his side of the vehicle, he nodded to the valet to open her door. Reaching over, he unbuckled her seat belt.

"Get out of the car, Alyssa."

His use of her given name had the desired effect. She passed the key fob to the valet and got out. When she'd fully exited the car, Carver unfolded his long frame from his seat, quickly meeting her at the front of the SUV.

She was correct. It was still relatively early by Vegas standards. Time would work in his favor, because they had things to discuss beyond how she ended up on a date with a douche who appeared to care very little about her. Even thinking about what the jerk said made Carver want to find the guy and pound his face in the way he desired in the restaurant.

Chapter Three

ONES AND ZEROS

As Alyssa walked into the hotel with Carver's big warm hand resting at the small of her back, memories flooded her mind from the last time she'd seen him in person. It was also at a hotel, but in a different city. She'd been in Chicago for a job interview. He was there to meet with his agent and a company seeking an endorsement.

Although it had been years, the remembrance was so fresh, it could have been yesterday.

Ten years ago

"Bit? Is that you? What are the chances I'd see you here?" Carver's South Georgia accent was no longer as thick as it was during their time at Tech. Likely influenced by the people surrounding him in his new home in San Diego. The hint of southern charm was still there though.

"Hey, Carver! This is a surprise." The face splitting smile he'd sported the night of the draft was still just as contagious as she returned it with a similar expression.

Walking away from the two men who stood at his side, Carver closed the distance between them and engulfed her in a tight hug. Being pressed against his hard body was a heady feeling. The hug was entirely unexpected since they'd been friendly in college, but not affectionately demonstrative. After all, he was dating her best friend. *Former best friend.* She mentally corrected herself. Her friendship with Mary Beth went south quickly after graduation and completely ended for a variety of reasons.

"I can't believe I ran into you like this. You have no idea how good it is to see someone from home."

The weight of his muscular arm dropped across her shoulders as he steered them toward the two men. Unsure of how to respond, Alyssa allowed herself to be led until they stood before the men who were strangers to her.

"Sorry about that guys." Carver said when they reached his companions. "I haven't seen Bit since my college graduation and I didn't want her to get away." He practically beamed as he said the words.

An unsmiling Carver looked like a hard man who'd never met a sunny day he didn't hate. But, a smiling Carver...That guy lit up the whole room. He was the sun brightening the day. His slightly larger bottom lip curved up stretching across his face in the most inviting way. It was downright mesmerizing.

It had only been half a decade, but the years had been kind to him so far. While he still looked like himself, his once baby face held more acute lines. Dark brows and thick eyelashes framed his emerald green eyes to perfection. Due to living in sunny Southern California, he sported a nice tan despite it being the dead of winter.

"Let me introduce you." Pointing to each man in turn, he introduced her to his agent and the man she'd pegged as his bodyguard. "Kevin, Jasper, this is Alyssa. Bit, meet Kevin and Jasper my agent and my...friend."

Carver didn't have to say the man, who made his six-foot four-inch muscular body look small in comparison, was his bodyguard. The look on Jasper's face when Carver said he was a friend was enough to confirm her suspicions.

"Hello. Nice to meet you." Alyssa said politely.

"Bit? As in the Bit you mention every time you have soup because you compare it to the soup she made you when you had the sniffles in college? That Bit?" Jasper asked with a twinkle in his eye.

Turning shocked eyes to a blushing Carver, Alyssa couldn't believe what she'd heard. *He remembered that? And, he told people about it?* She had no idea what to do with that information, so she remained silently glued to where he'd tucked her into his side.

That was another thing she found disconcerting. The way he held his arm around her made it seem like they were much closer than she thought they were in school. It also sent her insides tumbling in awkward confusion. As far as she knew, in the past, she'd never given any indication that she was attracted to Carver in the least. She'd freely acknowledged his appeal whenever Mary Beth brought up his physical appearance, but she'd stopped short of displaying anything resembling desire to know him as more than a friendly acquaintance.

After all, he was dating her best—*former* best friend. Alyssa would never break that bond over a guy. No matter how fine he was. But... Carver and Mary Beth split barely five months after they graduated. Also, Alyssa and Mary Beth were no longer friends.

She didn't owe her any loyalty. Not that Carver was offering her anything at the moment. He could very well be super excited to see someone from home. Although, they technically weren't from the same home town—just the same state. She was actually surprised he was so happy to see her. In solidarity with her friend, she'd cut off the limited contact she had with him after the two split. His excitement was a paradox.

"What do you say, Bit? I don't want to take over whatever plans you have tonight, but I'd really like for us to catch up. That's if you have some time to spare."

Realizing she had gotten lost in her thoughts and tuned out of the conversation, Alyssa's face heated with embarrassment. "I'm sorry, what?"

Apparently unbothered that she'd checked out on him, Carver replied. "I was just saying to Kevin and Jasper that since we were done for the night you and I could catch up."

"I'm sorry, what?" A line appeared between Alyssa's eyebrows as she tried to make sense of the words coming out of Carver's mouth.

Dipping his head closer to her, he gifted her with a lopsided grin. "I haven't seen you in a month of Sundays and I haven't seen anyone from home other than my family in almost as long. I thought maybe we could go somewhere and talk. You're bundled up like you're heading out, are you not staying here at The Drake?"

"Oh... No. I'm not. I met someone for dinner. I was just leaving to go back to my hotel."

"Well, I have a suite upstairs. We could head up and you can tell me what you've been up to."

What could it hurt? The thought drifted across her mind. Carver had never been anything but kind to her when they knew each other before. And, he apparently wasn't holding her cutting off contact with him against her.

"Sure. Okay. I can't stay long. I have an early flight tomorrow morning."

The sun was out in full force bathing Alyssa in its glow when Carver smiled at her agreement to join him in his suite. As a group, they moved through the lobby to the bank of elevators. Trying to keep her nerves at bay, Alyssa looked everywhere but at Carver or his small entourage for the entire ride.

Present

"Bit, we're here."

Carver's nudge at her lower back prompted her forward motion to exit the elevator to a part of the hotel she was surprised to learn didn't require special key card access. When he opened the door and ushered her inside, her eyes rounded. She'd admit to being slightly awed at the elegant display of wealth.

"Would you like something to drink?" Carver asked as he strode to the bar which sat to the right of an *actual* pool table.

Uncertain if alcohol would dull her senses or make her even more aware of the low throb that had invaded her center the moment he looked into her eyes, she declined the drink. She did however request water to combat the dryness she experienced when she considered the potential topics of conversation beyond how she ended up on a date with a guy who pretended to lose his wallet as a test of her character.

After he poured two fingers of whiskey into a tumbler for himself, he grabbed a bottle of water from the small fridge tucked beneath the bar for her. Softly thanking him when he passed it to her, she followed him past the spiral staircase to enter a sitting room with a plush sectional, an armchair and a big screen television mounted on the wall.

Extending one arm, he offered her a seat on the U-shaped sectional. Once she'd chosen a spot in one corner, he took the seat far enough away as not to crowd her, but close enough for her to feel the heat wafting off his body. Wishing she could put more space between them without being obvious, she fixed her eyes on the view of the city just beyond the windows which made up the entirety of one wall.

"So, wanna tell me what's up with you and that guy? Since he's not your boyfriend." Carver's question brought her attention back to him instead of the bright lights of the city.

"Not really."

Honesty is always the best policy, but from the look Carver leveled on her when she responded honestly, he wasn't a fan of her particular brand of honesty. Rather than give voice to his displeasure, he simply stared at her until she shifted uncomfortably on the sofa.

"Fine. We've been seeing each other for the past six months. Not exclusive. Nothing serious. Tonight was the first time he spoke to me that way and it will be the last."

Nodding, he took a sip from the tumbler as he watched her over the top of the glass. "Y'all were... as you say it 'seeing' each other for six months and you weren't ready to be exclusive? What's wrong with him? Besides the obvious asshole behavior I witnessed tonight. You said that was the first time, so that couldn't be the reason."

"Who says anything is wrong with him? Tonight excluded. It could be me."

"Nah...There's no way a man with half a brain, who got you to go out with him for six consecutive months, wouldn't try to make sure you knew you belonged to him." Leaning back, he threw an arm across the back of the couch, his fingertips grazing her shoulders sending a shiver down her spine.

"I don't." Gathering herself, Alyssa cleared her throat. "I don't *belong* to anyone. No one talks like that anymore."

"Sure they do, Bit. Most of them are just too chicken to say it aloud." The words unsaid between them twinkled in his eyes.

"If you say so."

"Oh...I say so, Bit."

"Can you please stop calling me that?" The nickname was too inti-mate. It implied a closer relationship than she thought they ever had. Well...except for that night in Chicago. And, that night didn't really count.

"No." His single word response sent a different type of shiver through her.

"Since when are you so mean? And pushy?"

"Mean? What have I done that's mean? Or pushy?"

"Carver, you picked a man up by his throat in a crowded restaurant. You call that being nice?"

"Considering what I really wanted to do, that was downright charitable."

"Wow..." She really had no words in response to that one. This Carver looked like the guy she knew, but she didn't remember this intense side of him.

"Bit, I know it's been a long time, but you can't possibly have forgotten how I feel about bullies. That guy was a bully—even if tonight was the first time he showed you that side of himself."

She was well aware of how he felt about bullies. The one serious argument she remembered between he and Mary Beth before they called it quits was due to the way he'd witnessed her treating another young woman on campus. In his view, Mary Beth's behavior was classic bullying and he was ready to break things off with her.

It took a lot of crying, cajoling and promises to do better for them to come to an agreement. Mary Beth never did anything similar again—at least not that Alyssa knew about. What Carver didn't know was that Mary Beth's behavior was a direct result of her jealousy.

The girl was in one of Carver's classes and had allowed him to borrow her notes. Mary Beth was convinced the girl was trying to steal him away and couldn't be persuaded otherwise. She'd never accuse Carver, so she took her anger out on his classmate.

"I remember, but you're also being more than a little bossy. Don't get me wrong. I appreciate your willingness to stand up for me, but don't you think you're taking this a little too far? I didn't have to come up here. I could've just gone home. We were never close enough for all this intensity you're giving off right now."

Placing the tumbler on the coffee table, he turned to face her fully. "We weren't close? Is that what you just said?"

The fire blazing in his eyes made her want to snatch the words back, but they were out there. They couldn't be recalled. Besides, it was true. At least her version of the truth.

Leaning closer to her, he captured her gaze. "If we weren't close, how do I know what it feels like to be inside of you? What you taste like on my tongue? How wet you get when I suck your nipples. If we weren't close, why do I know what sounds you make when you cum?"

Attempting to avoid the heat of his stare, Alyssa's eyes dropped to her lap. "That was one night, Carver. Ten years ago. It was just—"

"If you say it was just sex, me and you are gonna have a problem." His voice took on a deep, gravely quality as if the words were scraping across his vocal cords as he pushed them past his lips.

"Look at me, Bit." He waited for her to comply. Compelled by the steel underneath the demand, she lifted her gaze to his. "Are you seriously sitting here trying to convince me that we're little more than strangers with no real connection to each other? Is that the lie you told yourself to make you feel better for ghosting me?"

Alyssa had no idea how to respond to the revelation that Carver had held on to their one night in his suite at The Drake. He was one of the most sought-after bachelors in the country at the time. Heck, he probably still was. She'd told herself it was best for her to leave before he woke up.

After all, she had an early flight she couldn't afford to miss. Besides, with all the women throwing themselves at him everywhere he went, there was no way he was looking for something serious. She convinced herself he probably had one-night-stands regularly. Now, it seems their night together was imprinted on his memory as much as it was hers.

What in the world was she supposed to do with this new knowledge? Ones and zeros. Algorithms and macros. Those she could handle with her eyes closed. This. Whatever this is with Carver. It was unchartered territory.

Chapter Four

DON'T TRY TO RUN FROM ME, BIT

Carver still couldn't believe his luck. Less than forty-eight hours after landing in Vegas he'd run into Alyssa Ripley. In the years that had passed from the last time he'd seen her, he'd told himself he was putting too much stock into one night. Even if it was a night like none he'd had before or since.

Silence stretched between them as he waited for the impact of his words to resonate with her. He knew her much better than she thought he did. He could practically see the wheels turning in her mind as she replayed his statements in her beautiful analytical brain. To him, her intelligence was almost as sexy as the rest of her. Carver appreciated the female form in general, and Alyssa's form specifically.

Her beautiful medium brown skin glowed with such richness, his fingers curled with desire to touch it to verify it was a supple as it looked. The dress she wore accentuated the bountiful globes of the breast he longed to have in his hands again. It hugged her hips displaying her round ass and thick thighs to perfection. Sitting next to her and not touching her was pure torture, but he kept his eager digits to himself. Things couldn't go the way they did the last time. He wouldn't allow it.

. . .

Ten years ago – The Drake Hotel

The entire ride up on the elevator, Carver's nerves jangled. It took herculean effort for him to appear cool, calm, and collected. Of all places, he'd found Alyssa again in Chicago. After things went south with he and Mary Beth, of course Alyssa stood with her friend. He didn't blame her for breaking off what little contact they had with one another, but he missed her something fierce.

He hadn't realized how much until he saw her face, in profile, walking toward the exit. Breaking off his conversation with Kevin and Jasper mid-sentence, he called out to her. When she didn't immediately ignore him, he banked on her not wanting to cause a scene when he suggested she come up to the suite. He was so happy to see someone familiar and having that someone be his Bit, he momentarily forgot how their association ended. Thinking of Mary Beth put a sour taste in his mouth, so he pushed those thoughts away.

The elevator slowed to a stop and the doors opened with a ding. Stepping off, he guided Alyssa towards his suite with his fingertips pressing lightly at the small of her back. Kevin and Jasper followed a few steps before Kevin broke off to go to his own room. Jasper continued on with Carver.

If his presence bothered Alyssa, she didn't say so. But, Carver didn't think she would say anything even if it did. He'd learned early on that she was polite to a fault. When pressed further or too far past her comfort zone, then she'd say something. Otherwise, she watched and assessed the situation. Besides, he was certain she had figured out Jasper was his bodyguard and not just a friend.

Once he opened the door, Jasper swept the suite before excusing himself through the adjoining door to his connected room. Giving Carver a pointed look, he left them alone. He didn't consider Alyssa a threat, but his eyes told Carver not to leave the room without him. As much as it stuck in his craw to need a protection detail, Carver nodded in silent understanding. He was too well known to go off by himself, especially in such a large city.

When the door closed behind Jasper's hulkish frame, Carver went to where Alyssa stood at the window. Stopping behind her, he placed his hands on her shoulders.

"Let me help you with this."

Reaching around, he tugged at the lapels until she released them and allowed him to help her off with the calf-length peacoat and knit scarf. Beneath the coat, she wore dark slacks and a pale blouse which did nothing to hide the generous swell of her breasts. Their eyes locked in the reflection from the window. The corner of his mouth lifted in a half smile.

"Come sit down, Bit." Walking away, he draped her coat across the back of a chair. "Do you want something to drink? I'm sure there's something cool in the fridge."

"I'll have a water, if you have it."

Her soft voice still held a tinge of what he called proper Southern. She didn't drop consonants like most southerners. Her words were crisp, but you could still hear the slight drawl in her speech.

"Coming right up."

Smiling like fetching her a bottle of water was the highlight of his day, he quick-stepped to the small fridge. Snagging two bottles, he walked back to the sofa and sat. Not close enough to touch, but close enough for the scent of her perfume to waft his way.

"I almost didn't believe my eyes when I saw you downstairs. Until you responded, I thought I'd embarrassed myself by yelling out to a stranger." Shifting in his seat, he angled his body towards her. "Tell me, Bit. What brings you to Chicago?"

Tugging at one of her springy curls, she cut her dark amber eyes at him. "I'm here for a job interview."

"At night?" Carver's hackles rose protectively. He'd never heard of a nighttime interview for the kind of work he assumed Alyssa would do based on her major. She was a programmer, not an entertainer. Was some perv trying to take advantage of her?

"No. Well, yes."

"Which one is it, Bit?" He winced internally at how harsh the question came out. He had no excuse other than his immediate concern for her safety.

"The interview was earlier today. Tonight was more of a wooing situation. They brought a group of their younger programmers and engineers out for me to get to know them in more of a social setting."

"Oh. Ok." Still slightly suspicious, he didn't like the idea of her being out in a strange city alone at night. Although, it was technically early evening at barely eight p.m. It wasn't like they kept her out until midnight and didn't see her back to her hotel safely.

"They didn't have someone to escort you?"

"They did, but it's been so long since I've been to Chicago. I've never been to The Drake, I wanted to look around. I convinced them I'd be fine alone. I'm a big girl. I can handle myself. Besides, they have this new rideshare service that'll drive me anywhere I need to go."

"I don't like the sound of that, Bit. Jasper and I will take you back to your hotel when you're ready to go. No need for you to get into the car with some rando." Carver had heard of those rideshare things. He didn't trust them for himself. He definitely didn't trust them for her.

"Carver...Thank you, but it's not necessary."

"I'll decide what's necessary, Bit." Her eyes widened at the assertiveness in his tone, but he didn't try to soften his declaration. He was coming on strong as hell, but he couldn't pull it back.

Shifting gears, he shared his reasons for being in the Windy City. Time flew as they caught up on each other's lives since they'd last seen one another. Because his life was more in the spotlight than hers, he asked a lot of questions. A lot.

Finally, he couldn't take it anymore. He had to get the elephant out of the room. As loyal as Alyssa was, there was no way she would stay in his suite as long as she had if she and Mary Beth were still friends.

Over the course of their conversation, the space between them had shrank until she was less than an arm-length away from him. Stroking her shoulder, he broached the subject.

"Bit, what happened with you and Mary Beth?"

"What makes you think anything happened?"

Dipping his head, he peered at her through his lashes. "You forgot who you're talking to. I know you're a loyal friend. My name was mud to her after we ended things. Which means it was mud to you by proxy. You wouldn't be here all cozy with me, catching up like old friends if the two of you were still on good terms."

With her hands clasped together in her lap, she remained silent so long, he thought she wouldn't answer. Flicking him a closed off look, she finally broke the quiet.

"Let's just say we no longer saw eye to eye on certain things and leave it at that."

"That's it? Y'all had a disagreement? I'm not trying to get into your business." *Lie.* He was totally trying to get into her business. "But, I feel like there's more to it than a simple difference of opinion."

"Carver, can you just drop it?"

"Sure...when you tell me the truth." Edging closer to her, he bumped her thigh with his own. "Come on, Bit. Tell me what happened. I'm not looking to bash your friend—"

"She's not my friend. Apparently, she never was." Immediately after the words left her mouth, she clamped her lips shut as if trying to hold the remaining words inside.

"What does that mean?" Dropping a hand on her thigh, he gave it a squeeze. "Come on, Bit. Talk to me."

"Did you know she's married now?" The question seemed off topic, but he went with it. At least she was talking.

"Yeah. I heard through the social media grapevine. Married with a couple of kids, if I'm not mistaken."

"You know more than me. I didn't know about the kids."

"How did that happen? I thought the two of you were close."

"So did I. Right up until the moment I overheard her talking to her sister about me."

Carver's jaw ticked with emotion when he saw the shroud of sadness fall over her face. Mary Beth had bitchy tendencies that often made him wonder how she and Alyssa remained friends. Hell, he surprised himself with how long he put up with it. Knowing that telling him what happened was hard enough, he didn't rush her. Fighting against the desire to pull her into his embrace to comfort her, he waited for her to continue.

"It was four years ago. For as much as she said she loved you and wanted to marry you, she jumped into another relationship and was engaged within six months after the two of you called it quits."

Mary Beth's desire to get married was one of the reasons he'd broken things off with her. He refused to be pressured into a commitment. He was just starting a career. Marriage was the last thing on his mind.

Alyssa barked a dry, mirthless laugh and continued her story. "Ever the dutiful friend, I was helping her get things together despite having started a new job in a new state after graduation. I'd flown in for a fitting. I was trying on the ridiculously expensive bridesmaid dress.

I walked out to hear her telling Jayne that if I wanted to be in her wedding I'd need to lose weight, because she couldn't have anyone bigger than a size ten in her wedding pictures. For a minute, I thought I heard her wrong. So, I asked her about it later.

That's when I found out she'd never been my friend. Not really. A real friend would never say the things she said and she wouldn't try to make me change things about myself for such superficial reasons."

"Bit...Look at me." Carver kept his voice low, but steady. When she didn't comply fast enough to suit him, he slid a hand into the curls at her nape and turned her head with his fingertips. Her soft curls wrapped around his digits and he fought against the urge to tug at her tresses. There were things between them that needed to be said. First, he had to clear up any misconceptions she had about herself.

Capturing her eyes, his gaze bore into hers. He saw the uncertainty there, how she didn't quite believe his words. She always seemed so self-assured, but everyone had a soft spot. Apparently, Mary Beth had found Alyssa's and done what a true friend never would. She used it to try to tear Alyssa down.

"You are absolutely perfect. You were then and you are now. Mary Beth is a miserable person who isn't happy unless she thinks she's doing better than someone else."

Dodging the directness of his gaze, she attempted to avoid his stare. Not allowing it, he captured her face between both of his hands.

"I wouldn't lie to you, Bit. You're perfect."

The pinkness of her tongue swiping across her lips drew his eyes away from her amber pools. Tracking the motion, he groaned and gave in to his desire. Tentatively, he pressed his lips to hers. Their pillowy softness pulled at something inside of him. Swiping his tongue at the seam, he requested entry.

Given the slightest of openings, he took full advantage, darting inside to taste the sweetness of her mouth. His shaft lengthened in his pants. How long had he wanted to touch and taste her this way? Too long.

All of the pent-up yearning he'd pushed down came pouring out as he devoured her lips and luxuriated in her taste. He wanted more. Reluctantly, he released her lips and trailed kisses along her jawline nipping at her ear before skating pecks down her neck latching on to the pulse point at the base of her throat. Her gasps and soft moans let him know he'd discovered a sweet spot.

When her fingers landed on his chest, he prayed she didn't push him away. He'd stop if that's what she wanted, but it sure as hell wasn't what he wanted. He wanted to strip her bare and gaze on her luscious body. His fingertips itched to trace her silky-smooth skin, and his mouth watered anticipating tasting every delectable inch of her.

Through the fog of desire, he realized her hands on his chest were pushing not stroking. So, he released his hold on her sweetly scented skin. Pressing his forehead to hers, he trapped her eyes with his own. Not wanting to break the spell, he waited for her to tell him what she wanted.

Her voice was barely above a whisper when she finally spoke. "We can't do this, Carver."

"We can't do what? Kiss? I thought we were doing a pretty good job. But, with more practice, I'm sure we can do better." Smiling widely, he tried to quell the uncertainty he saw in her expression.

One corner of the lips he wanted on him tipped up. Swatting his chest in that way women do when they're mildly exasperated, but still flirty, she shushed him. "You're still such a smart ass."

"You expected that to change?" He quipped.

A smile tugged at the edges of her lips, although she didn't allow it to completely emerge. "You don't have to do this. My self-esteem is fully intact."

A frown drew his eyebrows together. "Wait...You think I'm kissin' you out of pity?"

He tightened his grip on the hair at her nape when she tried to turn her head to avoid his questioning gaze.

"Answer me, Bit. Do you think I kissed you just to make you feel better?"

"Did you?"

Defiance laced her voice, but the way she captured her bottom lip between her teeth told a different story. Whether she intended it that way or not, he took her words as a challenge. Grabbing her hand, he placed it on his rock-hard length. Even through the barrier of his jeans, he knew she felt it.

"Does this feel like pity to you? I can assure you, it ain't. It's taking everything in me not to strip you naked on this couch and plant my dick so far inside you that you'll feel it every time you take a breath for the next month."

Her eyes widened at his boldness, but instead of jerking her hand away, her fingers stroked him through the denim. Feeling her touch on him was everything he'd imagined and more. Even muted through his clothing, it set him on fire. He couldn't take it another minute.

They needed more privacy. While they were technically in his suite, only the adjoining door separated them from Jasper. Standing, he extended his hand to her. An entire conversation was held between them in a simple glance. Slipping her hand into his, she stood. Tangling their digits together, he led her through the doorway to the bedroom.

As soon as he closed them inside, he gave in to the urgency to see all of her. Quickly stripping her of the conservatively sexy top, heeled boots and slacks, he didn't stop until every inch of her was bare to his hungry gaze. Even though he was aware of the heat of his intensity, he couldn't rein it in.

With him still clothed and her naked, he didn't allow time for any shyness or indecision to creep in. Latching on to her lips, he began stoking the fire within her. Walking her backwards to the bed, he threw off the coverings and laid her across it with her legs bent at the knee and hanging over the edge.

He wanted to explore every millimeter of her sexy body, but time was of the essence. His dick could only take so much, and the torture of seeing her stretched across his bed was driving him mad. Carver knew once he was inside Alyssa, he wouldn't be able to be gentle. So, he had to do what he could to prepare her to take him.

Removing his sweater and undershirt in one smooth motion, he dropped to his knees. Spreading her legs to make room, he placed his lips to her moist center and gave it a suckling kiss. A combination squeak and moan from Alyssa reached his ears. Her hips wiggled and jerked like she was trying to squirm away.

Quickly wrapping his arms under her thighs, he gripped her hips and jerked her into position. "Don't try to run from me, Bit. This pussy is callin' my name."

With that declaration, he delved between her folds lapping at her labia and dipping his tongue into her honeyed center tasting her sweetness. She leaked for him, providing a continuous supply of her nectar. His shaft throbbed in objection to still being confined in his increasingly tighter trousers. When her precious pearl peeked from its hood, he latched onto it. Ignoring the fingers tugging at his hair and the jerking of her hips, he continued to suck until her cries reached their crescendo.

"Oh my...Oh SHIT! Carver!"

"That's it, Baby. Give it to me!" He growled against her folds.

She didn't have to announce that she was cumming. Her juices splashed against his chin and he quickly adjusted to partake in his well-earned dessert. He savored her sweetness until she was reduced to intermittent shivers and his cock was on the brink of mutiny. Hurriedly shucking off the rest of his clothing, he rolled on a condom before leaning over her relaxed form.

Trailing kisses over her rounded stomach, he made his way to her bountiful breast. Taking a moment to pay homage to the puckered peaks of her nipples, he continued upwards. Languid amber pools watched his progress. If he weren't so eager to join with her, he'd thump his chest with pride for the satisfied expression on her face alone. No time for that now.

Capturing her plush lips, he trapped her moan as he pushed the head of his shaft into her still spasming, heated channel. He wasn't even halfway inside, and he was about to burst. Releasing her lips, he kissed her eyelids before rasping out.

"I'm sorry, Baby. This round is gonna to be a lil' fast and rough."

Putting his words into actions, he plunged into her steamy depths. Her walls gripped him tightly while yielding to his rigid length allowing almost all of him to sink inside. Balancing on one arm, he wrapped the other around her leg bringing her knee to her chest. The angle allowed the last coveted inch to be engulfed in her delicious pussy.

Withdrawing, he watched his length, glistening with her juices. When only the tip remained, he snapped his hips thrusting into her hot canal. He set up a forceful rhythm and he kept his word. He wasn't gentle and the first round didn't last long. However, he made up for it in the rounds that followed.

He particularly enjoyed their time in the bathroom when he took her from behind while watching their reflection in the large mirror. When their eyes met in the looking glass, the unguarded passion in her gaze sent him over the edge. Dipping his fingers between her folds, he rubbed the little bundle of nerves while he continued to pound into her until she joined him by screaming out her own release.

After their explosive coupling, they moved to the shower before falling into a satisfied heap in bed with him promising to get her to her hotel in time to make her flight. Only, he never got the chance to keep his promise. When he opened his eyes the next morning, she was gone. The pillow she'd lain on was cool to the touch. Hopping from the bed, he searched the suite. Not one trace of her remained.

Sitting on the edge of the bed, he cursed to himself. He was so happy to see her, and be close to her, that he'd failed to get any contact information. Short of hiring a PI or stalking her family and friends, he had no way of contacting her. *Shit!*

Chapter Five

GIMME YOUR PHONE

Present

Just as sure as he knew his own name, he knew Alyssa was going to try to offer up some bullshit, flimsy excuse as to why he awakened alone all those years ago. He knew it, yet he waited—with as much patience as he could muster. Said patience was wearing thin, but he held firm.

As they sat on the U-shaped sofa in his far too big for one person suite at the Mandalay Bay, he watched the emotions flitting across her face. Once again avoiding direct eye contact, her gaze was fixed on the large windows displaying the excellent view of the Vegas strip.

He was certain her mind was probably running through all of the options before bringing her back to the truth they both knew. Reminding himself again that things had to be different this time around, he didn't allow the memories to overtake him or for the lustful undercurrent to prompt him into action prematurely.

After several excruciatingly long moments, his voice broke through the silence. "Alyssa. Look at me."

While his clipped words were hard, he didn't raise his voice. However, her reaction implied he'd barked the command. Jerking slightly, she swung her stare from the windows to him. Uncomfortable with even the appearance that he'd frightened her, he brushed his hand along her shoulder in what he hoped was a soothing motion.

"Sorry, Bit. I didn't mean to startle you."

"You didn't." She assured him, but his left eyebrow cocked in disbelief caused her to correct her statement. "Okay, you did a little."

"I apologize for startling you, but you're not off the hook." When two lines appeared in her forehead, he started their conversation up right where he left off.

"Why did you ghost me in Chicago? Things may have moved a lil' fast, but I know you felt the connection. There's no way you faked your response to my touch. I sure as hell didn't fake my response to yours."

"Carver...I'm not sure what you expect me to say."

"How 'bout the truth? That's all I need to hear. Anything else is unacceptable. I've never lied to you and I won't accept anything less than honesty."

Soulful dark amber eyes stared at him in response. He'd wanted her eyes on him. He'd demanded it, but he didn't take into account how having her solely focused on him would affect his traitorous libido. After years as a star athlete, he was no stranger to interactions with women he found attractive. It was rare for him to be ruled by sexual cravings, even when faced with naked temptation.

Yet, sitting next to a fully clothed Alyssa was wreaking havoc on his senses. Grinding his teeth, he steeled his resolve. While he'd been drawn to her in college, their chemistry hadn't been nearly as intense as it was now. That one night in Chicago, broke the seal and changed the dynamic.

There was no way to go back to the easy, laid-back interactions they'd shared in their early twenties. Quite frankly, Carver didn't want to go back. He wanted to go forward, but they couldn't do that until they cleared the air.

"What truth do you want from me, Carver? The truth that I have no idea how to feel right now? That I didn't know how to feel then? I was barely out of college and trying to really get my life started."

"You were twenty-five and you'd been done with school for four years. Try again."

"It might've seemed like that was plenty of time to you, but I was literally only two years out from living with my parents. In so many ways, I was finding myself."

"So, what was our night together? An experiment? An itch you needed to scratch?"

"No! I would never do that to anyone. Especially not you."

Even as he asked the question, he wasn't sure he was ready for her answer. Relief flooded him when she admitted he hadn't been a curiosity she'd sought to satisfy.

"Okay...So, tell me why I woke up curled around a cold pillow instead having you in my arms the way you were when I fell asleep."

Alyssa went silent once more. Carver thought he'd have to prompt her again, but she finally opened up.

"Carver...that night was...amazing. I never knew it could be that way. With anyone. Then, to have it be with you was beyond my wildest dreams. In fact, it felt like a dream. When I woke up, and felt the heat from your body beside me in that bed...reality set in, and I had no idea what to do.

You'd dated my best friend for more than two years. Granted, I no longer considered her my friend at that point, it still felt wrong. Being with you in that way was a sort of betrayal. Not against Mary Beth, but against the person I thought I was.

If you'd asked me before that night if I'd ever hook up with the Ex of a friend, my answer would've been a resounding 'no'. That's not who I believed myself to be. Only...I'd done exactly that. I couldn't face you. I didn't even want to face myself."

"So, you left me out of misplaced loyalty to Mary Beth?"

"No."

"You just said—"

"I know what I said. You heard me, but you weren't listening. It wasn't about Mary Beth. It was about me and the kind of woman I'd always thought I was. I don't owe Mary Beth a damn thing—least of all my loyalty."

Clamping his mouth shut on the words tumbling in his brain, he studied her. Her face. Her body language. She was absolutely telling the truth as she knew it. It wasn't the bullshit answer he expected. Once he internalized her statement, he understood.

Alyssa was a principled person. It still stung though. He'd never imagined they wouldn't have an opportunity to talk more the next morning. They'd lost so much time because he'd been so eager, he hadn't thought past the moment.

Of all the things he'd conceived since that morning, her blaming herself wasn't one of them. Her regretting their impulsiveness? Maybe. Even her thinking he wasn't serious about her occurred to him. He had a period of wildin' out when he and Mary Beth first called it quits.

He wouldn't blame Alyssa if she'd thought he was trying to add a notch to his belt—even if she should've known him better than that. However, her assuming all the responsibility for their actions and thinking poorly of herself behind it, didn't sit right with him.

"Bit, you have to know I didn't think less of you. It never crossed my mind that you'd see being with me as some kind of failin'."

As it had before, her gaze wandered to the view of the skyline. Her hands rested in her lap gripping the water bottle tightly. Grasping the top, he tugged the crumpling plastic from her fingers. Setting it beside his empty whisky tumbler on the coffee table, he drew her hands into his.

"Bit, look at me." His tone left no room for anything but compliance. When he had her attention, he continued.

"I'm not gonna pretend to know about the inner workings of women and their friendships, but it seems wrong that we'd have to consider each other off limits. Just because I used to date someone who used to be your friend years ago shouldn't mean the two of us couldn't have something. That don't make a lick of sense to me."

"It wouldn't. Men tend to be more open about their friends dating Exes. Some women are as well. I've just never been one to consider a friend's Ex as fair game. At least I wasn't..."

"You still aren't. It's not like you pursued me. Besides, like you said, you didn't owe Mary Beth a damn thing. So, there shouldn't be any guilt or thoughts about breaking girl-code."

Shaking her head, she tried to pull her hands away. "You really don't get it do you?"

"I guess I don't. Why don't you try explaining it one more time."

"Hooking up with you—"

"We didn't hook up. At least that's not how I saw it."

Shooting him side eye for interrupting she continued, "If I'd stayed after being intimate with you and we'd started something, it would've been a really bad look. There's no way anyone would believe that I hadn't been trying to get with you the whole time the two of you were together. They'd think I jumped on the first opportunity to be with you.

It wouldn't matter that years had passed since the two of you were together. Nor would it make a difference that I'd never made any advances toward you while you and Mary Beth were a couple. All they would see is her ex-boyfriend and best friend together, and they'd think the worst."

Detangling one hand from hers, he wrapped his fingers around her jaw to hold her face immobile as he glared at her. "You think I give a fuck what people think? I didn't then and I sure as hell don't now. I don't give two shits about people believing we had something going on behind Mary Beth's back. As long as we know the truth, they can kiss my ass and shut the hell up."

Attempting to pull away, she objected. "Carver, you don't mean that. You have an image to maintain."

"The hell I don't mean it. Nobody gets to dictate who I have in my life. Not a solitary soul." Leaning forward, he dropped his forehead to hers.

"Do you realize how much time we lost over some misplaced moral code?" Her lack of reply led him to slide his hand from her jaw to the nape of her neck. Finding the soft coils there, his fingers threaded into her tresses forming a loose fist.

"Do you?" He growled.

"Ten years." She finally huffed out.

"Ten years, three months and five days."

Her eyes rounded in shock at his revelation. Letting her know how closely he'd marked the time allowed her to glimpse a fraction of his obsession. He wouldn't tell her how it took many calls and talks with his mama to convince him it would be stalkery as fuck to hire a private investigator to track her down.

The weight of his admission settled between them. Her once tense digits relaxed in his hold. Instead of allowing him to hold her hands, she flipped them over tangling their fingers together. Softness replaced the trepidation in her eyes and her head tilted, leaning into his touch.

Unable to take the proximity a second longer, Carver closed the scant distance between them to capture her lips. Moaning at the feel of her full lips against his, he sought entry with a flick of his tongue. Now that he'd felt the suppleness of her lips, he had to taste her again. Giving the hair in his fist a gentle tug, he encouraged her to open for him. Her gasp provided him the space he needed to dip his tongue inside to become reacquainted with her sweetness.

Gathering her close, her body curved into his like it knew this was exactly where they were supposed to be. His cock lengthened and throbbed in protest to being encased in his pants. Feeling her plush body against his hardness was a heady experience. He wanted to devour every inch of her.

Tugging at the deep Vee in the top of her dress, he quickly pushed her bra down to expose one lush breast. The nipple puckered as if begging for his attention. Not squandering the opportunity, he drew the bud between his teeth and lashed it with his tongue. Biting down just enough to elicit a response, but not enough to hurt, he held it captive. An equal opportunity breast man, he plucked at the other nipple while he gorged on the first.

Her moans of pleasure spurred him on as she slid her fingers into his close-cropped hair and tried to pull it. Her gratified whimpers were an intoxicating aphrodisiac. Just when they began to get higher indicating she was close to her peak, he pulled away.

Ignoring her disappointed grumbles, he rolled her exposed nipple between his fingers. Sitting up, he pierced her with a hard stare.

"Gimme your phone."

Confusion clouded her already lust-hazed expression. "What?"

"Gimme your phone. This won't be like last time. This is as far as we go until I have a way to contact you."

"Carver…" The needful way she dragged out his name, almost made him cave.

"No, Bit. No orgasms for you 'til I know you won't run from me in the morning."

Was it an asshole move to get her all revved up and make demands? *Absolutely*. Did he care? *Nope*. Not if it got him what he wanted—a second chance with Alyssa.

"Carver…"

"Phone." Another twist of her nipple accompanied the demand.

"Oh shit!…It's in my purse." She panted.

"Get it." He continued to work on her breast with one hand while the other slipped beneath the skirt of her dress.

"I can't. I can't think with you doing that."

"I can stop if you want." He moved to withdraw his fingers.

Satin-smooth digits clamped onto his like a vice. "No. Don't stop."

"Then gimme what I want, Bit. Pull out your phone."

Shaking and fumbling with the zipper, she finally lifted the device holding it up to him.

"Unlock it."

Without complaint, she held the phone to her face. Once he saw the apps on the screen, he pressed a lingering kiss to her lips as he relieved her of the device.

"Good job, Baby."

Tapping the screen, he entered his phone number and called himself. Pulling his phone from his pocket, he created a contact from the phone call.

"What's your address?"

"Carver…"

"I'm serious, Bit. You're not runnin' from me again. What's your address?"

The desire in her eyes had faded somewhat since he'd stopped stimulating her, but he was confident he could get her back there quickly. They needed to handle a little business first.

Once she rattled off the information, he saved it, then put both phones in his pocket. Clasping her hands in his, he tugged her to her feet. The heels put her at the perfect height for him to swoop down and re-capture her lips with little effort.

After countless minutes, he pulled away from the drugging effect of kissing her. He laced their fingers together and walked her to the spiral staircase. They had lost time to make up for, and they needed space for all that he had planned.

Chapter Six

NOW, HOLD ON. THIS RIDE IS GONNA GET A LIL' ROUGH

Watching Carver's broad back as he led her up the stairs, presumably to his bedroom, Alyssa's mind raced with all the reasons she should grab her shit and leave. Yet, she didn't. She couldn't. Her pulse galloped causing a thudding in her ears. Her core slickened in anticipation of him delivering on the orgasm she'd been denied earlier.

Carver looked over his shoulder as if to check to make sure she was still there. Of course, she was there. Where would she go? Besides the fact that he held her hand firmly in his, her body would revolt if she so much as looked at the door like she was leaving. Her skin tingled with the memory of the last time they were intimate.

No matter how much her logical mind wanted to dispute it, Carver Jamieson was in her system and there was no cure. If ten years hadn't been long enough to purge his touch from her memory banks, it was a lost cause.

The prudish Southern Belle who occupied one small corner of her mind couldn't dissuade her by mentioning she'd started the evening with one man and planned to end it in the bed of another. Polly Prim and Pure could kiss the broad side of her ass. The sample Carver had given her moments ago was potent enough for Alyssa not to heed any words of rebuke or caution.

"Bit, I can hear you thinkin'. Stop it."

Telling her not to think was an exercise in futility. Her mind was always filled with thoughts and scenarios. She couldn't turn it off, much to the dismay of her sleep schedule. No matter how hard she tried, there'd always be at least three things kicking around in her head vying for dominance.

Tugging on her hand, he guided her into the bedroom where a king-sized bed was the focal point. Her eyes locked onto the big bed with the dark, plush bedding draped neatly atop the luxury mattress. Remembrances of the last time she and Carver were alone this close to a bed caused her breath to hitch. Or maybe it was him stepping into her space and grasping her breast that instigated her difficulty in breathing.

"I told you to stop thinkin' so hard, Bit. Looks like I'm going to have to give that big brain of yours somethin' else to ponder."

Not that she had the words to respond to his statement, but he didn't give her the opportunity to voice them. His lips took hers in a kiss that sealed her vocal cords leaving her unable to do more than moan. Her core clenched in anticipation of being filled even though they were both, regretfully, still completely clothed.

His touch inspired her boldness. Instead of waiting for him, she gathered the hem of her dress and began lifting, preparing to remove the first barrier between them. Cool air wafted across her thighs. The shiver it inspired increased when Carver's fingers joined hers taking over the task of ridding her of the garment.

"Who told you that you could take off your own clothes?" His deep, raspy voice tickled her eardrum when he chastised her for trying to undress herself.

Fighting against the lust trying to rule her, she attempted to inject sternness into her voice. "*I* did. In case you didn't notice, I'm a whole grown woman."

Ripping the dress off over her head, his long digits sought out and unclasped the closure of her bra.

"Oh... Baby...I'm well aware of just how grown you are. But I unwrap my own presents."

Confusion colored her expression as she looked at his serious countenance while he gazed upon her nearly naked form. A chuckle rumbled from his chest. Wrapping his big hands around the sides of her breast, he lifted them, flicking her nipples with his thumbs before kissing each one reverently.

"Every part of you matches every part of me perfectly. Your softness where I'm hard..."

His hands left her breast. Fingers trailing across the rounded swell of her belly. "Your plushness, where I'm lean..."

Skimming the waist band of her panties, he slipped his forefingers inside and slid them over her hips then down her legs. Resting on his knees in front of her. Tapping her inner thighs, he wordlessly commanded her to open for him. The tips of his long, thick, fingers glided between her folds.

"Your silky wetness always ready and available to quinch my thirst. How could you possibly be anythin' other than a gift made special for me?" Following the path of his fingers, he pressed his face right into her pussy. The tip of his Roman nose nudged her clit as he traced his way down to capture her nether lips between his, giving them a noisy suck.

"Mmmm... I missed your flavor on my tongue."

While her stance was wide enough for stability, Carver's assault on her senses weakened her knees. The way his scruffy beard abraded her thighs was more than she could handle and keep both feet planted.

Grabbing onto his head and shoulders to keep herself upright, Alyssa released a string of curses and encouragements for the way he dined on her pussy like it was his first meal in forever.

"Oh! Oh FUCK! Carver! You have to stop. NO! Don't stop! I'm gonna cum!"

At first, her words seemed to spur him on. At the mention of her pending release, he pulled away from his feasting and sat back on his heels. Frowning, she searched his face now glistening with her essence.

Sparkling jewel eyes met hers. One side of his mouth tipped up displaying a knowing smirk. He knew exactly what he'd done to her.

"It's not gonna be that easy, Bit. You'll get your orgasms. But...not until I say so."

No amount of willpower could stop the pout from forming on her lips. Uncaring about her distress, he regarded her with the confidence of a man who knew he could deliver on his promise.

Standing, he captured her lips again. Swiping his tongue along the seam, he requested entry into her mouth. Despite being peeved at his cum blocking taunt, she eagerly granted the entreaty. Sweeping inside, he shared her taste with her while his fingers resumed their pleasuring of her breast. Her center moistened even further under his erotic ministrations.

Releasing her from the kiss, he trailed nibbling pecks along her jaw until he reached the shell of her ear. "I guess I found a way to turn off that overactive brain of yours. You can't think of anythin' other than cummin', can you?"

A frustrated moan was all she could muster in reply. He was right. Getting to her release was her primary focus. All other thought ceased the moment he delved his tongue between her folds.

"Let's see what happens to it when I reacquaint your sweet pussy with my dick."

There was no time to process his challenging declaration. Sweeping her off of her feet, he laid her sideways across the bed. She couldn't revel in the soft caress of the downy bed coverings because Carver's hard body immediately trapped her beneath him. How he managed to undress in what seemed like the blink of an eye was a mystery she hadn't the focus to solve.

One moment, she was gasping in surprise at the quick position change, the next her breath was stuck in her chest as Carver thrust his entire length into her slick channel. As aroused as she was, her walls still clamped down on his thickness making his entry ride the delicious edge of pleasure and pain.

"Oh...Fuck... Carver."

"That's right, Baby. Moan my name while you take this dick. Feel it. Let it imprint on you so that you never forget. So you won't ever even *think* about walkin' away from me again."

If Alyssa was able to process beyond how he made her feel, she'd have a snappy comeback for his cocky statement. But, she didn't. She was utterly consumed with the sensations coursing through her. Forming a coherent thought let alone voicing it was woefully out of reach.

A vicious swivel from Carver's hips created a cascade of pleasure so intense her back arched crushing her chest to his, tipping her head back-wards and slamming her eyes shut. *Good gravy*! The man knew exactly what to do with the generous tools at his disposal. Long, with ample girth, his shaft filled her so full, she swore she felt his heartbeat along the length.

"Open your eyes!"

The growling animalistic quality of Carver's voice demanded that she immediately obey the command. Her wide eyes clashed with his heated emerald stare. Sweat beaded on his brow and glistened all over his broad shoulders and muscular chest.

Bracing himself on his elbows, he took her bottom lip hostage and lashed it with his tongue before delivering a suckling bite. Her responding pant gave him the necessary opening to reclaim her mouth with a kiss erotically timed with the thrusting of his shaft into her silky channel. Once again, the sensations were so overwhelming, her eyes slid closed.

"What did I tell you, Bit? Keep your damn eyes open. I wanna watch you watch me. I want you to watch us and see how perfect we are together."

His words, combined with the fire in his gaze was too much. Her hands roamed his body blindly seeking a place to land. Her thighs brack-eted his hips squeezing him in time with the hypnotic motion of his thrusts. He'd said she couldn't cum without his permission, but she was barreling toward her release with the speed of a fighter jet closing in on a target.

"You think I don't know what you're doin', Bit?" Carver pressed his forehead to hers narrowing her view to only his penetrating stare.

"You think I don't see you tryin' to cum without my say-so? Hm?"

"Carver, please. I can't—I have to."

"You can't what, Baby? You can't stop? You can't hold back? Is that it?"

Halting his forceful movements, he began a slow pace where he withdrew until only the head of his cock remained inside her. His re-entry was excruciatingly slow, punctuated by a hip rotation to stimulate her clit. It was enough to keep her on the cusp of orgasm, but not enough to tip her over the wall.

She wanted to fight him. Baring her teeth, she bit back the disgruntled words on the tip of her tongue. Sass wouldn't get her the release she sought, but damned if she didn't want to tell him what he could do with his big dick and demanding attitude.

"Gotta settle somethin' with you real quick, Bit. Then, you can cum. Okay?" Forehead still pressed to hers, he connected their lips in a quick peck. "Stay with me, Baby. I'll give you what you want."

"When?..." Her question was more akin to a whine than a distinct request.

"Real soon, Baby. Real soon."

Licking her slightly parted lips he teased her with a kiss he never deepened. With his constant demands to keep her eyes open, she was left with watching the emotions flit over his face as he tortured both of them with his measured thrusts.

"This right here. This thing between us, Bit. This isn't a one-time deal. Understand?" When she didn't answer immediately, he withdrew his length and plunged back inside in a much more forceful stroke.

"I can't hear you, Baby. Do you understand?"

Scrambling to recover what was left of her mental abilities, Alyssa rushed to respond as her body shuddered in anticipation. "Yes. Yes, Carver. I understand."

"No runnin', Bit. When I open my eyes in the mornin', the first face I wanna see is yours—laying next to me in this bed." Picking up the pace, he brought her back to the precipice of release.

At this point, thinking wasn't fluid for Alyssa, but she managed to rasp out an 'ok' in response. A swift shake of Carver's head told her it wasn't good enough. The jumble of words swimming in her brain finally arranged themselves into a sentence that she managed to push past her lips.

"Ok, Carver. No running. I'll stay with you."

"You said the magic words, Darlin'. Now, hold on. This ride is gonna get a lil' rough."

Grabbing one leg behind the knee, he pushed her thick thigh close to her chest and proceeded to work her pussy like he owned the deed, and all rights for future use. Unable to do anything but feel, Alyssa's cries rang out into the room spurring him on.

When she thought she couldn't take any more, he reached a hand between them locating the sensitive bundle of nerves peeking from its hood. Delivering a firm press then a squeeze, he flung her into her release. Chanting her name, he followed her over. His moans and growls vibrated against the side of her neck where his face was buried as he emptied his seed into her convulsing channel.

*Shit...*They didn't use protection. She didn't have the energy to think past that thought as exhaustion pulled her into the arms of the Sandman. She vaguely responded to Carver's pokes and prods to get her under the covers after he'd used a warm towel on her over-stimulated pussy. Telling herself she'd get up to do a more thorough job when she caught her breath, she drifted off into dreamland.

Sleep held her so tightly, she didn't see Carver take her clothing and stash it away before he climbed into bed beside her wrapping her in his arms. Without waking, she snuggled into his embrace and fell more deeply into slumber.

Chapter Seven

RUN LIKE FLO-JO

Sunlight filtered through the sheer curtains on the windows turning the backs of her closed eyes into a kaleidoscope of yellow, orange, and red. Slowly lifting her lids, Alyssa tried to get her bearings. Her gaze landed on the massive windows making up the entirety of one wall.

This wasn't her bedroom, nor was this her bed, and the arm clamped around her waist wasn't a part of her daily norm. Not by a long shot. Looking at the arm wrapped possessively around her middle, she visually traced the tattoos covering Carver's skin.

From her perusal the previous night, she knew he was inked from wrist to shoulder on his right arm. So far, his chest remained untouched, but she doubted it would stay that way. When she'd last seen him, he only sported the circular red, white and blue Captain America shield on the inside of his bicep.

A considerable amount of art had been added to his limb over the past ten years. Currently within her sight was an old school revolver with the barrel pointing down, toward his wrist. The butt of the matching revolver was barely visible past the tip of the dagger centered between the guns. Atop the blade was a vivid red rose.

The guns she sort of understood, considering he was a quarterback and the tattoos were on his throwing arm—his gun. The dagger and rose were a mystery. They hadn't exactly gotten around to discussing body art. Actually, after their conversation on the sectional, not much else was said.

Wait...Did she promise him they would be together? Like...together-together? *Holy shit!* Now, fully awake, Alyssa's mind whirled and her heart raced as she was flooded with recent memories. She'd fallen asleep after the first round only to be awakened from her short nap to Carver once again wringing orgasm induced promises from her. Her core clenched in response to the recollections and the twinge of soreness solidified her current reality.

She was lying in bed naked in the presidential suite of a Las Vegas hotel with Carver Wyatt Jamieson snuggled against her. A very naked Carver Jamieson, whose morning erection was pressed against her sore pussy. The greedy hussy had the audacity to slicken in preparation. Granted, she hadn't experienced Carver-level loving in...hell, since that night at the Drake. No one else had even come close. But, that didn't mean her pussy could sign up to be pounded like minced meat.

While she was contemplating her wayward sex trying to lead her down the pleasurable path to walking with a limp, she failed to notice Carver's formerly limp fingers had become mobile. By the time she caught on, they were plucking at her nipples and the traitors immediately pebbled under his touch.

"Mornin', Bit." Carver's sleep roughened voice tickled her eardrum.

Nuzzling the side of her neck, his stubble lightly scratched her skin as he peppered her neck and shoulder with slow kisses. As good as it felt, she had to put an end to it. Her girlie bits really couldn't take the 'good morning' Carver's touch pledged.

"Good Morning." Wiggling, she attempted to scoot forward out of his embrace.

Immediate lockdown was his response. The hand stimulating her nipple became a clamp holding her tightly to his chest.

"Just where do you think you're goin'?"

"Bathroom. I need to go to the bathroom."

That wasn't one hundred percent untrue, but it wasn't her most pressing need. His hold loosened, then he flopped on his back, giving her complete freedom. Not letting it go to waste, she hurriedly slid to the edge of the bed. Once there, she looked around on the floor for something to cover herself with.

"I thought you said you had to pee."

"I do."

"Then why are you still sittin' there?"

"I need something to put on. I don't see my clothes."

Sitting up, he placed his back to the headboard and looked at her perched on the edge of the bed with the sheet clutched to her chest. Reaching out, he tugged at the linens. From the expression on his face, the linens had done him a great offense by being her shield.

"You don't need your clothes. You're just goin' to the bathroom. Right?"

The way he said 'right' let her know he'd caught on to her evasive tactics. She couldn't refute him without letting on that she was indeed using her bladder as an excuse.

"I've already seen everything the good Lord blessed you with. So, you don't need to cover up on my account."

The wink and challenging twinkle in his eyes propelled her from the bed toward the ensuite. She didn't have to glance back to know he watched her the entire time. The heat of his stare warmed her almost as much as his touch. She didn't *have* to look, but she did. She couldn't help herself. Sitting up, biting one corner of his bottom lip, Carver's half-mast gaze was glued to her ass. His appreciation for her physique was painted plainly on his face.

Picking up the pace, she entered the bathroom and closed the door behind her. Ignoring his complaints about her disrupting his view, she actually went to the toilet to relieve herself. After she was done, she stood before the sink washing her hands and studying her appearance in the mirror. What she saw was a testament to the way she'd spent the previous hours.

Her once perfectly coiffed hair told of having Carver's fingers in it, rearranging it into a love-stroked tousled look. Areas on her neck and breasts were reddened from his arduous sucking of her skin. Seeing the red marks, brought back the vivid memories of how she received them. *Down girl!* She commanded her core when it fluttered in anticipation of a repeat performance.

No matter how much her traitorous body wanted to test her brain's theory, Alyssa knew she couldn't handle not even one more round with Carver and his magic stick. She'd never tell him that out loud, but that shit had to be magic. Alyssa Renee Ripley didn't do dickmatized, but that was the only explanation for the way she'd behaved and continued to behave around him.

A barely there tap on the door was followed by it swinging open. Carver walked in wearing nothing but his birthday suit. Alyssa was one hundred percent sure the suit didn't look like that when he got it though.

"Excuse you!"

"Excuse me for what? I knocked." Pecking her on cheek, he waltzed right past her, stood before the toilet bowl, and proceeded to urinate.

Her brain told her to turn away. Leave and let him have the privacy the situation required. Her brain gave the directive, but her legs didn't move. Hungrily, she perused his body paying special attention to the semi-flaccid pleasure pole in his grasp. Yeah...She really called his dick a pleasure pole.

It kinda was though. Just thinking about the places inside her that thing touched, made her almost forget her pretty place was too sore to try for round three, or was it four? Hell, she couldn't remember. Entranced, she missed that he'd finished. It wasn't until he crowded her against the counter to wash his hands that she snapped out of her daze.

"You're starin' at me like you wanna do somethin', Bit."

Penetrating her with a knowing look, one corner of his mouth tipped up in a smirk. *Cocky ass...*

"I don't know what you're talking about." Pushing against his chest, she attempted to put some space between them. "Excuse, me. I'm done in here."

Instead of moving, he grabbed her ass in both hands and lifted her onto the counter. Creating a gap between her legs big enough for his hips, he closed the minuscule distance between them.

"Don't play coy with me. We both know what you were thinkin' when you were gawking at my dick just now. Don't worry. I'm more than happy to let you spend some more time with him."

"You think an awful lot of your abilities, sir. I—"

Nuzzling her neck, he stole any other retorts she had to his state-ment. She really needed to stop this before they reached the point of no return. If she could just find the willpower to tell this man 'no', that would be great. But, willpower had packed up its shit and moved to another zip code. That bitch even changed her number.

Carver's hands left her ass, traveling up her torso, seeking out her rapidly hardening nipples. His lips captured hers, seemingly uncaring of their dreaded morning breath. She'd like to say she put up a good fight to be logical, but that's not how it happened.

When his lips left hers and latched onto her breast, her hands went on their own exploration. One stroked his stiffening length, while the other rubbed the back of his head—stroking his closely shorn hair. With zero coaxing, she was ready to ignore the limits of her body and let Carver fuck her on the bathroom counter.

Shrill ringing cut through the haze. It was her cellphone. Tugging, she pulled away from his embrace.

"Ignore it." Carver's gruff command was given without even lifting his head from her breast. His hips jerked when her fingers loosened on his shaft.

"It might be important." No one called her that early on a weekend unless something was wrong. Just as she was making headway in pulling out of his hold, the ringing stopped.

"See. It stopped." Apparently, Carver took it as a sign and resumed his activities with renewed vigor.

Less than a minute later, the ringing started again. It was joined by a tune from what had to be his cellphone. Cursing, he stood up straight and helped her down, muttering the entire time about cock-blockers with too much time on their hands.

Locating her phone on the nightstand next to his, Alyssa picked it up to see her best friend's bright smile on the display. Swiping to answer, she wondered what could be so important for Zaria to call her before eight a.m. on a Saturday morning.

"Hey Zee, what's up?" Next to her, Carver picked up his phone and walked away as he answered.

"Don't, 'Hey Zee, what's up me'. You're what's up, chick."

Frowning, Alyssa tried to figure out what Zee could possibly be talking about. How was she what was up?

"It's too early for riddles, Zee. What are you talking about?"

"You really don't know?"

"If I knew, I wouldn't ask."

"Don't get snippy with me." Zee huffed like she wasn't the one who called Alyssa entirely too early, blocking morning sex. Her not knowing Alyssa was about to get some was no excuse to call before ten a.m. on the weekend. Only her mother did that.

"Zee...what's going on? Why are you calling me before the chickens are up?"

"You play proper, but your ass still has some country in you don't you?"

"Zee!"

"Fine!" Alyssa heard rustling in the background before her friend spoke again. "Tell me why I was minding my business, lying in bed, perusing the innanets and I scroll up on a viral video featuring my bestie?

I had to find out from strangers that you not only know that fine ass Carver Jamieson, but he knows you well enough to jack somebody up on your behalf. Tell me why I had to find that out on the innanets, friend?"

Struck silent by Zee's revelation, fire licked up Alyssa's neck and settled in her cheeks. *Oh shit, oh shit, oh shit!* She knew people were recording at the restaurant last night, but she hadn't anticipated a viral post. Why hadn't she considered that? People love to put every part of their lives online. What would they care about posting her business? They wouldn't. *What the hell was she gonna do now?*

As her mind raced, she vaguely heard Carver's voice speaking to the person on the other end of his call. Quite likely, his caller was delivering the same information she'd received from Zee. Would he want to end things now that they'd been outed? Did they really have anything to be 'outed' for?

They'd literally only seen one another twice in the last fifteen years. Each time they'd ended up in bed together, but that was beside the point. They had no connection on social media until this stranger decided to post the interaction at the restaurant. And for what? Likes? Follows? *Ugh!*

Trapped in her thoughts, she hadn't responded to Zee who immediately launched into a play-by-play that Alyssa mostly tuned out. She didn't need a retelling. She'd seen it firsthand. Carver stepped out of the walk-in closet capturing her attention.

"Zee, I gotta go. I'll call you later."

"What? Ma'am! Don't you get off this phone without telling me what's up. I know where you live. Don't make me come over to your house."

"Zee, please. I promise I'll call you later, but I really gotta go now." Not waiting for a response, Alyssa ended the call.

Suddenly self-conscious about her nudity, Alyssa wrapped her arms around her middle and looked around the room searching for her clothes. She needed to be dressed for whatever conversation they were about to have. Not that the garments would be much of a hindrance if sexy time were put back on the agenda, but for now it would make her feel better to cover up.

"Where are my clothes?"

Instead of telling her, Carver responded with questions of his own. "Why do you want your clothes? You goin' somewhere?"

"No. At least I don't think so. I'd just rather put something on." Why couldn't she find her clothes? She knew they'd dropped them on the floor before they fell into bed last night. When she didn't see her dress on the floor, she assumed he'd picked it up, but she didn't see them on any of the available surfaces in the room.

"C'mere." Wrapping his arms around her, he pulled her flush to his front. "You've got that look on your face and I don't like it."

"What look?"

"The one that says as soon as you put on clothes, you're gonna run like Flo-Jo at the eighty-eight Olympics."

"I don't know who that is. I was one-year-old in nineteen eighty-eight."

"Why do you insist on tryin' me, Bit? You do know that I know you were raised around sports lovers right? I was only three in eighty-eight, but I've seen clips of the great Flo-Jo multiple times probably every four years during the track and field events at the Olympics."

Damn it. She'd forgotten he'd been around a few times when her family had come to campus to see her. Being an avid Tech fan, her dad talked Carver's ear off about stats before she was finally able to get them out of the apartment.

"Fine...I do know Flo-Jo, but that's not the point. The point is, I'd like to get dressed and I can't find my clothes."

Carver's watchful gaze bore into her as if he was trying to pry her thoughts from her brain. Much smarter than people gave him credit for, she was certain he was playing out scenarios before he responded. At this point, she'd deduced that her missing dress was his doing. *Figures.* Despite her promise not to get ghost the minute he closed his eyes, history meant it was possible she'd awaken remorseful and leave regardless of their agreement.

Keeping his arms wrapped around her, he walked them toward the bed. Only when they'd reached the side of it did he break contact. Even then, it was brief as he coaxed her back onto the surface and grudgingly pulled the sheet up for her. Sitting with her back against the headboard, the white sheets clutched over her breast, and her phone in her lap Alyssa waited for Carver to speak.

They had a lot to discuss. Considering his reluctance to provide her with her own clothing, she presumed they'd have to rehash their phone calls and decide how to move forward. She'd never dated anyone in the spotlight before. Not that she hadn't had the opportunity. She had. She avoided it because people were small-minded and simple. They couldn't comprehend the concept of privacy when it came to celebrities and they were insanely judgmental.

Alyssa had always been on the larger side of thick and she was okay with that. She was healthy, regardless of what the 'thin to win' crowd thought. Seeing a person like her with a wealthy, fit celebrity would set off the fragile egos of people who tied body size to beauty and date-ability. Alyssa could do without the kind of attention which went with being in that kind of spotlight.

Tugging her into the cradle of his arms, Carver rested his chin atop of her head of chaotic hair.

"Do you wanna go first, or do you want me to?"

There was no point in feigning ignorance. Settling against his chest, she listened to his heartbeat as she recounted her short call with Zaria. He listened without interruption. When she was done, he confirmed a similar call, not from a friend, but from his agent. Apparently, he and Kevin had parted ways when he stopped playing and he was represented by someone named Jonathan now.

Picking up his phone, he played the video he'd received. It was an accurate account of what happened, with some additional color commentary thrown in from the person doing the recording. Not wanting to ask, but needing to know, Alyssa broached the subject of his thoughts on the whole thing.

"Honestly, I think they're blowing it out of proportion. Jonathan is worried your ex is gonna press charges. He claims what I did could be considered assault." Carver's tone said he thought the idea ludicrous.

"Technically…"

"Don't tell me you agree with him."

"You did almost choke the man out, Carver."

"Nah…He could breathe. If I'd wanted to really choke him, he woulda been unconscious when he hit the floor."

Smacking his chest, she stifled a laugh. Carver gave zero fucks about his behavior with Torrence. "You're a mess. You could at least act like you're remorseful."

"Why would I? I'm not. Like I said before, I didn't do nearly what I wanted to do to him. He should count himself lucky."

"Anyway, I do agree with your agent. You need to be more careful. You can't go around laying hands on people like that."

"I'll do more than lay hands on anyone who thinks they can talk to you any kinda way. It's not okay. I won't stand by and listen to it. Actions have consequences."

"Yeah, yeah, Captain America. But, you can't go around fighting mine or anyone else's battles. Sometimes it's best to walk away."

"The fuck I will and that's all I'm gonna say about that."

"Carver…"

"I'm serious, Bit. New topic. We're done with this one. I won't bend on standing up for what I know was right, and it was right for me to defend you. Period."

Peeking up into his face, she noted the determined set of his jaw and decided to agree to disagree on this one. Moving on from his possible pending assault charges, if Torrence felt petty, she approached the other subject burning her brain.

"What are we gonna do now?"

"What are we gonna do about what?"

"If my friend and your agent are right about the number of views on that video, people are going to assume we're together."

"We are together." His words came out clipped and a bit rough. They left no room for argument even though she considered them presumptuous.

"Carver...We literally saw each other for the first time in ten years last night. Just because we had sex doesn't mean we're together. It takes more than sex to make a relationship."

Carver's entire body went rigid. Her assessment came out more severe than she intended, but she wouldn't take it back. She meant what she said. Sex couldn't and wouldn't be the totality of any relationship which included her. Setting her away from him, he peered into her eyes, the blaze in his emerald depths seared her down to her toes.

"Bit...I thought we worked this out last night. I'm gonna try to say this as nicely as I can...."

The silence stretched between them as she waited for him to continue. When he finally spoke again, she wasn't ready for what he said.

"Bit, I need you to cut this shit out. Stop trying to throw up road blocks and excuses. I want more than just sex with you. You know that. Hell, we both could get sex from anywhere.

What's between us is deeper than that and it scares the crap out of you. If you're scared, just say you're scared, Baby. Don't put what other people think between us. I told you before, I don't give two shits what anyone not named, Carver or Alyssa, has to say about us being together."

Cupping her face between his hands, he soothed his harsh words with a gentle caress.

"A few people on the internet don't get a say on you being mine. There are only two people who make that decision and both of them are in this bed. Are we clear?"

"Crystal."

Seeing the fierceness in his expression and feeling the determination in his hold, Alyssa couldn't do anything other than agree.

"Glad we cleared that up."

As soon as the words left his mouth, Alyssa found herself flat on her back with her legs thrown across Carver's broad shoulders.

"Let's get back to the real discussion. I didn't get a chance to give my girl her good morning kiss."

Tunneling between her thighs, he latched on to her clit giving the bundle of nerves a suckling kiss. Tossing her head back on the pillow, Alyssa gave herself over to Carver's expert morning greeting to her eager core.

Chapter Eight

IT'S ABOUT DAMN TIME

Carver sat at the dining room table in his suite reviewing some documents his assistant had emailed him the day before. He made a mental note to ensure the Realtor had properties with a home office on the list. He didn't want to work this way for very long. He needed his office chair and a desk.

Trying to focus on other work was difficult, because what he really wanted was to spend the day stamping his name all over Alyssa's body—specifically her pussy. She'd finally convinced him to give her the dress she'd worn the previous night. It took some...*persuasion* on his part, but she agreed to a date later.

With the commitment to see her again secured, he walked her down to the valet stand and watched her drive away. Thankfully, the press didn't know where he was staying yet. Knowing it wouldn't stay that way for long, he sent a quick message to the Realtor to see when she'd be ready to show him properties meeting his criteria.

He wanted somewhere he and Bit could be assured of privacy. She was skittish enough without adding nosey ass paparazzi into the equation. He thought he was done with that phase of his career. When he played and they were winning, it was nothing to step outside of a hotel to a crowd of cameras and people yelling out completely inappropriate questions.

That wasn't his life anymore. At least that's what he thought. After the viral video, his social media pages had exploded with new followers and comments on old posts trying to get his attention.

Some of the comments were from women shooting their shot. There were also comments from people of color and allies defending him against other commenters who had things to say about how he treated that douche Alyssa was dating. While his attackers attempted to make his reaction race based, those in his corner stated their appreciation for him standing up for black women.

The messages from people spouting racial bullshit about him and Alyssa were immediately blocked—along with anyone who had shit to say about her body. She was fucking perfect and he'd be damned if he'd entertain anyone who said otherwise.

It appeared as though he was going to have to hire someone to monitor his social media again. After he retired as a player from the NFL, things slowed down considerably on his socials and he didn't think it was necessary to pay someone to monitor the relatively light traffic to his pages. All of that changed overnight.

Carver spent the better part of an hour wading through the messages and comments before he was able to get started on anything else. He still needed to check with Alyssa to make sure she wasn't experiencing any backlash. So far, it appeared no one had named her, but he knew that wouldn't last long.

Closing the lid on his laptop, he gave up on getting any work done. He wasn't in the right frame of mind to give it the proper attention. He wouldn't get there until he knew she was protected from whatever bullshit was coming after his tussle at the restaurant.

Picking up his phone, he searched through his contacts until he landed on the name he wanted. Tapping the icon, he placed the call. It rang only twice before Jasper's raspy voice came across the line.

"What the hell did you manage to get into less than twenty-four hours after you moved to Vegas? Your ass is all over the internet. It's almost as bad as when that social media shit first got popular and every chick and her grandma were pulling crazy ass stunts to get a picture with you."

"Well, hello to you too." Carver groused.

Jasper wasn't wrong, but he could've at least let Carver ease his way into the conversation first. Not that it would have taken him long to get to the point, but he would've at least exchanged pleasantries before launching into his request.

"Don't act like you didn't call me because you want something. No need for all the small talk. It's Saturday and I have people to do, so tell me what you need."

Jasper was still based out of San Diego, but he'd expanded his security company to cover more parts of the country than just California. His crew of protection specialists had grown significantly from when Carver was a steady client. Carver used his services sparingly now, but they'd kept in touch because they'd developed a friendship as well as a working relationship.

"You have people to do?" Carver couldn't let the comment slide although he knew he should.

"I said what I said. Now, if you aren't gonna get to the point, I'll assume you really just called to shoot the shit even though we both know you need my help."

"Don't be an ass, Jasper."

"Get to the point, Carver."

"Alright. Fine. I'm sure you've seen the video. According to Jonathan it's on every social media platform and is possibly gonna be picked up by GMZ. Once that happens, Bit's name is gonna be everywhere."

"And you want her to have a detail."

"Yeah."

"Did you ask her if she wants a detail?"

"We haven't discussed it yet."

"Why don't you call me back after she agrees? You know I don't do reluctant clients. We don't have time to run people down in order to protect them. Either they understand our purpose and want us there, or we move on to clients who actually appreciate having us around."

"I'm gonna talk to her when I pick her up later. She's smart and reasonable. I don't foresee there will be an issue. I want something lined up before this hits."

"So, you're talking within the next twenty-four to forty-eight hours?"

"Preferably."

"You couldn't just talk rough to the guy? Did you have to embarrass him by dangling him off your arm like a puppet?"

"You sound like Bit. I'll tell you like I told her. Considering what I wanted to do, he got off easy. He was an asshole being completely disrespectful to her and talking shit to me about her. He's lucky to still be able to eat solid food."

"Aw shit... You finally got her didn't you? None of the one-night bullshit from Chicago. Like, you did the whole stake your claim she's your woman song and dance. Didn't you?"

"Whatever man. Can you have a team here by Monday or not?"

"Don't get all sensitive on me. I'm happy for you. It's about damn time. I would've found her for you years ago if you would've let me. You were pitiful that morning at the Drake. It took you months to stop searching for her online and I'm sure it was longer, you just stopped letting me see you do it after a while."

Carver really didn't want to dredge up those memories. He and Alyssa were making a new start in Vegas and he only wanted to look forward, not backward. Revisiting the past too often would only stir up resentment for the time they'd lost.

Although he experienced a great deal of growth over the past ten years, part of him felt he could've grown just as much if not more with her in his life. Either way, what's done is done. They had now and now was where he intended to live.

"Thanks for the insight into my past mental state, Jasper. Can you get a team here or not?"

"I'll have to check the roster and I'll get back to you."

"Great. Thanks, man. I appreciate it." Carver was sincerely thankful. He was aware putting a good detail together on short notice wasn't easy. However, if anyone could do it, it was Jasper. That's why his friend was his first call.

"One thing before we get off." Jasper's voice took on an even more serious tone, causing Carver's senses to tingle. *That ain't good.*

"What's that?"

"Before I put anyone on a plane and secure living quarters, I'll need confirmation from the lady herself that she's in agreement with this whole situation."

"Don't worry. She'll be okay with it once we talk."

"If you say so. Let me make some calls and I'll send you a contract asap."

"Great. Thanks again."

"Yeah... Later."

Carver was left holding the phone after Jasper's unceremonious conclusion of the call. He wasn't sure why Jasper was harping on getting Alyssa's agreement to have security. As logical and intelligent as she was, she would understand. Living near a city loaded with celebrities, she was familiar with how intrusive people could be.

There were brand new crazies in the world emboldened by the things they'd seen others get away with online. Bit would understand that aspect of being with him. While they had an unwanted spotlight on them, it would be in her best interest to have someone watching her back at all times. There's no way she wouldn't be on board. *Right?*

Wrong. He'd been so very wrong to think Alyssa would immediately agree with him about the need for a security detail. Like, more wrong than a parent expecting a toddler high on sugar to sit still during a four-hour movie. It ain't gonna happen.

"No."

"What you mean, no, Bit?"

Carver watched Alyssa across the table at the restaurant he'd chosen specifically for the privacy. Placing her fork on her plate, she crossed her arms over her chest and looked him right in the eyes and stood her ground.

"Exactly what I said. No. I'm not going to have people following me around at my job or while I'm grocery shopping or sitting around my house or anything else. Not happening."

He wanted to move his chair around closer to her and pull her into his arms. In the past, he'd been impressed by her tenacity. It wasn't easy for a woman in a male dominated field.

During college her male engineering counterparts had no issues treating her like she didn't belong. She didn't let that deter her. Studying alone many nights or in the small group of other black students, she'd blown them all out of the water gaining the praise from the professors the guys coveted.

"Bit...Baby. I've already called Jasper to have him get a team together. You remember Jasper don't you? His people are super discrete and you won't ever feel like they're smothering you, but they'll keep the idiots and crazies out of your face."

Knowing he couldn't just demand she accept protection, Carver tried to appeal to her logical mind. From the set of her jaw, he wasn't optimistic about it working.

Her words came out measured and even. "You had no right to call Jasper without speaking to me first. This is my life, Carver. I won't be moved around like a player on the field being told where to stand to catch your passes. I'm an adult. One who's managed to take care of herself just fine so far."

Huffing out an irritated breath, Carver ran a hand over his close-cropped hair. The conversation and the date weren't going according to his plan. At all. In his mind, they would have a nice meal where she'd agree that a security detail was prudent.

They'd leave and go for a drive around the city looking at the lights and talking. Then, they'd end the night at her place where he'd get to taste her sweetness and make love until their bodies gave out on them.

The way things were looking, the only thing that would go according to plan is the meal and that was only because he'd waited until it was almost over to bring up his security team idea.

"Bit... Listen...No one's sayin' you can't take care of yourself. It just doesn't sit right with me to know some overzealous asshole could walk right up to you at any time and there wouldn't be anyone to protect you."

"I don't see you walking around with a security detail. *You're* the household name. Not me."

Under different circumstances, he'd consider her pouty expression cute. Heck, he'd even deem it a challenge to put a smile in its place. Not this time though.

"Baby, the driver who brought us here isn't just a driver. He's private security. So, I am walking around with detail. He didn't come inside because Anton's has excellent security.

It's the reason I picked this place for dinner. The owner prides himself in providing his clientele with a safe, hassle free environment. Make no mistake though, Michael will be at the door when we're done."

Turning, Alyssa presented her face to him in profile. He didn't like it. The position cut him off from reading her expression, leaving him in the dark on what was possibly going on in that beautiful mind of hers. Was it possible he was making headway in convincing her to accept Jasper's team?

Abruptly, she swiveled to look at him. "I'm done eating. Can we go now?"

"Sure. If that's what you want." Raising his hand, Carver called for the check while watching Alyssa, trying to read her body language without much luck. Pulling out his phone, he sent a quick text to Michael to alert him of their movements.

Once he'd settled the bill, they exited the restaurant. Using his fingertips on the small of her back, he guided them through the understated opulence of the establishment. The light click-clack of Alyssa's heels bounced off marble floors as they made their way to the glass doors leading outside.

When they stepped through the automatic doors, Michael was there leading them to the back passenger side of the vehicle. Helping Alyssa in, Carver climbed in behind her. As if he'd been doing it for years, he reflexively reached out to help her with her seatbelt. Having gone through the routine on the ride over, she didn't protest.

For what seemed like an eternity, they rode in silence. He would've been fine with it, but it wasn't a companionable silence. With the words unsaid between them, it was tense. Breaching the physical distance, he clasped her hand in his. Bringing it to his lips, he kissed the back.

"Bit—"

"Carver—"

They both started speaking and stopped simultaneously. Although, his instinct was saying he wouldn't like what she had to say, he prompted her to speak.

"You go first."

Her grip on his fingers tightened with tension before she released a resolute breath. "I think we're moving way too fast and we should take a step back."

"No." Carver's entire body went rigid.

Pleading eyes met his as she sat next to him trying to backpedal out of the relationship they'd begun less than twenty-four hours prior.

"Carver, can you listen before you come to a conclusion?"

"Bit, I don't know if I can. I'm feeling like anything you say right now is coming from a place of fear and I'll be damned if I let fear keep us apart."

Clamping his fingers around hers, he resisted her tugging to free her hand. He couldn't let her run. Not physically or emotionally. They were done with that. When he wouldn't let go, she stopped pulling releasing a resigned sigh.

"Carver...I'm not saying I don't want to be with you."

"What are you sayin' then?"

"I'm saying we're moving at lighting speed for two people who haven't spent time getting to know each other. There are still aspects of me that are the same as the person you knew at Tech, but a lot has changed. I'm sure it's the same for you. We need time for you to get to know the new Alyssa and I need time to learn who Carver Jamieson is now."

"Why does doing any of that require us to take a step back? Isn't that a natural part of all relationships?"

"It is. But, what isn't natural is hiring a security detail for the woman you've only just entered a relationship with."

"Bit, it might not be everyday normal, but it's one hundred percent natural for a man in my position to want to ensure his woman has protection when he can't be around to do it himself."

"Then maybe I'm not cut out to be the woman of a man like you."

Glad the partition was up and Michael couldn't hear them, Carver worked to keep himself from losing his shit. Her words gutted him. They shouldn't have. He shouldn't be this invested this early on, but he'd wanted Alyssa in his life for more than a decade. There was no way he could find her and lose her in the span of a day.

No longer able to stand even the smallest distance between them, he released his seat belt and closed the gap separating their bodies. Cupping her face in his hands, he searched her eyes for answers. What he discovered was a bit of fear tinged with confusion, but there was still a softness there.

"Do you mean that, or are you lashin' out because things aren't goin' exactly how you want 'em to go?"

Long lashes dropped to cover the dark amber pools as she tried to hide what he saw in their depths.

"Look at me, Bit. Look me in the eye and tell me you don't think we should be together simply because I don't wanna take chances with your safety and well-being."

"That's not fair. That's not what I said."

"Well, it's what I heard."

A wry grin curled the corners of her lips. "You have a habit of hearing without listening."

"Then set me straight. But know this. Anything suggesting we should put the brakes on our relationship is a non-starter. We can comprise, but I ain't givin' you up. Not when we just found each other again. Don't ask me to do that, Baby. I can't."

Soft palms met his heated skin. Slender fingers, with blunt tipped nails curled around his wrists as he continued to hold her face in his hands.

"You're right. I had a knee jerk reaction to the security detail. I don't think it's necessary and I don't foresee any way that having people follow me around won't interfere with my day-to-day life.

I've led a very simple, but happy existence thus far. I've never been a fan of the way people treat celebrities and I've never desired to be in the limelight. All of this is a system shock.

There has to be a middle ground. You said your social media exploded with notifications. My accounts are all private. They always have been. Besides, no one has named me in the video. Only people who know me really well even recognized it was me."

"Just because your name isn't out there, doesn't mean people don't know who you are."

"Why don't we wait and see? I think this will die down and none of the things you're worried about will come to pass."

The smile on her face was so hopeful, Carver didn't want to crush her by explaining the harsh reality racing toward them. He'd give it a week, tops, before some dunderhead tried some bullshit that would have him considering wearing prison orange.

"Five days. We'll revisit this in five days."

"That's not even a whole week, Carver."

"That's as long as I'm willing to concede."

The tension of the exchange wasn't nearly as thick as before and he sighed internally when she released an acquiescent exhale.

"Fine. Five days."

"I'll let Jasper know."

"I didn't say yes, Carver."

"Sure you did, Baby." Pressing his lips to hers, he put an end to their first argument. He didn't deepen the kiss, because he was certain she'd object to sex when only the partition separated them from Michael. Maybe one day. A man could dream.

Chapter Nine

LIE TO YOURSELF ALL YOU WANT

When Alyssa left Carver's suite Saturday morning, she didn't make it home before her phone started to ring with calls from family and close friends. Turns out their little videographer had over a million hits on their video and climbing. *Oh joy...*

Instead of wading through social media posts the way Carver described, she dealt with calls and texts from people she actually knew. Honestly, she felt she got the raw end of the deal. It started with her mother. How someone who avoided social media knew everything that went on with the platforms continued to amaze Alyssa. She was halfway home when her mother called.

"Alyssa?"

"Hey, Mama."

"Where are you? Are you driving? It doesn't sound like you're at home."

"I am driving, Mama." It was mid-morning and she hoped her mother didn't delve into where she was driving to or from.

"Oh. Okay. Listen, Marcel sent me a video this morning saying the girl in it looked like you. I said, no ma'am. My baby is not in some video on the internet. But I looked at it anyway, because I knew she was gonna call trying to start something.

I thought she was lying, but she wasn't. Why didn't you tell anyone about this? Torrence cutting up on you in public and Carver wringing his neck."

"Mama, Carver didn't wring his neck."

"Looked like it to me."

"He didn't. Anyway. I didn't tell you because there really wasn't anything to tell. I don't call y'all every time some guy talks out the side of his neck. I can handle it."

"I don't like how that sounds. It sounds like stuff like that happens a lot."

"It doesn't happen a lot, but it happens. Maybe not on the scale Torrence tried, but they get butthurt and act out. Not all men are mature enough to deal with situations like adults. I can't come running to my parents every time some immature guy shows his true colors."

"Well, I still don't like it. We might not be able to do anything about it from the other side of the country but it's better to hear it from you than out in the streets."

"Yes, ma'am."

The censure in her mother's voice made Alyssa temporarily contrite. She didn't tell them some things because she didn't want them to worry unnecessarily. If it hadn't been for some nosey stranger, this conversation with her mother wouldn't have occurred.

"Mmhmm. Now, back to Carver. Ain't it funny that y'all ran into each other the same night we talked about him?"

"I guess you could say that."

"It's a good thing he was there. He gave that no-good so and so the what for. Talking about my baby like he didn't have the sense God gave a gnat."

Alyssa didn't bother to correct her about Carver. It wouldn't do any good to point out that she'd been in the process of walking away from Torrence and his drama when Carver butted into the situation. Maybe it would've escalated without him, maybe it wouldn't have. They'd never know.

"Well, you don't have to worry about Torrence. He knows we won't be going out again."

"Good. You were too smart and cute for him anyway."

"Mama!"

"What? Honesty is good. That little ferret was jealous of how smart and beautiful you are. I bet it stuck in his craw that he couldn't break you down to his level."

"If you say so."

"I do."

Knowing how her mama liked to have the last word, Alyssa didn't bother to reply. She'd finally made it home. Although she'd showered before she left Carver's she was still wearing last night's dress. She was looking forward to a nice long bath. Switching the call to her earphones, she exited the car.

"So... are you and Carver gonna see each other again?"

Alyssa almost tripped on the stairs entering her house. "What? Why would you ask me that?"

"I told you Marcel sent me the video. I'd have to be blind not the see how he wrapped his arm around you when y'all left the restaurant. That didn't look like any friend I have."

"Mama, I think you read too much into the situation. Carver has a thing about bullies. Torrence set him off. He was just looking out for me. That's all."

There was absolutely no way in hell she'd tell her mother she'd spent the better part of last night and this morning letting Carver blow her back out. They were close, but not that close.

"Tell me anything. I know what I saw. Mark my words. Now that the two of you are in the same place, he's gonna come calling."

"Mama, it's really not like that."

"Girl...Lie to yourself all you want. You don't have to lie to me though. Anyway. I just called to check on you. You go on and do whatever it was you were doing, put your groceries away or whatever. I'll talk to you tomorrow."

Once again, Alyssa didn't bother to correct her mother's assumption. It wasn't like she planned to tell her what she was really doing. Until she and Carver talked things out, there was nothing to tell.

Hours later, as Alyssa sat across the table from Carver at the exclusive restaurant inside Anton's high roller casino, she grappled with how her world had tilted on its axis in less than one planetary rotation. At the exact hour the previous day, she'd been on the phone with her mother assuring her that she and Carver were barely more than acquaintances.

Now, he sat on the other side of the expensive table scape telling her he was hiring a security detail for her. How in the hell had things switched up so quickly? Giving a relationship a chance was one thing; having strangers invade every aspect of her life was quite another.

The thoughts running rampant in her head weren't logical or reasonable. He'd asked her to stop putting up roadblocks and obstacles, then he turned around and tried to take over her life. *A security detail? Seriously?* Before she said something she'd later regret, Alyssa asked if they could leave.

Her appetite was gone. Besides, she'd finished most of her meal. Knowing Carver, he probably planned it that way thinking to soften her up before he lobbed his outlandish idea at her.

Struggling internally, she didn't want to see it from his perspective, despite the insistence of her analytical side. Their walk through the restaurant, then the casino, before reaching the exit was done in silence.

Regardless of her heart's objections she floated the possibility that she didn't belong with him. He quickly shut that idea down. Between his sheer presence, his refusal to accept her weak attempts to break things off and her own mind telling her she was being foolish, she didn't stand a chance.

He sat beside her in the back seat of the car making plans to have Jasper get a team ready and she hadn't even agreed to his plan. At least not verbally.

"I didn't say yes, Carver." Alyssa leaned away placing a hand on his chest.

"Sure you did, Baby." Carver's triumphant grin was followed by him placing those kissable lips on hers. The struggle to keep her head on straight was very, very real. Once his mouth took hers, all she wanted to do was climb in his lap and act like a teenager sneaking off with her secret boyfriend.

Only, they weren't teenagers and if Carver had anything to say about it, they wouldn't be a secret. Before her hormones took complete control, she managed to pull away from his drugging kiss.

"We have to stop."

"Why?"

"We're in the back seat of a car."

"You say that like there's not plenty of room to do whatever we want." In a motion much too fluid for her comfort, he unbuckled her seat belt and had her straddling his lap in a matter of seconds.

"Carver!"

"Don't play innocent, Bit. You know you like it." Grabbing two handfuls of her rear, he squeezed her cheeks.

Alyssa's voice held shock, but she was certain he heard the excitement in it as well. He pushed all of her boundaries and she wasn't positive she wanted to push back in this instance.

Thank goodness, she'd opted for a romper with full pants and not a dress. She felt the bulge of his erection beneath her center. Regardless of Michael's presence on the other side of the partition, if the only barrier between them had been her underwear, she wasn't sure she would've been able to resist taking Carver's magic stick for a quick ride.

Not giving her the chance to over think, he recaptured her lips while simultaneously tugging her hips rocking her pant-clad core against his stiffening length.

"See, Baby. You fit perfectly with room to spare on this big back seat. What do you have to say now?"

Nothing. She couldn't say a word. Her libido was campaigning hard to take the reins. Controlling her movements, Carver punched his hips up grazing his thickness against her. With her hormones vying for domination, Alyssa didn't resist. Their moans of pleasure issued out in time with the low music streaming through the speakers.

Her fingers trailed up his shoulders before wrapping around the back of his head. Her nails scraped across his scalp drawing a groan from deep within his chest. Bucking his hips in response to the stimulation, he wrenched his lips away.

"Fuck! If we don't stop this, I'm gonna strip this onesie off and fuck you right here." The strain of holding back was evident in his voice.

"It's called a romper, not a onesie."

"Romper, onesie. It doesn't matter. It's gonna be a pile of scraps if you keep testin' me."

"I'm testing you? You started it. I was fine sitting over there alone."

"Don't try to insert logic on me." His fingers clenched, released then clenched again on her ass. "You feel so damn good..." Briefly closing his eyelids, he moaned.

Dropping her head back exposing her neck, she rolled her hips grazing his covered cock against her obscured nether lips. If she kept going, she was confident she could cum while fully clothed. His hands clamped down, stilling her motion against him.

"Stop rubbin' my best girl on my dick like that if you aren't lookin' to get fucked in the backseat of this car."

Her eyes gleamed with mischief as she stared at him. "Oh, now you want me to stop? Did you bite off more than you can chew?"

His eyes popped open in a glare. "Make no mistake, Bit. The only reason you're still wearin' this onesie and not bouncin' on my dick is because I know you'd be embarrassed for Michael to hear you gettin' your world rocked in the back of his car. Now, stop pushin' me or that's exactly what'll happen."

The idea of torturing him titillated her, making her want to rock against his hardness even more. Only the knowledge that Carver didn't make idle threats kept Alyssa from tempting fate. The heat from his gaze was enough to burn their garments if he possessed such powers.

Sliding her hands down his chest, she pushed away attempting to retake her seat. Initially, his grip on her butt cheeks tightened, but he finally moved his hands to her hips to help her.

Her poor pussy did not appreciate her restraint and throbbed in protest of not being penetrated at that very moment. When she'd settled in her seat, he reached over to secure her seat belt before sliding over to fasten his own.

Glancing out the window, she watched their progress. Initially, Alyssa wasn't sure where they were going. She'd assumed Carver gave Michael an address, but as they progressed past the outlet mall her mother loved, she realized they were heading towards her home.

Turning to look at Carver, she sought confirmation. "Is the date over? You're taking me home?"

His long fingers lifted her hand from her lap and he tangled their digits together before kissing the back of her hand.

"I am taking you home, but this date is far from over." The promise in his expression broadcasted clearly. Another night of Carver's carnal delights was in her very near future.

~

Silence reigned between them during the ride, but the sexual tension was so thick it'd require a chainsaw to cut it. Traffic was surprisingly light, so they reached her place in less than thirty minutes. She'd opted for a two-story house on a corner lot, instead of the adobe style one-story homes prevalent in the area. She had more yard than many of her neighbors, but she figured the extra lawncare expense was worth it to not be able to reach her arm out of the window and touch her neighbor's house.

Okay... So the houses weren't that close together, but coming from a city where houses were placed on generously sized lots, having the large homes built on less than a quarter acre seemed cramped to her. As if they expected someone who wanted more space, the builders of the four-bedroom, three and a half bath structure placed it in the center of the almost half acre lot. It was virtually unheard of in the area.

The vehicle came to a stop in her driveway. By the time she and Carver were unbuckled, Michael had the door open and his hand extended ready to help her from the car. Thanking him, Carver stepped out first and turned to assist her.

Smiling to herself, Alyssa wondered what the hell she'd gotten herself into. The man couldn't bring himself to let his bodyguard touch her long enough to help her from the car. How would he make it when he found out she spent her days surrounded by men?

Things were slowly changing in the STEM fields, but the vast majority of her co-workers were male. The only women she interacted with professionally, on a regular basis, happened on conference calls. Somehow, she knew that bit of information wouldn't go over well. While she was sure he was aware of the gender gap, knowing it and seeing it were two distinctly different things.

With the heat from Carver's body at her back, she unlocked the front door. They entered her foyer and she immediately crossed to the keypad to disable the alarm. As soon as she pressed the last digit of her code, his hands were roaming her body while he kissed the skin exposed by the narrow straps of her romper top.

Before the lustful fog completely took over, she managed to disentangle herself from his hold. Stepping back, she kicked off her heels. His penetrating gaze never left her as he followed suit, toeing off his loafers without untying them. When he went to snag her around the waist, she side stepped him, moving toward the stairs.

"Wait..."

"Wait for what?" He grumbled closing the distance between them. "Don't you think we've waited long enough? As a matter of fact, we have some time to make up for."

Seizing her lips in a searing kiss, he moved them until her back was pressed against the wall. Trailing kisses along her jawline, he suckled at the skin just beneath it, driving her wild. His hands were busy as he slid one into the bodice of her outfit while the other lifted her leg, gripping her thick thigh high on his waist.

Her center gushed without even being touched. Simply from anticipation. Carver seemed to have a detailed map to all of her erogenous zones.

"Mm...Carver.... What about Michael?"

"I must not be doing somethin' right if you're thinkin' about another man at a time like this."

Somehow, she managed to dodge his attempt to recapture her mouth. "I'm serious, Carver. I don't want him sitting outside in the car waiting for you to come back and you're in here trying to get laid."

Making a noise which sounded suspiciously like growl, he lifted his head. "Number one, I'm not *tryin'* anything. Number two, Michael isn't just sitting outside. He's doing his job making sure the place is safe, then he'll leave until I call him back."

Frowning in confusion, Alyssa tried to understand why Carver's bodyguard would leave. "I thought he was supposed to protect you. How can he do that if he's gone?"

"Michael's very good at what he does. I'm positive he made sure we weren't followed on the way here and he'll make sure the place is squared away before he leaves."

Cupping her head between his hands he peppered kisses on her face starting at her forehead trailing down the bridge of her nose before taking her mouth again.

"Now, can you focus on the moment?" He mumbled against her lips.

"Can we at least make it to the bedroom?" Alyssa placed her hands on his chest to put the slightest amount of space between them.

Sighing, he dropped his hands and stepped back. "Whatever you want, Baby." Lightly grasping her shoulders, he turned her toward the staircase. Delivering a stinging swat to her butt cheek, he encouraged her to start moving.

Throwing him a glance over her shoulder, she was stuck between wanting to tell him about himself and being turned on by his high-handed behavior. Her hormones won the battle and she quickly ascended the stairs leading him to her bedroom.

"You gotta lot of rooms for just one person, Bit."

Alyssa turned to see Carver visually perusing the doorways leading to her home office and one of the spare bedrooms as they walked past them.

"It's pretty standard for this area. The number of rooms wasn't what drew me to the house. I was more drawn to the area and the lot. Having two spare bedrooms and an office was just a bonus."

Entering her bedroom ended their seemingly benign conversation. The Carver she'd encountered in the penthouse suite reappeared and he expeditiously unbuckled her belt and stripped off her romper as he placed kisses on her body for each place he exposed.

As was becoming a habit, he rid her of her clothing and laid her on the bed before attacking his own. The separation was brief. Their ardor didn't have a chance to cool since he was covering her body with his less than a minute after her back met the silky sheets. Paying extra attention to her puckered nipples, he lavished them with affection while kneading her globes.

Alyssa's core clenched in longing to be filled by the stiff length that grazed her thigh each time he shifted or moved. Leaving her breast with a suckling pop, he delivered pecks along her torso before shouldering his way between her legs. Gazing down at him, she watched as he stared at her pussy prior to kissing it reverently.

"How's my best girl? Did you miss me? I'm sorry you had to wait all day. I promise I'll make it up to you."

Carver spoke to her throbbing core like it was its own person instead of a part of her anatomy. Yet, she didn't feel slighted. Her walls slickened and moisture seeped from her channel without him providing the skillful oral pleasure she knew was coming.

Keeping his promise, he lapped at her folds before drawing her pearl into his mouth lashing it with such precision pleasure shot up her spine slamming her eyes shut with its force. Mindlessly searching, her fingers scraped through his almost buzzed hair, eliciting a growl from Carver which only served to ratchet her desire higher when the sound vibrated through her pussy.

When she was with him this way, shame was a foreign concept. But, if she had any, it would've washed over her after she reached her climax following his rumble of pleasure. Encouraged by her release, Carver hummed against her labia like he was partaking of the most delicious of delicacies.

"Mmmm!..." Alyssa's lips clamped shut over the moan as her head thrashed on her pillow.

"Don't try to hold it in, Baby. I wanna hear how much you love it. Ain't nobody around to be quiet for. Let that shit out."

Carver issued his demand with a gripping smack to her inner thigh. Immediately kissing the area to soothe it, he went back to his mission to turn her mind to mush. A mission he took very, very seriously. He didn't stop his oral onslaught until he'd wrung another voice snatching orgasm from her and greedily lapped up the fruit of his labor.

Giving a parting kiss to her folds, he trailed kisses up her shuddering frame. Kisses to the backs of her eyelids prompted her to lift them. Hovering above her with a Cheshire Cat grin was Carver's handsome face.

"No sleepin'. We ain't even close to being through."

Sharing her taste with her he slipped his tongue between her parted lips tangling it with her own. Partially dropping his weight onto her, he flexed his hips rubbing his shaft along her folds stimulating her clit.

Tipping her pelvis, she adjusted to allow him entry into her pulsing channel. Instead of accepting the invitation and putting them both out of their misery, he pulled all the way back. At her grumble of protest, he shushed her while reversing their positions to place her on top straddling his trim hips.

Startled at the sudden change, Alyssa squealed grabbing Carver's arms to steady herself and shifting her weight on her knees. His fingers gripped her hips and he bucked beneath her.

"You're wigglin' in all the wrong ways, Baby."

Handling her like she was several sizes smaller, Carver lifted her. Without ever touching his cock, he unerringly found her center and slid her down his shaft. His thickness stretched her slick walls robbing her of her breath.

"Damn...You're squeezin' me so tight; I feel like I'm gonna bust any second." Carver moaned, his fingers grasping and releasing her hips spasmodically.

Although her core wept to be penetrated, Alyssa had to take a moment to adjust to being filled so suddenly. The feeling of pleasure with the slightest edge of pain ricocheted through her. Experimentally, she undulated her hips in a small circle.

"Fuck, Bit baby. Don't mess around." The hands on her hips traveled to her ass where Carver began guiding her up and down his length.

"Ride this dick like you mean it. It's yours, Baby."

Raising his upper body from the bed, he threaded the fingers of one hand into her hair pulling her in for a soul melding kiss. Releasing her lips, he pressed his forehead to hers locking her gaze with his.

His intensity combined with the feeling of overwhelming fullness from his thick length imbedded in her channel to the hilt, made it difficult to keep her eyes open. She wanted to close them and allow the waves of bliss to crash over her, but Carver had made it clear he wanted to see her pleasure when he was inside her. He wouldn't accept anything else.

Smack!

The stinging blow did more than get Alyssa's attention, it caused her pussy to gush. Who knew she enjoyed having her ass spanked during sex? She hadn't. Not until Carver.

"Ride it, Bit. Bounce that ass and take my cock. Give my girl what she wants."

Damn she liked it when he got all demanding. She'd never tell him that out loud, but she didn't have to. Her pussy, apparently now known as Carver's best girl, told him exactly how she felt.

Without further prompting, she pressed her hands against his chest pushing him to lay down. Balancing with her fingers splayed on his pecs, she moved into a squat and complied with his request—bouncing her ass and riding his big dick. Determined to give him the same level of pleasure he gave her, she alternated her pace between long slow and short quick strokes.

Apparently, the way her cheeks clapped during the quick moments was his undoing. Slipping his forearms under her haunches, he held her aloft while he punched his hips up in a blinding rhythm forcing both of them over the edge. Her core spasmed around his turgid length as her essence coated his shaft and he painted her walls with his seed.

Their cries of completion echoed out into the room as they both reached their climax. A sheen of sweat covered them both as Alyssa collapsed onto Carver's chest breathing heavily. Lazily, he trailed his hands from her shoulders to the round of her hips and back up.

In a lethargic haze, they eventually rose from the bed to clean up before falling back beneath the sheets too tired to worry about stripping them. It could wait until morning. Snuggled into Carver's side, wrapped in his embrace, Alyssa drifted off into a well sated sleep.

Chapter Ten

MORNIN' BIT

As much as he wanted to make up for the years he thought they'd lost, Carver didn't follow his first inclination to keep Alyssa in a state of undress all day Sunday and simply order food when they required nourishment. That's not to say they weren't intimate. After all, his best girl needed her morning kisses. At least, as far as he was concerned, she did.

Licking his lips in memory of how he started his Sunday morning, he picked up the phone from the bedside table. He needed a hit of his Bit in some form to get his day started. How he'd managed all this time without her was an unsolvable mystery.

Swiping the screen, a picture of his Bit sleeping peacefully with her head on his chest greeted him. He'd snapped the photo the previous morning—right before he woke her with his head between her lush thighs. An unconscious smile stretched across his face. He hadn't been this damn happy in a long time.

Even though she'd insisted on sleeping apart Sunday night, he still felt like the luckiest guy alive. Taking the job with the Ravagers and moving to Vegas was turning out far better than he had anticipated. He got to continue to do what he loved, being around football, and he'd reconnected with the woman he feared he might never see again.

Damn... His mama was right. She told him, if it was meant to happen it would come back around. When they were supposed to reconnect, they would. He didn't want to hear it at the time and for a while he battled daily not to get Jasper or a private investigator to find Alyssa for him.

He was quite possibly obsessed with her. After just one night. Now that he'd spent the weekend learning about her in even more ways, he had to admit his mama was correct. While on one hand, he felt like they'd lost time, on the other he saw the way she'd blossomed even more since they'd last seen one another. He'd also grown and matured during their time apart.

Looking at the picture on his phone and thinking about her made him want to hear her voice to start his day. Checking the time, he tapped the screen to place his call. Putting the phone on speaker, he listened to the rings and waited.

"Hello?" Alyssa's sultry voice came over the line sounding much too sexy for her to be so far away from him.

"Mornin', Bit." The more he talked to her, the more his southern accent took over—especially in moments of high emotion. It was like she brought out the feeling of being home, and his accent came out in force.

"Good morning. Why are you up so early? I mean, I have to be in the office in an hour, but you don't have to go in today do you?"

Laying back on the big bed, Carver stretched out his legs and put his gaze on the view out of the massive windows in his bedroom.

"I couldn't sleep any longer. Somebody got me used to wakin' up beside her and then made me come back to this lonely hotel room and sleep alone."

Carver heard the tell-tale signs of Alyssa going about her daily routine. While he hadn't been privy to her before work rituals, he'd witnessed her weekend behavior the prior morning.

"You really want me to believe two nights was all it took for you to become adjusted to me sharing a bed with you? Pfft! Excuse me if I don't believe you."

The words he wanted to say were clamped behind his teeth. Not because he was afraid to express himself, but something told him hearing them would be overwhelming for her. He couldn't tell her he'd dreamt of falling asleep beside her. Nor could he tell her waking up next to her each morning had been a long-held desire since long before their night at the Drake. She'd think he was some kind of crazy stalker.

He couldn't have that. She was already skittish enough. While it wasn't possible to give her the full picture, he didn't let her comment slide completely.

"I do believe I'm the one in the position to know how I'm feeling at this moment, ma'am. And, I'm feeling like a man who wanted to wake up, kiss his best girl good morning and send his woman off to work with a smile on her face."

"Two out of three ain't bad." She quipped, forcing a chuckle from him before he could shut it down.

"You got me there. At least I get to hear your voice. It would be better if I could see your face, but I'll take what I can get."

"I still have a few minutes before I have to leave, we can video chat."

"You ain't said nothin' but a thang, Baby."

Ending the call, he immediately pressed the video chat icon. Sitting up in bed, he allowed the bedcovers to pool at his waist. After a second or two of the digital rings, Alyssa's beautiful face filled his screen.

"That's a million times better." Carver's eyes drank in her lightly made-up face. A pinkish gloss covered her lips making them appear even more plump and kissable.

"You're not so bad yourself...for a guy who's still lounging around in bed like a man of leisure."

"Take the day off and you can lounge with me for a few hours. Then, we can go look at the houses the Realtor has lined up for me."

"As tempting as the first part sounds, I'm gonna have to say no. I have a full day planned. We have a new client and I have to attend kick-off meetings. After that, I have to get started on the code changes for another client."

"Only the loungin' part sounds good? You don't want to help me pick a place?" He was being bold as hell, but he didn't care.

"I think selecting *your* home is entirely *your* decision. And honestly, I'm not one of those people who likes going on tours of houses for fun."

"Touring the houses might not be fun, but us being together could make it enjoyable."

He fought against saying the words he desired. Shit like, it was going to be her home too; so, she should have a say. And, he didn't want to get something that was only conducive to his lifestyle without considering hers. Talk like that would most definitely have her backpedaling and trying to exit their fledgling relationship.

Nope. Keep all that shit in, because losing Alyssa couldn't happen. If it meant he had to dial it back a little, he'd try. For a while at least. The jury was out on how long he'd manage it, but letting her walk out of his life again wasn't optional.

Placing the cap on her tumbler of coffee, she smiled at him indulgently. "I'm sure spending the day with you would be enjoyable, but I really can't call in to work last minute. Not today."

Although she hadn't gone into detail, Alyssa told him about her job with a mid-sized tech company specializing in gaming security. She worked mostly with slot machines and similar casino games. He wasn't even aware such things were needed, but he was more of a poker or black jack guy when he played games of chance.

They spoke a little longer while she had her breakfast and finished getting her things together. Not wanting to distract her as she drove, he ended the conversation after securing a commitment from her to join him for dinner that evening. He knew asking her to take the day off was a long shot, but he couldn't resist asking.

Although his contract was all ironed out with the team, he wasn't set to go into the facility until mid-week. He hoped to have his search for a home narrowed down by then. Since he was using a branch of the real estate firm he'd used in San Diego and New York, they already had an idea of his preferences.

Rolling out of bed to get his own day started, he threw on some athletic gear and hit the gym on the first floor of his suite. No longer being on the field full time didn't mean he completely stopped his regimen. Once he was done, he ordered breakfast and hopped into the shower.

Carver's meeting with the realtor was scheduled for ten a.m. He'd just finished speaking with Jonathan about hiring someone to manage his social media when he received Michael's text that he was on the way up. Turning off the notifications on his accounts had bought him some measure of relief, but he wasn't confident that it would last long.

Although he wasn't hired by the Ravagers for the Offensive Coordinator or Head Coach, it was common knowledge those positions were in his path. Due to those ambitions, he'd have to maintain some sort of social media presence if only through the official Quarterback Coach account. He wouldn't be able to turn those notifications off indefinitely.

As of yet, no one from the team office had called him about the incident. They either hadn't been informed, which was unlikely, or they were waiting to see what came of it. No matter what Jonathan said, for the most part, he was coming off as a hero. Not that he wanted attention or accolades for protecting his woman. It was what he was supposed to do.

The only thing that could turn this situation into a bad thing would be if the scrawny bully Alyssa had been on a date with decided to be a bigger asshole and press charges. All Carver could do was wait and see what would shake out. He wasn't worried. If that guy had the sense God gave a gnat, he'd crawl back into his hole and pretend he'd never met Alyssa Ripley.

Carver walked through the 21,800 square foot mansion equally impressed with the agent's ability to follow his instructions while simultaneously getting it completely wrong. Located in one of the nicer Vegas suburbs, the place was gorgeous. It's beauty wasn't the issue. Neither were the additional office spaces he wanted for himself and Bit. The home gym, theater room, game room and primary bedroom suite were things of beauty.

He was certain his dad would go absolutely crazy over the indoor gun range on the basement level, but he'd never get the chance to use it. In spite of the relatively low asking price for the eleven-bedroom, sixteen-bathroom house, Carver wouldn't be making an offer.

It was a showplace, not a home. No amount of sprucing and furniture arrangements would give it the vibe he wanted in the place he laid his head. A perfect place to hold parties and entertain, it felt more like a resort rather than a place people built their lives and raised families.

He fully expected to entertain in his home at some point, but he couldn't pick a place based solely on how impressive it would look when he had people over. Regret at not doing an online preview of the place filled him as he realized this was their first stop. If the other places were along these same lines, this process was going to take longer than he expected.

After the elevator ride back to the main floor, Audrey turned toward him smiling like she just knew she'd nailed it on the first try.

"You've been awfully quiet Mr. Jamieson. What do you think? I'm sure you can add some touches to make it feel more like yours. I have the name of some excellent contractors who could make any significant changes you might want."

Scratching his neck, Carver looked around at the expansive area that should have been the living room or den, but looked more like a hotel lobby than anything.

"It's a really nice place and it has everything I asked for, with a few bonuses added in."

Audrey's red curls bounced with the vigorous nodding of her head. Her smile was still intact, but Carver knew he was about to dim it a few notches.

Spreading out his arms, he gestured around the room. "It's gorgeous, but it doesn't feel like a home. I don't get the feeling anyone actually lives here. So, I can't picture myself living here."

As expected, her smile drooped a little, but she quickly perked it up. "Well, no worries! We'll just move on to the next location. Maybe that one will be more to your liking. It's smaller than this one, but has all of the features you requested."

"Sounds great." Extending his arm, he indicated for her to go first.

Nodding to Michael, Carver followed the agent from the house. After a twenty-minute drive, they entered the gates of another suburb. The homes weren't quite as large, but were still well over fifteen thousand square feet from his observation.

Before he even stepped out of the car, he knew that place wouldn't do, but he went inside anyway. Never one to waste someone's time, he didn't allow the full tour once he stepped into the sterile looking foyer.

Sure, he could hire a decorator to remove the monochromatic theme the current owner had going, but there was no decorating around the harsh angular lines of the rooms and odd placements of accent walls. He saw all of that after only five steps into the house. He didn't need to see any more, nor did he need Michael to look it over for any security issues.

After a similar outcome at the third and fourth houses, he almost called it quits for the day. Something told him to press on. Taking some of the blame, he knew much of this could've been avoided had he looked at them in advance online instead of trying to twist Alyssa's body into pretzel shapes all weekend. Damn if he'd regret choosing her over online house shopping. It was no contest.

As they approached the last place on Audrey's list, Carver got that feeling in his gut. The same one he had before the start of the college championship game and before all three of his winning Superbowl games. The suburb was a little further out from the city actually, but that wasn't an issue for him.

He knew privacy came at a cost and the cost usually included being removed from living directly inside the city. When he worked in New York, he lived in a penthouse and while he loved the amenities of the building, he hated not having a free-standing space of his own.

When Audrey had to supply Michael with a code to enter the gate, Carver felt even better about the house and he'd yet to set a foot inside. Once he did, he was ready to tell Audrey to draw up papers and make an offer. He didn't. But he was ready.

Sitting on a one-acre corner lot, the eight bedroom, nine bath mansion met every criteria on Carver's list. It even had a pool house his parents or other guests could use when they came for visits to give them more privacy. There was an office wing which included a conference room two offices and a security room. There was an additional office on the second floor of the house overlooking the foyer that would be perfect for Alyssa.

Was he jumping completely ahead of himself by mentally putting her in the house? Absolutely. Did he care? Not one iota. It might not be tomorrow, nor the next day, but they'd make a home together. Even if it wasn't at this particular house.

The price point was midway between the most expensive place he'd seen and the least at a cool $9.5 million. He'd already discussed potential purchase points with his financial advisor and it was well within the range. However, he'd hold off on making a final decision until he could get Bit over to see it. Based on their earlier talk, he was certain he'd have an interesting time getting her to agree to have a look.

Maybe knowing he only wanted her to look at one place would sway her. Checking his watch, he saw it was a little after two p.m. They'd skipped lunch. Since Alyssa wasn't due to leave work until five p.m. Carver suggested a late lunch to go over the next steps with Audrey to begin the process of making a bid. Nothing would be finalized until he talked to his Bit, but they could get the ball rolling.

Unlike when he'd taken Alyssa to Anton's for dinner, Michael came inside the restaurant with he and Audrey. Wanting to allow his bodyguard an opportunity to eat without as much concern about being on guard, Carver requested a private room. Heads turned as they followed the hostess through the establishment. He didn't have to look to know more than a couple of phones had come out and video or pictures were being taken.

He could only assume it was due to the viral video. Once he left the game as a player, he hadn't experienced this level of interest. It had only taken a few years for people to simply acknowledge his presence but not fawn over him aside from the occasional super fan. They would always want a picture or an autograph.

Normally, it didn't bother him. He remembered what it was like when he met the athletes he'd looked up to as a kid. He didn't begrudge anyone a moment, as long as they remained respectful.

They were seated in a room containing three tables and curtain covered floor to ceiling windows leading out onto a private patio. Placing their menus on the center table, the young woman informed them of their waiter's name and assured them that he would be with them shortly. A kid, who barely looked like he was out of high school, came into the room moments later. Introducing himself, he filled their water glasses.

"Do you need a few more minutes to look at the menu, or do you know what you'd like?" Placing the water pitcher on a stand near the door, he turned to them ready to assist or take their orders.

"Ladies first." Carver indicated to Audrey.

"I'll have the Cobb salad with the balsamic vinaigrette dressing."

"Very good, ma'am. Would you care for anything else? Perhaps an additional beverage?"

"Yes, I'll have a diet soda please."

"Yes, ma'am. And you, sir?"

The server turned to Carver who immediately ordered a steak with a loaded baked potato. Michael ordered lighter fare, something Carver was certain he'd done so he could finish quickly and wouldn't make him sluggish. It was a miracle he'd even accepted the offer to eat lunch with them instead of posting himself outside the door of the room.

Had he not agreed, there's no way Carver would've closed himself alone in a room with Audrey. No matter how badly he needed the privacy to discuss business. They'd order food and have the meeting at the real estate office before he did such a thing.

It was too easily misconstrued—by onlookers and by the woman herself. This wasn't a date. It was business. Speaking of, he asked Michael's opinion on the last property from a security standpoint.

"It already has some good features. I can see making a few adjustments, but it has a solid point to start with."

"How long would it take to implement those adjustments?" Carver asked.

"Before anyone does anything, I would suggest going back with a team to really look it over and check it out for any vulnerabilities. The walk-through today was too quick to perform an accurate evaluation."

"Okay. Thank you for your insight."

Michael didn't work for Jasper's firm directly, but he was a skilled security specialist the team recommended. He and Carver got along well, and Carver had checked him out with Jasper. His friend vouched for Michael's abilities which was enough for Carver.

As their food came out, Carver's smartwatch buzzed on his wrist. Looking at the face, he read the short message from Alyssa.

> Bit: Not feeling well. Came home from work early. Can't make dinner. I'll need a raincheck.

Pulling his phone from his pocket, he immediately tapped out a reply.

> I'm sorry you're not feeling well, baby. Is there something I can bring you? I'm done with my house hunt for the day. I can come over and take care of you.

> Bit: You don't have to do that. I'll be ok. I'm just gonna lay down.

Tired of the back and forth, Carver excused himself from the table and strode to the patio door. Michael immediately stood and followed remaining close enough to reach him quickly, but far enough away to give him a modicum of privacy.

The electronic tones played in his ear as he waited anxiously for Alyssa to answer the phone. She'd just texted, so he expected an immediate response. Finally, the call connected.

"Carver...I'm okay. I just need to be alone." Her voice held the unmistakable sound of tears.

"Bit, baby. Talk to me. What's goin' on? Are you cryin'?"

"No...Yes, but I'll be okay. I just need to lay down."

"I'm on my way."

"Carver—"

"Somethin's wrong enough that you're cryin'. I'm on my fuckin' way."

Ending the call, he turned to Michael who held the glass door open already on alert to move. Barely stopping to offer his apologies to Audrey for cutting their meeting short, he assured her he'd be in touch. Speaking to the maître d on the way out, he left money for their meal and for them to call a car service to take Audrey back to her office.

When he walked out of the door, Michael had already pulled the car around. As they maneuvered through the afternoon traffic, Carver's mind was in overdrive trying to unravel what could've have happened to bring Alyssa to tears.

A multitude of scenarios played out in his head and he didn't like either one. His watch buzzed a few more times. He read the messages, but refused to respond. Whatever it was, Bit would have to tell him to his face. She may be used to going at things alone, but that shit was over. If he had anything to say about it, she'd never fight a single battle. He'd be her shield and protector. Anyone who fucked with his Bit would have to deal with him.

Chapter Eleven

WHAT?

Alyssa's day started out great as far as Mondays went. Despite her very active weekend with Carver, she wasn't sluggish when she awakened. She sprang right out of bed when her alarm went off and began her daily routine.

After her unexpected, but welcome, 'Good Morning' call from Carver, she went in to work wearing a smile and looking forward to her reward at the end of her day. This time last week, if anyone had told her she would be in a full-on relationship with Carver Wyatt Jamieson, she would've laughed in their face.

Carver had always seemed larger than life and while he'd never been anything but friendly and kind to her in college, she had not one inkling there could be more until their night in Chicago. Even that, she took as a one-off until they reconnected at the restaurant.

As much as she wanted to avoid living in the public eye, she had to admit she was more than enamored with Carver. Although she would've never made a play for her friend's boyfriend, she conceded he was not just a gorgeous face and body. His basic principles aligned with her own.

In college, they had very few one-on-one interactions by design. She figured out pretty quickly how easy it would be to fall for him, so she worked to ensure there wasn't an opportunity for her to slip up—embarrassing herself and ruining her friendship. In hindsight, she didn't have a friendship to worry about.

Traffic wasn't terribly heavy on her drive to work, and she was able to find decent parking. Another plus to add to the good day column. *Secure Pull* was a mid-sized information technology company whose claim to fame was their ability to design virtually unhackable code and components for slot machines and other similar casino games.

It's possible the company could garner more of the market if they went after it, but it was still run like the family-owned business at its roots. Although it was now publicly traded, they only had two branches and less than a thousand total employees.

Considering the technology they were sitting on, it didn't make sense to Alyssa. But...they didn't pay her to consider such things. They paid her to design systems and write security code—which she did quite well. So well she was often requested by clients. Granted the recognition was great, she had to frequently remind her manager she wasn't the only member of their department capable of doing either task

It's understandable he'd want to honor the client's wishes. However, he didn't try to convey the scheduling issues that could arise from having too many customers looking for one engineer to complete their requested design and build.

One thing her daddy always told her was that you teach people how to treat you. Though she did her job to the best of her ability, what she wouldn't do was work herself into an early grave by taking on too much trying to please others. She had to *teach* her manager that his inability to manage the client's needs with his available resources, didn't equate to her essentially living in her office to get a mountain of projects closed out.

Walking through the dark, double glass doors in the front of the building, Alyssa greeted the security guard behind the desk in the reception area.

"Good Morning, Miss Barbara!"

She stopped briefly to engage the older woman. Fifteen years Alyssa's senior, Barbara Gibbons was a former Marine who retired after putting in twenty years. At barely fifty, Alyssa thought she should be head of security, but she seemed content being the first person people saw when they entered the automatic doors.

"Hello, Ms Ripley. How are you today?"

No matter how many times they went over it, Alyssa couldn't get Barbara to be less formal. She persisted in calling her Ms Ripley while also insisting Alyssa call her Barbara. Alyssa added the *Miss* because her mama would cut her serious side eye for addressing an elder without a handle—as she put it.

"I'm doing well, thank you. If Kent didn't send you an email already, we're expecting a few people from *Components and Games* this morning around nine a.m. They should be in the system already."

"Now you and I both know Kent hasn't said boo to me. He hasn't made it in yet either."

Smiling in understanding, Alyssa shook her head. "I'll send you a list of names when I get to my office."

"Thank you. If you leave it up to these men, I won't hear a word until strangers are on the doorstep trying to get in."

"No comment." Alyssa responded with a wry grin.

Continuing on into the building, she entered the stairwell on her way to her second floor office. The three-story building had an elevator, but she rarely used it. She didn't see the point unless she was carrying packages—which was rare.

Normally, she arrived fifteen to twenty minutes early. Her morning conversation with Carver had put her slightly behind, but not so much that she was late. She stepped out of the stairwell with five minutes to spare before her work-day officially started.

Traversing the maze of cubicles, she noticed the conversational hum, but didn't think much about it. Some mornings, it was library quiet on her floor. Others, it buzzed like a colony of busy bees. Nodding to those who made direct eye contact, she didn't stop to chat on her way to one of the sought-after offices.

As promised, once she logged into the system, she sent Miss Barbara the list of names for the people arriving for the meeting. At the designated time, she gathered her things and went to the conference room. Again, she paid little attention to the level of conversation nor to the people who openly stared at her when she walked by.

The meeting went well. She, Kent, and the representatives from *Components and Games* discussed the scope of work, assignments and all the necessary moving pieces to get things going. The group dispersed at the scheduled time, and Alyssa decided to venture out for lunch instead of eating at her desk.

Settling on the Tex-Mex restaurant a five-minute drive from the office, she asked for a seat outside to enjoy the nice spring weather. It hadn't gotten too hot for such luxuries yet. Eating alone never bothered Alyssa. She went from her classmates being predominately male to the same environment in her professional life.

As things were in college, she didn't socialize much with her male counterparts. She was polite and endeavored to have good working relationships, but they rarely broke bread together. Which was why she was surprised when one of her co-workers, Ballard Grimes, approached her table, pulled out the chair across from her and took a seat.

"Hey there, Ripley."

"Ballard."

Alyssa placed the menu on the table and stared at the stocky blond man with features strongly resembling a turtle. Ballard was the kind of guy who called most people by their last name. It didn't bother Alyssa. After all, it was her name.

"If it's not too forward, I have a question...well...kind of a request."

That was new. She interacted with Ballard on an as needed basis. Something about him was off, so she avoided him whenever possible. The hairs on the back of her neck stood up.

"What kind of request?"

"So...I'm seeing this chick, I mean woman, and we were hanging out the other night." Looking down, he started rearranging the condiments in the center of the table.

Alyssa listened watchfully without interrupting. She didn't see how his love life had anything to do with her. Who he spent time with wasn't remotely in her realm of thought.

"Well, you know how things are now, you make small talk about your work then eventually you start talking about current events and things you've seen on the internet."

Shifting the tabasco sauce and the little rectangle filled with sugar substitutes, he continued. "She asked if I'd seen this viral video with Carver Jamieson beating up some black guy at some restaurant on Friday night."

Alyssa's stomach dropped to her feet. She'd hoped the incident with Torrence would die down, it had only been a few days, but other than family and close friends, she hadn't spoken to anyone about it. Until today.

Taking measured breaths, she waited to see where Ballard was going with his story. Part of her hoped he was just angling for an autograph or a photo op to impress his new girlfriend.

However, the icy tendrils of dread creeping up her spine said it wouldn't be that easy. Trying to stay in the moment and wishing Ballard would get to the freaking point, she remained mute.

"So, I told her I hadn't seen it and she pulled it up on her tablet and I watched it." Giving Alyssa a smile that didn't improve his appearance, he kept spilling his word vomit and not getting to the point.

"I couldn't believe a class act like Jamieson would beat someone up in public, and I was right. He shook the guy up a little, but it wasn't a beat down."

Alyssa experienced a brief moment of relief. Ballard didn't buy into the hype that Carver assaulted Torrence. Well...he kinda did, but he didn't beat him up like Ballard's girlfriend said.

"Anyway, I'm sure you're wondering what this favor is that I need and I'm just rambling." Ballard huffed out a nervous chuckle.

A snarky retort was on the tip of her tongue; however, Alyssa simply nodded in agreement. The server picked that moment to come back and take her order.

"I'll have a quesadilla fajita with extra guacamole please. And, could I get some more water to drink?"

"Sure thing. And for you, sir?" The server turned to Ballard.

"Oh no, I'm not staying. I'm meeting someone."

"Ok. I'll get this put in for you right away, ma'am. I'll be back with your water as well."

"Thank you." Alyssa smiled at the young woman politely.

Clearing his throat, Ballard started back in with his never-ending story. "So as I was saying, I watched the video on Stacey's tablet and I was surprised to see you in it.

I almost didn't recognize you with the dress and your hair all different, but it was you wasn't it? I didn't know you knew Carver Jamieson."

Regarding him with skepticism, Alyssa weighed her words and decided to go with bluntness. "There are many things you don't know about me, Ballard."

Done with him beating around the bush, she grabbed the bull by the horns. "Listen, Ballard, if you're angling for an autograph or a picture with Carver, I can't make any promises."

She had no intention of even asking Carver, but she wouldn't tell Ballard any of that. Her wish at the moment was to get him away from her table before her order arrived.

"Oh no. I'm not looking for an autograph, although that would be cool." Leaning forward on the table he spoke his next words as if he were letting her in on secret.

"See, Stacey works at the local news station, but she also has her own blog. She's hoping to break out and maybe get with one of the major networks. When she realized I knew you, she asked if I could introduce you two."

"Introduce us for what?"

"Um...an interview? I told her all I could do was ask. When I saw you here for lunch, I thought it was fate since I'd invited her to meet me."

Ballard had the audacity to look like he wasn't sure when she was certain he damn well knew what his little girlfriend wanted when she asked him to introduce them. She's a reporter. When a reporter wanted an introduction, they were trying to get an interview.

Heat licked up Alyssa's neck. She was sick and tired of men making decisions and asking her about it after the fact. Well, she wasn't sticking around and he could explain her absence to his little friend whatever way he wanted.

Looking around, Alyssa tried to locate the server. Apparently, she was taking her food to go. She couldn't believe this joker tried to ambush her. Finally catching the eye of her server, she called her over.

"I'm so sorry, but could you package my order for take out? I've decided not to eat in today."

"Sure. No problem." Seemingly unbothered by the change of plan, the other woman walked away to put in the order change.

"Wait, you're leaving? Why?" Adding obliviousness to his audacity, Ballard looked genuinely shocked.

"Ballard, in the four years we've known each other, how many one-on-one conversations have we had?"

"Uh..."

"None. The reason you can't think of any is because there haven't been any. We've exchanged pleasantries in the breakroom or at the table in the conference room, but we've never really talked.

Yet, you thought nothing of invading my lunch to ask me to grant an interview as a *favor* to you. What part of your brain made you think that was a good idea?"

Ballard sat across from her looking like a whipped puppy. Nope. That was an insult to puppies. They were far cuter than Ballard could ever dream of being.

"Oh...I get it. You *weren't* thinking with your big head. You were thinking with your little one." Disgusted, she opened her purse and fished out cash for a tip. Placing the bills beneath the basket of complimentary nacho chips, she stood to leave.

Ballard placed a hand on her forearm when she turned away. "Wait! You're leaving? Come on, Ripley. What is it you say? Help a brother out."

This jerk is unbelievable. Shooting him a withering glance, she shifted her eyes from his face to the hand on her arm. Saying nothing, she stared at him until he removed his fingers from her person.

She was so angry she almost forgot her food. If she hadn't run into her friendly server before she reached the front door, she would've left and felt terrible about it later. Blindly handing the woman two twenty-dollar bills, she accepted her order and walked out of the restaurant.

"Miss Ripley? Alyssa Ripley?" A stocky man with short brown hair called out to her from the edge of the walkway.

Alarm bells went off in her head and the 'Stranger Danger' talks from her parents blared in her ears. While his voice sounded friendly enough, the phone he held in front of him indicated he was recording their interaction.

Fuck!! Alyssa wanted Carver to be wrong. She needed him to be wrong... Rather than confirm he had the correct person, Alyssa pivoted away in the direction of her vehicle. Instead of the quick escape she planned, she walked right into a small crowd of people whose eyes lit up with sadistic glee when they saw her.

Gripping her keys in one hand and her takeout order in the other, she tried to ignore them as they began firing questions at her. Intrusive questions they had no right to ask. Questions referring to comments about her and Carver from social media posts she never read.

One guy pushed in front of the others and thrust a tiny microphone into her face. "Do you have anything to say to the people who think you staged the incident at the Lupo on Friday night?"

What?

Chapter Twelve

THAT SHIT HURT

Carver clenched and released his fingers as he watched the Vegas scenery fly by. Michael dipped in and out between vehicles to cut through the traffic to get them to Alyssa's as quickly as possible.

She'd told him not to come. He ignored the texts she sent when he hung up the phone. The tears combined with the sound of defeat in her voice galvanized him. His gut told him whatever caused her distress was linked to their relationship.

They'd ended their earlier call on a happy note, so he was certain it wasn't something he'd done. Which meant it could only be the thing he dreaded when the video went viral...Her social media shit storm had struck. His body was coiled in tension ready to spring out of the seat as soon as the SUV rolled to a stop.

Normally, a position coach for an NFL team wouldn't warrant such interest. However, Carver knew he wasn't just any position coach. In his almost ten years in the league, he'd been a fan favorite going to the Pro Bowl each year, won three Super Bowls and was awarded MVP four consecutive years.

When Alyssa said he was a household name, she wasn't trying to inflate his ego. The spotlight shone brightly on him for many years. One thing the gossip media hungered for the entire time was the thing he never gave them—a scandal. Not one during his career of having women and men throw themselves at him shamelessly in an effort to obtain even residual attention from the interactions.

Jasper joked about him getting into situations, but he'd led an extremely tame existence in comparison to other professional athletes. Not to say he was a saint, but they'd have a hard time digging up dirt. The most they could come up with were questions about how quickly he and Mary Beth broke up when he moved to San Diego. Since their situation was pretty common, it didn't gain much traction.

When Michael swung the vehicle into Alyssa's driveway, Carver barely allowed time for him to put the gear in park before he was opening his door and bounding up the paved walkway to her front door.

Certain he looked like a madman, he knocked on the door and rang the bell. The doorbell was equipped with a camera so there could be no question as to who was on her doorstep.

When the heavy maplewood door swung open, he was over the threshold in a flash gathering her into his arms and hugging her close. For a few moments, she did nothing more than grip the sides of his shirt.

In careful movements, he relocated them from the entryway to the sofa in her living room. The click of the front door closing alerted him to Michael's presence. Only sparing the other man a quick glance, Carver returned his attention to the woman in his arms.

Her downcast eyes were slightly puffy and red rimmed. The loose springy coils which normally encircled her head were smushed on one side indicating she really had been laying down when she texted him. Tendrils of angry heat licked up his neck. Trying to keep himself under control, he took a measured breath before speaking.

"Bit...Baby...Look at me." When her lids lifted, the sadness in the depths of her cognac-colored eyes tore at him. "What happened? Talk to me."

"Can we not...I don't want to talk."

Everything in Carver wanted to push the issue. She was closing him out and he didn't like. Not at all. However, seeing his Bit look defeated tugged at his heartstrings. While he could press her to get her to open up, adding to whatever caused her wounded expression wasn't something he could live with.

Apparently, this was one of those times his dad told him about when he'd have to push his desires to the side and just be there. The muscles in his jaw flexed under the clenching pressure, but he managed to keep himself under control. He really wasn't a hothead, but anyone causing Alyssa a moment of sadness, let alone tears, took him from 'zero' to 'fuck shit up' in a ridiculously short amount of time.

There was no denying he had it bad for her. Which meant the limits on what he'd do to protect her were very few. Finally nodding his agreement to her request, he tenderly kissed her forehead.

Standing from the sofa, he helped her to her feet and led her to the stairs. He didn't stop until they were standing beside her bed. Helping her beneath the covers, he quickly discarded his shoes and clothes before climbing in beside her.

Curving his body around hers, he held her as she cried softly into her pillow. Internally raging at his inability to do more, he alternately stroked her hair then kissed her head and shoulders. They lay that way until her sniffles tapered off and her breathing evened out indicating she was asleep.

Although he'd disrobed, his original intention was to cuddle beside her until she was in deeply enough for him to move without waking her. It didn't quite work out that way. One minute he was stroking her hair, the next he was waking to her snuggled into his side with her head on his chest.

Checking his watch, he saw a couple of hours had passed. The slight motion of lifting his arm stirred Alyssa and she squirmed, tucking her head beneath his arm before rolling to her side again. Taking the freedom offered, he slipped from the bed, re-dressed and went downstairs to see about dinner.

He entered the kitchen to see Michael seated at the table with a laptop open in front of him. Video surveillance images were on the screen displaying viewpoints from the front and back of Alyssa's house.

Nodding at the screens, Carver started to ask how Michael obtained the feeds, then remembered who he was dealing with and opted for the next question.

"Do you think that's necessary?" Carver didn't object to him keeping an eye on things. However, he wasn't positive Alyssa would share the feeling.

"While you were sleeping, I made some calls and did some rooting around online."

Taking the empty seat across from him, Carver urged him to continue without speaking.

"It looks like a few of the more aggressive paps in the area ambushed her outside of a Tex-Mex place at lunchtime. She didn't answer any of their questions, but that didn't stop them from asking and taking pictures. I'm not sure which part upset her, but what I saw would've had me executing some well-placed punches in more than a couple of faces.

I haven't figured out how they knew she was there or why they were so aggressive. I do think it's necessary to keep an eye out though. Property listings are public record. She's buying not renting. Since they have her name, it won't take long for them to get her address. I'd feel better if she had more than these two *Circle* cameras, but at least the community is gated."

Carver didn't have a great deal of faith in the gated access of Alyssa's neighborhood. There wasn't a security guard at the gate; a person simply required a code to enter. They'd gained access using the guest code Alyssa gave him previously.

"Did you save the videos you found?"

"Of course."

"Let me see."

After a few clicks of the mouse, Michael turned the laptop around so Carver could see the screen. Watching, took him right back to the brink of rage. The boldness of the men and a few women in the questions they hurled at Alyssa would have shocked him had he not lived through how invasive paparazzi could be.

Alyssa never answered any of their questions. The only words she uttered were, 'Excuse me' and 'Please move'. She didn't even give them a perfunctory 'No comment'."

Carver's jaw turned granite and his teeth clamped together when an average height white man with floppy sandy-colored hair stepped directly into her path and shoved a tiny microphone in her face. The man's question about the run-in between Carver and Torrence at the restaurant being a set-up didn't faze him.

No. It was the way the fucker kept blocking her each time she tried to get around him that set Carver off. He didn't stop until a large man walked up next to Alyssa and stiff armed him out of the way.

Angry he wasn't able to be there himself and happy someone else filled in, Carver took note of the restaurant logo on the guy's polo shirt. Pausing the video, he turned the screen to Michael and pointed at Alyssa's rescuer.

"Do you think you could find out this guy's name?"

"Sure thing. I'll make a call."

"Thanks. I appreciate it." Returning to the video, Carver finished watching, committed the name of the person who posted it to memory and slid the device back to Michael.

Pulling his phone from his pocket, Carver looked at the other man. "I'm going to order some dinner. Would you like something?"

"No thanks. I'm going to switch out with Blake in about an hour, if that works for you."

"That's fine. Thanks."

Blake was Michael's back up. Carver had established a routine with the bodyguard since he didn't expect him to be at his back twenty-four hours a day. With Alyssa's home potentially being a soft target, he was grateful Michael thought to call Blake.

Goodness knows, he didn't need to add going to jail for assault to the list of things to worry about. If any overzealous paparazzi showed up at Alyssa's doorstep, Carver would need someone to deal with them to keep from personally laying hands on whoever may come.

After searching through the list of options, Carver placed an order on the Food King app using an alias. It might seem like overkill, but in this instance he was exercising extreme caution. If there was a dollar to be made, an unscrupulous person wouldn't have any issues mishandling information obtained from a delivery service.

Blake had just closed the door after the Food King driver dropped off the dinner Carver ordered when they heard Alyssa's footfalls on the stairs. Blake returned to the kitchen with the bags to finish comparing notes with Michael, and Carver walked to the bottom of the stairs to wait for Alyssa.

Looking slightly better, but still a little sad, Alyssa's gaze met his. Dressed in leggings and a t-shirt she was outfitted in a relaxed fashion, even if she continued to carry tension in her shoulders. When she reached the last step, he clasped her hand.

"I ordered food. Come have some dinner. Then, we can talk."

A nod was her only response to his statement as he tugged her behind him into the kitchen. Stopping beside the table he pulled out a chair for her to sit.

"Bit, baby. This is Blake. He's going to stay when Michael leaves. Blake, meet Alyssa Ripley."

"Ma'am." Blake tipped his head to Alyssa.

"Hello, Blake." Alyssa responded—her voice slightly hoarse from sleep.

Snagging plates from the cabinet, Carver placed them on the table before opening the containers to begin dishing out food onto a plate for Alyssa.

"Are you guys sure you don't want any? There's plenty." He offered again.

Both men declined. Gathering his devices, Michael said his good-byes and rose from the table. Blake followed him to the door leaving Carver and Alyssa alone in the kitchen.

They ate their meal, consisting of pasta, steamed veggies and garlic bread, in companionable silence. As much as he wanted answers, Carver didn't press her. He was happy to see she was at least eating and the wetness around her eyes had dissipated.

Trying and failing not to watch her every move, as soon as she laid her fork down on her empty plate, he scooped it up and placed it in the sink with his own. Taking her hand, he helped her from her seat word-lessly leading her into the living room.

Seated next to her on the sofa, he cupped the side of her face examining her expression. "Can you tell me what happened? I've seen a little on a video outside a restaurant, but I want to hear it from you. I know there has to be more than what I saw considering the state you were in when I got here."

Her eyes skittered away from his briefly before returning. The vulnerability in them squeezed his heart.

"It didn't start at the restaurant, although what Ballard did was messed up, it was simply one piece of the puzzle."

"Who's Ballard?"

"Ballard Grimes. A jackass who works in the engineering department who thought I would *help a brother out* by giving the chick he's trying to fuck an exclusive interview."

Alyssa's free hand made air quotes around the *help a brother out* statement. Ballard Grimes. Another name to add to Carver's shit list.

"We aren't close or even cool like that, but he felt comfortable asking me to meet some reporter to talk about you. He didn't say those exact words, but that's what he wanted. It came out later that, when he overheard where I was having lunch, he called his little girlfriend. He told her to show up there if she wanted that interview. She was either too dumb or excited to keep it to herself. That's why those leeches were waiting for me when I left.

I thought I was going to have to punch someone to get past them until the manager of the restaurant came out and helped me get to my car."

Rubbing the back of her hand, Carver tamped down his anger so he could get the entire story. "I wondered how they knew you were there."

"I have Ballard and Stupid Stacey for that highlight to a messed up day."

"What else? You said the restaurant wasn't the beginning."

"It wasn't. It started when I first got to work, only I didn't know it. My co-workers were passing around the social media posts and talking amongst themselves, but no one said anything to me.

I don't socialize with my co-workers, so it didn't strike me as odd for them to dip in an out of one another's office's and cubicles without including me in the discussion.

So, while I went about my day in my meetings, little did I know, they were sending instant messages to each other speculating about my sex life and what a man like you could possibly see in me."

"The fuck?" Carver growled.

"Oh yeah. They had plenty to say—to each other—about you being so famous, rich and handsome and me being a fat nobody with an average face."

White hot anger coursed through him, but Carver fought to keep it in check. Alyssa didn't need his rage; she needed his comfort and reassurance.

"I wouldn't have known anything about it if someone hadn't accidently put me in the group chat when I returned from lunch. When the first ping came in, I thought it was about a project since I recognized a few names on the list as members of one of the teams I've been writing code for.

I was eating my lunch, so I didn't open it. It wasn't until the fourth consecutive ping within five minutes that I opened the messages and read them."

Tears gathered in her eyes and he hugged her to his chest. Knowing whatever she'd read hurt her so deeply tore at him.

"Usually, I don't let what people think of me get inside my head... But the things they wrote...That shit hurt...

I've worked with these people for more than six years. In some cases, I pulled their ass out of a sling more than once, but it took very little prompting for them to jump in on tearing me down.

Everything from my looks, to my race, my intelligence, and how I really got my big office, were up for debate. I say debate, but no one was advocating for me or for the rest of them to stop running me down.

Someone eventually realized I was in the thread and the messages stopped. Not before I took screen shots though. Screen shots I promptly sent to myself and my HR rep.

After that, I had to get out of there. I sent my supervisor a message to let him know I was leaving for the day, got my stuff and left. I don't know if I even want to go back. I'm not sure I can work in close contact with people who are so cruel."

Carver heard what she said and what she didn't say. The 'people' she worked with were predominantly male and white. She didn't say so. She didn't have to. Alyssa also failed to tell him what came of sending the screenshots to her HR rep.

A student of history, he knew if nothing else, white men had audacity and a sense of entitlement. They'd been waiting for an opportunity to call her ability into question. History also taught him that the HR representative, whoever they were, would try to talk Alyssa out of filing a dispute. Rather than calling the bigoted assholes on their behavior, they'd attempt to get her to agree to let it go.

Fuck if she would. Not if he had anything to say about it. Regardless of if they intended for her to ever find out, their actions contributed to a hostile work environment.

Fury churned in his gut. Rationally, he knew he couldn't go to her place of employment and knock people's heads together. It didn't stop him from wanting it though. Instead of acting on the impulse, he stayed where he was, comforting his Bit.

His gentle stroking of her back belied his inner thoughts. He'd be damned if he'd pined after this woman for years just to have their relationship be fraught with idiots trying to tear them apart simply because it didn't suit their ideal aesthetic.

"Bit...What did your HR rep have to say about the screen shots?"

Chapter Thirteen

WHO THEY CAN'T FUCK WITH

"Huh?"

Alyssa pulled back from Carver's embrace giving him a quick glance before training her eyes on the black television screen mounted on the wall opposite the couch. She'd purposely skipped over the part of her story where she walked down to speak with her HR Representative about what she'd seen.

"Don't do that, Bit." Banked fury blazed from Carver's eyes, but his voice wasn't harsh. "Don't pretend or try to avoid answering my question. What did your rep say when you went spoke to them?"

How the hell did he know she wouldn't leave without speaking to the rep to follow up on the email? Was she that transparent? The way he seemed to know her so well was a little unnerving. It made her wonder how closely he'd paid attention to her all those years ago and if he'd harbored more than friendly affection for her back then.

Cupping the side of her face, he continued to give her the entirety of his focus. "You don't have to shoulder this alone. Even if I can't help fix it, I can listen. Let me be there for you, Baby."

Somehow, and for good reason, Alyssa didn't think Carver would stop at simply listening—no matter what he said. Still her heart melted a little from his words. Leaning on someone outside of her family was done sparingly, especially after the debacle that was her *friendship* with Mary Beth.

Zaria was the only other person she confided in and it took a few years of friendship before Alyssa trusted her enough to share anything of consequence. Carver was seemingly immune to the barriers she erected. He either sidestepped them or bounded right over as if they were only a mild deterrent.

"She, my Representative, so much as said I was blowing it out of proportion. She didn't use those exact words, but that was the gist of it."

"What kind of representation is that?"

"The kind where she doesn't want the good old boys to remember she's not one of them. I never would have thought she wouldn't support me. If I hadn't sat in her office and heard her speak with my own ears, I'd find it hard to believe.

We weren't friends, but she made it a point to assure me she wasn't like other HR people who only looked out for the company. As a woman of color, she had a unique perspective and she used to make certain we were treated fairly."

"She's black?" Carver asked incredulously.

"Not hardly." Alyssa shook her head. "She's Asian-American. When we met, she proudly told me how her family immigrated to this country in the 1800s and earned their way doing jobs no one else wanted to do.

According to her, the way they were treated was partially the reason she wanted to go into a field that looked out for the little guy. I guess I don't count as the little guy in her mind. I walked into her office hoping for a solution and came away realizing I had no allies there."

"So, she suggested doing nothing?"

"Oh, she said she'd look into it, but then turned around and said it might be in my best interest not to pursue it since they didn't say those things to me directly. If I hadn't accidently been put in the thread, I'd never have known. In her words, I should just shake it off and chalk it up as boys being boys."

"The fuck?" Carver's expression of disbelief was almost identical to Alyssa's when Meredith had the nerve to suggest she *shake it off*.

"That's what I said. I can't unsee the things they typed or implied about my character. They know that I know and I have names to go with who wrote what in that chat. Why am I the one who has to play nice? They wrote that shit in a company chat, on a company network, during company time. They obviously didn't care if there was a record of their racism and misogyny. Anyway, when I realized she wasn't going to be helpful, I went above her to the HR Manager.

He was even less helpful. I sent him the same screen shots that I sent to Meredith. He read the first few, then had the audacity to ask me what I expected him to do about it. Isn't he the head of HR? Shouldn't he be the one telling me what the next steps are?

He pointed out that the chat included almost half of the engineering team. Did I expect him to fire half of the engineering staff? I never asked him to fire anyone, but I'm not comfortable working with anyone who speaks of me the way those men did.

When he tried the same old *boys will be boys* line, I got up and walked out. I grabbed my things from my office and left. I gave my Manager the courtesy of an email letting him know I was leaving for the day, but that was all."

Carver gathered her close kissing her forehead before resting his cheek atop her disheveled curls.

"I'm so sorry this happened. The internet has made people brave to the point they forgot there are real people hurt by the things they say and do. Even though I'm used to it, I never wanted it to touch you."

Pulling back, Alyssa rested her hands on his chest and looked into this face. "This isn't your fault. You didn't tell them to be assholes. It didn't take much for them to start trading lies about me and breaking down my body parts in that chat."

His body tensed under her touch. "Who are they?"

"Who are who?" Alyssa responded evasively. There was no way she was giving Carver those idiots' names. She wouldn't have him ruining his career seeking revenge on her behalf.

His lids lowered until only the slightest hint of green was visible through the slits. "Don't play with me, Bit."

"I'm not giving you their names." Clamping her lips shut, she crossed her arms over her chest.

Silence stretched between them before he grudgingly nodded. "Fine, what's Meredith's last name? Better yet, the head of HR, what's his name?"

"Carver, I'm not giving you that information."

"Why not?"

"Because, you're angry and spoiling for a fight." Placing her hands on his pecs, she traced the muscles before moving her fingers up over his clavicle to clasp them behind his neck.

"As much as I appreciate you wanting to defend me, it's my issue to deal with."

"No, it's not. It's ours. It wouldn't exist if folks would just mind their own damn business. Since they can't, those shitheads at your job need to recognize who they can't fuck with. Number one on that list, is you."

Carver's insistence on protecting and defending her did something to her insides, but she couldn't let him risk his contract over her jealous co-workers. Now that her head was clearer, she understood most, if not all, of their comments stemmed from jealousy.

"Carver...No. You can't go to my job cutting up because a few guys with fragile egos hurt my feelings."

"Bit—"

"I'm serious. I won't be responsible for you losing your contract before you even step foot on the practice field."

Using the strength she marveled at, Carver relocated her to his lap, facing him with her legs bracketing his.

"Bit, baby... I know this thing between us seems fast to you, but there's omething' you need to understand. There is no one more important to me than you. I'm sure as hell not worried about a job I don't need."

He was right. It did seem too fast to her—warp six at least. Having an idea of his answer didn't stop her from asking. "What are you saying?"

Those hands, those ones he'd used to grip the football for years, cupped her hips and squeezed reassuringly.

"I'm sayin', I'm all in with you, Bit. Now that I have you in my life, without anyone between us, I'm not allowin' anyone to hurt you. Not when there's omething' I can do about it."

Alyssa's heart galloped. There was no way she'd heard what he said correctly. He hadn't uttered those three pivotal words, but he might as well have. His reference to someone between them could only be about Mary Beth which caused her mind to race.

He was essentially admitting he'd wanted more with her in college. *What the hell was she supposed to do with that information?* She'd barely admitted to herself that she had to have some attraction to him back then. Otherwise, she wouldn't have fallen into bed with him so easily in Chicago and she would *not* be seated in his lap now with her ass being rubbed by his magical hands.

"Carver...I care about you too much to let you jeopardize your future. You're still young and coaching is important to you."

"I'm going to overlook you dodging your feelings to let you in on a little-known secret. I don't need a coaching job. I do it because I like being near the game.

Besides making a crap-ton of money playing, I had endorsements, modelin' gigs, and investments. I also didn't spend my money on stupid shit like some guys. I'm not worried about losing a paycheck."

"What about your reputation?"

"What about it? Anyone who really knows me will expect me to defend my woman's honor."

"I don't need you to defend my honor."

"No, you don't, but *I* need it." His warm hands traveled up her back and he sank his digits into the hair at her nape. "No one, and I mean no one, causes a single unhappy tear to fall from your eyes without suffering any repercussions.

If it makes you feel better, I won't beat their ass. I'll just buy the company. Then I'll fire all of them—including the dipshits in HR."

"Carver!"

"What?"

"You can't go around buying companies and firing people."

"Who says? Actions have consequences. They're never too old to learn."

Alyssa couldn't believe her ears. Carver was sitting on her couch casually suggesting buying a company simply to be able to fire the people who hurt her feelings. *His ass is crazy.* That was the only explanation. Normal people didn't consider such drastic measures to exact revenge.

Hell...whoever said Carver was normal though? He'd been lauded for the freakish nature of his athletic ability for years. Normal wasn't a word typically associated with him because he'd made his life on crushing norms.

Miraculously, he'd avoided many of the pitfalls that swallowed young professional athletes whole. The shiny baubles dangled before his face hadn't tempted him down a path which would leave him penniless as they had a number of players. Still...buying a company was out there. One glance at his stubborn expression was enough to know that he was absolutely serious.

"Carver...Do you hear yourself? You're suggesting making a major financial decision on a whim."

"It's not a whim. It's an option. Consider it another investment. Casinos aren't goin' anywhere anytime soon. So, there'll be a need for the games people like to shove their money into. Havin' a company that caters to the needs of such a lucrative business is pretty smart if you ask me. You get the casino cash without the hassle of dealin' with the people directly."

That was incredibly insightful. If he hadn't made his proposition in such an offhanded manner, she'd have no problem with it. But he hadn't and she did.

"You can't do that."

"I can and I will. Unless..."

"I'm not giving you their names."

"Then I guess I'm buying a company."

"You've got to be kidding me. I—"

Alyssa's sentence was interrupted by Carver's ringing cellphone. Pulling it from his pocket, he held it up. Easily reading the screen, she saw Blake's name on the display.

"What's up, Blake?"

Alyssa heard the rumble of Blake's voice on the other end of the call, but couldn't make out the words.

"Ok. I'll tell her."

"Tell her what?" Alyssa asked before Carver could end the call.

Tapping the screen, he cut the conversation with the bodyguard

"Blake says there's a Zaria Coleman outside. She says she's not leaving until she sees you."

"Oh shit!"

Scrambling from Carver's lap, Alyssa stood and rushed to the front door. Zaria never showed up unannounced—no matter how much she threatened to do just that. Uncaring if he followed her, Alyssa slipped her feet into the flip flops she kept near the entrance and hurriedly opened the door.

Her friend stood in front of Blake's hulking frame with her arms crossed, tapping her foot in agitation. *That's not good.*

"Hey Zee!" Alyssa called out to her friend as she stepped onto her front porch. "Blake, please let her pass. She's always welcome here."

"Somebody better tell him." Zaria huffed as she cut Blake severe side-eye while she walked past him.

"Since when do you have a bodyguard and why haven't you answered my calls? I've been worried sick. I've called you no less than twelve times in the last two hours. What the hell is going on?"

By the time Zee finished her rant, she was standing before Alyssa on her small porch. Her normally smooth brow was wrinkled in concern which made Alyssa's gut clench in remorse. After Carver showed up, she'd turned the ringer off on her phone and hadn't checked it for hours.

"I'm sorry, Zee. I've been asleep for hours and when I got up, I didn't think to check my phone."

Turning to walk back into the house, she met Carver's chest. Pushing lightly, she wordlessly asked him to move. Stepping backwards into the house, he moved to the side to allow both women to pass.

"Zaria, this is Carver Jamieson. Carver, this is Zaria—"

"Her best friend." Zaria interrupted. Extending her hand, she finished introducing herself. "Zaria Coleman, Esquire; and you, sir, are a big bag of good-looking trouble."

"I'm sorry. What?" Carver's voice vacillated between laughter and surprise.

"You heard me. You're pretty to look at, but you're trouble."

"Zaria!" Alyssa hissed.

"I know they say lawyers lie all the time, but I'm an advocate of truth telling. And, the truth is, since he showed up, you've been all over the internet."

Dread once again crawled up Alyssa's spine. "What do you mean?"

Walking into the living room, Zaria pulled her phone from her purse before dropping the bag on the nearest chair.

"I overheard one of the paralegals talking. Normally, I wouldn't have stopped since I had a meeting, but I overheard his name." Her eyes pointed to Carver before she returned her gaze to Alyssa.

"Since the two of you have been linked, when I heard his name, I slowed down. They were looking at a video on a cellphone. A video of you. Being chased by paparazzi. I immediately reversed course going to my office to call you and I've been calling you every fifteen minutes since then.

I finally decided to invoke the IMBD clause in our friendship and used my code to get into the gate."

"IMBD?" Carver asked.

"I might be dead." Alyssa supplied in a monotone.

Zaria didn't have any family in the area. Although Alyssa had her two cousins, they weren't close enough for them to check on her regularly. She and Zaria had come up with IMBD as a sort of insurance that someone would care enough to make sure they were still breathing.

It sounded hella morbid, but they filled a gap for each other. Alyssa felt even worse when she considered what was going through Zaria's mind after seeing the video and not being able to get in contact with her. Closing the distance between them, she hugged her slightly shorter friend.

"I'm sorry, Zee. I didn't mean to worry you."

"Mhm...Don't do that shit again. If something pops off and you want some alone time, at least give me a heads up. I know how to give people space."

"I know. It won't happen again. I promise."

"Good." Releasing Alyssa from the hug, Zaria turned to Carver. "So what do you plan to do about the shit storm you stirred up in my bestie's life?"

"Zee!"

"What?"

"That's not fair. This isn't Carver's fault."

"Who says?"

"I do!"

Tugging her hand, Carver tucked her into his side wrapping his arm around her possessively. "Shh...Bit. She's right. I brought the media frenzy into your life. It's my job to protect you from it."

Their Saturday night conversation came rushing back in a tidal wave. *Fuck*! She knew what was next and she didn't like it.

Tipping her head, she glared up at him. "No."

"Yes." He bit out; his gaze just as fierce as hers.

"No, Carver. I mean it."

"You promised, Bit. Are you going back on your word?"

"I didn't promise. I agreed to five days. It hasn't been five days."

"That's because it didn't take five days for the vultures to circle."

"Excuse me. What are you two talking about?" Zaria held up her hand like she was in class vying for the teacher's attention.

"He thinks I need a security detail. I disagree."

"It doesn't matter if you agree. You need it. I told you. I won't take chances when it comes to your safety, and I meant it. I'm calling Jasper."

"Grrr!" Alyssa gritted her teeth in frustration. Today wasn't the best day, but he was going overboard.

"Did you just growl at me?" The laughter hovering at the corners of his lips didn't help the situation.

"You're not being reasonable." Folding her arms across her midsection, she stopped short of stomping her foot in protest. Just barely.

"Girl! What the hell is wrong with you? Of course you need security. At least one of you has some sense."

Alyssa's mouth hung open in shock. Zaria was her friend. She was supposed to have her back. Instead, Zaria directed a pointed look at Alyssa before looking at Carver.

"I guess I take back my original assessment. You do have a plan."

"Umm...Thank you?" Carver replied.

"You should thank me. I'm gonna help you out." Pulling on Alyssa's folded arms, she tugged until she had Alyssa's hand in hers.

"Come with me. We need to talk." Assuring Carver that they'd return soon, Zaria hustled Alyssa from the room.

Entering Alyssa's home office, Zaria closed the door behind them.

"Why are you acting like one of those ditzy characters from a rom-com on the romance channel? You know damn well if you're going to be with a man in the public eye, you need someone to watch your back."

Offended by her friend's blatant statement of the facts Alyssa tried to ignore, she stood mutely. Arguing with Zaria wasn't in anyone's best interest. She's an attorney. She made her living arguing.

"Uh-uh. You don't get to do that. Don't crawl inside your head and act like I'm picking on you for no reason. Number one, I'm not picking on you. Number two, if you weren't so busy trying to keep your routine from being disrupted, you'd see this from our perspective."

"Our?"

"Yes. In this case, Carver and I are on the same team. That man is richer than you realize, and he is not shy about letting people know how into you he is. He's not denying you and he won't. So, that makes you a target. Not just for paparazzi trying to get a story, but for some idiot trying to use you to get to him and his money.

Let's not forget the delusional people who are fixated on him and might see you as the only thing standing between them and Carver declaring his undying love to their crazy ass."

Alyssa didn't bother to ask how Zaria knew Carver's financial status. Having people investigated was part of the package for her work. She wouldn't think twice about using it to help Alyssa. That's how Alyssa knew Torrence didn't have the money nor position he'd bragged about. She'd never let on that she knew the truth, because she didn't seriously consider a future with him.

Zee was right though. Alyssa's determination to maintain her independence was blinding her to the things Carver tried to explain when he brought up the security detail. *Damn Zaria and her damn logic!*

"Do you get it now?" Zaria asked softly. Alyssa's only reply was a mute nod. Rubbing her arm, Zaria switched modes to offer understanding and encouragement.

"It's hard to make such drastic changes in your life, but if you're going to be with Carver, this is a concession you'll have to make. At least for a little while."

"I know. I don't like it though."

"We all do things we don't like sometimes. I don't like doing squats, but they help my ass sit up nice in my jeans. So, I do them."

Bumping her hip against her friend's, Alyssa laughed at the incomparable analogy. Having come to a realization that her life had to change, they left the room for her to concede. Although she was certain Carver was already on the phone with Jasper, she followed Zaria from the room ready to speak to the man who'd turned her world upside down in just three days.

Chapter Fourteen

DON'T PLAY DUMB WITH ME

It had been a solid week since Carver laid eyes on Alyssa in that restaurant. To say things had been up and down was an understatement. After the paparazzi/co-worker tornado of fuckery, he'd gotten on the phone with Jasper. Thankfully, her friend managed to get Alyssa on board; because Jasper's stubborn ass still refused to send a team until he heard it from her personally.

It chapped Carver's ass and he told Jasper as much. Not that Jasper cared, but it made Carver feel better to say it out loud. The next day, the three-member team showed up to introduce themselves to Alyssa, Carver and Michael. Carver considered switching services, but he'd established a rapport with Michael and Blake. No point in disrupting it. Besides, he knew Jasper was probably already working on recruiting them.

Carver stretched his legs out in front of him as he lounged in the oversized chair in Alyssa's living room. The better part of the morning had been spent at the kitchen table going through emails and trying to stay on top of paperwork. Now, he was supposed to be looking at game film and studying the players he'd begin coaching over the next few weeks.

He'd only been back to his suite once to grab a some items. He'd placed an offer on the house, but it would take a few weeks for everything to be settled for him to move in. In the meantime, he didn't want Alyssa alone and vulnerable. Sure, she had a security detail, but until she got adjusted, he wanted to be close to her. At least that was the excuse he was using.

Alyssa hadn't been back in the office as of yet. She'd worked from home instead. Carver was happy it was an option since it saved them an argument. He had every intention of finding out the names of the co-workers who participated in the group chat.

Jasper had someone looking into them as well as the overzealous paparazzi who blocked Alyssa outside of the restaurant. Carver hadn't forgotten about that fucker either. He wouldn't escape the lesson of keeping his hands to himself and respecting boundaries.

The Human Resources Representative and Manager were already on his radar. Discovering their names had been easily accomplished by looking at the company's webpage. Of course, Alyssa had no idea what he was doing. He'd done his detective routine while she worked and he was supposed to be at the team offices getting acclimated to his new digs.

His Business Manager, Michelle, had been given some background information on *Secure Pull* when he asked her to look into buying up shares. It really was a sound investment. So, Michelle didn't balk at the request. Buying enough shares to gain controlling interest in the company would take little longer than he'd like, but it would be done before the season kicked off.

Dropping the remote in his hand, he picked up his cellphone from the side table when it rang. Checking the display, his father's smiling face was on the screen.

"Hey, Pops. What's going on?"

"Oh, nothing. I was just telling your mama we hadn't talked to you since you moved to the desert. I thought I'd give you a call to check in."

While it was true Carver hadn't talked to his parents in over a week, he was certain his father's call wasn't just to touch base.

"Are you sure, Pops? I told you it might take some time for me to get settled here. All the paperwork wasn't finalized until earlier this month.

So, I cut it a little close for when I actually had to show my face at the team office."

"Yeah, yeah. I remember. How's that going?"

Sitting back in the chair, Carver crossed his leg with one ankle on the opposite knee. "It's going ok. I went in, met the other coaches and looked at the shoebox they gave me for an office. Everything's good. We have some meetings lined up over the next couple of weeks with the coaching staff and players. We're right on top of Spring training. So, my schedule will pick up pretty quick."

"Oh. You can handle it. You're a born leader. I'm sure it won't take long before they're offering you the Offensive Coordinator job."

"I think you're getting ahead of yourself, Pops. That job isn't on the table. Besides, I've only been coaching for a little over five years."

"Five years, five months, or five minutes. It doesn't matter. The spot will be vacated and you'll get an offer. I give it two years tops. McIntyre is ready to move on.

He's been OC for three different teams. The Ravagers are his last stop in that seat. Besides, they'd be foolish not to see that you can do more than coach one position."

Carver's chest tightened listening to his father speak of his pending success with such absolute certainty. No matter how often his old man built him up, it still warmed his heart. Both of his parents had been super supportive when he wanted to seriously pursue sports instead of taking up farming, as was the tradition in his father's family.

"I appreciate the vote of confidence, Pops. We'll see how it plays out."

"We sure will. Mark my words though."

Carver chuckled instead of continuing to debate the subject.

"So...Jessie came by yesterday."

"Oh, yeah?" Carver set the notebook he was holding on the small table next to the chair.

Now they were getting to the real reason for the call. Carver's cousin Jessie was the family gossip. If she'd shown up in person instead of calling, she must have had what she thought was sensitive and juicy information.

"Yeah...You know how she is. She was talking to your mother about stuff going on at the church. I didn't really pay her no mind until she asked if you were okay because she'd seen a video on the internet where you were getting physical with a man in a restaurant."

His dad's South Georgia accent came through so that the word 'video' came out as vid-ja. As he listened, Carver clenched his teeth. *When was that damn video going to die?* Since the incident happened in a public place there was no way to get it squashed. Besides, it had been out there too long.

"Of course, your mama called me over and we watched it together. I don't see why they're making such a big deal about it. You were defendin' a lady's honor just like you were raised."

"I don't either Pops. I was hoping things would die down. It's causing unwelcome attention."

"Oh yeah?"

It was the moment of truth. Carver had to give up the rest even if his gut was saying his father already knew why he went caveman in the restaurant.

"Yeah...Pops, did you recognize the woman in the video?"

"If my eyes weren't playing tricks on me, and your mama was positive they weren't, wasn't she your college girlfriend's roommate? Bit?"

"Alyssa." Carver corrected with an unexpected bite in his voice.

"Alyssa? I could've sworn you always called her Bit?"

"*I* did and *I* still do, but her name is Alyssa."

"Mhm. Oh...Ok, son. I get it. Anyway, that was her wasn't it? She was the reason you nearly choked a man out in a crowded restaurant."

So tired of people blowing things out of proportion, Carver didn't even correct his father's statement about choking Torrence.

"Yeah, Pops. Alyssa was the woman in the video."

"Well, you know Jessie wouldn't have come if it was just that. She was saying the press is hounding that young lady and to top it off, that girl who was supposed to be her friend is making those Ticky Tockies sayin' some pretty shitty things about the both of you."

Uncrossing his legs, Carver bolted upright in the chair. *Fuck!* They get one situation under control and another rears his head. He didn't need to hear the name to know his dad was talking about Mary Beth. Even if he did get the name of the app wrong, Carver got the gist.

There was no way Alyssa knew. Hell, he was on social media more than her and he hadn't seen them. He wouldn't have though. He followed very few accounts and rarely posted. Rant videos from bitter ex-girlfriends wouldn't come up in his feed without him being tagged. He really needed to hire a social media manager to shut some of this shit down.

"Things like what?"

"I don't remember all of it, but she said somethin' about Alyssa just trying to get attention and that she always had a thing for you. She claims Bit, I mean Alyssa, made a play for you but she shut it down. Then some stuff about the two of you sneaking around behind her back."

Fuck. Fuck. Fuck!! Mary Beth should count herself lucky he didn't believe in hitting women. He would, however, find a way to shut her up and make her regret speaking their names from her selfish mouth.

"I know you didn't believe any of that, Pops."

"Of course not. I didn't raise you to sneak around. Besides, I may not have spent a lot of time with her, but what I remember of Alyssa is that she was a loyal friend. Even when Mary Sue was being a brat, she still supported her. If you ask me, Alyssa was Mary Ellen's friend, but that girl was only her own friend. Your mama says the same. You know she never like Mary Kate anyway. Said she was more in love with the idea of being an NFL wife than she was with you."

In the past, Carver might have corrected his father when he got Mary Beth's name wrong, but he couldn't care less now. In what he knew was a bid for relevance, she'd gone on social media trying to ruin Bit's reputation. That shit absolutely wouldn't fly.

"I know. I figured that out when she blew up on me because I didn't get down on one knee at graduation."

"You dodged a bullet the size of an eighteen-wheeler with that one, son."

"Facts..." After a brief pause, his father spoke again.

"What do you plan to do?"

"About what?"

Carver's mind was already on who he could call to get this under control and how he could shield Alyssa from it. She had enough to deal with without her former friend using her name clout chasing.

"Son...Don't play dumb with me. How are you gonna to shut this down?"

"I'm already working on getting a social media manager. I'll take care of it."

"What are you gonna to do about your woman?"

"My woman?"

"Carver Wyatt Jamieson, I've known you since before you drew breath on this earth. We normally talk every other day, yet I haven't spoken to you since the day before your flight to Vegas.

It didn't take much for me to put it together, especially after I saw the way you wrapped your arm around her in that restaurant. That combined with the way you looked at her in college when you thought no one was paying attention, your mama and I came to the same conclusion. You were staking your claim. It took you long enough."

Carver bristled under his dad's words, but didn't rebut them. Yet another person who thought he dragged his feet on going after his woman. It didn't matter. They were together now. Despite the time gap, he still felt like following his mother's advice was the right move. Had they come together sooner, he would've come on much too strong.

That thought made him chuckle seeing as how it wasn't like he was easing them into a relationship now. The difference was Bit. She was much more confident than she was ten years ago. She also had no problems standing up to him. Depending on the subject matter, he found that personality trait sexy as fuck.

"I can't hide anything from you, can I?"

"Why would you even try, son?"

"I don't know, Pops. It's...things are still new, and all the attention isn't making it easy for us to simply be a couple and do things couples do getting to know each other and finding out how they fit together. You know?"

"I get what you're saying. Given your job has you in the media crosshairs, you're gonna have to do something to protect your family. And by family, I'm not talking about me and your mama. I have things under control down here."

Swallowing the lump in his throat at his father alluding to Alyssa being his family, Carver nodded as though his dad could actually see him. Finding his voice, he eventually vocalized his thoughts.

"I know, Pops. I called Jasper. She has her own team for now."

"For now?"

Craning his neck to look out into the hallway, Carver listened intently to make sure Alyssa wasn't nearby before speaking again.

"The only way I could get her to agree to the security team was to say it was for a limited time."

"She sounds as stubborn as your mama."

"I didn't say that. You did."

"I'm not sayin' anything about my loving wife that I wouldn't say to her face. She's got a stubborn, independent streak the size of Texas. If your little lady is half as bad, you're in for a ride."

"Tell me about it. Getting her on board with there being an *us* took some doing, then the internet craziness started. Since Jessie was over there telling everyone's business, did she tell you about the paparazzi ambushing Bit earlier this week?"

"What? Naw. She didn't say anything about that."

Carver spent the next half hour relaying to his dad all the happenings over the past week—including a partial disclosure of Alyssa's issues with her co-workers. The colorful words coming from the other side of the phone were enough to assure Carver that his father felt much the same as he did regarding the situation.

As they were winding down, Carver glimpsed Alyssa walk past the doorway. Quickly ending the call, he slipped the device into his pocket and followed her into the kitchen. When he crossed the threshold into the room, he found her standing in the center of the space staring blankly.

"Bit?"

"Oh!" She exclaimed. Whirling around, she pressed one hand to her chest.

Rubbing her arms comfortingly Carver peered into her eyes. "You okay? I didn't mean to scare you."

Relocating her hand from her chest to his, she stroked him absently.

"It's okay. I walked in here, then forgot what I came looking for. I didn't hear you come in."

Drawing her closer into the circle of his arms, he pressed a kiss to her forehead. "No worries, baby. Just as long as you're okay."

Her arms slid around his waist and she laid her head on his chest. "I'm okay. I remember why I came in here now. I'm thirsty, but I didn't want water. I was debating on making tea then I went down the rabbit hole of thinking about dinner which led me to the last time I bought groceries. From there, I went to my to-do lists and before I knew it, I was staring into space trying to organize my life."

Carver could only laugh at her explanation. It wasn't the first time and probably wouldn't be the last that her thoughts led her down a path that made her forget what she was doing to begin with.

It was something he was happy to see hadn't changed about her since college. It used to happen in the midst of conversation. She seemed to internalize it more these days, but he could see the effort to remain on topic sometimes when they were discussing mundane things.

"So, do you want tea? I can put the kettle on for you and you can go back to your office."

"No, thank you. I'm done for the day. Besides, I don't want warm tea. I want sweet tea and I think I'm out of the good tea bags."

"The good tea bags?"

"Yeah... The ones in the yellow box."

"The yella box? As in Lipton? Woman, that's blasphemy. You like British tea over the perfect blend from Louisiana right here in the U S of A?"

"I'll drink the Louisiana tea, but I prefer the British tea, as you call it. Either way, I'm sure all I have are the herbal teas that I drink hot."

Pulling out of his arms, she walked to the cabinet to the right of the stove. Opening the door, she reached inside removing a tin cannister. When she tipped the cannister in his direction, one look confirmed her original statement. It was empty. The ensuing pout on her face had him pulling out his cellphone ready to place a Food King order to have her tea delivered within the hour.

"What are you doing?"

"I'm gonna put in an order to get you some tea."

"What? It's not that serious. I'll add it to my grocery list and pick it up in the morning."

"Give me your list and I'll order everything now."

The glint in her eyes should've been a clue, but he didn't catch on.

"It's fine, Carver. I can get everything myself when I go to the store." Putting the empty cannister back into the cabinet, she closed the door and turned to walk away.

Snagging her around the waist as she attempted to pass him, he pressed his front to her back. He didn't receive any pushback, but she didn't melt into him the way he wanted.

"I know you can get things for yourself, but I can also get things for you. So, why don't you give me your list and that's one less thing you'll have to worry about?"

Turning in his arms she looked up at him for a few beats before speaking. "I appreciate everything you're doing, but you don't have to bubble-wrap me. Going to get my own groceries isn't a hardship."

"I'm aware, but I seem to remember someone sayin' she didn't want a bodyguard following her around the store while she does her grocery shopping. I was just tryin' to help."

Her brow creased and her eyelids dropped into a squint. "They're seriously going to follow me around the grocery store?"

"Bit...baby. What is it you think I hired them to do? Walk you to the door and wait for you outside? Whenever you set foot out of your front door, they go where you go."

"Everywhere?"

"Everywhere, Baby. Shopping, work, gym...Hell if you go into the public restroom, there will be someone to sweep it first. That's why there's a woman on the team."

He saw the retreat before she started shaking her head.

"No. That's too much. There hasn't even been one attempt to even say anything to me since Monday at the restaurant."

Blowing out an exasperated breath, Carver walked them to the island and pulled out a chair. Taking a seat, he tugged her between his legs.

"Bit...We're not doing this again. You can't keep trying to back out every time things get slightly inconvenient. You agreed. You understand why we need to take these precautions. I'm not gonna keep hashing this out over and over again."

Fiery dark amber met his gaze, but her lips were clamped firmly shut. That was fine. So long as the message sank in, he'd deal with a little resentment.

"I don't like it."

"Understood, but it's how things are right now. I won't compromise your safety."

Unwilling to allow her to stew in her anger, he threaded the fingers of one hand into her hair while he used the other to clamp onto her ample bottom drawing her closer into the vee of his legs. Meeting her halfway, he placed gentle kisses on her lips before licking the seam requesting entrance.

The tension in his shoulders released when Alyssa opened just enough to allow him entry. Taking full advantage, he swept his tongue inside, relishing in her yielding to him. One kiss turned into two which led to Carver stripping her leggings off, bending her over the island and lining himself up behind her.

Despite ending almost every day of the past week buried inside her heat, his cock was hard with very little provocation. It stood out ramrod straight straining toward her glistening folds and the treasure which lay beyond.

Just as he went to slip inside her velvet walls, she placed a hand out to stop him. "Wait. Not here. What about the guys?"

"Here is fine, Baby. Don't worry. They're not coming in unless I call them."

"Carver..." Alyssa borderline whined his name as she unconsciously rocked her hips back. Her body wasn't in agreement with her words and Carver had every intention of giving her body what they both wanted.

Ending her weak protest with a searing kiss, he guided her back into position and sank his length inside her channel to the hilt. Groaning at the way her pussy gripped his dick, he held still with his hands holding her hips to halt her backwards undulations.

"Mmm...Carver...Please move, Baby." His Bit was working her Kegels on his sensitive cock since he'd stopped the motion of her hips.

"Fuck, Bit baby!"

Carver barely recognized his own voice when the words flew from his mouth. If she kept that up, he'd come before he took her to nirvana. He couldn't have that. Lifting his left hand, he brought it down on one cheek with a sharp smack. The responding clenching of her walls on his rigid shaft felt so good his balls tightened and he had to close his eyes to regain his composure.

Without his consent, his hips began a shallow sawing motion. Dropping his head forward, he lifted his lids. Anytime they were together, he couldn't resist watching his lightly tanned cock delving into her dark folds to pierce her bright pink pussy. As much as it heightened his arousal, it was also what made him grit his teeth as he concentrated on not cumming until she got hers.

This time would be quick. He knew it when they started. He'd had an undeniable desire to reassure himself of their connection after their little dust-up. Her response to his touch and kisses was all the incentive he needed to keep going.

Snaking his arms around her, he lifted her shirt to latch onto her breast with one hand while he used the other to worry the little bundle of nerves. His hips never stopped moving, driving his thickness into her heat as his fingers caused havoc to her other senses stimulating her breast and clit.

A well-executed swiveling thrust of his hips, merged with the movement of his digits, brought his woman to orgasm. Her combination wail and moan bounced off the walls bringing a cocky grin to his lips.

"That's it, Baby. Cum all over my cock."

Carver's self-satisfied smile was short lived as the spasming of her walls pulled him over the edge with her. His sac released and his essence shot down his shaft into Alyssa's clasping channel. Jerking intermittently, he emptied himself into her all the while holding her body tight to his to keep them connected.

As he felt himself soften, he stood up straight tugging her upright. He rained gentle kisses along her shoulders unable to stop himself from putting his mouth on her.

"Mmm...Now we can go upstairs. I guess you win. We'll go grocery shopping in the morning."

Her lazy agreement was enough for him. She'd probably protest in the morning, but at the moment, he'd fucked the fight out of her. He counted it as a win. Placing her discarded leggings in her hands, he swung her into his arms and headed toward the stairs. They'd figure out dinner later.

Chapter Fifteen

SHUT YO MOUTH

Alyssa rolled over and stretched in the bed trying to get the stiffness from her limbs. Carver's distraction tactics were blatant, but she fell for it anyway. She'd probably keep falling for it as long as he continued to deliver the levels of pleasure that he was dishing out.

Following their kitchen activities, they eventually came up for air to eat. Then, they spent the evening cuddled in bed watching episodes of her favorite Sci-Fi show on a streaming service. He had no clue what was going on, but he watched with her anyway.

This morning, he'd awakened her with kisses to her lower lips as he dispensed morning greetings to his *best girl*. Why he insisted on referring to her vagina by that nickname, she didn't know. So long as an orgasm was her wake-up call, she wouldn't complain.

The fact that she had free range of motion alerted Alyssa to Carver no longer being beside her in the bed. She vaguely recalled him mentioning something earlier about a workout or run while she drifted back into dreamland. Levering herself off the bed, she trudged into the bathroom to start her day.

After revitalizing herself under a warm shower and slathering moisturizer on her body, she stood in front of the sink brushing her teeth. Her eyes landed on the organized chaos that was the countertop. In one corner, near the outlet was an electric toothbrush on its charging station. Carver's toothbrush. Her gaze roamed over the space taking in the personal items that had migrated from his overnight bag.

Finished with her teeth, she rinsed with mouthwash taking note of the amount remaining. She mentally added a new bottle to her shopping list. Pressing a towel to her face to dry it off, she caught a glimpse of the dark blue terry cloth robe hanging on the hook beside the door. Turning in a slow circle, Alyssa leaned against the counter as a realization began to dawn on her.

No. That's not what it was. Denying what her eyes were seeing, she left the ensuite and stepped into her walk-in closet. Her clothes hung, neatly separated by use and color. Sliding open the top drawer of the built-in cabinet, she pulled out underwear before retrieving a pair of shorts and a t-shirt from the next drawer down.

Turning to walk out of the closet, a tidy stack of shirts and shorts in one of the open cubbies grabbed her attention. Next to that section of the organizer, button down shirts and pressed trousers hung efficiently above the shoe rack which once only contained her heels and now also held two pair of large, expensive looking loafers. There was an empty space which she knew with certainty was where he'd put his sneakers.

Quietly, stealthily and without her even noticing, Carver's ass had moved into her home. Well...almost. The few items in her closet and bathroom weren't the extent of his belongings. However, there was no mistaking that he'd made himself at home. Stumbling over her feet, she entered the bedroom and struggled into her clothes while looking for her cellphone.

Alyssa needed someone to talk her down. Her rational mind said all of this was too soon, but she couldn't say anything to Carver. She knew he was getting fed up with her balking. Hell, she was getting on her own nerves. Her feelings for him scared the shit out of her, so any little excuse to push him away would do. Her heart thudded, the sound reverberating in her ears at the thoughts racing through her mind.

Locating her phone, she didn't get a chance to make a call. The screen displayed missed messages from Zaria.

Zee: Girl...you aren't going to believe this shit.

Zee: I just scrolled up on some bull on that clock app.

Zee: Call me.

Tapping the screen to place the call, Alyssa perched on the side of the unmade bed waiting for her friend to answer.

"Girl, give me a second. I need to send you this video I scrolled up on during my Saturday morning perusal of the innanets."

"Uh...Ok."

"Here it comes."

Zaria had apparently been awake for a while because her voice was sharp and held no trace of sleep. A few clicks and a ding later, Alyssa placed the call on speaker to access her messages.

"Did you get it?"

"Yes. What is it?"

"Watch it. It's a TikTok of some broke down looking chick talking about she was your best friend in college and you stabbed her in the back. I know that bitch is lying. She looks at least fifteen years older than you. Unless she was a non-traditional student, there's no way."

Dread coiled in the pit of Alyssa's stomach. *This shit*. This shit was the reason she watched her shows, read her books and stayed the hell off of social media.

Using her thumb, she lightly tapped the screen starting the video. Initially, when Alyssa saw the woman, she had no idea who she was looking at, but the voice was familiar. As she spoke, the woman flipped her bleached blonde hair over her shoulder, pushing sunglasses to the top of her head revealing her face fully. *Mary-fucking-Beth*.

Closing her eyes, Alyssa clenched her jaw. This week had been a terrible mix of shit and sunshine only to be capped off by absolute fuckery in the form of her ex-best friend. Great. Just great.

Alyssa listened as Mary Beth asserted that she hadn't wanted to say anything, but after seeing pictures of Carver and Alyssa all over social media combined with people saying how sweet and protective he was, she felt compelled to speak out. Mary Beth claimed she felt obligated to let people know Alyssa wasn't as innocent as they were making her out to be and that she'd probably set it all up once she found out Carver had moved to Vegas. How else would he have been right there when Alyssa just so happened to need a big strong man to rescue her? *What in the entire fuck?*

"What pictures is she talking about?" Alyssa asked Zaria.

Instead of answering, Zee countered with her own questions. "You actually know her? She's not lyin'?"

"Yes. I don't recognize the username she's using, but that's Mary Beth. I told you about her. She and Carver were a thing their last two years of college."

"Shut yo mouth! The same Mary Beth who had the audacity to expect you to lose weight to be in her wedding?"

"The same." While Alyssa had shared the bare bones of how her friendship with Mary Beth ended, she hadn't gone into explicit detail with Zaria.

"I thought you said she was only a couple of years older than you?"

"She is."

"Well, age took a stick and beat her across the face with it, because she looks like she could've been one of your teachers instead of a classmate."

Had Alyssa been in a different frame of mind, she would've laughed. Zee had a way with words.

"Zee...the pictures?"

"Oh, right." Zaria huffed and mumbled under her breath. Alyssa heard rustling as if her friend were shuffling through papers.

"What was that, Zee?"

"I was saying, I told your ass you need to start paying more attention to what's going on in these internet streets, but you don't listen."

Ignoring the rebuff, Alyssa latched on to what sounded like an admission on Zaria's part.

"You saw stuff and didn't tell me?" Alyssa's voice carried a tinge of hurt. Thinking Zaria had knowledge of potentially harmful information and didn't tell her stung.

"No. Until today, I didn't know about any pictures—only the video we'd already talked about. My algorithm is set to messy, comedy and sexy men. I had to follow a few of the hashtags she used to see what she was talking about."

Slowly, Alyssa released the breath she held tensely. "So, where are the pictures and what are they?"

"Nothing bad, from my perspective, but I see what set her blondeness on fire."

"What?"

"Apparently there were people at the Lupo who took pictures instead of video and a few more avid video watchers took still images. They have shots of you and Carver staring into each other's eyes. There are also a few of the two of you leaving the building together."

"I don't understand why that would inspire a rant. I mean...Mary Beth has her own life with a husband and two kids. Why the hell would she care if Carver had my back when Torrence acted an ass?"

"Oh, I'm getting to that part. You remember when I called you last week right?"

"Yes."

"I told you how the video was all over the place. There were people in the comments saying fucked up shit, but there were also people talking about how great it was to see a man standing up for a woman. Not just any woman, but a black woman.

The buzz obviously fed into the neverending discussion of how black women are the least protected group. I hadn't seen the half of it in my feed, but when I followed those hashtags, I saw some heavy hitting influencers weighing in on the whole thing."

"But why? It's not that interesting."

"Girl, don't play. Carver is a future hall of famer and is considered one of the most eligible bachelors—period. His fine ass didn't just jack a man up for flapping his gums about you. The way Carver looked at you in those pictures...Girl...It made me want to end my dating sabbatical to put out an ad for one just like him.

Anyway, back to my point. The swell of support, from people that matter in the social media world, is what I think triggered the bottle blonde. It seems like when too many people stick up for black women someone has to come along and try to tarnish us in any way they can."

Zaria's observations were most likely accurate. In hindsight, Mary Beth had never really been Alyssa's friend. Any time it remotely appeared the spotlight might shine on Alyssa instead of her, she found a way to re-direct it. Severely introverted, nerdy Alyssa only thought her friend was saving her from uncomfortable situations. Now, she saw it for what it was, selfishness laced with possible narcissism.

"I'll be so glad when these folks find something else to talk about. It's bad enough for me to deal with people on my job creating whole ass chat groups to discuss my personal life, now I have former friends out there spreading lies trying to get five minutes of fame.

None of this would be a blip on anyone's radar if it were just two regular people who had an altercation. It might've gotten five seconds of chatter and speculation, then died."

Alyssa's voice carried the weight of her frustration with the entire debacle. The conversation with Zee made her want to crawl back into bed and avoid people for the next twenty years at least. Maybe by then society will have gotten over their obsession with celebrities. Then, she and Carver could be left alone to simply enjoy being together. Total pipe dream, but a girl could dream. Right?

Against her better judgement, she asked Zaria to send her the photos. Part of her believed, even Zee, was reading more into the images than was really there. As her phone notified her of the incoming messages, Alyssa heard heavy footfalls on the stairs. Carver was back from his run.

"Hey, Zee. Let me let you go."

"No problem. I was done anyway. We'll talk later."

"Sure. We're overdue for dinner and drinks. We should get together one day next week."

"Cool Beans. I'll call you."

Ending the conversation with Zaria, Alyssa placed the device on the nightstand and stood from the bed. As she tossed the weighted blanket to the floor, she made a mental note to change it out with a summer weight comforter. The warmth of Carver's body alerted her to his presence before he engulfed her in his arms from behind.

Squirming, she stepped away. "Ew! You're sweaty!"

Closing the distance between them he clasped her hand tugging her forward. "You like when I'm sweaty."

"Not when I just had a shower. No, sir. Back away." Alyssa pulled her fingers free and skirted the bed putting up her hands to ward off his amorous attention.

"Keep callin' me sir and you're gonna to end up needing another shower." Carver's head dropped giving, her a suggestive wiggle of his eyebrows.

"Carver, be serious."

"Why?"

"Because... we can't spend all of our days having sex."

"Who told you that nonsense?"

He moved to advance on her again when an electronic ping garnered their attention. The noise was the reminder she needed to tell him about her talk with Zaria. She'd intended to bring it up as soon as he walked into the room, but as usual, her thoughts scattered when he touched her.

Putting her hand on her hip, she cocked her head to one side. "It's not nonsense. As enjoyable as it is, fucking can't be our whole relationship."

"Not the *whole* relationship, but I don't see why we have to deny what we both want."

Slipping an arm around her waist, he plastered her body to his and captured her lips in a drugging kiss. When his fingers slipped into the waistband of her shorts, she found the strength to pull away.

"Mmm! No. Not right now, Carver. We need to talk."

Immediately, he pulled his hands away and stepped back. "Just so you know, those four words never lead to anythin' good. I don't like 'em."

Walking around the bed, giving Carver a wide berth, Alyssa picked up her phone and located the video Zaria sent her. Holding it out to him, she showed him the still image.

"Look what Zaria sent me." Nudging the phone in his direction, she urged him to take it.

"What's this?" Carver accepted the device with a crease of his brow.

"A TikTok that Mary Beth posted talking about us. Well mainly me, but she mentions you as well."

If she hadn't been staring directly at him, Alyssa would have missed the twist of his lips accompanied by the guilty flick of his gaze to hers before he fixed his face and tapped the screen. Once Mary Beth's voice filled with faux southern charm filtered from the phone, Alyssa turned away and went back to stripping the bed. By the time she'd gathered the sheets for the laundry, her former friend's voice had ceased in polluting the air in the room.

"Bit, baby. You know nothin' she says matters, right? It's just her making an attention grab."

"I know."

Alyssa walked past him to drop the sheets at the doorway. She'd take them down to the laundry room after she made the bed. Walking into the bathroom, she grabbed fresh sheets from the linen closet. Returning to the bedroom, she laid the sheets on the chair near the window before turning to Carver.

"What I don't know is why you didn't tell me about it when you found out."

To his credit, Carver didn't deny it. Scratching his neck with one hand he pierced her with a wary stare.

"I didn't know about it until yesterday evenin'. I didn't see it online. I found out from my nosey cousin by way of my dad."

"Yesterday evening? You mean right before you tried to fuck me into forgetting how my life is being disrupted?"

Tossing the phone to the bed, Carver closed the distance between them. "Those two things have nothing to do with each other. I wasn't keepin' it from you. I just wanted us to have a moment to breathe without another trainwreck to navigate."

Stepping into her space, he unfolded her hands from her waist, placed them on his chest and slid his arms around her waist. Dropping his forehead to hers, the pleading look in his eyes almost made her fold. She didn't. Him withholding things from her wasn't cool. If she let him off too easily, he'd simply keep pushing her boundaries.

"If you weren't hiding it, why did I find out from Zaria and not you?"

"Because I was hopin' Jonathan woulda called me back with the name of a Social Media manager. Then, I'd be able to tell you what was goin' on and show you my plan to take care of it."

"Considering how things are metaphorically exploding around us, you can see how that wasn't the best move to make, right?"

"Yeah, Baby. But I also know how you love a good plan. I didn't want to stir you up without offerin' options."

Her fingers splayed against his pectorals as she pushed him without any real venom.

"I may be rusty on the rules of relationships, but we're supposed to discuss options and come up with plans together. I told you. I don't need you to fix things for me."

"And I told you, *I* need to do whatever I'm able to do to protect you. Part of that is lookin' into shit before I bring it to your attention. You're my woman, Bit."

"That may be so, but I'm not a child. I don't need to be handled with kid gloves."

"*May* be? **May be**?" Carver growled.

Alyssa gasped when his grip tightened, holding her impossibly close to his hard body.

"I coulda sworn I told you we weren't gonna keep re-hashing the same thing over and over." His digits delved into her hair forming a fist in her coils then tugging. "Ain't no **may be**. You're **my** woman. I'm **your** man. We may disagree, but those are two facts we need to be on the same page about. Do you understand me?"

Alyssa's pulse raced and she had difficulty holding on to her thoughts. The fire blazing in Carver's eyes was enough to snatch the breath from her lungs. When combined with the fierce way he held her, it was enough to strip everything away until she was left with only absolute compliance with his every word.

Damn. She wanted to push back. Assert her independence. But, she couldn't. He was right. She was too. However, she was doing exactly what they'd argued about last night before he bent her over the island in her kitchen. She was putting up barriers and Carver Wyatt Jamieson wasn't having it.

"Do. You. Under. Stand. Me?" Carver gritted out delivering stinging smacks to her covered backside with each word.

Jumping a little with each swat, Alyssa attempted to ignore the tightening of her core which clenched in time with every stinging blow. While not hard enough to do any real harm, her ass tingled beneath her clothing.

"Answer me, Bit." Carver demanded, his warm breath brushing the shell of her ear as he skated kisses down the side of her neck until he reached the crook where he latched on with a bite, giving just enough pressure for her juices to leak from her walls yearning to be filled.

"I...ummm..."

"You what, Baby?" Using his hold on her hair, he tipped her head back exposing her neck more for his exploration. With one more rub to her burning cheeks, his other hand traveled up her torso to land on her breast.

"Focus, Baby." The command was accompanied by a pinching twist of her nipple.

"Oh shit!" Alyssa gasped out in response. *How the hell had she let him turn this around on her again?*

Carver's responding chuckle stirred a twinge of indignation, but it was quickly squashed by arousal.

"That didn't sound like the answer I was looking for. Let's try this again." Raising his head, he peered into her passion clouded eyes. "I need to hear the words, Bit. Tell me that you understand, and we aren't gonna keep doin' this shit. I'm your man. You're my woman. Say the words, Baby."

For a split second, the fierceness in his eyes faded and she glimpsed his vulnerability. In his own way, he was just as scared as she was. Cupping his chiseled jaw in her hands, she gave him what he required.

"You're my man. I'm your woman." Alyssa's voice came out clear and strong.

Once again, Carver dropped his forehead to hers. Closing his eyes, he spoke just above a whisper.

"I know you're scared, Baby. This is unchartered territory for both of us." Emerald clashed with amber when he lifted his eyelids. "I'm sorry for not telling you when I found out, but you have to cut me some slack. My first instinct will always be to protect you. It's my primary responsibility in life. It's part of who I am. You can't ask me to step back from being myself."

Rubbing the stubble on his face, Alyssa saw the words swimming in his eyes. He loved her. *Hard.*

Chapter Sixteen

I HAVEN'T DONE ANYTHIN'

Carver sat in his office blankly staring at the wall mounted monitors. He was supposedly reviewing player information, but was actually trying to convince himself not to call Alyssa again. It was her first day back at work after a little over a week off, and he was more anxious than she was. Or at least it seemed that way to him.

For a change, she'd awakened before him. He was tugged from slumber by the delicious feel of her lips wrapped around his morning wood. A guy couldn't ask for a better wakeup call than his woman pleasuring him. Her moans melded with his and she appeared to enjoy the act as much as he relished in receiving it. Once she'd sucked his soul from his body he'd gotten payback. No morning was complete without him giving his best girl a kiss.

Following round two in the shower, they'd parted ways before eight a.m. It was now half past nine and he'd called twice to see how things were going. After the second time, she told him under no uncertain terms not to call back.

He was behaving like an over possessive ass, but he couldn't rein it in. This past weekend, he was a hairsbreadth away from telling her he loved her. Too much, too soon. At least for her. He was excellent at reading the room—unless he didn't want to.

It took less effort than he anticipated for *Secure Pull* to get on board with her personal security team being on site. It's a good thing they came around though. Carver wasn't above using whatever influence he had to get them to see reason. Without some guarantee of her safety, she wouldn't set foot back inside that building. Not if he could help it—and he had the means to make it so.

An email notification popped up on his laptop screen. Happy For a distraction, he opened the message from his manager's assistant. Johnathon finally had a list of names for a social media specialist to handle his accounts.

Urena Black's photo accompanied the profile document Carver was sent. Pretty, with an engaging smile, she looked no older than twenty-five, but her list of client references was impressive. One of the names on the list was very familiar to him. Denzel Reed.

Placing an earbud in his ear, Carver scrolled through his contacts and tapped the screen to make a call. On the second ring, he heard his longtime friend's voice.

"You finally crawled from between that woman's legs and remembered there were other people in the world, huh?"

"Fuck you."

"I do believe you called the wrong number for that. Maybe I should hang up and let you try again."

"Cut it out smart ass. It's been less than a month since the last time I saw your ass. If you recall, I was your wingman while you were trying to pick up that actress you've been salivatin' over."

"Some wingman you were. You didn't distract her friend worth shit and all I was able to get was a follow back on Insta."

"A follow back is something. You shoulda slid into her DMs"

"I don't slide into DMs. People slide into *my* DMs."

"And that's why you're sitting alone with *angry dick* mad because the woman you want isn't rolling around on her bed callin' out your name like Whitley. Den-Zelle! Den-Zelle!"

At the image he conjured, Carver didn't attempt to contain his laughter. Denzel didn't find it nearly as amusing.

"Whatever, bro. Why did you call me? I know it wasn't to rub it in that you're getting laid by the woman you want, while I'm not."

Tapering off his chuckles, Carver cleared his throat and started over. He did feel a twinge of guilt for not being better at keeping in touch with one of the people he truly considered a friend. Other than a few quick texts, they hadn't talked since he moved to Vegas.

"No. I didn't call you to rub it in. All jokes aside, you know I wouldn't do that. I wanted to run a name by you and get your input."

"Hit me."

"Urena Black."

"What about her?"

"She's been recommended to manage my social media accounts. You're listed as a reference. What are your thoughts?"

"She does solid work. She has a very low bullshit meter, but she'll make you look like whatever you want to the public. If there's a fuck-up going viral she's excellent at shutting that shit down. How do you think I managed to keep the crap my ex tried to pull from making me look like the biggest asshole ever?"

"That was her?"

"Yup."

"Cool. Thanks. I'll reach out to her."

"If you'd called me sooner, I would've recommended her."

"I see you're not done bustin' my chops."

"No, I'm not. Keeping a healthy friendship requires communication. You can't just show up once every few months and be my wingman at a bar."

"Been talking to that head shrinker again?"

Denzel's deep voice was sober in it's seriousness. "I have. Your wild ass should see someone too. If people knew half the shit I know about you..."

"You know shit because I trust you. Besides, I'm well-adjusted and self-aware. I'm good."

"If you say so."

"I do." Carver bit out. "Moving on. What have you been up to besides speculating on my personal life?"

"Nah... playa...Don't try to shift the subject to me. I wouldn't have to speculate on your personal life if your ass picked up the phone, and don't say it goes both ways. I called you. You sent me to voicemail. You were probably so damn happy to be up in that woman's face, you couldn't see straight."

Carver's lips stretched into a wide smile. There were very few people aside from his parents who knew about his feelings for Alyssa. Denzel was one of those people.

"My bad, man. You know how it is. You've seen the way the paps lost their damn mind over one inconsequential dust up in a restaurant."

"Oh, I saw it. That's why I called. To talk your mean ass off the ledge. As we speak, you're probably plotting against no less than ten people for even daring to breathe her air. Tell me I'm lyin'." Denzel challenged.

"I don't know what you're talking about." Carver refused to confirm his friend's statement.

"Bro... you forgot who you're talking to. I'm the guy who told you to dump Mary Beth's social climbing ass long before she started hearing wedding bells. I knew then you were into her friend more than you would admit. What is it you used to call her? Lil' Bit?"

"Bit. Just Bit."

"That's it! You had a cute little nickname for the *friend* of the girl you were dating, but the closest you came to a pet name for your *actual* girlfriend was to call her 'Babe' on occasion. You were so fucking obvious."

Carver sat mutely, seething at Denzel calling him out and knowing nothing the man said was a lie. Since the day he'd starting referring to Alyssa as 'Bit', he rarely called her anything else. While he sparingly called Mary Beth anything outside of her given name.

He and Denzel played together first at Tech, then for a few years in San Diego. Denzel had only been out of the league for a couple of years. Majoring in sports journalism, he'd gone the analyst route when he retired. Maintaining their friendship while respecting a professional distance on some subjects was sometimes trying. However, Carver trusted his friend not to break his confidence.

"If I saw it, you know damn well your girl saw it. And by your girl, I mean the one who hung on your arm, not the one who was so loyal to her friend she walked around with blinders on."

"You know what? No one asked you for your in-depth analysis. This isn't one of your sports shows."

Chuckling at Carver's discomfort, Denzel kept running his mouth. Carver figured he was making up for all the calls they missed over the past month.

"I also saw that your lovely ex crawled from under a rock trying to use your lady to snag some spotlight for herself. What do you think is up with that?"

Running a hand through his hair, Carver scratched his scalp in renewed irritation with Mary Beth. "I don't have a clue. It's been fifteen fucking years since I laid eyes on her in person. According to Bit, it's been almost as long since their friendship ended.

Why she thinks anyone should care about me and Bit bein' together after all this time is beyond me. But, I can tell you this. She's gonna learn to keep our names out of her fucking mouth."

A thundercloud settled over Carver's face. An intern walking past the glass wall of his office caught a glimpse of his expression, pivoted in the other direction and damn near sprinted away. Carver felt a little bad. Poor kid looked like he might wet himself.

"CJ...Man...What are you up to? You don't make idle threats." Silence stretched across the phone line as Denzel waited for a response that didn't come. "Come on, Bro. I hear it in your voice. What did you do?"

"I don't know what you mean. I haven't *done* anythin' and I'm not *up to* nothin'."

Ignoring the warning in his tone, Denzel pressed a little more before giving up and changing the subject to a safer topic. Carver spent the next half hour catching up with his friend. They discussed his search for a home which led to real estate purchases in general as Denzel had also invested his NFL earnings in various areas—real estate being one of them.

Carver was certain his friend didn't need the analyst jobs he had with a few of the major sports networks, nor the podcast revenue. Denzel loved the game. He was a student of the sport which made him one the best wide receivers Carver had played with during his career. Hands down.

"Oh yeah, guess who I saw last week?" The excitement in Denzel's voice had Carver sitting up taller in his seat.

"Who?"

"Big Bama Boy."

"Big Bama Boy as in Ash? Asher Peterson? Are you serious? We talk a few times a year, but I haven't actually seen that guy in person in at least eight years."

"Same. I almost didn't recognize him. He has one of those mountain men beards and he wears his hair long now. Dude had an actual man-bun when I saw him. Looking like an Instagram model or some shit."

Carver, Denzel, and Asher all played together for a couple of years before Ash left football to pursue a career in law enforcement of all things. When they all played together, Ash was always clean shaven with a haircut that resembled a Marine high and tight. Denzel joked about Ash's model good looks like he didn't have people literally running into walls because they were so busy staring at him they weren't watching where they were going. True story.

"How is he? I'm gonna have to touch base with him. The last time we had a decent conversation, he was going undercover and didn't know when he'd be done with that assignment."

"Well, if he's not done, he sure as hell blew his cover the night I ran into him."

"What happened?"

"Check this out. I was sitting at the bar in this upscale rooftop club at one of those ritzy hotels downtown. I can't remember the name. Anyway, this beautiful and I mean Amazonian level fine sister walks in."

Carver didn't wonder if the mention of the woman had a purpose. Many of Denzel's stories began with a woman one way or another.

"Bro...I nearly swallowed my damn tongue trying to keep it in my mouth she was so fine. So, she walks over to the bar and lucky me, the only empty seat was to my left. She asks me if the seat is taken. Of course, I say no and I reach out to hold the back steady while she sits down.

Man, before she can sit down good, a big catcher's mitt ass hand clamps on mine and shoves it off the back of the chair. I look over, ready to throw down, only I'm staring at a big fucking barrel chest instead of a face. I look up and see his huge ass glaring at me.

He doesn't say shit and I don't say shit because I'm trying to figure out how I'm gonna handle it. And like I said, I didn't immediately recognize him. Anyway, the Amazon whips her head around and tells him to mind his business. To which he replies, 'You are my fucking business.'

At this point, I'm trying to decide if I'm gonna have to fight this oversized motherfucker for disrespecting me or for pushing his attention on a woman who didn't want it. That's when he finally looked at me and realized who I was.

I ain't gone lie. I was relieved I didn't have to fight his big ass. He's still just as solid as he was when we played. He has to be tipping the scales at a minimum of three-seventy-five."

Carver laughed at the obvious relief in Denzel's voice even in the retelling of the story. Ash was the kind of big no one wanted to tussle with. It was a whole lot easier to shoot him—with large caliber bullets. Not that Carver had considered it.

Okay, maybe once, but he quickly dismissed it. Asher was as Denzel said, 'cool people'. So, actual physical altercations with him were never really on the table.

They talked a little while longer, before Carver had to hang up to go to a meeting. Looking at the time, he was surprised to see an hour had passed. He'd made it to almost lunchtime without calling Alyssa again. Apparently Denzel was the distraction he needed. Making a mental note to do better with keeping up with his friends, he grabbed his tablet, a notepad and a pen, then left his office.

As much as he wanted to cut his day short and try to convince Alyssa to do the same, Carver grabbed a quick lunch and went back to his office. He was one of the few coaches who stayed on the premises after the meeting, but he didn't want to go to his hotel suite. Besides, Alyssa said she had a late meeting and wouldn't be home until after five p.m.

Seated at his desk, he opened his laptop. Pulling up the email with

Urena Black's info, he located the phone number. Seeing as he needed someone on the chaos that was his social media accounts, he called the number listed.

On the third ring, the call connected and a pleasant, somewhat throaty, voice answered. "Urena Black speaking."

"Ms Black. This is Carver Jamieson. I believe my manager Johnathon Rhodes reached out to you about possibly taking on the management of my social media accounts."

"Hello, Mr. Jamieson. I received an inquiry from Johnathon, but we didn't set up anything firm."

"Please, call me Carver."

"Okay, Carver. You may call me Urena."

"Great. Now that we have the pleasantries out of the way, Urena. Do you think you'll be able to help me?" Carver asked, getting straight to the subject at hand. If she couldn't take him on, there was no point in dragging it out.

"You're just as direct as I've heard. I like it." Although he couldn't see her, Carver heard the smile in her voice. "I've reviewed each of your verified accounts as well as the official coach's accounts the team set up for you. Although those have no posts yet.

I've noticed one thing consistently across your personal accounts." She paused. He assumed to allow him to speak, but he waited for her to finish her assessment. "You've been reactive. You haven't made a single post to address the videos and photos floating around the internet of you and the woman that I'm guessing is important to you, Alyssa Ripley."

"What am I supposed to say? Stay out of my business? I didn't think any of the assumptions and speculation deserved a response."

"They don't, but that doesn't mean you shouldn't get in front of it and shut it down. Your silence is making the internet trolls even bolder and allowing them to shape the narrative."

Carver slowly closed his eyes and clenched his fists. *Fuck*. She was right. Of course, she was. She was the expert. In some cases, silence was golden, but in this case, his silence was allowing people to think he wouldn't protect his woman beyond physical altercations.

"So, what are you suggesting?" He asked gravely.

"Before I tell you what I think, let's discuss my rates and my rules."

Leaning back in his chair, Carver's cheeks puffed as he blew out a deep breath. He had the feeling her rates wouldn't be an issue so much as her rules.

"Let's hear it."

"I like to speak to people face to face when discussing this type of business. Is it possible for us switch this call to a video chat? I only have about twenty minutes before my next meeting, so I'll be brief."

"Sure."

"Excellent. Click the link I just emailed you."

"What li—" the electronic notification from his laptop drew his eyes to the notification bubble. "Never mind."

Clicking the link, he disconnected the call as Urena's face appeared on the laptop display.

"Now. That's better." She smiled. "I've also sent you a rate sheet along with what each tier of service entails. I must inform you that while I oversee many accounts, it could be me or a member of my staff that may handle traffic to your accounts at any given time.

If that's an issue for you, please let me know now. I assure you that my staff is well trained and they all have signed airtight NDAs in order to work for me."

"I don't have a problem with that." Opening the document as soon as it hit his email, Carver immediately read over the terms for the top tier of service. If he was doing this, there was no point in fucking around with the basic packages.

"Good to hear." The smile on Urena's face was genuine and her demeanor inspired confidence. Carver didn't really care how much the services cost, although he considered the prices reasonable. He simply wanted to absolve himself of the headache and protect Bit from being hurt in the crossfire of people's ignorance.

They spent the remainder of the meeting with Urena giving her honest evaluation of his situation, which she said could be much worse. Her immediate recommendation was something he would've never considered, but she assured him would draw the attention his way and away from Alyssa where she and her team could manage it better.

Her suggestion made his petty side grin like a Cheshire Cat while his protective instincts kicked into high gear about potentially exposing Bit to even more attention from intolerant assholes. But, Urena was the expert. She assured him it would turn the tide. Now all he had to do was convince Bit.

Chapter Seventeen

HER

Standing on the balcony of Carver's hotel suite, Alyssa tried to figure out how she let him talk her into this. The sun was setting, and a light breeze reminded her that Spring wasn't officially over. Dressed in her third outfit of the day, she wanted to tell the photographer to kiss her butt then go hide under the covers.

Carver's media specialist, Urena, was more than a simple social media manager like he originally said. She was a strategist. A really good one from what Zaria told Alyssa when they had drinks on Thursday. Urena offered a multipronged approach to giving the media what they wanted in the least intrusive way to make following she and Carver around less appealing. At least that is what Alyssa hoped.

First, Urena coached Carver through a post for all of his social media platforms. He did one of those, *Let's Clear the Air*, videos. Alyssa wasn't sitting at his side like some prop, of that she was appreciative. Urena advised that he needed to make the first post alone.

Now, they were in the second or third phase of the plan. Alyssa wasn't one hundred percent sure because of the whirlwind of activities. They'd had a photographer shadowing them for the past two days snapping candid shots of them as they went about doing couple things together. For Alyssa's privacy, everything took place in Carver's suite or while they were out together in public.

They'd had a busy Saturday. First, they took a helicopter ride to watch the sun come up over the Grand Canyon. It was entirely too early when they left, but it was worth it when she saw the kaleidoscope of colors painting the sky over one of the Seven Wonders of the World.

In all the years she'd lived in Nevada, she'd never taken the tour by bus or helicopter. Their guide was great and she was almost able to forget the photographer constantly snapping images.

After the Canyon tour, they'd had breakfast before changing clothes and embarking on another adventure. It was like Carver was trying to do all the things before she cried uncle and refused to leave the house. Urena had strongly suggested that they stop hibernating, but the go-go-go of the day was taking its toll.

Alyssa didn't flinch when Carver slid his arms around her waist leaning down to kiss her cheek. She'd heard the sliding glass door open. Besides, she'd grown accustomed to his need to touch her in some fashion when they occupied the same space.

"What's going on in that head of yours, Bit? Getting tired of our entourage?"

"Which one? The security team or the photographer?"

"Both."

Turning in his arms, she gazed into his concerned face. "Believe it or not, I've gotten used to the security team."

"So, it's the photographer."

"Oh God, yes!" Dropping her forehead to his chest, she rubbed it back and forth against him. "Why does he need so many pictures? Are we doing a layout in multiple magazines or something?"

Laughing, Carver stroked her back. "Nothing like that, Baby. He's just making sure to get options. Aren't you happy we haven't had to go through them all though? Urena will take care of whittlin' them down just like she did the ones that were posted from last night."

"That's something at least."

Pressing her cheek to his pectoral, she listened to the even thudding of his heart, enjoying their moment of peace. After Carver's post addressing the viral videos he hadn't made any follow ups or personally answered any questions. It was taken care of by Urena's team based on the stock responses he'd agreed to.

They weeded out the crazies, trolls and the outright rude. Of course, there were still some people speculating, but he was on record leaving no room for people to put words in his mouth. Listening to Urena instruct him was interesting and entertaining. Carver gave zero fucks. Still, Urena provided talking points that kept him from actually admitting to assault.

Being unashamed of his actions, Carver didn't want to parse his words. But, Urena was trying to keep him from being sued—which Alyssa appreciated. What she didn't appreciate was the uptick in phone calls from relatives she rarely spoke with. Those she could do without.

When Carver hired Urena, he came home and talked to Alyssa about it the same day. Afterwards, they set up a joint call with her. As it happened, he wanted Urena to manage social media for both of them. Alyssa's social media footprint was tiny. Her accounts had been private since the option was available.

She'd never even bothered to set up a TikTok. She had to create one. She had a whopping five followers, Carver, Zaria, her brothers and her mother—who created a TikTok just to follow Alyssa.

During the creation process, Carver made a point to tell her she wasn't allowed to block him like she'd done on the other two platforms she used. Although she'd long since removed the block and accepted his requests, he wouldn't let her live it down. He shamelessly used it as leverage to get her to make a few videos that they would post in intervals on his page.

She couldn't believe she let him talk her into doing those transition trends. It was fun to play around, but she knew someone would find a way to try to steal their joyful moment and turn it into something ugly.

"Michael is going to bring the car around whenever you're ready to go."

Loosely holding her in his arms, Carver nuzzled the crook of her neck as he spoke. The action sent a shiver of arousal down her spine. Pulling away before it took hold, she patted his chest.

"Let me check my hair and freshen my lipstick and I'll be ready."

"Sure thing. I'll wait for you in the den with the guys."

When they re-entered the bedroom, she crossed the room heading toward the ensuite bathroom while Carver went toward the door leading to the hallway.

He had his cellphone in his hand and Alyssa heard what sounded like music playing as he walked out. He'd developed a mild TikTok addiction in the past few days since having to be more active online. He couldn't simply let Urena's team post on his behalf, he *had* to look for himself. To his credit, he did manage to restrain himself from responding.

Shaking her head, she walked into the bathroom. Her hair was a little windblown, so she had to do some repair work. After she finished, she was re-applying her lipstick when Carver walked into the bathroom. Stopping behind her, he slid one arm around her waist. The way he held the phone let her know he was recording.

He'd been doing that off and on, so she didn't think much of it. Smiling when he kissed her cheek, she reached back hooking an arm around his neck and turning her head for the kiss he brushed across her lips. At that point, he lifted his head, looked into the mirror at their reflection and said one word.

"Her."

Using their reflected images, Alyssa watched Carver as he stepped back tapping away at the phone in his hand. Not giving his actions much thought, she put away her hair care products and put the lipstick into her small clutch purse.

It wasn't until she heard a man's voice say, "Name something that you do that makes people irrationally angry," that she began paying closer attention to what Carver was doing.

Seated in the chair near the door, he wore a smirk as he avidly looked at his phone. She recognized the guy's voice from the TikToks they'd watched together. He was always posing questions for people to stitch and give their answer.

She made it to Carver's side just in time to see that he was looking at the recording he'd just made of the two of them. From her vantage point, she saw the way Carver looked at her before the video version of herself noticed him in the mirror. His eyes devoured her before locking with hers in the looking glass.

When she heard his voice say, "her", she realized she wasn't simply looking at a play back of his recording. He'd actually posted it to the platform. Closing her eyelids, Alyssa took a deep fortifying breath.

"Carver, please tell me you didn't just post that." Her eyes pleaded with him, but his expression was void of anything resembling remorse.

"Can't, because I most definitely did."

"Why?"

"Why not? If they're gonna be hatin' assholes, I don't see why we can't fuck with 'em a little."

"Why poke the hornet's nest? It's one thing to craft an image of us to give people enough of a peek to leave us alone, but that video is not a peek."

"Nope. It's a statement that I stand behind."

"What statement is that?"

"We see you. We see your ignorance, your bigotry, and intolerance. So...Fuck you, and the horse you rode in on. I hope that broke down nag gives you fleas."

Rolling her eyes in exasperation, Alyssa gave up on trying to reason with Carver.

"That's a lot of inference in just one word."

"What can I say, Baby. I'm talented like that."

Standing, he drew her into his arms pilfering another kiss before leading her from the room. Their ride down the elevator and short trek out to the waiting vehicle was relatively uneventful. A few people stared, but there were no over-eager fans or paparazzi.

Most of the looks were probably garnered simply because of the entourage and Carver looking like sex personified. Wearing a casual slate blue suit with a fitted black shirt underneath, in lieu of a button down, his green eyes stood out against his tan skin. Although practice hadn't officially started, he'd spent some time outside deepening his tan.

No doubt Carver was an attention getter. Not that she wasn't killing in her figure-hugging black dress which stopped just above her knees showing off her shapely calves accentuated by four-inch faux snakeskin heels. The vee in the front displayed her girls to perfection. If she wasn't aware of her appeal, the way Carver ate her up with his gaze was enough to make it clear.

They weren't in the car more than five minutes before Carver's phone dinged with a notification. When he pulled it from his pocket to check it, Alyssa couldn't avoid seeing the message.

Urena: Call me.

Alyssa knew it was only a matter of time before the social media manager made contact. While she had no proof, Alyssa was certain Carver hadn't run his little *fuck you haters* video by Urena before he recorded and posted it.

Cursing under his breath, Carver tapped the screen to place the call. "Excuse me for a second, Baby. I need to talk to Urena."

Nodding her understanding, Alyssa turned her gaze toward the passing scenery while tuning her ears to the conversation between Carver and Urena. Considering how closely they sat to each other and the lack of any outside noise in the vehicle, her being able to hear both sides of the call was inevitable. She heard Urena's voice clearly when she answered.

"Hello, Carver."

"Urena."

"Naomi was monitoring your accounts just now and noticed that you posted a video to TikTok."

"Yep. Did you like it?"

"It doesn't matter if I like it or not."

"Sure it does. You have an eye for these things. You know what will do well and what won't. If you like it, it'll do great."

"There's no doubt it will get plenty of views, but you created additional work for Naomi to clean up. This weekend was supposed to be about curating a narrative that gets the tabloid media out of your hair. If you're on social media thumbing your nose at the trolls, you're stirring the pot even more."

"So, what are you sayin'? You think I should take it down?"

"No. I'm not saying that. Besides, it's too late. It's been up for less than fifteen minutes and it already has thousands of views and the shares are steadily climbing."

"So, what do you want me to do, Urena?"

"Stop being a pain in my ass, Carver."

The giggle burst from Alyssa before she could call it back. Carver's hand landed on her thigh and squeezed. When she met his eyes, he winked and gifted her with one of his sunshine smiles.

"I'll do my best, but I can't make any promises. Sometimes being spontaneous is the way to go."

"That may be so, but I'm trying to help you reach a goal remember? I can't do that if you don't at least clue me in when you call an audible. Can we agree to that? You're a grown man, so you can do what you want, but we've got to be on the same page."

"Okay. I can agree with that."

"Thank you. Have a nice evening and give my best to Alyssa."

"Sure thing."

Once Carver disconnected the call, Alyssa's face wore an expression similar to the one she gave her brothers countless times over the years. He looked at her in confusion.

"What?"

In a voice reminiscent of her eight-year-old self, she sang out. "You got in trouble..."

Her words were followed by a fit of giggles which escalated into shrieks of laughter as Carver commenced to tickling her sides as punishment for taunting him.

When they arrived at Anton's, Samira, one of Alyssa's bodyguards materialized next to the car door to let them out. She accompanied them inside while Michael stayed with the car. Alyssa was long past wondering why they did things the way they did. So, she didn't question why Samira escorted them inside when they'd not had anyone with them the first time they went to *The Rooftop* at Anton's.

Samira was excellent at blending in, so it was easy to forget she was there. Alyssa wished she could just as easily ignore the photographer trailing them everywhere. She thought he was done, but he still hovered on the periphery.

Over the past week of having Samira with her while she went to work and around the city, Alyssa gained appreciation for the non-disruptive way Samira did her job. During Alyssa's first day back at work, more than a couple of the guys from the group chat tried to stop by her office.

She only knew it happened because they sent her emails when they were denied access. Emails she immediately forwarded to her manager as well as HR. Despite their ineffectiveness, Alyssa knew the game and was leaving a trail to denote the pattern. No one was dumb enough to repeat the things they'd said to one another, but they weren't adept at apologizing without incriminating themselves.

Still on the fence about continuing to work for a company where she didn't feel completely safe or heard, she'd spoken to her manager. That's when she learned no one from HR bothered to speak to him about the situation. She could practically see the wheels turning in his head as he calculated the possibility of losing contracts if she left *Secure Pull*.

The location of her office was such that anyone going to her manager's office had to walk past her door. When she bothered to look up from her computer, she noted the individual members of the group chat walking in that direction.

Their return path was done with a much wider berth than their approach. Alyssa was certain Samira had something to do with that. While Samira had been the one to accompany her inside, Kai and Remi alternated doing whatever it is they did outside and in the lobby of the building. The team had established a good rapport with Ms Barbara, which made Alyssa feel better about having them around. Very little happened at *Secure Pull* that Ms Barbara didn't know about.

Alyssa looked around the first floor of the Casino as Carver led her to the bank of elevators. Anton's wasn't the normal High Roller Casino. Sure, they had games for people who couldn't afford to drop one hundred grand on one round of poker, but even their slots had a minimum that would make the average person think twice before pulling the handle or pressing the button.

Alyssa was on the list of people who were unable to play slots. It was a condition of her contract with *Secure Pull*. Her name and photo were probably in the database of every casino around the country. Having written the security code and reviewed the algorithms for numerous machine styles, they could never be sure if she'd manipulated the system or not. It was a good thing for her, she had no interest in playing.

Despite the pricey buy-in, the casino floor was packed. Another oddity for an American Casino was the fact that Anton's was a completely smoke-free facility. They didn't have designated smoking areas. Smoking wasn't allowed anywhere on the premises. As far as Alyssa could see, their business didn't appear to suffer from the restriction.

There was much less of a crowd when the elevator opened onto the floor where the restaurant was located. Her heels clicked on the marble floors of the foyer, then sank into the plush carpet runner leading from the hostess' station into the restaurant.

Carver barely said two words to the woman wearing a designer pencil dress with her dark hair pulled back in a severe bun. She had the look of a traditional ballet dancer. All she needed was the toe shoes.

The young woman led them to a table in a private alcove outside instead of inside where they'd eaten previously. It was much more intimate and they had a view of the setting sun. The colorful sky was a perfect backdrop of which the photographer took advantage.

Alyssa was curious how any of the photos would be used. It gave the feel of being staged, but she could honestly say the man had never given either of them any instructions. He sincerely appeared to simply capture moments throughout their day.

Dinner was delicious. *The Rooftop at Anton's* was a place she and Zaria came on occasion to splurge. Not too often, but her first dinner there with Carver wasn't the first time she dined in the exclusive restaurant. Although, if her eyes didn't deceive her, this would be the first time she met the casino owner in person.

Walking toward them with a confident stroll was Andrei Antonov himself. *Good gravy.* The pictures in the magazines didn't do him justice. He wasn't what anyone would call pretty, but his features collaborated to form the definition of masculine beauty.

A strong jawline, covered by a neatly trimmed beard, a prominent nose that didn't dominate his face, high cheek bones and piercing ice blue eyes which sat below dark thick eyebrows, combined to create a face that was hard to ignore. He exuded power to a degree that Alyssa was certain terrified many people without him ever speaking.

Following her gaze, Carver noticed the walking advertisement for bigger, taller and scarier magazine. Okay, that wasn't a thing. But it should be.

"Bit, if I didn't know you weren't the kinda woman whose head was turned by every pretty face, I might be jealous of how long you've been looking at my pal Andrei."

Snapping her gaze back to Carver, Alyssa felt her cheeks heat. She didn't realize she was staring. "I was just surprised to see him. In all of the times I've eaten here, this is a first."

"Uh-huh."

Carver cut her side-eye before turning his attention to the man who now stood next to their table. It was hard for Alyssa to ignore that Andrei was slightly taller than Carver with a bulkier frame.

"Carver Jamieson, in my establishment, twice in the same month. To what do we owe the honor?"

Chapter Eighteen

IN MY DAMN FACE

Standing, Carver extended his hand to Andrei. The two had met years ago at a Super Bowl celebration. Carver almost didn't go, but changed his mind at the last minute. The entire team was attending, it wouldn't have looked right to skip it even if he wasn't in the celebrating mood.

At the time, Andrei remarked that he didn't look like a man who'd just won another coveted title and been named MVP. He was right. The victory felt a little hollow. That was actually the moment he decided he'd play one more season and hang it up. He loved the game, but his heart wasn't into playing it the way he needed it to be.

"I didn't expect to see you down here amongst the commoners, Andrei." Carver joked as they shook hands.

"One cannot spend all of his time in the ivory tower, my friend." Andrei replied, smirking at Carver before turning his gaze to Alyssa. "Good evening, Ms Ripley. I hope you are enjoying yourself—despite your present company."

Don't hit him. Carver chanted to himself as Bit blushed under Andrei's words. He hadn't even given her a real compliment and she was grinning like he'd whispered sweet nothings. Knowing he sounded like an irrational asshole, even to himself, Carver didn't voice any of his internal thoughts.

"I'm having a lovely evening. Thank you." Alyssa responded politely.

Neither of them was phased by Andrei already knowing her name. Besides the social media speculation surrounding the two of them, it was Andrei. A man in his position made it his business to *know things*.

"Very good. If you encounter any issues tonight or in the future, do not hesitate to let me know." Reaching into his pocket, Andrei produced a business card and passed it to Alyssa.

"I know you aren't giving my woman your phone number right in my damn face."

Try as he might, Carver couldn't stop the flames licking up his neck. Okay. He didn't actually try to stop them.

With a grin that didn't quite reach his eyes, Andrei regarded Carver. "I am going to give you a pass because I can tell you are crazy about this woman. Emphasis on the crazy." Squaring his shoulders, he smoothed his tie.

"I am simply letting her know she has resources if she has any issues in my establishments. It is an olive branch, not a proposal. Lighten up."

"Thank you, Mr. Antonov." Alyssa touched Carver's hand garnering his full attention.

She didn't say anything more, but he read her expression. While he wasn't making a scene, he came close. He needed to get his shit together. Flying off the handle any time another man spoke to his Bit wasn't going to cut it.

"Yeah, thanks." Instead of retaking his seat, Carver held up a hand signaling their server. When the young man approached, he asked for the check.

"No, Cirrol. Do not worry about bringing the check. Their meal is on the house." Andrei stated.

"I appreciate it, Andrei. But, it's not necessary."

Waving a hand in his direction, the big Russian brushed him off. "Do not mention it. In spite of your...overzealous protection, it is good to see you. I did not get a chance to speak with you the last time—when you two came in for lunch."

Ignoring Andrei's dig, Carver held his hand out to help Alyssa from her seat. Murmuring her thanks to Andrei, she rounded the table until she stood at Carver's side. Pressing his fingertips to the small of her back, he guided her from the restaurant.

Andrei walked them out making small talk. "Ms Ripley—"

"Please, call me Alyssa."

"Thank you, you may call me Andrei if you would like."

Working on taming the beast churning jealously in his chest, Carver remained quiet. His rational mind knew his Bit would never openly flirt with another man in front of him, but the green dragon inhabiting his brain didn't see logic. He saw a man who could legitimately turn his woman's head.

As if Carver wasn't standing between them, Andrei continued their conversation. "Alyssa, feel free to extend my offer to Ms Coleman as well."

"Ms Coleman?" Alyssa's eyebrows dipped with confusion.

"Although it is not what I would call regular, you two have frequented *The Rooftop* a number of times. Correct?"

"Yes..." Alyssa answered warily. Her eyes filled with questions.

Carver wondered if Andrei realized he'd tipped his hand. Hearing him refer to Alyssa's friend, Zaria, had the tension draining from Carver's shoulders. Andrei's slip up gave Carver something his logical brain couldn't supply—understanding. Andrei's approach had nothing to do with Carver and Alyssa, and everything to do with Alyssa's feisty friend. *Interesting*.

They exited the restaurant approaching the elevator to take them back down to the casino floor. Before they reached it, Alyssa excused herself to go to the restroom. Samira accompanied her.

"A little friendly advice..." Andrei placed a hand on Carver's shoulder. They matched in height, but Andrei was heavier than Carver. "Ease off. You are going to give yourself an early heart attack or run her off. I am sure you do not want either of those things to happen."

Initially, Carver simply looked at Andrei with a single raised eyebrow.

Nodding in understanding, Andrei tapped Carver's shoulder. "It is your grave. Dig it however you like. Have a nice evening. Please extend my goodbyes to Ms Ripley."

"If you want an introduction to Zaria, you could've just said that instead of sliding my woman your number." Carver's lips tipped up in a knowing smirk.

A storm descended onto Andrei's face. "I have no idea what you are talking about. I do not need a spokesman." Leveling Carver with an annoyed expression he turned to leave. "Get out before I change my mind about comping your meal."

Chuckling at his buddy's discomfort, Carver's face stretched into a wide smile as he called out goodbye to Andrei's retreating back. When he turned to face the direction Alyssa had disappeared, he ran into a small soft body.

"Oh! Excuse me. I didn't see you there."

Instinctively, he put his hands on the woman's shoulder's to steady her. When the woman looked up, he realized he knew her.

"Audrey?"

"Hi, Carver. I'm so sorry. I'm such a clutz." She smiled, placing a hand on his chest.

Once he was certain she was steady, Carver, release her shoulders and stepped back to put some space between them.

"No problem. No harm done. Are you okay?"

"Other than being embarrassed about literally running into a client, I'm peachy." Smiling at him, she flipped her hair over her shoulder.

"No need for embarrassment. Accidents happen."

"Thank you. Well, it's good I ran into you. It appears we are going to be in position to wrap everything up with your property before the end of next week. If I'm not mistaken that's just ahead of your schedule."

"That's great news. Send me the details on the meeting, and I'll adjust my schedule."

"Sure thing. I'll do it now." Pulling her phone from her purse, she tapped the screen a few times.

The ding in his pocket alerted Carver to the new message. Retrieving his phone, he acknowledged receipt.

"Okay. Well, again. My apologies for bumping into you and I'll see you later in the week."

"Sounds like a plan." Looking up from Audrey's smiling face he saw

Alyssa and Samira returning. "Excuse me. Have a good evening, Audrey."

Leaving the agent standing, he stepped around her. Once he reached Alyssa, he took her hand leading her to the bank of elevators.

"Guess what, Baby?"

"What?"

"I just talked to the real estate agent and it looks like I'll be able close on my house next week."

"That's great! Congratulations!"

"It's a little ahead of schedule. I'll need make a few calls to get it furnished the way I want, but it looks like I'll be able to check out of the suite sooner rather than later."

"That sounds awesome."

Alyssa's expression was one of genuine happiness for him, but he wondered if she realized what it meant for them when the purchase was complete. He couldn't see himself sleeping away from her in essentially the same city.

Damn societal norms. Carver wanted her with him. Under the same roof. How he was going to manage that was the question. The time remaining for him to figure that out was dwindling.

It wasn't like she hadn't seen the house. He'd taken her on an online tour using the realtor's photos and they'd driven by so she could see the neighborhood. She'd had nothing but positive things to say.

During his time in the NFL, there had been no shortage of women vying for his attention and using every ounce of their wiles to attempt to entice him. Had he done the things he'd done with his Bit with any one of them, they would've called the leasing office to cancel their contract. The ones who owned their homes would put their houses on the market.

Him sharing details about his future home and asking their opinion would've been taken as a sign that he wanted to cohabitate. Not his Bit though. She simply expressed excitement for him. He'd bet money the thought never crossed her mind to consider that he'd purchased that house with her in mind.

Reaching the first level of the casino, Carver halted their small entourage before they exited the building. He had a couple of options for what they'd do next, aside from him spreading Alyssa across the bed like a buffet. An option he hadn't considered was gaming activities at the casino, since it was one of the few places they'd be guaranteed to not be bothered.

"Bit, baby do you wanna play for a little while before we go? I don't mind if that's what you want."

Shaking her head, she declined. "Thanks, but I'm not allowed to play slots and while they've never specifically said so, I'm sure they'd have issue with me at the other gaming tables as well."

"Not allowed? Is it because you work at a gaming company? That can't be fair."

"It's not simply the fact that I work for a gaming company. I design, program and troubleshoot gaming software—mostly from the security side. However, I know enough that they consider me a gaming risk. Andrei, may be your friend, but I don't think even he would bend those rules for me. Besides, gambling really isn't my thing."

"Hmph. I never considered how that worked." Checking his watch, he made his final decision on their next location. Once they were ensconced in the backseat of the car, he fired off a couple of quick texts. One to confirm and another to reschedule. They'd still do the other activity, just not tonight.

Holding Alyssa's hand, he watched her as she took in the bright lights of the strip as if it were her first time. She had lived in Coryville for over half a decade. Being that close to Vegas, there was no way she hadn't seen the strip at night. In less than twenty minutes they circled the Mandalay Bay.

Once the vehicle came to a stop at the valet station, they exited. Tugging Alyssa away from the elevator which would take them to his suite, he slipped her hand into his.

"I have a surprise for you."

Seeing Alyssa's eyes light up was worth the effort it took to set up the entire day's events.

"Another one? This whole day has been one big surprise."

Using a finger to tip her face up to his, he dropped a lingering peck on her full lips. "Well...get ready for one more."

Rounding the corner, they encountered a young African American man who Carver knew was waiting especially for them. Approaching them with a broad smile displaying even white teeth, he extended his hand to introduce himself.

"Good evening, my name is Quentin. I'll be your VIP host this evening. Is there anything I can get you before we start your virtual tour?"

Carver looked at Alyssa whose mouth hung open in shock as she realized they were standing outside of the VIP entrance for the *Michael Jackson ONE* Cirque Du Soleil show.

Mentally patting himself on the back, he squeezed her fingers to get her attention. "Bit, anything Quentin can get for you before we start? Want a drink or something?"

Jolted from her silence, Alyssa blushed prettily and shook her head declining the guide's offer. Releasing her hand, Carver slipped his arm around her giving her a quick kiss to the forehead.

"Looks like we're ready when you are, Quentin."

It had taken some doing, but Carver's assistant had managed to secure them a VIP pass which included private accommodations. So, they wouldn't encounter anyone else until the actual show began. Even then, he'd bought a few extra seats to keep them insulated.

While Alyssa's eyes were fixated on the screens as she listened to Quentin's well-rehearsed speech, Carver watched her. He drank in her unfiltered responses to the things she saw and heard. When she smiled, so did he. Her joy in each moment was all that he needed to see. He couldn't describe one thing displayed on the monitors or tell anyone a word Quentin spoke.

During the actual show, he managed to tear his eyes away from Alyssa long enough to enjoy the rhythmic, acrobatic presentation from the cast members. For those ninety minutes, they were immersed in all things MJ. In that space in time, they were just a regular couple out on a date. Nothing and no one else could pierce their bubble.

When they entered his suite later that night, they barely made it over the threshold before Alyssa was shoving his jacket from his shoulders and attacking his belt buckle to get to the button on his pants. That he recalled, there was nothing overtly erotic about the show they'd seen, but something had flipped a switch on his Bit and he wasn't going to complain about the results.

Grabbing him by the front of his shirt, she pulled him around the corner to the u-shaped sofa. Allowing her to push him back onto the couch, he spread his legs for her to come closer while simultaneously lowering his zipper. Tugging at the waist band of his boxer briefs, he allowed his erection to fall out of the underwear.

Regarding Alyssa as she watched his every move, he stroked his length from base to the mushroom-shaped tip.

"See something' you want, Baby?"

Teasing her was torture for him. Thankfully, she wasn't in the mood for torment. Kicking off her shoes, she dropped to her knees between his spread legs and licked the pearl of precum gathered at the head of his shaft. His eyes threatened to close, but he forced them open.

He didn't want to miss a second of his Bit's lush lips taking his cock deep into her mouth. Replacing his hand with her own, she glided her fingers around his thickness as far as she could.

"Fuuuuuuck..."

The word was drawn from his throat as she suddenly engulfed half of his length into her mouth hitting her throat. The unexpected change coupled with the suctioning draw on his cock had his sac drawing up ready to spill everything stored inside.

Humming around his shaft, amber clashed with green as she held his gaze while pleasuring him spectacularly. Too spectacularly. Tangling his fingers into her curly tresses, he tugged until she released him with a grumble.

"I was enjoying that." She whined.

"So was I, darlin', but I need to be inside your sweet pussy when I cum." Removing her fingers, still stroking his hardness, he lifted until she stood before him.

Not bothering to remove her dress, he hiked it up quickly discarding the panties underneath. Before the coolness of the air could register on her sweet pussy, he scooped her onto his lap.

"Ride me, Bit. Take what you need and give me everything you have." Carver encouraged. Holding two handfuls of her lush ass, he guided her onto his stiff rod.

As each inch of his cock was encased in her heated channel, the battle to hold himself back became more difficult. The feeling of being wrapped inside her velvet walls, while her thick thighs bracketed his hips was heavenly. He couldn't think of anything that brought him greater pleasure, aside from tasting her sweet cream on his tongue.

Ignoring the ripping noise, he pulled at the vee neck of her dress and bra until her breasts tumbled out into his hands.

"You're so fucking beautiful…"

Lifting her breast to his lips he practically swallowed the turgid peak he suckled so deeply on it. Alyssa's sharp inhale followed by a guttural moan told him he'd struck the exact amount of pressure to give her the most pleasure.

Bucking his hips below her, he reminded her of her assignment.

"My dick ain't a thermometer. It ain't there to take your temperature, Bit. Shake that ass and ride it." Punctuating his demand with a gripping smack to her ass, he transferred his oral affection to her other breast.

Apparently galvanized into action, Alyssa grabbed his shoulders to balance herself as she began to lift and lower herself on his cock. The swivel of her hips had him touching places inside her which set her off. Her essence coated his shaft, dripping down his balls as she rode him like an experienced jockey poised for a marathon ride.

Only, this couldn't and wouldn't be a marathon. At least not this round. The way her pussy walls clamped down on his dick each time she reached the base, guaranteed they'd reach the precipice in more of a sprint.

The first round would be fast and that was okay. They had all night. Holding her nipple between his teeth, he bit down just enough to stimulate, but not enough to actually cause her pain. Her response was exactly as he expected.

"Aah! Oh shit! I'm gonna—you're gonna make me—"

Grabbing her hips, Carver buried his face in the crook of her neck and growled. "That's it, Bit. Give me everything. Drown my cock in your cum."

Rolling them on the couch, he quickly changed their position. He knew what she needed to finish. Hooking an arm behind her knee, he pressed it toward her chest and plunged his thickness into her depths to the hilt.

Grinding his pelvis against her pearl, he watched as her eyes rolled back and her voice was snatched silent. Her walls undulated along his length sucking his seed from him in torrents.

Breathing heavily, he pushed her disheveled hair from her forehead before gently kissing her lips. Soon, the gentleness disappeared and his tongue delved into her mouth to duel with hers. Moaning, she rocked her hips into his.

Breaking the kiss, he pinned her with his gaze. "Damn, Bit baby. Are you trying to kill me?"

"Are you saying you can't hang?"

Reminding her that she was still very much full of his cock, he swiveled his hips.

"That sounds like a challenge. You know how competitive I am."

"Bring it." Biting her bottom lip, she grinned mischievously.

"You ain't said nothin' but a thang, Baby."

Chapter Nineteen

WE WERE ROOTING FOR YOU

Carver was acting strange and Alyssa didn't think it was due to his coaching responsibilities with the team. Although he'd done the final paperwork for purchasing his new home, he had his assistant doing everything else in relation to communicating with the interior designer and setting up utility services. So, she didn't think home-buying stress was the cause either.

At present, he was in New York attending meetings. He'd only been there for a little over twenty-four hours, but it felt like forever. How had she grown so accustomed to seeing him daily that she couldn't make it a full day without missing him?

Sleeping without his arm curled around her waist, wrapping her in a human cocoon, was essentially pointless. She managed to doze off, but was never able to reach REM sleep. It was all his fault.

Before Carver and his comforting body heat, she was at least able to get her brain to calm down enough to allow for six solid hours of sleep. Now, not only was Alyssa's brain torturing her, her body was in on the gig. It missed his. She didn't even want to think about what they'd do when the mini-mansion he'd purchased was ready for him to move in.

It was irrational to purchase all of that house and continue to spend his nights with Alyssa in her much smaller home. No, it didn't make sense. As a matter of fact, it was downright wasteful. She guessed his trip to New York would help them begin to re-acclimate to not spending every night together.

Sitting in her office at work, she tried to refocus on the code for the new security program she had designed. The sections of the wall which bracketed the door of her office were glass and her door stood open. So, she had a view of the cubicles which made up the engineering floor at *Secure Pull*. Thanks to the tempered glass windows on either side of the area, there was an abundance of natural light.

There were people moving between the dividers more than usual, but Alyssa refused to inquire as to why. She was sure she could ask Samira. The woman had bionic hearing. Without ever leaving her post outside of Alyssa's door, she seemed to have her finger on the pulse of everything happening on that floor.

The notification ding from Alyssa's phone reminded her that she'd forgotten to put it on vibrate. She swiped the screen first, before checking to see what had the device pinging. While she hadn't developed Carver's TikTok addiction, she had started following trending topics.

She wasn't interested in being glued to social media, but she also didn't want to be caught off guard again. As Urena predicted, Carver's stunt the prior weekend quickly went viral. The stitches and duets were so numerous, she wouldn't even attempt to watch them all. Of course, Urena's staff made certain only the positive responses got any attention on either of their accounts.

Tapping the notification, Alyssa saw that #CarverJamieson was trending more than usual on the application. Despite knowing she'd probably regret following the link, she pushed her earbuds into her ears and touched the hashtag. Her screen populated with videos. According to the counter near the top, there were almost a thousand and counting.

Biting the bullet, she selected the first one. The electronic voice read the words on the screen. ***"What the hell, Carver? We were rooting for you."***

A series of photos populated the screen of Carver and a petite redhead. The first showed him beside her as they walked through a restaurant, the next showed them standing in the circular driveway of a house Alyssa didn't recognize, another was of him opening a car door while she climbed inside, and the last was the redhead standing close to him with her hand on his chest. His hands were holding her shoulders.

A pretty young African American woman appeared on screen. She looked over her shoulder as if looking at the image projected behind her. Then, turned back to look into the camera.

"Do y'all see this? He's out here making videos proclaiming his commitment to his woman and now look. No shade to the woman in the pictures, but she doesn't look anything like the queen he's had all over his social media for the past week.

Something in the milk ain't clean. Let me know what you think in the comments. I mean...I guess these pictures could be innocent and easily explained but that last one looked mighty intimate."

Alyssa's first instinct was to immediately close the app. The creator was correct. The last photo did look intimate, but his clothing in the photos was very familiar. She recalled each day vividly.

The first set of pictures was taken the day she'd been ambushed by the paparazzi. Adding two and two together, she deduced the woman pictured with him was the real estate agent he'd told her about. The other was likely taken a couple of days ago when he went to sign the paperwork to close on the new house. The polo and slacks were what he was wearing when they parted ways on Wednesday morning.

The last photo had to be taken on Saturday while she was in the ladies room at Anton's. He was wearing the same suit and the elevators could be seen in the background.

Perusing a few more videos only served to make her angry. People really had nothing better to do than be in someone else's business. Standing, she closed the door to her office as she shut down the app then opened her contact list.

Hoping she wasn't in court, Alyssa called Zaria. She trusted Carver, but she knew the optics were horrible—especially considering the agent met the physical standard of beauty society expected someone like him to be with.

Answering on the second ring, Zaria didn't bother with a greeting. "What's wrong?"

"Why do you assume something's wrong?" Alyssa shot back.

"It's ten a.m. on a Friday morning. You don't call me at this time of day. Text maybe, but not a phone call."

Leaning forward in her chair, Alyssa sent a few links to her friend. "Take a look at what I just sent you. It's trending."

Zaria was quiet on the line as she did as Alyssa asked. Since Alyssa couldn't hear anything, she assumed Zee was viewing the videos on her tablet, or PC. Tapping her fingers against her desk, she waited.

"People get on my last damn nerve." Zaria's words suddenly cut through the silence. "It would've taken them all of three seconds to image search this woman, which I did, and see that she's a real estate agent. He just moved here. Of course he'd be seen with a real estate agent if he doesn't want to live out of a hotel room."

The sound of Zaria sucking her teeth hit Alyssa's ears. She must be good and ticked off if she was doing that. She only sucked her teeth when she was angry.

"Tell me you aren't letting these gossiping people get to you. You don't believe this shit do you?"

"Absolutely not. I trust Carver. I didn't believe for a second he's been seeing someone else."

"Ok, if you don't believe it, what's up with the phone call?"

"I don't want to look stupid."

"And how, pray-tell, would you look stupid? Carver is all over the internet letting the world know he's about everything Alyssa Ripley."

"True, but perception is everything. His behavior could easily be construed as love bombing to make up for doing something shitty."

"You and I both know he's doing no such thing. And since when do you care what other people think?"

"Normally, I don't..."

"Then don't start now. None of this is worth the energy you're giving it. That man's nose is wide open. There's no way he's doing anything to jeopardize his chance to be with you. Not after waiting fifteen years."

"I know all of that, but having his name trending because of pictures with him and another woman just adds fuel to the fire."

"I really don't want you worrying about this. You can't control people's ignorance. Didn't Carver hire someone to manage social media for the both of you?"

"Yes."

"Have you spoken to them? If it's trending enough for you to notice, I'd bet money they have a plan for how to counteract it."

Tapping her forehead with her palm, Alyssa kicked herself for not thinking of Urena and contacting her for advice on what, if anything, she should do in regards to this new development.

"I haven't spoken to Urena. I should probably give her a call. Thanks, Zee."

"Anytime. I'll bill you."

Laughing at Zee's mention of billing her, Alyssa ended the call and sent Urena a message asking for a quick meeting. While she was waiting for a response, there was a knock on her door.

Certain no one had gotten past Samira, Alyssa called out for her to enter. Stepping inside, Samira closed the door behind her.

"There's a Ballard Grimes asking to see you. He's being pretty persistent, otherwise, I would've just sent him on his way."

Scrunching her face in distaste at the very mention of Ballard's name Alyssa shook her head. "Tell him to send me an email. There's nothing we need to discuss. We aren't on any projects together and I don't associate with him socially."

"Yes ma'am."

Turning on her heels Samira opened the door. Standing immediately outside was Ballard, who attempted to speak around her as she maneuvered him backwards and away from the doorway. *What in the entire hell is that about?*

Alyssa had enough on her mind without adding whatever petty machinations Ballard had going on. After what he did to her at the restaurant with the press, he was the last person she wanted to speak to on any given day. Even if she did, his timing was terrible.

At this moment, Alyssa's primary focus was on the spotlight that seemed to follow Carver and, by association, her. Until they got together, she'd happily lived her life in relative obscurity. Their relationship was in its infancy. Could it survive under this kind of scrutiny?

She cared about Carver deeply, but was what they had enough to withstand being under the microscope? As much as he tried to shield her, would Carver's best efforts be enough? Questions about whether or not she was cut out for this kind of life swirled in Alyssa's head.

Guilt flooded Alyssa, making her feel disloyal for even considering that Carver wouldn't be able to keep his word regarding protecting her from the ugliness. After all, it was why he hired her security detail and had Urena managing their social media. In her heart, she had confidence in him, but he wasn't the unknown variable in this whole thing.

The people poking their noses in her and Carver's business were the problem. The digital, social media, age brought about many good things as far as joining the global community and providing access to knowledge. However, what it also brought was the expectation that everything was for public consumption. That was the part Alyssa was concerned would eventually drive a wedge between her and Carver.

Chapter Twenty

WHO DOES THIS SHIT?

Outside the window of her smallish office, the sky was cloudless and the sun shone brightly. It was in contrast to the internal turmoil Alyssa experienced. She was grateful for Zaria's words of wisdom, but as she waited for Urena to call her back, Alyssa couldn't force the niggle of concern to go away. Was she strong enough to stick by Carver when, to the rest of the world, it looked like he was making a fool of her?

Thanks to Samira's forethought, the door to Alyssa's office was closed when her phone rang. It meant she had privacy for her conversation with Urena. The social media manager had gotten back to her sooner than she expected.

"Hey, Urena. Thanks for calling me so quickly."

"No problem. I actually thought it would be Carver first, but I figured I'd speak to one of you soon."

"So, you saw?"

"The #CarverJamieson trending online? Yes. I did. We're already working to counteract it. We simply have to get our narrative in front of the right influencers and it'll overshadow those speculating and outright lying."

"What does that entail exactly?"

Alyssa was genuinely curious. Her understanding of the dynamics surrounding social media was limited. She was one of those rare people who used it mainly to keep up with family, with a few friends sprinkled in the mix.

"We have creators we work with on the app who have influence in different areas. We supply them with an inside look and the details we want distributed, they do the rest. In return, we help them when they need it, quid pro quo.

No money exchanges hands. It's a symbiotic relationship. Many of them like being the first to know what's really going on and they like being ahead of things that will drive their interactions higher. Win-win for us."

"I never would have thought it. I just assumed these things happened organically."

"In a perfect world, people wouldn't be so quick to jump to conclusions and there would be time for the whole story to come out without having to be so strategic. Unfortunately, that's not how things work in reality.

I don't want you to concern yourself with what's going on with Carver's name trending. The stories floating around are so full of holes, that the only people who really believe them are those who wanted to believe the narrative they made up in their own minds.

They don't care if it's true. It fits what they want to believe. On a positive note, not all of the posts under the tag are speculating about your relationship. There is a growing number of them that are calling out how harmful and invasive people have been in regards to your privacy. So, there's hope yet."

"That's good to hear." Relief flooded as she listened to Urena's assessment.

Alyssa's phone buzzed alerting her to a new message, so she thanked Urena for her time and ended the call.

> Carver: Hey, Baby. I'm about to board the plane coming home. I'll see you this evening. I have to stop by the office when I land.

> Ok. Safe travels.

Carver: I was thinking we'd stay in tonight. I have early practice in the morning.

That's fine with me. I'll order dinner.

Carver: Sounds good. I missed the hell out of you, woman. I don't wanna share you.

I missed you too.

She debated on saying more, mentioning his name trending, but figured it served no purpose. He was about to get on an airplane and he had enough on his plate. There was no sense in riling him up while he was thousands of miles in the air. Besides, Urena and her team were already on it.

They exchanged goodbye messages and Alyssa tried to focus on her work for the rest of the morning. Completing the code ahead of schedule, she decided to take the rest of the day off. The code would need to be stress-tested, but that could wait until Monday.

She had an urge to throw something on the grill instead of ordering in. A trip to the grocery store and the butcher were in order. Sending Samira and the guys a message to let them know, she emailed her manager as well.

While her email was still open, she noticed a few messages. None of them were from project managers or team members, so she opted to let them wait until she returned after the weekend. Gathering her items, she left her office, locking the door behind her.

The eyes on her as she passed were noticeable and now that she'd seen the trending topic, she was able to put together why there was more activity earlier in the day. Alyssa didn't want to hear anyone else talk about the way women gossip. There were only two other women with offices on the same floor. So, it was men who were flitting around buzzing about her personal life.

By the time she was seated in the back seat of the SUV, she'd decided that she would work from home going forward unless her presence in the office was required. Of course, she'd have to speak to her manager about it, but she doubted there would be any pushback.

There hadn't been a peep out of him or anyone else when it came to her personal security. He'd probably be happy to have the distraction removed. Although Alyssa was certain, Samira and the guys weren't doing anything to disrupt or distract people from doing their jobs.

Their trip to get the items she needed for dinner was uneventful. Her early day meant an early day for them as well. The additional security measures Jasper had insisted on for her home meant she didn't have a person with her twenty-four hours a day.

Standing at the sink washing her hands, Alyssa had just finished putting her blended spice rub on the ribs when she heard Carver calling out to her. Frowning, she checked the time. He was early. He must have come straight from the airstrip.

"Bit!"

"In the kitchen!"

Carver entered the room in long strides not stopping until he was in her personal space. His eyes raked over her probingly before he cradled her face between his hands and took her mouth in a scorching kiss. Uncaring of her wet digits, she grabbed onto his shirt holding on for dear life.

The kiss bordered on frantic in its intensity. He held her face in his hands as if he thought there was a chance she may reject him. After a few moments, he pulled back delivering parting pecks to her kiss-swollen lips.

"Hey." Alyssa's voice cracked slightly with the greeting.

"Hey, yourself. I've been calling you. Why didn't you answer?" Still holding her head immobile, his gaze locked on her.

"You did?"

"I did."

With the limited motion available to her, she attempted to look for her phone. Patting her pockets confirmed it wasn't there. "I must have left my phone in my purse. It's upstairs."

Finally releasing her from his hold, he stepped back. Carver ran his hand down his face and Alyssa noticed the tension in his face for the first time. When he entered, he was on her so quickly, she didn't have a chance to get a good look at him. Reversing their initial pose, she reached up to cup his face between her hands.

"Hey...What's wrong? Why do you look so stressed?" As soon as the words hit the air, she understood. He'd found out about the rumors online. He assumed the worst when she didn't answer his calls.

"You saw the stuff online?"

"Yeah."

"And when I didn't answer the phone...?"

"I thought you were mad, or hurt, and didn't wanna talk to me. I came straight from the airstrip."

Slipping her fingers around his head, she tugged as she lifted onto her toes to place a kiss on his lips.

"I'm okay." She pecked his lips again in reassurance. "We're okay."

Drawing her closer with his arms around her waist, Carver dropped his forehead to hers. "That's Audrey in the pictures. The real estate agent that helped me find my house. I'd never do somethin' like that to you. You know that right?"

His eyes searched hers for understanding. She had work to do if he thought she'd so easily believe something she heard from strangers on the internet.

"I know that, honey. You're not that kind of man." Rubbing the back of his head, she smirked at him. "If you were, it wouldn't have taken you five years to kiss me the first time."

Growling, he grasped the back of her thighs, lifting and forcing her to wrap her legs around his waist. "Don't bring up old stuff. It reminds me of the way you ran from me. When I think about that, I remember you still haven't made up for all the time we missed."

Absently stroking the almost buzzed strands at his nape, she gave him half a grin. "Things happened when they were supposed to. Besides, I'm not gonna let you put Pinkie on bed rest because you think you can plant yourself inside me enough times to make up for the years we were apart. That's not how this works."

Walking until he placed her on the countertop, he planted his hands on either side of her, and nuzzled her neck. "I think we oughta test that theory Miss Engineer."

Alyssa's objection was cut off when Carver suddenly lifted her on his shoulder in a fireman's carry heading upstairs to the bedroom. Balancing against his lower back, she smacked the rounded cheeks of his perfect ass. Her little act of rebellion earned her a stinging swat to her own posterior.

Almost tossing her onto the bed, Carver followed immediately covering her body with his. Insinuating himself between her legs, he attacked her neck with suckling kisses. He was well on his way to hitting all of her best spots, but something was digging into her back.

"Carver...Carver, wait. Something's poking me."

Sitting up on his knees, he pulled her up to look beneath her. When he reached behind her and produced her phone, she smiled.

"Oh. That's where it was all this time."

Taking it from him, she unlocked it to clear the missed notifications. She didn't attempt to read any of the messages. Most of them were from Carver and he was here now. When she noticed the latest notification, she frowned.

"What is it?" Carver asked, looking from her face to the phone.

"Nothing. A message from Torrence. I thought I blocked him."

"Open it."

"Why?" Alyssa was sincerely confused. It didn't matter what Torrence had to say. The only reason she'd open a message from him would be to be certain she put him on the blocked caller list.

"Let's see what he wants."

One look at his face told her he wouldn't let it go, so she opened the message.

"What the **FUCK?!**" Carver gritted out. "I'm gonna break that shit off and shove it down his throat. Who does this shit?"

Where Carver was furious, Alyssa was stunned and confused. Why the hell had Torrence sent her a picture of his dick? There was text in the message as well, but she didn't bother to read it. She had other shit to think about. Like how she was going to keep Carver from following through on his threat.

Chapter Twenty-One
YOU ABOUT TO LOSE YOUR JOB

Carver had heard the phrase, *so angry they saw red*, but he'd never actually experienced it. Until today. His vision was literally tinted red. Who the fuck did Torrence think he was sending Bit a damn dick pic?

"Bit...Why the fuck does he think it's okay to send you this kind of shit?"

Carver's voice was gritty with anger. He knew he couldn't blame Alyssa for someone else's behavior, but that was the question burning his brain.

"Hell if I know. I've never requested nor accepted shit like this from anyone, especially not him. I blocked him, or at least I thought I had."

"Call him." Carver snapped out.

"What? Why? I don't want to talk to him."

"You don't have to talk. I'll do the talkin'."

Shaking her head, Alyssa tried to deny him. Somewhere deep inside, a small voice attempted to convince him to think about what he was doing, but Carver ignored it. There was no way he'd let another man get away with doing shit like that to his woman.

"Call him, or I'm goin' to his damn house to beat his ass right now."

"Carver—"

"Alyssa!"

He felt the smallest tinge of remorse when she jumped after he yelled her name. Closing his eyes, he made more of an effort to get himself under control. Despite how it seemed lately, Carver didn't typically fly off the handle or let his anger get the best of him. However, when it came to Bit, his fuse was extremely short for the bullshit. It set him off. Quickly.

Lifting the phone from her fingers, he tapped the number at the top of the screen placing the call himself—on speaker. Getting off the bed, he moved away from Alyssa and her pleading eyes.

Answering after only a couple of rings, Torrence immediately launched into his bullshit when he answered. "I figured you'd call me after that white boy showed his true colors. I just wanted to show you what you were missing."

"She ain't missin' shit motherfucker. The fuck is wrong with you sendin' my woman pictures of your shriveled up junk?"

"Fuck!" Torrence exclaimed and his obvious fumbling of the phone could be heard clearly. "Shit! Fuck. Listen, man—"

"No. You listen, dipshit. I don't know who the fuck raised you, but you picked the wrong one to fuck with."

"I'm sorry, man. I don't know what to say."

Carver didn't know why Torrence's dumb ass was even still on the phone. He thought he would've hung up when he heard Carver's voice instead of Alyssa's. Anger still churned in his gut, so he took the opportunity to go into explicit details of the many ways he would tear Torrence's world apart.

Was he threatened by Torrence's presence? Absolutely not. However, once he was able to see past his own anger, he saw Torrence's actions for what they were—assault. Sure, he hadn't put his hands on Alyssa. But, he thought it was okay to subject her to unsolicited pictures of his dick. That shit couldn't fly.

"I'm sorry, man. I promise, I've never done anything like this before, and I won't do it again. You don't have to do anything. Please tell Alyssa I'm sorry and she won't hear from me again."

"Damn right she won't hear from your ass again. You'll be lucky to still have access to a cellphone when I get done with you."

Without waiting for a reply, Carver disconnected the call. Although he had no desire to see Torrence's naked cock, he quickly took a screen shot of the message, logged into to his secure drive and saved it to his Shit List folder. When he took the screen shot, Carver noticed the text message that accompanied the picture.

> Torrence: You should've known that white boy wasn't going to be satisfied with a fat black chick. No matter how pretty you are. If you're done letting him play you, hit me up. I might take you back.

The fuck she will. Carver fumed. This motherfucker didn't know when to leave well enough alone. He's gonna learn today.

After Carver saved the screenshot to the folder, he deleted it from Alyssa's phone. The entire time, he mumbled under his breath about the other man's audacity and blatant stupidity.

"Do you feel better now?" Alyssa asked from her position on the bed. She sat with her legs folded, elbow propped on one knee, and her chin resting on her fist as she watched him.

"What?"

"I asked if you feel better now that you've had the chance to cuss Torrence out to his face."

"Baby, that cussin' was just the start of what I'm going to do to that slimy bastard."

"Carver..." Unfolding herself from the bed, she stood before him, slipping her arms around his waist looking up at him.

"I love the way you're so ready to protect me. I do. But, I think Torrence gets the picture that he fucked up. I doubt very seriously that I'll hear from him again."

"You're damn right you won't hear from him again, and it's absolutely necessary that he faces the consequences of his actions. He's supposedly a grown ass man. Yet, he's sending out dick pics and messages trying to get with a woman who told him she didn't want his ass. And not just any woman. *My* fucking woman."

Rubbing his back, she quirked an eyebrow at him. "Yes, but is sending a dick pic worth ending his career?"

"He should've thought of that shit before he sent it."

"True, but you told that man you hoped he had money saved because he'd be living with his parents again before the end of the month. How do you plan to do that?"

"He will, and you don't need to worry about the details. Just know any time he even thinks of you he'll get the fucking shakes."

"Carver..."

"I said what I said, Bit. You don't worry about any of this. I got it."

Denzel said it best when they spoke previously. Carver was definitely plotting. Torrence just put himself at the top of the list.

While he was still pissed, his anger had cooled a little with her cuddled against him. Bit had always had a way of calming him with the slightest touch. He tried not to think about how the text message had deflated his hard-on and essentially cock-blocked their little reunion.

If he thought about it too hard, he really would call Michael to pick him up and go to that bastard's house to beat his ass. Instead of giving Torrence any more of his energy, Carver kissed Alyssa's cheek and buried his face into the crook of her neck—simply breathing in her presence.

In one of those breaths, he thought he detected the scent of charcoal, but that couldn't be right. Although, he knew the rules about sticking his hands in a black woman's hair, Carver lifted Alyssa's curly strands to his nose. Yeah...That was charcoal.

"Bit, Baby?"

"Hm?"

"Why does your hair smell like charcoal?"

Jerking away from him, her eyes went wide. "Oh shit! The grill! I was getting ready to put some meat on before you came home. I forgot!"

Pulling out of his embrace, she shot out of the room. Standing there, he watched the place from where she disappeared. She'd said this was his home. He wondered if she realized it. With a sappy grin on his face, he followed her from the room.

Monday morning, before he went in to the team offices, Carver had Michael make a detour into the business sector of Las Vegas. As a general rule, he didn't bother his assistant on weekends. However, he asked Katherine to secure him a meeting with the managing partners of Nichols, Gardner and Hack, the accounting firm. He'd given her permission to insinuate that he was in the market for a new accounting team. He wasn't, but they didn't need to know that.

Carver entered the building to the normal low hum of a typical office environment. After checking in with the receptionist, he was led to a conference room. As he moved past the offices and cubicles, the office noise tapered off to silence, occasionally interrupted by excited whispers.

"Mr. Jamieson, I'm Walter Nichols." A tall African-American man extended his hand in greeting. "These gentlemen are Neal Gardner and Carl Hack, the other managing partners."

"Gentlemen." Carver shook the hands of the other two men.

Nichols gestured to the conference table. "Care to sit? Then we can discuss how Nichols, Gardner and Hack can be of service."

Accepting the offer, Carver placed his leather folio on the table and sat in one of the large executive style chairs.

"Mr. Nichols, I'm not certain how your firm can be of service, but I think I can help you."

Confusion cloaked the man's expression as he sat back in his seat. "How's that, Mr. Jamieson? We were given the impression that you were looking for a local firm to handle your accounting needs since you've relocated to Las Vegas."

Flipping open his folio, Carver removed a file folder. "Well... about that. I do have my business manager scoping out potential partnerships, however, I witnessed some behavior from one of your employees that made me wonder exactly what kind of people make up this firm."

"I'm not sure I understand." Nichols regarded his partners who returned equally confused looks.

"You have an employee by the name of Torrence Phillips, correct?"

Holding his hand in front of him in a slow down motion, Nichols interjected. "If this is about the video on the internet, we've already spoken to Torrence about his role. We were very disappointed in some of the things we heard.

While his personal affairs are his business, he didn't comport himself well and he's been made aware it won't be ignored in his bids for advancement. NGH doesn't harbor people of poor character. He has assured us it was an isolated incident that wouldn't be repeated."

"Oh yeah?" Carver flipped open the file folder. "Well, he lied. He sent these to the same woman within the last 72 hours."

Sliding the folder to the partner closest to him, he watched for their reaction. Carl Hack quickly flipped the page with the picture over and reviewed the message printout. Carver could've simply told them the picture accompanied the text, but seeing is believing. For everyone's sake the image was blurred, but it was clear enough to get an understanding of the content of the photo.

"This is outrageous! Why would you show us something of this nature?" Neal Gardner asked as red tinged his neck creeping up his face.

"Mr. Gardner, the question is why a seemingly professional, adult male would think it was perfectly okay to send this to a woman, without her consent? Then to add insult to injury, he sends a disparaging text message along with it."

Foregoing flipping the picture over, Mr. Nichols read the message. Thunderclouds settled over his face. Slamming the folder closed, he stared at his partners in a non-verbal conversation. After a few moments, he pressed an intercom button on the built-in console.

"Margaret? Could you ask Torrence to come to the conference room?"

"Yes, sir." The feminine voice replied.

"Oh and Margaret?"

"Yes, sir?"

"Tell Keith to come up as well."

"Yes, sir." The tone of Margaret's voice said she understood the assignment and the gravity of it.

Carver had no clue who Keith was, but he read the room like he read the players on a football field. Torrence was about lose his job. Unbidden, the catchy tune circulating around the internet floated into his mind. It took actual effort for him not to bob his head to the imagined beat... *You about to lose your job.*

"Mr. Jamieson, I can assure you, Mr. Phillips' behavior isn't the standard here at NGH. Although I'm sure it doesn't come close to alleviating the trauma experienced by the young lady, we are deeply sorry."

As Carver nodded his acceptance of Walter Nichols' words, the door to the conference room opened and Torrence slowly entered. His body language screamed his discomfort. However, when he laid eyes on Carver, his entire being went rigid. For his part, Carver only stared at him, not bothering to hide his intense dislike of the other man.

Watching Carver warily, Torrence walked farther into the room and put his hand on the back of a chair as if to sit down.

"No need to sit, Mr. Phillips. This won't take long." Walter Nichols' deep voice held obvious disdain.

"Oh. Ok." With his eyes flitting around the room nervously, Torrence released the chair.

"Mr. Phillips. Your time with NGH has come to an end. Effective immediately, you are no longer employed with this firm. Keith will be here momentarily. You will have ten minutes to pack up your belongings, then he will escort you out of the building."

"What?! Why? I work hard for this firm. Long hours, weekends during tax season with no complaints." Torrence's words came out shakily. Carver couldn't tell if it was anger, fear or a mixture of both.

"Mr. Phillips, as you are well aware, Nevada is a *work at will* state. We don't have to give you a reason for terminating your employ." Carver admired the calmness with which Mr. Nichols handled the other man.

"I know that, but you gotta tell me something." Torrence's gaze swung to Carver. His eyebrows drew together and his nose flared in a fierce scowl.

"You! This is your fault! I told you I was sorry and it wouldn't happen again. Why couldn't you just let it go? Why did you have to come to my job, man? Her pussy ain't good enough to wreck my career over."

It took Herculean effort for Carver not to jump across the table and beat the scrawny fuck's ass, but he stayed in his seat. Torrence was lashing out hoping Carver would lose control and make him look like the victim. Carver wouldn't allow himself to be played.

Did that mean Torrence would get away with his little dig? No. Carver would simply make certain there weren't any witnesses.

"Torrence! That's enough! It's obvious to us that you aren't a fit for our firm. Your behavior just now makes it even more clear that you lack personal accountability and character. You need to leave. Immediately."

Carver had no idea what kind of relationship the older man had with Torrence, but the way he spoke to him hinted at a disappointment which only came from a mentor. *Sucks for them.* They're both being let down today.

The conference room door opened once more and a stocky man with a Marine high and tight entered. Michael stepped aside to make space for the new occupant.

"Keith, can you escort Torrence to his desk to gather his personal belongings, then retrieve his credentials and escort him from the property?"

"Yes, sir." With a brief nod, Keith held his arm out for Torrence to precede him from the room.

Shooting Carver one final glare, Torrence walked out with the security guard on his heels. Following his exit, the partners once again offered their apologies for any harm that Carver and Alyssa experienced due to Torrence's actions.

Accepting their apology, Carver retrieved his folio, shook hands with them and exited. They remained behind. He was sure they had a great deal to discuss. Today had taken a turn they couldn't have possibly predicted. He applauded their immediate action. Carver considered speaking to Michelle about seriously putting them on the list to handle one of his accounts.

Chapter Twenty-Two

HE'S MY MAN

Alyssa's gaze drifted from the lines of code on her monitor to the window to her left in her home office. As she anticipated, her manager gave no pushback to her switching to a primarily work from home situation. So long as she kept her project pace and attended the meetings, he had no issue with it.

From their conversation, Harrison was aware of Alyssa's reservations regarding staying on at *Secure Pull*. If working from home kept her moving forward on their major projects, he wouldn't throw up road blocks. That was good. While she wouldn't make any sudden decisions, leaving the company all together was still on the table.

With a few clicks of her mouse, she started the simulation to test the code she'd spent a considerable amount of time writing. If it performed well under simulation, she could send it to the test lab to be downloaded into an actual gaming station. She wasn't involved in that aspect of the project. When it reached that stage, she moved on to the next project while she waited on feedback from the test engineers.

Her cellphone dinged with a notification. Saying a quick prayer that it wasn't another alert to Carver trending or a message from Torrence, whom she made absolutely sure was blocked, she pulled it closer and swiped the screen. Seeing her mother's name flooded her with relief.

Although Carver had appeared calmer when he followed her downstairs while she checked on her barbeque grill, it had still taken some time and effort to get him to lower the threat assessment from DEFCON 1. The man was scorched earth when it came to her.

The small, uber-logical, voice inside her said she should be concerned with his intensity, but the other, now louder voice, was cheering him on. As fearful as she was that he'd do something to damage himself in defense of her, Alyssa admitted that it felt good to have someone so fiercely protective of her. Once she got past trying to handle everything herself, she was relieved to have someone she could trust to be on her team. And Carver was one thousand percent Team Alyssa.

> Mama: Hey Baby. I know you're working, but call me when you get a minute.

Swiping the message, Alyssa called her mother. The code simulation would run with or without her watching it. So, she had time to talk to her mama.

"Hey...I didn't expect to hear from you so soon." Her mother answered on the first ring.

"Well, I had some down time. I figured it wouldn't hurt to go on and call. What's up?"

They'd had their normal Sunday evening call the previous day, so Alyssa's curiosity was piqued. It couldn't be an emergency. Her mother would've simply called in that situation.

"Honey...I just got off the phone with your Aunt Teresa..."

"Oh yeah? How's she doing?"

"She's doing fine. She asked about you. I told her I'd just spoken with you yesterday and you were doing well."

"Okay..."

"Are you at home? Your background noise sounds different."

Trust her mother to pick up on the slight difference in noise level from Alyssa's work environment to her home office. The difference in the noise level was negligible to Alyssa since she normally closed her door when she took calls.

"Yes, ma'am. I'm working from home for the foreseeable future. I'll only go into the office if I'm needed for a face-to-face meeting that can't be handled over video conference."

"Oh? You didn't mention it yesterday. What brought on the change? This internet stuff? I thought you said they weren't bothering you at work anymore?"

"They're not, but I don't have good vibes there. You remember I told you how people were buzzing between the cubicles and watching me whenever I walked by. It got on my nerves. Since I don't have to physically be there to do my job, I worked out something with my manager."

"Do you think other people will complain that you're getting special treatment?"

"I don't know, Mama. And, I don't really care. How they advocate for themselves is between them and Harrison."

"You're right about that one. As long as you're good, that's all I care about. Anyway, that's not why I called. When I spoke to your aunt, she mentioned she'd asked Ulysses and Braxton about you, but they both claimed you were ducking them. So, they hadn't talked to you in a while."

"What? I haven't seen those two since Super Bowl Sunday. When their plans for the game fell through, they stopped by because they knew I'd put something together—even if it was just for me and Zee. I've talked to them via text, but I haven't physically seen them in two months."

"Those little rascals! I knew it. I knew you would've mentioned it at least once when we talked if they'd been by. I told Teresa her boys don't show up around you until they're between women or wanting a meal."

"Mama!"

"What? No point in lying to her. She raised 'em. She knows. Anyway, it took her about twenty minutes, but she finally got around to the reason she called."

Before her mother said the words, Alyssa already knew what she would say.

"She was trying to pick me about what was going on with you and that man of yours. Since her boys hadn't been around you, they couldn't give her anything, so she came to me."

"Lord..."

Propping her elbow on her desk, Alyssa placed her folded fingers to her temple resting her head. She'd primarily ignored the family members who started calling and texting out of the blue when Carver made his *F U haters* TikTok.

"Right. I'm sure one or both of those boys will be in touch seeing as I didn't give her anything either. I don't know what made her think I would gossip about my own child, but she tried it."

"Mama, I know it's a stretch, but maybe she was genuinely concerned." Alyssa tried to give her aunt the benefit of the doubt.

"Listen, you know your aunt in a totally different way from the way I know her. She's your elder, your conversations only go so far. I know what she was doing. Let's just leave it at that."

"Yes, ma'am." Alyssa zipped her lips. Her mother's voice held a tone projecting her absolute certainty in her words. Far be it for her to tell her mother that she knew exactly how nosey Aunt Teresa was. Alyssa was simply trying to think positively.

"I'll give them to Wednesday at the latest before they come calling." Her mother continued. "There's no telling what kind of guilt trip she laid on them for not keeping in better touch with their little cousin—as if you aren't a grown woman."

Alyssa listened to her mother's mini-rant with a smirk on her face. Anna Ripley wouldn't allow anyone else to question Alyssa's ability to take care of herself. Ironic, since she, herself, frequently expressed concern about Alyssa living so far away from the rest of the family.

"Mama, it's cool. I'll be on the lookout for them. Though, I doubt they'll do more than shoot me a text or something."

They chatted for a few more minutes until Alyssa's computer notified her that the simulation was complete. Ending the call with her mother, she immersed herself in checking the data, noting areas that would require adjustment.

After grabbing a quick lunch, she dove right back into her work. She hadn't realized the passage of time until her doorbell rang, pulling her from her trance-like focus. Wrinkling her brow, she checked the feed from her doorbell cam.

What do you know? Her mother was right on the money. Ulysses and Braxton stood on her front porch. Checking her watch, Alyssa realized it was just after five p.m. It was time to call it a day anyway. Locking the computer, she walked out of her office.

The moment she swung the front door open, her older cousins started speaking at once.

"Lyssa, what the hell is going on?"

"Lyssa, why you got Mama calling us?"

Holding up her hands to halt the barrage, she cocked an eyebrow looking at them.

"Excuse you. I can't hear, if you're both talking at the same time. Besides, you need to fix your tone. The last time I checked, my father's name was neither Braxton nor Ulysses. You don't get to come at me like this."

Ducking their heads sheepishly, her cousins mumbled something that nebulously sounded like an apology. Nodding, she stepped back to allow them into the house.

"Who wants to go first?" Alyssa asked as she led the duo into the living room and took a seat.

Taking his privilege as the eldest, Ulysses spoke first. "Lyssa, why did you tell us everything was cool the last time we texted?"

Looking bewildered, Alyssa stared at him. "Because...it is..."

"It can't be. If it was, our mama wouldn't be calling us getting on our ass about not looking out for you better." Braxton picked up the conversational thread from his brother.

"Why is what your mother does my fault?"

"Uh-uh. Don't try that Jedi mind trick stuff on us. I see you trying to deflect. This isn't about what she did, it's about you telling us you were good, only for us to get chewed out." Ulysses slid forward in the chair pointing his finger between Braxton and himself.

"Right, you know the only reason we laid back was because you said everything was under control. Now, Mama is in our ass." Braxton added. "So, what's really going on? Are things worse than you told us? Do we need to kick that little accountant's ass? And what about Jamieson? Is he out here trying to play you?"

"Look...Have things been a little rough the past month? Yes. Am I ok? Also, yes. You don't need to do anything to Torrence, I blocked him after that night." She absolutely would *not* **tell** them about the dick pic.

"No, Carver isn't playing me. That was someone petty trying to make it look like he was doing something he wasn't. The woman in the pictures was the real estate agent who helped him find his house.

Nothing has happened that I haven't been able to handle. Which is why, when you asked, I said everything was okay. Because it is. Besides, I can't come running to you every time someone hurts my feelings. Y'all are acting like Ny and Kee right now."

At the mention of Alyssa's older brothers, Nyland and Keegan, the two exchanged looks. Because of her brothers' overprotective ways, Alyssa hadn't dated at all in high school. She went to prom with a group of girlfriends.

College was only moderately different. She dated some, but nothing seemed to really take off. Which is how she found herself occasionally being the third wheel with Carver and Mary Beth.

Shaking off memories of those awkward times, Alyssa assessed her cousins. Ulysses and Braxton were twins. Ulysses was the eldest by three and a half minutes, which he lorded over his brother despite their now forty years on earth. Sometimes, it was still difficult to tell the two apart.

"Cuz..." Braxton started.

"Uh-uh. Don't *cuz* me. Every time you call me cuz like that, you try to talk me into something you know I'm not gonna be cool with. No, thank you."

"It's nothing bad."

Folding her arms across her chest, Alyssa regarded him suspiciously. Of the two, Braxton was the mischievous one. Whenever Zee was around, he loved to stir her up by stating the opposing view of whatever topic was under discussion.

"You don't want us in your business. You're grown. We know that. We have our own lives as well. But if stuff is getting back to the old folks, without social media, we need to see that everything is on the up and up with our own eyes."

Quirking an eyebrow, she stared at them alternately. "What's that supposed to mean?"

"We wanna meet him." Ulysses answered. "Sooner. Rather than later."

"I'm not fifteen." Alyssa's chin jutted out stubbornly, not at all projecting the *all grown up* image she was going for.

"We're aware." They said simultaneously.

She couldn't believe this. After basically leaving her to her own devices with intermittent check-ins, her cousins now wanted to assert their roles as pseudo-guardians. Following a few tense moments of silence Alyssa finally caved. Agreeing was the only way she would get them out of her hair.

Besides, if she didn't agree, she'd hear from her own mother once they told Aunt Teresa that Alyssa must be hiding something if she didn't want them to meet her man. That wasn't it at all.

Despite the number of years she and Carver had known each other, they'd essentially only been together as a couple for a month. Their relationship had been hit with a lot in such a short amount of time, so it seemed longer, but it was still very new.

"Fine. I'll talk to Carver and we'll coordinate our schedules to have dinner or something. How does that sound?"

"Like you're trying to put us off." Ulysses sat back in the chair crossing his legs ankle on knee. "You aren't slick, Lyssa."

"I'm not putting you off." Alyssa's objection was met with expressions of disbelief. "Ok. Fine. Maybe I was, but my relationship with Carver is new. I don't recall anyone asking either of you to introduce your women to the family when you hadn't been together at least six months."

Braxton chuffed. "U would have to keep a woman longer than six months for that to apply."

"Who's talking? What's your average, B? Eight weeks?"

"Nobody asked you that U."

"You're the one volunteering my history. I'm just saying, you don't have the best track record yourself."

Stopping their tiff before it devolved into more of a tit for tat comparison, Alyssa interjected.

"Neither of you are in any position to make demands on me about my relationship is all I'm saying."

Putting his hands out in front of him in a conciliatory manner, Braxton tried again. "If everything's good. You don't have anything to worry about. We know you're gonna do whatever you want, regardless of what we say. We just want to look the man in the eye and see for ourselves."

As Alyssa weighed her options, which she recognized were limited, the sound of the front door opening drew her attention. Two sets of footsteps sounded against the hardwood floor in her foyer before Carver and Blake came into view. The bodyguard hung back in the doorway while Carver walked farther into the space.

Carver's eyes swept around the room before landing on Alyssa's. Ulysses was seated in the chair Carver favored, while Braxton sat on the end of the sofa closest to his brother. Popping up from the opposite end of the sofa, Alyssa walked over to Carver.

Fully aware of how it looked, she didn't spare her cousins a glance. Carver hadn't said a word, but the gaze he leveled on her called her to him. Tugging her into his left side, he placed a peck on her cheek.

"I didn't know we were having company tonight." He rumbled in her ear.

"Neither did I. They just dropped in a little while ago." Alyssa replied softly.

The clearing of throats burst their little cocoon causing them to turn their attention to Alyssa's cousins. Biting the bullet, she made the introductions.

"Carver, these are my cousins, Braxton and Ulysses. Guys this is Carver Jamieson."

Carver tensed slightly beside her, but she caught it. She hadn't put a label on who he was to her, but she didn't know what to use. They were too old for boyfriend-girlfriend and 'my man' sounded like something out of the nineties. Still. It was all she had at the moment.

"Carver and I are together. He's my man."

When Carver's posture shifted and his fingers flexed against her hip, Alyssa knew she'd made the right call—despite how corny it sounded to her ears. Somehow, when he called her his woman, it sounded sexy. But, when she said he was her man, out loud, she sounded like a little girl playing dress up.

Releasing his hold on her, Carver stepped forward to shake their hands. "Gentlemen, to what do we owe the honor of your visit?"

Carver asked the question as if Braxton and Ulysses weren't in her home being nosey. He also phrased his question grouping he and Alyssa together as a unit. Something which didn't go unnoticed by her cousins.

She was also certain they'd taken note of him entering without ringing the bell—which meant he had a key. The events leading to her giving Carver that key seemed eons ago, but it didn't look great considering how she'd told her cousins she and Carver were too new for introductions. Too new to be introduced to family, but apparently established enough for him to enter her home at will. *Shit*. They were definitely gonna tell Aunt Teresa that part.

Chapter Twenty-Three

I AIN'T STUPID

The last thing Carver expected after spending part of his morning making sure Torrence felt a portion of his wrath, then the rest of his day at the office, was to come home to unexpected guests.

"What do we have here?"

Blakes's question drew Carver's attention from his phone to see what his bodyguard was talking about. Following the direction of his gaze, Carver noticed the big black Chevy Silverado with chrome trim. Alyssa hadn't mentioned having guests over. Besides, it was a Monday. The start of the week wasn't usually when company dropped by.

"I have no idea. Why don't we go inside and see what's going on?"

Following the upgrades Jasper had implemented, he was certain the truck's owner had to be someone Alyssa knew and trusted. It didn't necessarily mean she invited them though. Seeing the vehicle and having no clue who was inside made him regret not gaining access to the security feed or at least the doorbell cam. He'd have to remedy that—even if he didn't plan for her to live there much longer.

Now that he knew the *'guests'* where Alyssa's cousins Ulysses and Braxton Ripley, Carver felt only marginally better about the situation. However, hearing her refer to him as her man made his heart soar. It didn't matter what he said they were and what he wanted them to be, up until then, she hadn't publicly claimed him the way he'd claimed her.

He hadn't realized what a difference it made until she said the words. Automatically, he stood straighter and felt taller. Love was a helluva drug. He was intoxicated with it and emboldened by it.

"Gentlemen, to what do we owe the honor of your visit?"

Carver asked, while already having a pretty good idea what was going on. Hell, he was surprised it had taken so long for them to make an appearance. Without a doubt, he knew if her brothers were closer, they would've already shown up at her house or the hotel looking for him to explain his intentions toward their little sister. He didn't fault them. He'd do the same for his own sister, if he had one.

"We would say we were in the neighborhood,"

"But we weren't."

One twin started the sentence and the other finished it. Although they weren't dressed the same, they were identical, so Carver had to remind himself who was who when they spoke—despite it being less than five minutes since Alyssa made the introductions.

"We came to check on Alyssa." Ulysses finished, crossing his arms across his chest.

At that revelation, Carver turned his gaze to Alyssa. His grip on her waist tightened. Flexing his fingers into her side, he drew her eyes to his.

"Bit, is everything okay? Has something happened since I left this morning?"

Carver was genuinely confused. He thought they'd moved past her keeping things to herself and trying to handle them on her own.

"Everything's fine. Just like I told these two when they texted, but apparently, they had to come look in my face to be sure."

"What exactly were we supposed to do when our mother calls us concerned because she's seen a video of some guy talking shit to you, then another of this guy here hugged up with another woman after he's been all over social media saying you two are together? You saying you're okay didn't match the information we had. For all we knew, you were in over your head and too stubborn to admit it."

While Carver understood the man's position, he didn't appreciate

Braxton's tone or the implication that he wasn't taking care of Bit like he should.

"Now, hold on." He leveled a stare at Alyssa's cousins. "You have a right to be concerned, but you don't get to talk to her like she's a child."

"Carver..."

Undeterred by the warning note in Alyssa's voice, Carver shook his head; his jaw hardened in determination.

"No, Bit. I know they're your family and they care about you, but you're a grown woman. They need to remember that when they speak to you."

"Carver, they know I'm an adult."

Carver could see he wouldn't really get to the bottom of their visit with Alysa in the room running interference. He knew they were there to take stock of him. The thought, of them possibly being there to try to convince her he wasn't worth the trouble, flit across his mind. But he dismissed it.

"Bit, baby, can you give us a minute?" Cupping her face, his gaze probed hers. "I think it might benefit me and your cousins if we talked man-to-men."

"What?" Tilting her head back, she began shaking it in the negative. "If you're talking about me, I should be here."

Lowering his voice, he whispered in her ear. "Please, baby. Let me handle this. Your cousins and I need to talk. I promise to remain civil. They're you're family. I don't want bad blood between us."

Raising her eyebrows skeptically, Alyssa assessed him for a few moments before acquiescing. Issuing pointed looks to him, then to her cousins, she stepped out of the room. Blake stepped out into the foyer, but he remained in Carver's line of sight. Carver didn't expect a physical confrontation with the two men, but Blake took his duties seriously.

Carver was certain Alyssa wouldn't venture too far out of earshot. His assertion was confirmed by the sound of cabinet doors opening and closing moments later. Once he was certain she wouldn't storm back into the room, Carver returned his attention to Ulysses and Braxton

"Listen, man." Ulysses put his hands out. One landed on his brother's shoulder while the other hung in the air between he and Carver. "It seems like we're getting off on the wrong foot. We all care about Alyssa.

Our concern may come off as overbearing, but we have the same goal—
make sure she's safe and protected."

Carver bristled at Ulysses attempted olive branch. It still stunk of
them saying he wasn't protecting her, so they had to step up.

"She is safe. And protected. By me. If you two were so concerned,
why are you just now showing up?" This is why he didn't want Alyssa in
the room. He didn't want to censor his questions or responses and he
expected they didn't either.

"I know this dude isn't—"

"B! Stop it. We didn't come here for this."

"Why *did* you come?" Carver latched on to Ulysses' statement.

"Like my brother said earlier, our mom called. She was concerned
about the things she saw online. All we could say was Alyssa told us she
was okay. After what our mom said on the phone, we decided it would
be best to come over and see for ourselves."

"Uh-huh." Carver didn't believe for a second that was all there was
to it. "What else?"

"Excuse me?" Ulysses frowned in apparent confusion. Yet instinct
told Carver he wasn't close to being confused.

"What's your other reason? My gut says there's more to your lil' pop
up visit than a wellness check."

"He's smarter than he looks."

"B... Stop trying to goad him."

Ulysses needn't have worried. Carver wasn't even tempted to do
anything other than smirk at the other man. He wouldn't stress his Bit
out by putting hands on the only family she had in the state. Instead of
taking Braxton's bait, he folded his arms and waited.

After the day he'd had at the team offices, locked in intense debate
about potential picks for the upcoming draft, the last thing he wanted
to do was come home and do anything other than be with his woman.
Yet here he was. Standing in Alyssa's living room, waiting for the other
shoe to drop surrounding their unexpected visitors.

"We wanted to meet you."

"Why?"

"To look you in your face and make sure you were being straight up with Lyssa. That you weren't out here playing in her face or stringing her along."

Carver gritted his teeth. It wasn't hard to figure out where they got the idea that he wasn't being faithful to Alyssa. The fucking *internet*. It was the gift that kept giving even when you specifically told that bitch to stop.

Ulysses' words hit their mark. One of the last things Carver wanted was for anyone in Alyssa's life to believe the lies they saw online. Her belief in him was most important, but he didn't want her embarrassed even by a mistaken perception of his actions.

That thought led him to push his resentment to the side. Gesturing to the sofa, he indicated they should sit once more. Making eye contact with both men, he tried again to put himself in their shoes. Adult or not, they saw Alyssa as someone they were supposed to look out for. It was something Carver could respect.

"I'm not stringin' Alyssa along. Nor am I playin' her." Sitting back on the couch, Carver made a decision about fully opening up to the brothers. "I've known Alyssa for more than fifteen years. We met in college. I've had feelings for her the majority of those years.

In college, things were...complicated. So, we were friendly, but never went beyond that. We ran into each other after college when we were both on business trips and I thought we had a connection. Only it wasn't meant to be at that time.

When I happened to see her again after I moved to Las Vegas, I was determined not to let her slip away again. Somehow, I managed to convince her to give us a real chance."

Piercing them with a granite stare, he continued. "Do you really think, after spendin' the majority of my adult life wantin' to be with her, that I'd jeopardize it? I may not be the smartest man, but I ain't stupid."

"When you put it like that, no. But as a man, I've seen guys do some dumb shit even after they've spent time and a grip of money trying to get a woman. So, I had to ask."

Ulysses sat back in the chair, regarding Carver with an expression he couldn't define. A quick glance at Braxton confirmed the other man wore a similar expression. Carver briefly wondered if they were doing the twin thing, which was why they were both so quiet.

"So, you two wanted a chance to feel me out. I can respect that. I have another question for you two though."

The two men locked eyes with one another briefly before looking at Carver, waiting for him to continue. He was one hundred percent certain they were doing the twin thing that time, but he didn't call them out.

"Is a phone call from your mother really the only reason you two showed up today, or was it just your excuse?"

"You've never met our mother." Braxton deadpanned.

"True, but *mommy told me to*, seems like a flimsy excuse for two grown men."

Again, they locked eyes with one another before Carver called them out. "Stop it with the twin shit. I've been honest with you. So, spill it."

Finally, Braxton sat forward, bracing his elbows on his knees with his hands clasped together. "You said you met Alyssa in college, do you ever recall her dating during that time?"

Carver worked to keep his expression neutral. He remembered moments that he wasn't very proud of. There were guys interested in Alyssa, but not many were brave enough to approach her. The ones with enough courage to take the leap, didn't last very long.

At the time, he blamed his relief at hearing the potential relationships had petered out on concern for her being with guys he didn't think were good enough for her. She never knew about his teammates who asked him about her. There was no way he'd let her go out with any of those man whores.

Instead of enlightening her cousins, he gave a neutral response. "I recall her going out with a few guys. Never anything serious though."

"Well, she didn't go out at all in high school. Like not once."

"It was mainly because of her brothers threatening anyone who looked at her too long, but we might've helped a little."

"A little?" Carver quirked an eyebrow at Braxton.

"Ok... A lot. We came on kind of strong then. It might've continued some into college with her brothers randomly popping up during her freshman and sophomore years."

Carver met Alyssa's brothers, Nylan and Keegan, a couple of times in college. He didn't meet Alyssa until first semester of their junior year though. After he and Mary Beth started dating.

"Her parents were concerned about her being on campus by herself at such a young age."

"I can understand. She was sixteen her freshman year right?" Carver recalled being impressed that she was in their class, but two years younger than them.

"Well...I'll admit, we all smothered her so bad, that when she graduated, she didn't stay around for very long before she took a job out of state. B and I moved here before she did. One of the conditions we had to agree to, before she accepted the job with *Secure Pull*, was to respect that she's an adult and give her space.

We try to take her at her word. If we check in and she says she's fine, we let it go. The last thing we want is to push her away. Besides, we have lives of our own. We can't spend our days getting in Lyssa's business."

Whether consciously or by design, Ulysses picked up where his brother stopped.

"We should've gone with our first mind when we saw the video with you jacking up the accountant, but we let it go when she said she was fine. Every time we sent a text, her reply was the same. *'I'm okay.'* When Mama called, we had the ammunition we needed."

"So... because of your perception that she has very little experience with men and relationships, you don't trust her judgment? Is that what I'm hearing?" Carver stared at them, offended on Bit's behalf.

"I wouldn't say that." Ulysses shifted in the chair uncomfortably.

"You might have not said it, but the implication is clear." Carver gritted his teeth in irritation. "You don't give Alyssa nearly enough credit. I'm starting to think despite you knowing her almost two full decades before I met her, I still know her better than you."

"I doubt it." Braxton huffed.

"No...I'm pretty certain. You two, and possibly her brothers, think her intellect only extends to book knowledge which helps her be successful in her career. You couldn't be further from reality. Bit reads people exceptionally well. Even if it looks like she's not paying attention. She is. It's true that she was naive in college, but she's not in college anymore. It took a hard lesson for her to get it, but we all know one thing about her—she only needs to get the lesson once for it to stick."

Nodding in agreement with the last part of his statement, the brothers seemed to relax slightly, but there was still an edge to their posture. Stretching one arm along the back of the couch, Carver turned his hand palm up.

"Now... ask me whatever you need to ease your mind. Giving up Alyssa isn't an option for me, so we need to find a way to at least make nice. I'd say we have roughly five minutes before she's had enough of being exiled and comes barging back in here."

His last remark, garnered a couple of chuckles. However, their response to his humor didn't stop them from taking him up on his offer. Their questions were in line with what he'd expect and Carver was positive they would report the entire conversation to her brothers. He doubted very seriously they'd relay the same level of detail to their mother though.

It didn't take long for them to exhaust their questions. By the time Alyssa came back into the room, they'd moved on to trying to pump him for information about the Ravagers preparation for the upcoming Draft. Carver simply allowed them to speculate without giving anything away.

Although he did share their opinion that they should spend their first picks on a quarterback, left tackle and guard. In fact, he'd spent the afternoon arguing his case with the rest of the coaching staff. But that was work stuff. He was home with his woman. Work was the last thing he wanted to discuss.

Thankfully, Alyssa broke up their information seeking by telling them she'd put something together for dinner. She didn't mince words when she informed them, the next time they showed up uninvited, she would revoke their gate access. Internally cheering her feistiness, Carver followed behind the group.

Chapter Twenty-Four

SAY SORRY REAL PRETTY

Alyssa puttered around in the kitchen partially fuming at being asked to leave the room, and relieved at not having to referee between Carver and her overzealous cousins. She honestly didn't know which one she was more concerned about popping off at the mouth—Carver or Braxton. It was toss-up.

When she didn't hear elevated voices, some of the tension in her shoulders released. Only hearing indistinct sounds of conversation was a win in her eyes. She'd been absently opening and closing cabinet doors trying to determine if she wanted to put in any effort to making a meal. Since they showed up without warning, Ulysses and Braxton shouldn't expect anything.

However, her mother's lessons in southern hospitality were ingrained. It was dinner time. Considering a meal for only herself and Carver would be rude. The two of them had existed on leftovers and take out through the weekend; Alyssa wasn't interested in either at the moment. So, it appeared she would be cooking dinner.

She tried not to think about how easily they'd fallen into a routine and how obvious it was to her cousins that she and Carver were far more serious than she wanted them to believe taking into account the length of time they'd actually been together as a couple.

The normal, new relationship giddiness was still there, but their level of comfort and the way they communicated was more like two people who'd been together for years instead of weeks. It's possible, they'd skipped a stage because of their existing foundation.

As Alyssa went through the motions of pulling out ingredients to make a quick Jambalaya in her trusty quick-cooking pressure cooker, her mind drifted to a day in she and Carver's past. It was in the first semester of their junior year, and one of the rare times they had a one-on-one discussion without Mary Beth.

October 31, 2003

Alyssa stood before the whiteboard with a marker in one hand and an eraser in the other. Her brow furrowed in concentration as she stared at the collection of ones and zeros scrawled on the board's surface. Two taps to the door frame drew her attention. She could've sworn she closed the glass door to mute any noise from the other students.

When she turned to see who knocked, she discovered Carver Jamieson leaning casually in the open doorway. It was odd considering it wasn't simply a Friday night, it was a big party night due to it being Halloween. Also, she was in a study room at the library. It was the last place she'd expect to bump into the school's starting quarterback who also happened to be her best friend's sort of new boyfriend.

"Um...Hey Carver."

"Hey, Alyssa. What are you up to?" Carver's normally fierce looking features weren't as intimidating for some reason. His eyes left her face to focus on her markings on the whiteboard.

"Oh. Nothing much. Just working on an extra credit assignment for my microprocessing class."

Alyssa was well aware of how boring it sounded that she was in the library doing extra credit work instead of home getting ready to have a wild night of partying. It was what most normal college students were doing. Heck, even some of the professors let class out early for the occasion.

The thing was, Alyssa wasn't a normal college student. She'd come to terms with being an unapologetic nerd. Her interest in learning and doing things like extra credit had long since ceased to be a source of embarrassment. The flush she felt under her skin had more to do with her awkwardness at being one-on-one with Carver in the tiny study room. It didn't help matters when he stepped fully inside and closed the door.

"What's a microprocessing class and why do you have to do extra credit?" Dropping his backpack onto the table, he walked around it to stand before the board.

Since her textbook was laying on the tabletop, she slid it closer to him. Her eyes skated back to the whiteboard.

"Microprocessing is essentially the study of the circuit board level of computers and how different components are used to process information."

She honestly thought he'd tap out after her brief explanation. Usually, people wore glazed over expressions immediately following the words 'circuit board'. Instead, Carver propped his hip against the table while flipping through the pages of the book before putting it down and looking at her.

"Ok. Computer stuff. Makes sense. You're a Computer Engineering major right?"

"Yes." Grabbing her book, she put it back next to her notebook.

"Mary Beth says you're super smart. Why are you in the library doing extra credit? It's Friday night. I'd think you'd be home getting all dolled up for a night out."

"Because I want to."

Alyssa knew her response was stiff, but she couldn't help it. Having him point out how lame her current activities were, made her very self-conscious. Which also made her a little snippy.

"You do realize you're in the same library I'm in right? Even if you aren't here for the same reason, you aren't home doing whatever guys do to get ready to go out."

"Touché." Carver winked and pointed at her. "Since we have an off week, and I have a few papers due while I'll be out of town for our next game, I thought I'd go on and knock them out."

Before she could stop herself, Alyssa blurted out, "wow...an athlete who's actually serious about his classwork."

Slapping a hand over her mouth, she stared at him with wide eyes. "I'm so sorry! That was rude. I don't know why I said it."

Brightening the room and easing her discomfort with a broad grin, he chuckled. "Don't worry about it. There's an unfortunate truth to it. Many athletes aren't encouraged to take their coursework seriously. That's not how I was brought up."

Silence settled between them. Alyssa had no idea why he was hanging around, but she kept quiet in hopes of not putting her foot in her mouth again. Mary Beth really liked Carver. Alyssa didn't want her friend to feel like she couldn't bring her boyfriend around because her roommate might do or say something offensive.

Standing, Carver moved to the other side of the small table where he'd dropped his backpack. He continued speaking as if they hadn't had the moments of silent tension.

"Most of the athletes live in the same apartment complex. I knew I wouldn't get a thing done if I stayed at my place. Not with my roommate and most of my neighbors gearing up to party like it's nineteen-ninety-nine. So, I came here."

"Oh..." Biting her lower lip, Alyssa simply stood there. She had no idea what she was supposed to do now. Carver had been friendly the previous times they'd interacted, but she couldn't say they were friends.

"So, let me rephrase my question. Why do you want to do extra credit?" His expression held no indication that he was humoring her, so Alyssa relaxed a little.

Turning back to the whiteboard, she studied the ones, zeros and lines she had drawn on the surface. "Professor Thigpen puts this series of binary characters on the board once a semester. To date, no one has ever solved it."

"Wow. Is it that hard?" Out of her periphery, she saw Carver take a seat in one of the four available chairs.

"Converting the numbers from binary to hex isn't that bad, but it's also a riddle. Once you solve the riddle, you have to put your answer in binary code. For me, the hardest part is the riddle."

Holding up his hands, Carver made the universal time-out motion. "You lost me at binary. Take pity on a poor history major."

Smiling at his exaggerated southern drawl, Alyssa turned to look at him. "Seriously? You really want to know?"

Spilling sunshine into the room with his smile, Carver propped his chin on one hand. "Sure. I enjoy learning new things."

So...that's how Alyssa found herself spending her Halloween Friday night explaining, binary and hexadecimal numbers and why it was important for computer engineers to have a good grasp of both.

Present

Three sharp beeps pulled Alyssa back to the here and now. Turning the knob to release the pressure on the cooker, she moved to the stove to remove the cornbread from the oven. The spicy aroma of the food prompted her stomach to grumble. It was a quick and easy meal, but it always hit the spot.

Slicing a few pats of butter on top of the cornbread, she moved on to putting the salad and bowls on the table as it melted. Once that was done, she drizzled honey on the bread and placed it on a trivet in the center of the table.

Her mother's teachings only extended so far; so, she didn't fix anyone's plates. Instead, she poked her head into the foyer to ask Blake if he'd like something to eat. As usual, he declined dinner, but accepted her offer of a to-go box which she fixed and placed on the small table in the foyer.

Carver and her cousins had been in her living room talking about heaven knows what the entire time she'd been in the kitchen. Enough was enough. Striding across the hardwood floors, she stopped in the doorway. She arrived just in time to hear her cousins pitching their recommendations for how the Ravagers should use their picks in the upcoming NFL draft.

Braxton was going on about the quarterback out of Texas who she knew the Ravagers didn't stand a chance in hell of getting. Their position in the selection order was too far down. The guy was exceptional. There was no way he wasn't going in the top three.

"Braxton, that's enough of you trying to pitch your dream team. Dinner is ready."

As the three men stood to follow her from the room, her eyes raked over Carver's face and body. Seeing his state of relative relaxation, she turned to leave the room.

"By the way, if you two show up uninvited on my doorstep again, I'm changing the codes for the gate so that you can't get in without calling me."

"What?"

"Come on, Lyssa. Don't be like that."

Ulysses and Braxton tripped over one another objecting to her declaration. Smacking the back of Ulysses' hand when he went to lift the top off the pressure cooker, she shot him a glare.

"Wash your hands."

As she chastised her cousin, she noticed Carver strolling into the kitchen drying his hands on a paper towel. Ignoring the smirk on his face, she passed him a plate. While Braxton and Ulysses went to wash up, she and Carver scooped portions of Jambalaya onto their plates before moving to the kitchen table to perform the same routine with the salad.

Alyssa was cutting the cornbread into squares when her cousins re-entered the room. Since they were no longer in over-protective mode, their banter had returned to normal. They teased one another about their portion sizes and jokingly moaned about there no longer being leftovers with Carver around.

She didn't contradict them, because it was true. Before Carver, they would've taken his and Blake's portions home with them. Although they seemed attached at the hip, the two didn't live together. So, they were somewhat serious when they compared who got more of what. Unfortunately, they reverted to five-year-olds during those times.

Despite her cousins' attempt to ambush her, they had a pleasant meal. The two didn't waste any time leaving after eating though. Shaking hands with Carver and offering their final player recommenda-tions, they left.

It wasn't long afterwards when Alyssa heard the front door open and close again. She assumed it was Blake leaving for the day. Just as Alyssa placed the last dish in the dishwasher and closed the door, she felt Carver's hands on her hips. Standing fully, put her back flush to his front.

Wrapping his arms around her waist, he leaned down to speak directly into her ear.

"Do you want to tell me where Samira, Kai and Remi are?"

Alyssa stiffened in his embrace. Somehow, since he hadn't mentioned it before then, she thought he was going to overlook the absence of her security detail.

"Um...monitoring remotely?"

Turning her around, Carver pierced her with a disapproving scowl. "Why weren't at least one of them here when I arrived?"

Feeling and probably looking like a guilty child. Alyssa peered up at him. "Because...I knew I wasn't going anywhere today. Besides, with all the security upgrades they've done around here and at the gate, I thought having them sit around the house with me was overkill."

"Baby, you can think whatever you want, but you don't send your protection away without talking to me about it. What if it had been someone other than your cousins who managed to get past the gate today? Or better yet, someone managed to convince those two to let them in when they entered.

Do Ulysses and Braxton know all of your neighbors? Would they be able to tell whether someone was trying to use them to gain access to you? Hell, do they even know there were supposed to be people here assuring your safety?"

Alyssa's back went up immediately when he mentioned talking to him first before dismissing her detail, but her anger dissipated almost as quickly when she considered the remainder of his statement. So, instead of arguing her point, she remained silent.

She really didn't have an angle which couldn't immediately be shot down. Also, despite the anger in his voice, she knew concern for her was the root of his position. God she loved him, but she hated feeling like she was living under a microscope. Her internal thought stopped her cold and she went rigid again in his embrace for an entirely different reason.

While she'd only admitted it to herself just now, it was true. She loved Carver Wyatt Jamieson more than she thought possible for her to love anyone romantically. It scared the shit out of her. *What if she messed it up? What if he got tired of her being contrary and called it quits?*

Misreading the reason for her stiffness, Carver shook his head. Green eyes blazed as he launched into the reasons she shouldn't go back to resisting the extra safety measures. Placing her hands on his chest, she began rubbing in small circles. After a few moments of her quiet soothing, he stopped talking and simply stared at her.

"I'm sorry. I won't do it again."

Her voice was soft and as soothing as the caresses she placed on his pectoral muscles. Raising an eyebrow, he regarded her skeptically. His lack of certainty that she meant what she said was something she earned. Unlearning the habit she had of pushing back, when it wasn't smart, was a process. However, she was willing to try. For him.

"I'm not just saying what you want to hear. I wasn't thinking it all the way through when I told Samira and the guys not to come today. I'll get with them tomorrow and discuss how we need to adjust with me working from home. I should've done it when I made the arrangements, but I'll take care of it."

At his continued doubtful expression, she knew she'd have to do more. Sliding her hands up his chest, she clasped them behind his neck, tugging him down. Lifting onto the balls of her feet, she kissed him.

"I will. I promise." She pledged between kisses.

Eventually, his lips lost their severe slant and he opened his mouth over hers. Accepting his invitation, she opened as well, allowing their tongues to tangle together. His hands traveled from the small of her back to his second favorite place—her ass.

Moaning under his caress, she wasn't prepared for the sting of pain to one butt cheek. The pain was immediately followed by the pleasurable zing to her core. Jerking back from his lips, a gasp tore from her throat. Her gaze flew to his face. His smirk greeted her.

"Did you really think you could say sorry real pretty and I'd fold?"

Well…yeah. She did. Alyssa was smart enough not to say so out loud though.

"Na-uh. It ain't that easy. Get your ass upstairs. I'll be there in a minute. Don't take off one stitch. That's my job."

Desire settled into her center preventing her from delivering a snappy comeback. The set of Carver's jaw told her he was very much serious with his directive. He wasn't angry, but he was definitely giving off the vibe that his brand of punishment was in her near future.

Alyssa had zero shame with how quickly she made it to her bedroom. Torn between going to the bathroom to freshen up or turning down the sheets, she ended up standing beside the bed doing nothing. Her imagination ran away with her contemplating exactly what Carver had planned.

The jingling sound of Carver's belt buckle pulled her from her trance. She turned just in time to see him stepping out of his slacks and stripping off his socks. Tossing his clothing off haphazardly, he advanced on her. Holding her captive with his gaze, he didn't stop until he stood mere inches in front of her.

Grasping her shoulders, he pointed her toward the mirror situated above her dresser. She watched as her loose-fitting blouse was removed and her bra was quickly dispensed with. Carver rid her of her tights and panties simultaneously. Soon, she stood staring at her naked reflection with him partially hidden behind her.

"We need to have a lil' talk." The gruffness of his voice sent a shiver down her spine.

Alyssa didn't question how a conversation required them to see their reflection in the mirror. Her arousal was already at an eight. It wouldn't take much to get her to a ten and push her over the edge. Considering her response to his commanding ways, one might think she pushed him purposely to get this result.

She didn't, but she wouldn't run from the consequences. While she was certain he'd torture her in some way. He'd also deliver mind blowing pleasure.

His hands roamed her body from her thighs up to her breast, where he stopped, cupping the globes in both hands. Vaguely, she wondered when their talk would start, but she didn't utter a word.

Finally, he spoke again. "Do you see that gorgeous woman there? The one with the body that drives me crazy. The one with the brain that makes me wanna put at least six babies in her womb because I find her intelligence just as sexy as I do her body."

Alyssa wanted to shut her eyes against the intensity of his stare, but she held on. The raw emotion in his gaze set her heartbeat to racing. It took every ounce of focus she possessed to keep her eyelids open.

"There is nothing I won't do to keep that woman safe. There is no bridge too far to assure she's wrapped in protection at all times. That's my job and I take it very seriously."

Pinching her nipples, he gave them a twist before abandoning one breast to seek out her pearl with the blunt tips of his fingers. That's when Alyssa lost her battle and closed her eyes. His digits slipped into her channel giving her a preview of what was to come.

His words penetrated her brain, but also her heart. Another, harder, pinch to her nipple made her cry out. Slickness flooded her channel coating his fingers.

"Open your eyes and look at me."

Trying with everything in her to comply with Carver's demand, Alyssa slumped against his chest ready to beg him for the release hovering around the edges of her desire.

"This shit ends today, Bit."

"Mhmm." Her acknowledgement of his words sounded more like a moan than agreement.

"I'm not fucking around, Baby."

"Mmm...I know. I understand."

"Do you?" The growling quality of his words went straight to her core.

"I do. I promise..."

"You promise what?"

"I'll be good."

"What else, Baby?"

Watching him through her lashes, she tried to stay attuned to his questions. The motion of his fingers in her sheath stopped, dragging a pleading moan from her throat.

"What else are you going to do, Baby? Talk to me."

Panting with frustration at being brought so close to the edge of her orgasm without achieving the goal, Alyssa searched her brain for what she knew Carver needed to hear. When she finally landed on the words, she could've cried from relief.

Meeting his gaze in the mirror, she gave him the words. "I won't try to send them away again. I'll trust you to keep me safe."

Her validation had a galvanizing effect on Carver. He doubled his efforts delving between her folds to stimulate her clit sending her flying into her orgasm. As her body trembled from the effects, he held her upright.

When she was finally able to control her limbs again, he stepped back, smacking her on the ass. "Get on the bed, Baby. I'm not done with you."

Chapter Twenty-Five

YOU KNOW THAT'S NOT NORMAL, RIGHT?

It was moving day and Carver still hadn't broached the subject of their living arrangements with Alyssa. That was okay though, because he had a plan. One he'd already put into motion. His belongings from his place in New York and some of his things from San Diego were enroute and most of the furniture had been delivered. She'd previously offered to help him get settled. All he had to do was remind her of the final move date and she rearranged her work schedule to make herself available.

After their talk Monday night, he stayed around on Tuesday morning until her team showed up. It wasn't a matter of him not trusting Alyssa to keep her word, Carver wanted to make certain the team wasn't reporting anything back to Jasper which would cause him to pull the contract. Jasper may be his friend, but he was serious about not wasting resources on people who resisted protection.

Once everything was squared away on that front, he mentioned them coming by the new house to check out all the bells and whistles in the control room. All done under the guise of them working alongside Michael and Blake when Alyssa was there. Since, she'd agreed to be there to direct traffic or whatever he needed during the move, she now stood in the foyer near the open front door staring at the newly transformed area.

Walking up behind her, Carver tugged her into a loose hug. "Want to take a quick tour before the movers get here with the rest of the stuff?"

"We can do that. Things look a lot different with the staging furniture and decorations removed."

"Yeah, the decorator had a few ideas to make it look less like a museum and more like a place someone would live. I think she did alright."

Nodding as she looked around, Alyssa's eyes didn't settle in any one place. "She did a much better job than I could've. Decorating isn't my thing. Heck, Zaria is the reason I have pictures on my walls. The first time she came over, she said my house didn't feel lived in with the bare walls.

After that, she basically pulled up one weekend, pushed me into her car and took me all over the city finding pictures and other knick knacks. Honestly, when we were done, I admitted she was right. My house looked like I hadn't finished moving in before the changes. With the artwork and framed photos, it became a home."

Taking her hand, Carver walked Alyssa around the lower level. Briefly, they stopped at the home gym and attached sauna as they made their way to the back. Heading outside, they stopped at the guesthouse located on the other side of the pool. From there, they went to the office space security would use which was next to his office and a small conference room.

Other than to comment on the number of monitors mounted on the wall of the control room, Alyssa said nothing other than a quick word of acknowledgement to Kai. He was parked in front of the monitor array cycling through camera views as they entered.

When they finally made it to the second floor, Alyssa slowed to a stop outside of a set of glass double doors. They'd just cleared the top of the spiral staircase. The wrought iron railing at their back overlooked the foyer on the first floor. Alyssa's gaze wasn't focused on the view. It was on the room beyond the large glass doors. Carver didn't volunteer any information, he simply waited.

"Carver...What's this?"

"What does it look like?" Her lips pursed at him answering her question with a question, but she didn't call him on it.

"An office, but not like the other one at the back of the house." Her voice trailed off and Carver waited for her to make the connection.

The room was nothing like the office he'd shown her on the ground floor. The colors were much lighter and the furnishings had curvier lines. One wall contained a floor to ceiling bookshelf which stretched the length of it, while the opposite wall held two huge whiteboards. There was an executive desk situated in front of a large window overlooking the front of the property.

A chaise lounge was placed a few feet front of the bookshelf with a throw blanket draped across the back. Wren, the designer, had carried out his instructions to the letter. The room wasn't a duplicate of her office at her house. It held all of the same things, along with some additions he knew suited her personality.

Pushing the door open, she walked inside a few steps then turned to look at him. "Is this for me?"

"Yeah. You like it?"

Her eyes swept the room before coming back to his face. "I love it, but you didn't have to do this."

"Sure I did." Carver closed the distance between them. "I want you to be comfortable here. To me, that means you need a space that's for you. I have my office and a conference room."

Carver stopped himself from elaborating further. It was on the tip of his tongue to give her a complete rundown on why it was absolutely necessary for her to have an office.

Her soft palms cupped the sides of his face. "You didn't have to do this."

"Bit, baby. Just say thank you, then gimme a kiss."

Shooting him a cheeky grin, she complied. The moment her lips touched his, he took over the kiss. With her body flush against his, he was certain she felt the rise of his cock through his loose-fitting training shorts. Reluctantly, he pulled away with a few parting pecks to her plush lips.

"Come on. I want to you see the rest of what Wren did around the place."

Still looking a little kiss drunk, Alyssa allowed him to tug her behind him to explore the rest of the second floor. Going off-script, Carver took her directly to the main bedroom suite. The only furniture yet to arrive for the room were the sofa and recliners he wanted for the lounging area.

Stepping over the threshold, he walked directly to the garden doors leading out onto a private balcony.

He pressed a button on the wall and the curtains slid open exposing the windows flanking the doors. Through the glass, two outdoor lounge chairs and a small table were visible. The view was of the pool area and the expanse of grass large enough to be converted into a tennis court with some room to spare.

Behind him, he heard an audible gasp. Turning, he saw Alyssa standing at the doorway to the ensuite bathroom. A sly grin took over his face as he watched her. He'd had a similar response to the room the first time he saw it. Although he'd grown accustomed to certain things over the years, even he'd been impressed by the added details in the space.

"You could fit the entire second floor of my house into just this room and bathroom." Alyssa looked over her shoulder at him before stepping all the way into the ensuite.

"It's definitely not short on space." Following behind her, he propped one hip against the black marble counter which held three sinks instead of the standard two. "Truth be told, it was one of the key selling points for this place. There were other factors, but this main suite sealed the deal for me."

"I can see why."

Walking across the porcelain tile, Alyssa stopped at the bottom of the three stairs leading to massive jetted tub. With concerted effort, he beat back the images of her inside the tub with water glistening on her silky skin. He regained control in time to watch her walk to the best feature, in his humble opinion. The shower.

Besides being so large that if he stood in the center, he couldn't touch either wall with his impressive seven foot wing span, it had five shower heads and a steaming function. Two of the showerheads were on opposite sides while a third was in the ceiling for the waterfall effect. The two remaining were at more of a body level rather than being angled from above.

There was built in shelving to hold whatever shower implements deemed necessary. Carver's eyes were drawn to the bench seat along the back. Once again images assailed him of all the things he and his Bit could do in such a space.

This time, Alyssa's voice pulled him back into the moment.

"Carver, why is this closet filled with women's clothing?"

Shit! He was so lost in his thoughts he hadn't noticed her move toward the walk-in closet on the left side of the bathroom.

"Oh, about that." Scrubbing his hand across the back of his neck, he approached her with a half grin half grimace on his face. "I bought some things for you, so you wouldn't have to worry about havin' somethin' to wear whenever you came over."

"So, you duplicated my closet?"

Her tone suggested she thought his actions were high-handed at best and creepy at the worst. She didn't have to say it aloud. He knew her well enough to figure it out.

"Nah...Nothing like that. I mean...they might be similar because they're in the same style or color. But, nothing is identical."

Trailing her fingers along the neatly hung garments, Alyssa walked deeper into the closet. Her original assessment was an exaggeration. It wasn't *filled* with women's clothing. It was only partially filled. He'd left ample space for when she brought the rest of her things from her place.

Carver knew buying clothes and hanging them in her closet was a gamble, but he really couldn't bring himself to care. He was well aware of how it looked. Yet, he'd do it again.

Alyssa stopped inspecting the contents of the closet and turned toward him. Bracing her hands on the waist high cabinet in the center of the room, she pierced him with a look he couldn't decipher—which meant it probably wasn't a good thing for him. He stood framed in the doorway, waiting for the inevitable.

"Carver...I'm trying. I really am. Everything between us has been pedal to the metal from the moment we saw one another at the restaurant. The speed has been scary, but that's because I'm not accustomed to the type of intensity we have. I'm not running from it, but it's taken some adjustment—especially the part about being in the public eye.

I've accepted the changes because I want to be with you. I want what we have together. But when you go off and do things without consulting me..."

Leaning forward she narrowed her eyes. "Tell me the truth, Carver. Did you buy this house with the intention that we'd live here together?"

"Yes."

Carver couldn't lie to her. No matter how much he'd avoided actually discussing it with her directly, he couldn't deny her honesty when she asked frankly.

As it turned out, his plan was shit. Although he hadn't actually run it by his father, he could still hear his pop's voice in his head telling him to do better.

Carver imagined the day in some sort of dream fog where he'd get her here, and involved in the process of making the house a home. The office was phase two, but the bedroom, specifically the contents of the closet wasn't supposed to come until later. Much later.

After all, he'd watched her pack an overnight bag earlier and hadn't stopped her. He'd even carried said bag to the car for her. In hindsight, that was an opportunity to mention he'd taken the liberty of getting a few things for her that were already here. Okay...saying it was just a *few things* was a stretch. Still, he missed an opportunity.

"You know that's not normal, right?" Although she'd asked the question, Carver could tell she didn't really want an answer. She proved him correct when she continued speaking.

"If you want a multi-million-dollar home for yourself, fine. But, doing so with the express intent that it would be a place for the two of us without saying as much to me is way out of bounds."

"That's not completely true, baby. You don't remember us talking about me searching for a place? Or when we looked through pictures of listings once the realtor narrowed them down and I'd gone out to look at them in person? Has that slipped your mind?"

"Of course not, but I thought I was just giving you my opinion. Being helpful."

Tipping his head to the side, it was his turn to stare at her. However, his expression matched his next words. "Alyssa Renee Ripley, you are many things, but dumb ain't one of 'em."

Walking fully inside, he stopped once he was standing beside her.

"Now, I would never accuse you of being like other women, but I can't imagine any woman being included in a discussion about a man looking to buy a house who wouldn't consider that he may be askin' for their input because he wants her there with him. Maybe not immediately, but in the future."

"Carver, it's only been a—"

"If you bring up how long we've been a couple one more time, I'm gonna put you over my knee and spank that ass red."

Her sharp inhale at his threat said she wouldn't find the experience entirely unpleasant.

"It ain't gonna be the good way, so get that thought outta your head."

"You don't know what I was thinking."

Leaning closer, he spoke directly into her ear. "Sure I do, Baby. You were thinking about me making that ass red, then kissing it to make it better."

Standing up straight, he regarded her with only the slightest hint of smugness. "Now, stop tryin' to distract me and answer my question. Did you think I was talking to you about this place as a courtesy or somethin'?"

"Are you trying to say I should've read something into it? It's not like I went on any tours with you." Alyssa snapped out of her haze so quickly it almost had his head spinning.

"Carver, we had one, maybe two discussions about it and you showed me some pictures. It wasn't like we spent hours poring over list-ings looking for the perfect one.

If we'd done that, yeah, I might've read something into it. As it was, we didn't spend any significant time talking about this house. You can't put this on me not picking up on context clues. At least not entirely."

This discussion was heading perilously toward an argument and that's not what he wanted, nor what they needed considering the trucks should be arriving with the rest of his things at any moment. He needed more time, but what he had was right now. There was no point in drag-ging it out. Slipping his arm around her, he nudged her until she relaxed against his side.

"What is it that's really bothering you? That I didn't come right out and say I wanted us to live here together or the thought of us *actually* living here together?"

Laying her head on his chest, she toyed with the material of his t-shirt for a few moments before she answered. "It's a little of both, but it's mostly the second part."

Releasing a sigh, Carver wrapped his other arm around her enclosing her in a loose hug.

"Bit...Baby, I'm sure you've noticed the only time we've slept apart since the first night I stayed at your place was when I spent those few days in New York. Essentially, for the past month, we've been living together. We were simply doing it at a different address."

When she didn't respond, he nuzzled the top of her head, then slipped a finger under her chin to tip her face up toward his.

"I'm not asking or even suggesting that you put your house on the market or anything like that. I'm just saying that thing that bothers you most is a thing we're already doing. It's just in a place where the deed is in your name. If it eases your mind, this deed can be in your name too."

As soon as the words hit the air, Carver knew that last little part was too much. But, he wouldn't take it back. He meant it. It didn't matter to him whose name was on the deed as long as she was beside him when he laid down at night.

Pulling back and placing both hands on his chest, a line appeared between her eyebrows as she drew them together.

"You know that's not normal either, right?"

Shrugging, he offered her a lopsided grin. He wondered if that being her only question meant he had successfully navigated the emotional minefield. He didn't have long to think about it because his cellphone buzzed in his pocket. Taking it out he; he swiped the screen. Reading the message, he slid it back into his pocket.

"That was Michael. The movers are here."

"We aren't done talking about this, Carver."

"I know, Baby."

Pressing a kiss to her forehead, he stepped aside and extended an arm for her to precede him from the closet. Sure, he had some work to do, but she hadn't completely come unglued on him. Carver marked it as a win, even though he knew there was still work to be done.

Chapter Twenty-Six

I'M TALKIN' TO MY BEST GIRL

Alyssa preceded Carver from the room with her mind ablaze. Different facets of herself battled internally. He'd gone too far, and what made it worse was he didn't see it. Or at least he didn't see the magnitude of what he'd done.

It wasn't a doubt in her mind that Carver loved her. Even if they hadn't exchanged the words she felt it. But this...It was too much. Way too much. Way too soon. What she knew about relationships was that they're all different. So, she didn't really expect the two of them to be like everyone else or follow someone else's timeline.

Carver was a man who was accustomed to getting his way. Not because of who he was, but because he worked hard to earn the things he wanted. She learned that long ago when she watched as he put in extra time practicing beyond the requirements. The hours he put in, watching film of not just himself but other teams and other quarterbacks who were performing at the level he aspired to, was admirable.

Still, it almost felt like he was trying to put them where they would've been if she had stayed that morning at The Drake instead of leaving while he slept. That thought took root as she walked down the curving staircase to see Michael standing next to the open front door.

Alyssa stopped in the foyer while Carver continued on through the doorway. She heard him speaking to whom she assumed were the movers, but didn't go outside to investigate. Instead, she walked into the living room looking around with fresh eyes.

Like she'd told Carver earlier, decorating wasn't her thing. The most she could do was look at the label on the box and point people in a direction. But she was there to help. That's what girlfriends and significant others did. *Right?*

The morning progressed quickly as the movers efficiently did their jobs. As she expected, she didn't do more than direct traffic. Her one major accomplishment was getting the massive television wired and connected to the network once it had been mounted to the bedroom wall. The home theatre and remaining TVs were connected by the provider when the account was set up. The one for the main bedroom was a custom build that Carver had shipped from his house in San Diego.

By lunchtime, it was only Carver and Alyssa together in the kitchen. They were seated at the semi-circular table next to the island eating take-out. They hadn't said much to one another since she confronted him in the closet that morning. It wasn't due to avoidance. The activity level in the house was high, so there weren't many opportunities for conversation. Which was fine.

What she needed to say to him wasn't for public consumption. Alyssa didn't miss the awestruck way a few of the movers stared at Carver anytime he walked by or spoke to them directly. The way they looked at him told her they probably couldn't wait to rush to social media and post about how they'd met a future Hall of Famer.

Finished with her portion of Kung Pao chicken and rice, Alyssa stood to toss the nearly empty container into the trash. When she returned to the table, Carver glanced up at her as he ate the last of his Dim Sum. Retaking her seat, she waited.

Once he'd taken his final bite, he wiped his mouth and tossed the napkin into the empty container. Setting it to the side, he folded his arms on the table.

"You've been awful quiet, Bit. You still mad at me?"

"I'm not mad at you, Carver. I never was. Shocked. A little hurt maybe. But, not mad."

Leaning forward with his elbows pressed into the table, a wrinkle of concern appeared in his brow. "Hurt? I hurt you?"

Alyssa's gaze raked over his face taking in his expression and posture. "You really don't see it do you?"

"See what?"

"That what you did, what you're doing, is manipulative."

"What?"

Holding up a hand to stop the barrage of words she saw building behind his eyes, Alyssa considered what she had to say before she spoke again.

"Carver, instead of talking to me about what I wanted...No. Instead of coming out and telling me what *you* wanted, you tried to maneuver me like a chess piece.

I'll take part of the blame because I should've said something when your belongings started showing up at my place. I didn't. Things were a little crazy with the media, but beyond that, I was selfish. I liked having you there."

"If you liked having me at your place, what's the difference with us being together here?"

Alyssa pressed her palms against the sides of her head in a mild show of frustration. She wasn't getting through to him. Hell, even she heard the correlation. By that logic, why did the location matter?

"While you were at my place most nights, you still had the suite. You chose to be with me instead of there. I didn't say anything, because I got to stay inside my comfort zone. But, I should've said something."

"Why?" The single word question held so many layers.

"I'd already told you I felt like we were moving too fast, but you brushed it off. I let myself be swept up in the concept that we didn't have to do things by anyone else's timetable. It's true. So, it didn't take much to convince me."

"So, you think I bulldozed over your concerns and manipulated you to get what I wanted. But you didn't say anything because you wanted it too. Help me out here, Bit. I'm confused."

She couldn't blame him for being confused. Her actions and words weren't lining up.

"I'm scared, Carver. I need something and you aren't giving it to me.

You can't protect me enough to compensate for it. You can't sex me enough for me to overlook it. And, I know you don't like to hear it, but I need time."

Pressing her hand to her chest, she continued.

"My feelings and emotions are only one aspect of me. I need time to wrap my mind around where we are and where we're going. This isn't me trying to throw up roadblocks or barriers. This is me telling you that I can't deal with you making moves behind my back and thinking all you have to do is apologize to make it all better.

Hell, you didn't even apologize. You turned it around on me like I should've known. Maybe I should've, but it doesn't let you off the hook for not actually having the conversation with me and allowing me to *choose* what I wanted to do."

"Fuck..."

Carver's normally vibrant green eyes were dull when he looked at Alyssa following her disclosure. His shoulders slumped which made her feel terrible. Yes, she was hurt, but she didn't want to exchange hurt for hurt. She simply wanted him to understand things from her perspective.

Internally, she fought against the desire within her to say or do something to ease his discomfort. However, Alyssa knew it was in both of their best interests if she remained quiet and let him work through it in his own way. She'd laid everything out there. Now, they had to talk about it like adults in a healthy relationship, so they could navigate through the situation.

"Bit...Baby... You know what I want most is for you to be happy, right? I would never intentionally hurt you any more than I'd stand by and let someone else hurt you.

I know I didn't handle this the way I should've, but it was never my plan to manipulate you into moving in. I just wanted to present you with options and hope that you chose the one that had us living in this big ass house together. Where I could be more confident that you're safe when I'm not with you."

The chairs, which came with the house, were on wheels. Using that to his advantage, Carver grasped the arm on the side of Alyssa's chair and pulled her closer to him. He didn't stop until one of his knees was wedged between hers and vice versa. Staring at her, he seemed to search her eyes for a few minutes before he spoke again.

"Ok. Baby. Talk to me. I'm listening. I'm clear about what I want. You. Here with me. Everyday. What I need is the assurance that you'll be here or on your way here when I get home. But, I want you to have what you want. What you need.

When you say you need time, it sounds an awful lot like you sayin' you wanna take a break. *Is* that what you're sayin'? You want us to step back from each other? I gotta tell you, that don't sit right with me."

Carver's hands engulfed hers as they rested on her thigh. The heat of his palm against her cool skin was comforting even while her stomach churned. She hadn't meant to give him the impression she wanted to back away from their relationship, but she couldn't seem to express herself in a way he'd understand.

"I'm not saying that I want to take a break from us."

"What are you sayin' then?"

"I'm saying I can't move in with you. At least not now."

"If not now, when?"

"Carver..."

"Bit...Baby...If we discount the time following graduation, do you understand that we've allowed ten years to go by that we could've been building a life together?"

"I know, but we can't get that time back."

"No, we can't. But we shouldn't waste the time we've been given either. You're still worryin' about what other people will think or say about us."

"That's not true. I don't care what strangers think."

"I'm not talkin' about strangers. I'm talkin' your family. Your friends. Those closest to you. You're worried they'll think poorly of you. That they'll ask why a good girl like you is shackin' up with a man."

Heat flooded Alyssa's cheeks. She had been raised as a *good girl*. Cohabitating prior to marriage was a big no-no in her parents' eyes. However, many of her family and close friends had grown to see it as an antiquated belief. Carver had drilled down to the core of her fear. Her eyelids lowered trying to cover the secret he'd unearthed.

Cupping the side of her face, Carver stroked her cheek with his thumb. Pointing his finger back and forth between the two of them, he breached the silence.

"This. What happens with us. Ain't got shit to do with anyone not named Alyssa and Carver. *We* decide what's best for us. Not society and not our families. Understand?"

His fingers flexed against the nape of her neck. Alyssa nodded her agreement.

"Uh-uh. I need the words, Bit."

"I understand."

"Now...tell me what you would do, if you weren't worried about what your mama and daddy would say."

"Don't say it like that. It makes me sound like a kid."

"When it comes to our parents, we'll always be their kids."

His smile, while not at full wattage let her know he wasn't holding her fit of nerves against her. His words were a call back to something similar her mother said to her whenever Alyssa pointed out that she was no longer a baby.

"Even if what my parents would think wasn't at the back of my mind, I'd still want time."

"Time for what?"

"For us to learn each other as the people we are now. The past couple of months, we've clocked a lot of face time, but moving in together is a major step."

"It is, but we took that step weeks ago."

"No, what we've been doing was more of an extended sleep over."

"Is that the lie you've been telling yourself?"

"Absent a discussion like the one we're having now, the two of us never agreed to living together."

Carver's lips thinned into a hard line. "I got a question for you, Bit. Before me, how many men have you allowed to *sleep over* at your place for consecutive nights?"

Alyssa's head jerked in the hold he still had on her. "What? How does who I've slept with before you factor into this?"

"I'm not asking about a damn body count. I don't give a shit about that. I'm asking about who you've allowed to be in your space the way

I've been there. I already know the answer to my question. I just want **you** to say it out loud."

"If you know, why don't you tell me?"

"None. Before me, you never let anyone sleep over, at least not for consecutive nights. And never for weeks at a time."

Trying to avoid his penetrating stare, Alyssa looked to the side. She had never felt more exposed. At least that's what she thought until Carver spoke again.

"Bit, baby, look at me. Can you honestly say what we have isn't different? That it's unlike anything either of us has experience before?"

Alyssa couldn't deny him. She wouldn't. "It's not."

Carver's gaze softened. His right hand left hers to cup the other side of her face. Her eyes tracked the bobbing of his Adam's apple before training on his lips as he formed his next words.

"Baby...we've said a lot of things to each other and done just as many, but we've danced around the elephant in the room long enough."

His thumbs stroked her cheeks while his fingers flexed against the base of her head.

"Bit, baby. I love you so much sometimes it's hard to for me to breathe. I smile when I hear your name and I look forward to every single second I get to spend in your presence. I don't want to go back to a time when I didn't get to go sleep with you in my arms. I don't want to purposely wake up without you lying next to me."

Alyssa gasped at his words. Tears welled in her eyes as he declared the depth of his feelings for her. Although he had shown her in numerous ways, hearing the words had a different effect.

"Please tell me those are happy tears, darlin'. Tell me you aren't lookin' for a way to let me down easy."

Clutching the front of his shirt, Alyssa tugged him forward. Looking at his expressive eyes, she said the words she'd held close to her heart. "I love you, Carver Wyatt Jamieson. So much."

Anything else Alyssa may have said was swallowed by Carver's kiss. He took her lips with an urgency she'd never experienced from him. When they finally broke away, his forehead dropped to hers.

"Damn, Baby. I think this calls for a celebration." Standing, he held out a hand to help her from her chair. "What say we go upstairs and try out that brand, spankin' new bed?"

Alyssa core clenched in anticipation from Carver's suggestion. He wiggled his eyebrows and his fingers until she took him up on the offer for assistance. Taking the stairs beside the kitchen instead of walking through the massive foyer, by the time they made it to the bedroom, they were both naked. The touches and kisses delivered enroute had her walls thrumming with desire.

Lifting her off of her feet the moment they crossed the threshold, Carver laid Alyssa on the bed. Pushing her legs apart, he settled between her thighs with his nose inches from her now throbbing center. Alyssa felt the air stir on her mons, and saw Carver's lips moving, but she couldn't hear anything above the blood pounding in her ears. *Why wasn't he touching her already?* As the thought crossed her brain, words tumbled from her lips.

"Why aren't you touching me?" Alyssa's hips undulated without her consciously performing the action.

"Shh, Baby. I'm talkin' to my best girl. I'm apologizin' in advance for what I'm gonna do to her."

Turning his gaze back to her pulsing pussy, he placed a kiss on her lower lips. "I promise I'll make it up to you."

The murmured words were followed by another kiss to her folds and a lick to her sensitive clit. Climbing up her body, he gripped the underside of her thighs pressing them out and up. Notching the bulbous head of his cock at her opening, he snagged her gaze holding her captive with his emerald stare.

With their eyes locked on one another, Carver thrust his entire length into her hungry walls. Her tight sheath clung to his cock caressing it as he swiveled his hips once he was buried inside her to the hilt.

"Tell me again." He ground out as he withdrew his thickness before driving back into her depths. "Tell me!"

She didn't have to ask what he wanted to hear. Alyssa knew. "I love you, Carver."

Releasing his hold on her legs he dropped forward with his forearms bracketing her head.

"Again" he demanded as he pumped into her at a steady unrelenting pace.

Trailing her hands from his chest to rest at the sides of his face, she saw his love for her shining in his eyes. "I love you."

The more she said it, the more he wanted to hear it. Soon she was screaming it out into the room as she reached her climax. Following behind her, he filled her with his seed. Raining kisses on her face, neck and shoulders, Carver didn't withdraw from her still spasming channel.

"I love you so fucking much, Baby." Carver's words tickled her ears and covered her heart with a warmth Alyssa hadn't known she needed.

Carver's gentle kisses soon turned more erotic. His cock thickened once more. Instead of starting round two, he pulled out then stood from the bed. Grabbing her by the ankle, he tugged her to the edge.

"Come on, Bit baby. Let's test out that couch in your closet."

Chapter Twenty-Seven

WHAT ARE YOU LAUGHING AT?

Carver was floating on cloud nine. To say the last four months had been life altering would be an understatement. The last thing he expected when he accepted the position with the Ravagers was that he'd end up in the same city with the love of his life.

With his means and connections, Carver could've kept tabs on Alyssa during the years they were apart, but he didn't. He trusted the process. There were also times when he'd almost convinced himself that it was possible they weren't meant to be. That load of horseshit didn't last more than a month at a time.

Fate had brought him to Las Vegas and sent him down to get a bite to eat where he encountered the woman who'd plagued his dreams for a decade. Carver shook his head when he thought about it. He deserved a fucking medal for his restraint.

But, all of that was in the past. Now, when he came home each day, his Bit was there. Sometimes, she was still in her office working; others she was preparing dinner or binge watching one of her beloved sci-fi thrillers. No matter where she was, or what she was doing, she was there. In their home.

Once she'd come around to his way of thinking, he wasted no time getting things set up to bring the rest of her belongings over. He didn't care that she wasn't putting her house on the market. What mattered most to him was having her with him in a place they shared.

Before training camp started in July, they'd taken their first vacation as a couple. Carver took Alyssa to the Amalfi Coast in southern Italy. While she'd traveled extensively, it was somewhere she hadn't been. It was also a place they could be certain of having anonymity. So, no worries about viral videos or people infringing on their privacy.

They had an amazing two weeks yachting and exploring the nearby historic cities, since Alyssa was fascinated with the architecture. Carver admitted he marveled at the way the homes seemed to be built right into the side of the mountain. Without prying eyes, Alyssa was so carefree, he almost didn't want to come home. But, they each had work and responsibilities.

The team was in the last weeks of training camp before the start of the pre-season games in August. Due to him fighting for certain offensive draft picks, the team selected a quarterback and a left tackle to add some depth to their lineup. Unfortunately, they used their first picks on defensive players, so the offensive players they drafted were late second and early third round selections.

The kids had raw talent, but they had played for coaches who didn't properly develop them. Carver didn't doubt he could share knowledge which would help them be successful in the league. The question was if they'd be receptive.

"Gallagher! If I have to tell you again to stop palming that football like you're playing hoops, I'm gonna tape your fingertips to the ball. And, have you even studied the play? Where the hell were you throwing that pass?"

Taking long strides, Carver approached the third string quarterback. The kid was lucky to even get any snaps and he was blowing it by not being prepared. Gallagher had heart, but it took more than heart to make it in such a competitive sport.

He'd done well in college because he could scramble and run the ball better than half the running backs in the league. But, if he wanted to run, he should've tried out for that position instead of quarterback.

Gallagher had a great arm, but as Carver said, his technique was shit.

How he'd made it this long without being taught properly was a question to which Carver didn't like the answer he came up with.

"Sorry, Coach. I can't seem to get my fingers to do it the way you said. It doesn't feel natural." Catching the ball being tossed back by the receiver, he rolled it around on his large hand.

Taking the ball, Carver demonstrated again. With Gallagher's long fingers, it should be child's play, but he kept slipping back into his old habits.

"It doesn't feel natural, because you haven't been practicing it enough. You've spent, what twelve, thirteen years, doing it the way you first learned? Which was wrong. You've gotta overcome that training, no matter how many times it seemed to work for you in the past."

Getting into his stance, Carver sent the receiver out on the route again. Dropping back, he cocked his arm and released the ball. In a perfect spiral, it sailed through the air before landing in the hands of the receiver at the exact spot it should have fifteen yards away.

"If you want results, you have to put in the time. Not just during practice. Before practice. After practice. On your day off. Until it's muscle memory."

Piercing the young QB with a hard stare he let his words sink in for a minute. Gallagher's expression was closed, so Carver had no idea if he was getting through to him. What he did know is he only had a certain amount of leeway before he'd be forced to cut him. The kid had promise and he really didn't want to do it. But, if the young quarterback couldn't master the basics in order to contribute to the team, Carver would have to do it.

As the receiver jogged back with the ball tucked under one arm, the head coach called an end to practice. When Gallagher went to walk away with the rest of his teammates, Carver tapped his shoulder.

"Practice is over for them. Not you."

Calling out to the nearest member of the equipment crew, he asked them to hold off on putting the bins of footballs away. Instead, they moved two of them to the fifty-yard line. Catching a couple of assistants before they could leave, he had them pull two of the throwing nets onto the field as well.

"Grab a ball." Digging into the bin closest to him, Carver waited until Gallagher also held a football.

"Your net is on the left, mine is on the right. We're not leaving until we empty these bins. Twice."

To his credit, Gallagher didn't complain. He simply walked over to the other bin.

"The first round, you throw them the way you've always done it. Then, switch to the way I showed you. If you're more accurate your way, and hit the target at least half as many times as me, I'll shut up about it."

Gallagher perked up at the suggestion that Carver might ease off of him. He nodded while tapping the side of the ball he held. Carver tried not to be offended that the kid thought he stood a chance. Carver's single season pass completion record still hadn't been broken.

"But...If you're more accurate using my method, you have to stop fighting it and put in the work. Do we have a deal?" Holding out his fist, Carver waited.

"Deal." Gallagher's responding fist bump was done with such confidence Carver almost felt bad for him. Almost.

Having stayed back, the Receiver's coach, Octavius Pierce, blew his whistle to get them started. After sinking the first few balls into the target effortlessly, Carver stopped to look at Gallagher.

"This isn't about speed. It's about accuracy. Take your time." As of yet, the kid hadn't hit either of the five available spots on the large net.

Grabbing another ball from the bin, Carver resumed leisurely sending bullets into the openings in the net. For the next half hour, he preceded to put on a clinic. When they were done, Carver had proven his point with Gallagher. Gripping the ball and adjusting his stance the way Carver showed him yielded the young QB a significant improvement in precision.

"Thanks, Coach. I know you didn't have to take extra time to work with me. I appreciate it."

"Thank me by remembering what we worked on and not sliding back into bad habits."

"You got it, Coach."

Breaking into a wide smile, Gallagher tapped Carver on his right shoulder before jogging off the field. He was so excited he missed the slight grimace Carver couldn't hide at the contact. Gallagher missed it, but Octavius didn't. Hearing his chuckles, Carver glared at him, but Octavius gave zero fucks.

"What are you laughing at?"

"Your old ass."

"If I'm old, you're ancient. You've got at least ten years on me."

"And that's long enough for me to know not to put my almost fifty-year-old ass in competition with a twenty-two-year-old."

"I'm still in shape. I could suit up tomorrow."

"I'm sure you could. Then you would spend the next week damn near in traction trying to recover."

"Fuck you."

"Nah...Not me, but maybe if you go home and beg your woman, she'll take care of your boo-boo and give you some pity sex. It might make you feel better about getting old."

White teeth shone starkly against his dark brown complexion as he threw his head back and laughed unashamedly at Carver's discomfort.

"It's really not that funny. And age has nothing to do with it. I work out, but I haven't put in that many reps throwing the ball in a long time."

"Whatever you have to tell yourself, man." Octavius lightly punched Carver's left shoulder as he walked away.

Gently rotating his shoulder, Carver alternately cursed himself for forgetting to warm up before he got started and Octavius for laughing at his pain. However, one thing the other man said brought a smile to Carver's face. His Bit was home with her magic hands. Yet another perk to them living together.

~

Senior Year

Carver walked out of the locker room with his backpack thrown over his left shoulder. His right shoulder ached like a bitch. He'd taken a quick shower, but he just wanted to get back to his apartment to take a longer, hotter shower to let the water beat down on him to hopefully help with the soreness.

The opening notes of Snoop Dogg's *Drop it Like it's Hot* emanated from his pocket. Denzel thought it was hilarious to keep changing the ring tone on Carver's cellphone to the various tunes he downloaded from some website. Pulling the phone from his pocket, he saw Mary Beth's name on the screen.

"Hello?"

"Hey, Babe! You all done with practice?"

Of course he was. He didn't have his phone with him on the practice field. Carver didn't bother to point out the obvious. There was no point to it.

"Yeah. I'm walking to my car to head back to my place. What's up?"

"I was checking to see if you were still coming over to hang out."

"Uh...I don't think so, Mary Beth. I'm beat and my shoulder is sore as hell from all the reps today."

"Ohh...Sweetie...Please?! We haven't spent any time together all week. I miss you."

"I know, but I'm really not feeling up to being social. Besides, I have a couple of assignments to finish." Reaching his second-hand GMC Yukon, Carver opened the door and dropped his backpack into the passenger seat.

"You can do your homework here. We can work together. I promise I won't bother you. And. And. Alyssa's making dinner. You know she always cooks way too much for just the two of us."

At the mention of food, Carver's stomach grumbled. He weighed the options of a home cooked meal against a hot shower and alone time. The meal won. He didn't even ask what Alyssa was cooking, he simply told Mary Beth he was on his way.

Carver didn't dwell on the way he perked up at the mention of Alyssa. Her cooking dinner was just a bonus. He felt like a complete asshole for it, so he couldn't think about it too long.

Although he sometimes wondered why, he did care about Mary Beth. So, anything happening with the way he was drawn to Alyssa was a non-starter. Besides him not being the kind of guy who cheats, she wasn't the type of girl who went after her friend's boyfriend. She was much too sweet and loyal for something like that.

In the short drive from the practice stadium to Mary Beth and Alyssa's off-campus apartment, Carver ran through what he still had to do before he could lie down for the day. From the looks of things, it would be a long night. It was a good thing he didn't have an early class the next day.

Mary Beth answered the door almost as soon as Carver lowered his hand from the doorbell. If he didn't know better, he'd swear she was watching from the window timing his trek from his truck to their front door. Accepting her offer of a quick peck on the lips, he entered the apartment.

Savory scents assailed him before he stepped over he threshold. He thought it was his mind playing tricks on him when he smelled the unmistakable scent of lasagna while he walked up the stairs. But, once he entered the small common area he realized he hadn't been imagining things.

Dropping his bag on the floor next to the nondescript coffee table, he walked toward the half wall separating the common area from the galley-style kitchen.

"Hey there, Bit. That lasagna smells delicious." His stomach rumbled on cue and he pat it while smiling.

Placing the rectangular shaped glass dish on a folded towel on the countertop, Alyssa looked up at him returning his greeting.

"Hey, Carver. Thank you. It looks like you're just in time. I just have to put the garlic toast in the oven. How many pieces would you like?"

"I'll take two if you don't mind."

"None for me. I don't want garlic breath."

Mary Beth offered her choice with a pinched look on her face. Alyssa simply nodded and went about putting four pieces of the pre-packaged toast onto a baking sheet. Tugging on his arm pulled his attention away from Alyssa. Grimacing, he grasped Mary Beth's hand removing it from his bicep.

"Ow." Immediately responding to his exclamation, she stepped closer.

"What's wrong? Did you get hurt in practice? Are you not going to be able to play this weekend?"

"Of course I'm playing this weekend." Carver frowned. *Why would she immediately assume he'd been benched by injury?*

"My shoulder and arm are sore from the extra reps I put in today. I might have pushed it a little too hard."

"I don't know why you work so hard. You're the best quarterback Tech's had in years. My dad says so and he's like the biggest Tech fan ever."

Settling onto the couch with Mary Beth sitting safely to his left, Carver looked at his girlfriend. "While I appreciate your dad's vote of confidence, I work hard because I want to be the best quarterback I'm capable of being. The only way to do that is for me to put in the effort."

Snuggling closer to him, she rubbed his left arm. "What can I do?" When he stared at her blankly, she added, "to help. Is there something I can do to help with the soreness?"

"Nah...I have a routine the trainer gave me. I'll go through it when I get to my place."

"You're not staying after dinner?"

The pout she directed at him was his warning that she was going to keep asking until he gave in or left amid a possible argument.

"I told you I had a couple of assignments to finish."

"I know..." Gnawing on her lower lip, she suddenly perked up. "I've got it! Alyssa can work her magic on your arm and shoulder, then you'll be able to finish your assignment without pain and we can hang out tonight like we planned."

"Mary Beth, you can't just volunteer Alyssa that way. Who's to say she doesn't have something she needs to do?"

So far, Carver had managed to keep his interactions with Alyssa friendly and platonic. He'd only admitted to himself how appealing she was to him. If she put her hands on any part of him, he couldn't be certain he wouldn't embarrass both of them with his response.

"Alyssa doesn't mind. Do you Alyssa?" Mary Beth raised her voice so that it carried into the kitchen.

"I don't mind what?" Alyssa stepped around the half wall wiping her hands on a paper towel.

"Carver has some arm and shoulder soreness from practice. You wouldn't mind rubbing it for him would you? I would do it, but you know I'm terrible at massages."

Alyssa's eyes landed on his before moving back to her friend.

"Umm...Sure. I guess."

"Don't worry about it, Bit. I'm gonna do the ice then heat thing when I get home and put some cream on it. It'll be fine."

He tried to let Alyssa off the hook, but Mary Beth was bound and determined. After a few more minutes of back and forth, Carver relented—with Alyssa's assurance that she was okay with it.

In hindsight, he probably should've stuck to his guns. After scarfing down the delicious meal Alyssa cooked, Carver was already far too relaxed. Disappearing into her bedroom, Alyssa came back out with a tube of analgesic cream in one hand and a short stool in the other. Stopping next to the sofa, she spoke softly.

"You'll need to take your shirt off and lie down on your stomach."

Mary Beth hopped up to make room. His long legs made it impossible for him to stretch out completely, so his shins rested against the arm on the opposite end. Mary Beth's phone rang and she dashed into her bedroom to catch the call.

"You really don't have to do this, Bit." Carver tried one last time to let Alyssa off the hook.

"It's no problem. You look really uncomfortable."

Placing the stool beside the couch, she sat and unscrewed the top from the tube. The moment her fingers touched his skin Carver was simultaneously relieved and disgusted with himself. He didn't know if it was because it was her or if she was really that gifted, but it was by far the best massage he'd ever had in his life.

He couldn't suppress his moans of enjoyment. In an effort to not make it even more weird, he turned his head away. If he hadn't he was certain she would've read his expression. Carver isn't sure how it happened, but he fell asleep. Considering he was hard enough to drive a hole into the cushions below his hips, that was a minor miracle.

Carver woke up to Mary Beth leaning over him. Sitting up, he searched for Alyssa, but she wasn't there. The door to her bedroom was closed. Checking his watch, he noted how late it was. Declining Mary

Beth's offer for him to stay the night and ignoring her pouting as a result, he pulled his shirt on.

Grabbing his backpack, he rotated his shoulder marveling at how much better it felt. Saying his goodbyes to Mary Beth, he left their apartment. His mama was right, the good Lord watches over children and fools. It was the only way he could explain him falling asleep in lieu of embarrassing himself with Bit.

As good as the massage had felt, he'd have to avoid having her touch him that way in the future. If he didn't, more than one friendship would suffer. Climbing into the truck, Carver turned the nose in the direction of his apartment. He still had homework to get done before he could call it a night.

Chapter Twenty-Eight

WHERE ARE YOU GOING?

Having completed all she intended to do for the day, Alyssa went through her routine of shutting down programs. She worked from home almost exclusively now. It was better for her and not just because Carver had outfitted the office with everything she could even think of wanting for her comfort. There were less distractions. The arrangement actually stayed her decision to leave *Secure Pull* and focus on her side endeavors.

Just as she was about to close her email, a notification popped up. *Ballard Grimes*. Ballard had been sending her emails saying they needed to talk and asking her to call him for months. She'd ignored him since they had no reason to communicate. They didn't work on any teams together, but she was tired of his messages.

Being that they worked for the same company, and it was possible they may be paired together in the future, she couldn't block his messages. So, she did the next best thing. Picking up her earpiece, she placed it in her ear and tapped her phone to make a call.

Harrison answered the call on the first ring. "Hello, Alyssa. I'm surprised to hear from you so late in the day."

"Hey, Harrison. Sorry to call so close to the bell, but I have a question."

"It's not a problem. I'm not leaving for another thirty minutes. What's up?"

"I've been getting persistent messages from Ballard saying we need to talk. Do you know what could be going on? We don't work on any projects together and we were never friendly enough to chat about anything not related to work."

Even though she couldn't see him, Alyssa heard the frown in Harrison's voice. "Ballard Grimes? He's been calling you?"

"No. Not calls. He was sending messages through the company chat, but now it's just emails."

"Alyssa, we let Ballard go two months ago. There's no reason he should try to contact you. Unless he wants a reference. But even then, why contact you? As you said, you two didn't work on the same projects."

Alyssa's jaw dropped at Harrison's revelation. Ballard had been fired? She guessed working from home had her out of the loop of company gossip. Clicking on the email, she looked at the address again. That's when she noticed the extension on the address was for a free email service and not the standard @SecurePull.com.

"I had no idea. That makes this even stranger."

"He never says what he wants to talk to you about?"

"No. It's the same message every time along with a phone number."

"Well, maybe you should respond or block him—whichever one works for you."

Since she now knew he was no longer employed by *Secure Pull,* she didn't have to worry about the ramification of blocking him. So, with a few clicks of the mouse, Alyssa did just that. Although part of her wanted to know what had him so eager to speak to her, she followed her instinct. It told her nothing good could come from entertaining Ballard Grimes.

"I don't see a reason to speak to him, so I blocked the email address." Clicking around on the screen she went back to shutting everything down. "If you don't mind me asking, why was Ballard let go?"

Technically, she knew Harrison wasn't supposed to tell her about personnel decisions. She asked on the off chance he didn't care about the policy in this case.

"You know how it is around here. Clients get to meet the engineers working on their projects. They request certain people—like what happens with you a lot."

Alyssa ignored the pride in Harrison's voice when he mentioned how often she was requested by clients. This wasn't the time for him to try to butter her up to take on more work. However, he apparently didn't want to let the opportunity pass.

"Anyway, with Ballard, something happened that I haven't seen the entire time I've been with the company. We had clients call and ask that he be removed from their projects.

When I tried to assign him to others, the same thing happened. Once the client learned he was on the team, they asked for him to be removed. We couldn't keep him on if clients refused to work with him."

"Wow...I've never heard of that either." Alyssa wanted to ask if Ballard was that inept, but she felt she'd pushed enough. Anything more would be gossip. So, she wouldn't ask. However, if Harrison volunteered the information, she wouldn't stop him from sharing.

"It was the oddest thing. Now he didn't perform your level of work, but he wasn't completely incompetent. I wouldn't have kept him in my department if he was. All I can think of is that he pissed off the wrong client. Quiet as it's kept, the gaming community is small. If he got on the wrong person's bad side, there's not much I can do to help him in this industry."

"Does he think I can?"

"I have no idea."

Alyssa waved her hand despite knowing Harrison couldn't see her. "Oh, sorry. That was rhetorical. I didn't mean to say it out loud."

"No problem."

Alyssa heard Carver's voice as he ascended the stairs. He hadn't said her name, so she assumed he was talking on the phone as well. She wrapped her up call with Harrison, just as Carver stopped in front of the open door to her office. He held a duffle in his hand, and she saw the white tip of his earbud poking from his ear. With a smile on his face, he dropped the bag and entered the room.

"Ok. I'll call you tomorrow morning and we can discuss the details." He walked around the front of her desk and placed a kiss on her cheek. "Hey, Baby."

Standing up straight, a frown creased his brow. "What? Why the hell would I call you baby? What is it you like to say to me? Get off my phone with that bullshit. I'm talking to my woman."

There were a few beats of silence before he spoke again. "I'm not telling my woman that shit. I'll tell her you said hello like a civilized human being. By the way, I'm gonna kick your ass the next time I see you."

Tapping the bud in his ear, Carver ended the call. Swiveling her chair, Alyssa watched him and waited. Once he removed the earbud and pulled out his case, she spoke.

"Hey, Babe. Are you not going to tell me what Denzel said?"

Grinning, Carver tangled his fingers in hers tugging gently until she stood in front of him.

"Like I told him, I'm not telling you that. He said, hello—among other things."

"And I don't get to know what those other things were?"

"No."

Stepping closer, she dragged her fingers across his chest. "You're really not going to tell me?"

"No. But I will tell you something else." Sliding his arms around her, he rested his hands at the small of her back with his fingertips grazing her ass.

"What's that?"

"According to Den, I should be getting a call from Tech soon..."

Alyssa was certain Carver's pause was for dramatic effect. Tapping his chest, she cocked one eyebrow at him. "And...? What else?"

"They're inducting a new class into the T-Club and the University Hall of Fame. His source said both he and I are on the short list."

Alyssa's jaw dropped for the second time for an entirely different reason. "That's awesome, Babe! Congratulations! It took them long enough. You should've been inducted years ago."

"Everything happens when it's supposed to. But, I appreciate your vote of confidence." Pilfering another kiss, he hugged her to his chest.

"Anyway, if it's true, I should get a call within the week. They typically hold the induction during homecoming."

"I remember. I'll make sure my schedule is clear for the last week in September."

"Bit, baby, I love how sure you are that it's a done deal."

"You should be sure as well. You're Carver freaking Jamieson. Like I said, it should've happened long before now. You were eligible five years ago. If anything, I'm a little pissed at the way they dragged their feet."

Alyssa punctuated her statement with a tap to his right shoulder. She didn't miss the slight wince that followed her action.

"Hey...What's wrong? Why did you wince like I hurt you?"

Grinning bashfully, Carver tipped his head to the side. "Well...What had happened was..."

"Carver. Wyatt. Jamieson. Don't play with me. What's wrong with your shoulder?"

"I may have strained it a little at practice today."

Shrewdly assessing his expression, Alyssa now saw the tension hovering at the edge of his eyes.

"Carver, you're a coach. How does a coach get injured at practice? Did someone tackle you by mistake?"

Backing up to the chaise lounge, he pulled her to sit on his lap. Initially she resisted, but he gave her *that look* and she reluctantly perched on his thigh. Glancing at her from the corner of his eye, he arranged her the way he wanted her before speaking again.

Alyssa raised her eyebrow again at his grimace when he moved his right shoulder. He caught the look and gave her a slight smile. Then, he went into how he'd thrown over two hundred passes working out with one of the quarterbacks.

"Carver! What were you thinking?"

"I was thinking, some people can't learn by tellin'. You have to show 'em."

"Yeah, but—"

"I would be fine if I hadn't forgotten to stretch beforehand. Besides, it's nothin' a little heat treatment, icing and a rubdown won't cure." When he said rubdown, he lowered his head giving her a puppy dog stare.

"I know what that look is about." She playfully swatted at him, giggling at his shamelessness. When her laughter tapered off, she cupped the sides of his face.

"Babe, I know you're all, Captain America and Superman, in your heart. But in the real world, you're a retired quarterback. Emphasis on the *retired*. If you want to get in reps with the kids, you can't start with so many straight out of the gate. It's been a long time since you put in work like that. Your body needs to build up to it. If that's what you want to do that is."

"I get what you're saying; but, Bit baby, this kid is really talented. He just hasn't been properly coached. If I didn't do something to get through to him, I'd have to cut him. That would be a huge blow to his career and an even bigger loss for our team."

"He's that good?"

"Better."

"Do you think what you did today made a difference?"

"I believe it did. Only time will tell."

Pecking his lips, Alyssa beamed at him. "I love how you try to bring out the best in those around you."

Returning the kiss, he smiled. "Thank you, Baby. I simply do what I can."

Patting his cheek, she gave him another parting kiss. "Come on. Let's get you into a hot shower and I'll put the gel packs in the freezer for later."

Carver's face lit up. "Does this mean I get a rubdown?"

Standing, she grasped his left hand, pulling him to his feet. "If you play your cards right, I'll do more than just your shoulder."

Giving him a saucy wink, she walked out of the office flicking off the light switch along the way. Parting with Carver on the landing, she went to get the gel packs to ice his shoulder while he went to their bedroom to shower.

Deciding it was counterproductive to join him in the shower, Alyssa went about prepping the bedroom for Carver's massage. As she grabbed the oil and lotion she liked, her mind drifted back to the last time she'd tended to him and his over-worked throwing arm. They were in college, and she was still relatively naive about many things.

Then, she'd been nervous to perform such an intimate task for her friend's boyfriend. However, she'd reminded herself that people paid strangers to massage them all the time. It was no different. Except it was. She wasn't getting paid and being so close to Carver did funny things to her insides. Things that made her feel disloyal to her friend. She didn't like it.

It was different now. Shaking off the memory of her loyalty to a person who'd never given her the same, she turned down the duvet and sheets. Spreading out two of the overly large bath sheets, she was happy she'd insisted on getting them even though they hadn't used them up to now.

"Now, how do you expect me to not think of things other than my aching shoulder when I walk out to a view like this?"

Looking over her shoulder, Alyssa raised up from her position leaning over the bed. She knew her ass had been turned up offering him a perfect view of her ample backside when he entered the room. It hadn't been her intention to put on a show for him. Placing her hands on her hips, she shot him a warning look.

"Don't start none, won't be none." Carver simply laughed at her warning. Whipping the towel from his hips he strode toward her.

"Excuse me, Sir. There is no reason for you to be completely naked."

"Keep callin' me, sir, and we're gonna skip the massage."

"Oh really? And do what when every time you shift your right flank you grimace?"

When he reached her side, he displaced her hands with his hands on her hips and erased the remaining distance between them. "We both know the use of my shoulder isn't required for you to take this dick."

Ignoring the tingling his words and proximity induced, Alyssa pushed back from him. "Please lie down. I know you're in pain. Let's take care of that first."

"Wait!" Stopping him before he climbed onto the bed, she passed him a water bottle and the two ibuprofen she'd grabbed when she put the gel packs in the freezer. "Take these."

Without argument, Carver tossed the pills back and chugged the water. Once he was done, he stretched out on the towels she'd spread across the bed. Scooping up her supplies she crawled onto the bed next to him, resting on her knees. Opening the massage oil, she poured a little into her palm and rubbed her hands together.

Although she was no longer a timid twenty-year-old and they were in a full-blown relationship, Alyssa's stomach still flipped when touching Carver's heated skin. Her eyes raked over the colorful tattoos on his arm before she forced herself to focus on the task at hand.

Carver's vivid green eyes stared at her watchfully as she gently ran her fingers across the top his shoulder, then down to the blade and along his side, testing to see where he was most tender. Part of her wished he'd turn his head away as he'd done all of those years ago, but the other part got a bit of a thrill from the possessive way he looked at her.

Heat crept up her neck and she felt herself losing the battle to keep things PG under the weight of his sultry gaze. His guttural moan when she massaged a particularly sensitive spot would've made her flood her panties, if she was wearing any. Most days, unless she knew she was leaving the house, she went commando.

Thankfully, he closed his eyes while he tortured her with his noises of appreciation. After a few minutes of his moans and her sharp inhales, he lifted his eyelids piercing her with a heated stare.

"If you don't want me to fuck you right now, I suggest you talk to me about something to take my mind off of how hard my cock is."

"Carver!"

"What? You know I'm right."

"Your mouth is reckless and if you don't want to be so stiff you can't move tomorrow, I suggest you figure out a way to get your mind off of your nether regions."

His stare intensified before he shifted his gaze to just over her shoulder. "Fine. Who were you on the phone with when I got home?"

His question surprised Alyssa. He rarely asked her about her phone calls unless he heard his name.

"It was my manager. Harrison."

"Oh. So, work stuff."

"Kinda, but not really."

"What does that mean?"

"It means, I thought it was work stuff, but it turned out not to be that way."

"Ok, so what was it?"

Alyssa shifted under Carver's penetrating stare. She hadn't told him about Ballard's attempts to contact her. Knowing how overprotective he was, she didn't want to cause any unnecessary issues. It was easiest just to ignore Ballard. She figured he'd eventually get the message and stop. She guessed wrong.

Releasing a pent-up breath, she bit the bullet. "I called Harrison to ask him why Ballard would need to talk to me."

Carver's muscles tensed beneath her hands. "Ballard? As in that little shit that brought the paps down on you at a Mexican restaurant?"

"Yes..." Drawing the word out reluctantly, Alyssa stopped the motion of her fingers.

Turning to his side, Carver sat up to face her. "Did he call you or something?"

Reaching out a hand, Alyssa tried to calm the explosion before it built. "No. No calls. He sent emails asking me to call him. I never did."

"How many?"

"I don't know."

"Bit..."

"I didn't count. It's been on and off since I started working from home. It was enough that I called Harrison to see what's going on. That's when he told me that Ballard was fired two months ago."

"You've been working from home for almost five months, Bit. When were you going to tell me about it?"

Silence stretched between them. Alyssa wouldn't lie to him, but she couldn't bring herself to tell him the truth. She didn't have to. He read her silence correctly.

"You weren't going to tell me; were you?"

"There was no reason to, Carver. He was a co-worker who sent a few messages. It was no big deal. Nothing to tell you about, since I didn't actually speak to him or respond to his messages."

"The fuck!"

Initially, Alyssa jumped at the volume of his voice. Then, she squared her shoulders and looked him in the eyes—almost daring him to yell at her again.

Raking a hand over his almost buzzed hair, Carver took a deep breath. "Alyssa...someone contacting you a few times and stopping when you don't reply is no big deal. This was more than a few times. That's some stalker shit and you should've told me about it."

Alyssa felt like he'd slapped her in the face when she heard her given name fall from his lips in that tone. She literally rocked her head back on her shoulders. *That shit hurt.* He rarely called her anything other than Bit, Baby or some other sweet nickname.

When she started to respond, he held up his hand to stop her. "No. Don't make excuses. Yes, you have a detail and working from home affords you even more security, but it's my job to protect you. How can I do that if you keep things like this from me?"

"Because I didn't want you to overreact. Like you're doing right now. Ballard is a nuisance, but he's not a physical threat to me."

"How can you say that when he didn't give two shits about telling a hoard of strangers your location? The only way you were able to leave that restaurant unharmed was because of the guy who came out to help you."

Alyssa hadn't forgotten about that day, but she knew it wasn't in her best interest to point out that, technically, Ballard hadn't given her location to a media hoard. He'd told an attention hungry gossip girl. She'd told the paps. Alyssa knew pointing out that discrepancy would hurt more than it helped. Instead, she took a different tact.

"I apologize. I really didn't think it was anything to worry about. Once Harrison told me he no longer worked at *Secure Pull*, I blocked him."

Carver simply stared at her and shook his head.

"What?"

"I thought we'd moved past you shutting me out."

Finally noticing the hurt in his eyes instead of the angry set of his jaw, Alyssa reached out to touch him. When he pulled away and climbed from the bed, she dropped her hand in her lap.

"Where are you going?" She was uncertain if he'd answer, but she asked anyway.

Stopping in the doorway, he turned to look at her. "Did you just hear anything I said? Ballard Grimes is a threat, Bit. The team needs to be aware. We need to know what the fuck he's been doing and why the hell he thought it was okay to keep trying to contact you when it was obvious you didn't want to speak to him. I'm gonna put some clothes on and go down to the office to talk to Samira and the guys. Then, I'm gonna call Jasper."

Clamping her lips shut, Alyssa watched his back as Carver disappeared into the bathroom presumably on the way to his closet to put on the clothes he'd mentioned. She couldn't really say anything. It was clear she'd royally screwed this whole thing up. Now, she wished she'd said something the first time Samira had to tell Ballard to go away.

Chapter Twenty-Nine
GET YOUR ASS UPSTAIRS

Carver was fucking livid. It was hard to believe that less than five minutes ago, he'd been about to flip over and put his hard cock to use. Now, it wagged flaccid in the wind as he stalked into his closet to tug on pants and a t-shirt.

He knew his woman was independent and prized being able to handle things on her own. However, Carver really thought they'd moved past her keeping things from him because she thought they didn't matter. Knocking back the voice of reason telling him he'd essentially done and continued to do the same thing, he slipped his feet into a pair of trainers without putting on socks.

When he exited the bathroom, Alyssa was no longer sitting on the bed. She stood beside it with a bundle of towels in her arms. Ignoring her pleading expression, he walked out. Carver knew he couldn't look at her too long or he'd fold. He'd never been able to see her with sadness in her eyes and not try to fix it. They'd talk it out eventually, but he couldn't do it at the moment.

When he entered the security office near the back of the house, it appeared they were in a meeting of their own. Samira sat at the desk directly below the monitors while Michael and Kai occupied two seats at the small conference table.

"Am I interrupting?" Carver asked as he closed the door behind him.

"No. We're just doing a quick recap and pass on."

Carver expected that Michael would've left already. He'd been with him all day which far exceeded an eight-hour shift since Carver's day started at seven a.m. It was after five p.m.

"Anything I need to know about?"

Samira swiveled her chair to fully face him as he took a seat at the table opposite Kai. "Nothing unusual. There was a pap trying to use one of the trees along the street to get a peek onto the property. We took care of it. Now, we're discussing how to prevent it going forward.

Although it's technically a public sidewalk, this is a gated community. So, we'll need to get with the HOA and the security at the main gate to see how they made it inside in the first place."

Despite knowing paparazzi would attempt to invade their privacy, it irritated Carver to hear there were still people looking to use them for a quick payday. For the most part, he and Alyssa led very uneventful lives. It was hard to understand the fascination, even though he'd spent years in the limelight.

"Ok. Let me know if they get more aggressive. In the meantime, I have a different situation for you to be aware of and keep an eye out for."

Carver allowed his gaze to drift around the room so it was obvious he wasn't only speaking to Samira.

"I just spoke to Alyssa and she told me a guy named Ballard Grimes has been trying to contact her. He worked for the same company until he was let go a couple of months ago."

Michael sat up straighter in his seat while Kai flipped open a notepad and began writing.

"Did she say why?" Kai's pen was poised to write Carver's answer in his little notebook.

"She said she didn't know why, but I have a feeling I do." As much as he didn't want to do it, Carver knew he'd have to give them some details. Forewarned is forearmed.

Samira sat forward with her elbows on the arms of her chair. "Wait. That name is familiar..." She tapped her electronic notebook a few times then nodded. "I knew it was familiar. When Miss Ripley was still working at the *Secure Pull* headquarters, he stopped by her office one afternoon. When I asked her if it was okay to let him in, she told me to tell him she was busy. So, I turned him away."

Heat licked up the sides of Carver's neck. Trying to keep his anger in check, he modulated his voice when spoke. "You didn't think that was worth reporting?"

"At the time, no. It was how things were when she was in the office. Sometimes, she would allow people in, others she'd tell me she was too busy to see them. Looking at the date on this one, it was her last day officially working in the office.

He hadn't tried before then, and I guess since she didn't come back, he moved on to other ways of making contact. I don't have access to her electronic correspondence, so there was no way for us to know he'd continued."

Michael interjected when Samira finished her explanation. "Carver, are you saying this guy is a physical threat to her?"

They'd long ago dispensed with formality in their relationship; so, Michael calling him by his first name didn't faze Carver.

"I'm saying he could be if he gets desperate enough. Him losing his job wasn't a coincidence."

Carver sat back in his seat tapping the table with his forefinger. Pointing between Kai and Samira, he continued. "You two weren't on the team yet, but Michael remembers the day Alyssa was bombarded with paps outside of a restaurant while she was on her lunch break.

Ballard Grimes was the reason why. When the video of me and Alyssa went viral, he saw it as an opportunity. He followed her to lunch and let a reporter know her location. The rest I'm sure you're aware of."

"So, the company fired him for that?" Kai looked confused, but Samira and Michael's faces wore the same knowing expression.

"No. They fired him because none of their clients wanted to work with him."

"And I'm sure you had nothing to do with that, right?" Michael leaned back in his seat shaking his head. Carver didn't need his judgement. He needed him to help protect Alyssa from a potential threat.

"Whether I did or didn't isn't the issue. I need to know what he's up to. She's blocked him from contacting her. As soon as he realizes that, I'm sure he'll try other methods. Alyssa thinks he's harmless. I want to be certain he can't cause harm."

They spent some time going over possibilities and discussing contacts for getting more information. Once they were done, Carver thanked them and rose to leave the room. Michael stood to follow him out.

They met up with Blake in the doorway. Although surprised to see him, Carver didn't comment. Their disclosure of the pap in the tree meant they'd have to be more diligent during the night. He fully expected the reason Remi wasn't around was because he'd join Blake at some point for a night shift.

Veering from his normal path off the property, Michael walked with Carver through the house. He didn't allow the silence to linger long.

"We don't have the kind of relationship where you have to tell me what you did to make that man lose his job, but can you tell me I'm wrong in my assessment?"

Looking around, Carver insured their conversation was still private before he answered.

"You're not wrong, but his response to it is proving my gut instinct right. Normal people take the 'L' and move on. What he's doing is obsessive behavior."

At Michael's look, Carver almost said 'Fuck you' out loud, but managed to catch himself. He didn't need anyone to tell him he was obsessive and possessive when it came to Alyssa. It wasn't normal and he didn't care. Anyone who harmed her had to suffer consequences.

"We aren't talking about me."

"I didn't say anything."

"You didn't have to."

Once they reached the foyer, Michael continued to the right in the direction of the garage, while Carver continued on to the kitchen. His steps faltered when he saw Alyssa standing next to the sink washing her hands. *Had she heard their conversation?*

He couldn't tell if her stiff posture was due to overhearing or the way he'd stormed out on her earlier. His temper remained on a low boil regarding the whole thing—especially after finding out Ballard had attempted to get to her in the office. The more he thought about that, the harder it became for him to remain silent.

"Bit, when were you going to tell me Ballard tried to get to you at work?"

Turning toward him as she toweled her hands dry, Alyssa's brow furrowed. "What?"

Taking a few steps to close the distance between them, he searched her face.

"I just finished talking to the team. Samira said Ballard tried to get her to let him in to see you while you were still working in the office. Why didn't you tell me?"

Huffing, Alyssa dropped the towel onto the countertop and walked past him to the refrigerator.

"Carver, I'm not going to keep doing this. I didn't say anything because there was nothing to tell. He stopped by. I was too busy to see him. So, I told Samira I didn't have time."

Opening one of the doors, she looked at him over her shoulder. "You seriously expect me to tell you every time a coworker stops by my office?"

His logical mind, knew the correct answer to her question was 'no', but logic wasn't his strong suit at the moment.

"If it means some creep doesn't get a chance to stalk you, then yes."

Closing the door forcefully, Alyssa folded her arms across her chest. Her glare should've burned the shirt from his back it had so much heat in it.

"Do you hear yourself? My work environment is ninety-percent male. It doesn't make sense to tell you every time one of them stops by or is denied a meeting request because I'm too busy.

Besides, since I don't go into the office anymore, this discussion is moot. Everything we're talking about happened in the past. It can't be undone. I can't go back in time and change it."

Walking toward her, Carver didn't stop until her back was pressed into the refrigerator and their fronts had less than an inch of space between them. The set of her jaw was stubborn, but there was a hint of uncertainty in her eyes.

"Tell me somethin', Bit. Do you need one of them to sell a fake story to a tabloid or put you in a position where you feel unsafe for you to get it? If you're workin' on a team with someone, I expect you to have contact with them in meetings and what not. But, if y'all ain't on a team together and they keep tryin' to meet with you, that's a problem. That's the shit I need to know about."

Stroking her cheek with the back of one finger, he stared into her face. Understanding shown in the depths of her dark amber gaze. When her fingertips skimmed his sides, he dropped his forehead to hers narrowing their vision to only see directly into the other's eyes.

"You're used to takin' care of yourself, Baby. I get that. But, I'm used to this life of people bein' backstabbin' shit heads who'll do anything for a buck. You can't assume *anyone* is harmless."

Her voice was so low when she spoke, if he hadn't been all in her personal space, he wouldn't have heard it.

"Okay."

"Okay what, Baby?" Capturing her face between his hands, he compelled her to meet his gaze.

"If someone who normally doesn't speak to me tries to make contact, I'll tell you about it."

"Don't just tell me what I wanna hear."

"I'm not." Lifting on her tiptoes, her lips brushed his. "I apologize. I truly didn't think it mattered."

"Bit, baby. You really have no idea the hell I would reign down on any motherfucker who tried to hurt you do you?"

Her gasp made him realize he'd fisted two hands full of her thick hair. Loosening his grip, he pecked her plush lips in apology.

"You are so intense..." Alyssa's expression told him her statement wasn't an insult, but an awe filled observation.

"When it comes to you, there are no limits. Don't expect anything less than one hundred percent of me."

"Is that so?..."

Her fingers floated down his sides, then latched onto the waistband of his loose-fitting pants. The mercurial change in her expression to one of desire was swift, but Carver stayed ready for his woman. Clasping her hands before she could slide the elastic over his hips, he halted her movements.

"Uh-uh...Not so fast. You don't get a reward for keepin' secrets."

"But, Carver..."

Not giving in to Alyssa's whine, he whipped her around and lifted her onto the island. Ignoring the twinge of pain from his shoulder, he wedged his hips between her legs. The countertop was at the perfect height.

Capturing her lips in a blistering kiss, he poured all of his feelings into it. Trailing lingering pecks along her jawline he moved until he reached the crook of her neck where he nipped the sensitive skin. Her short nails scraped the back of his head as he moved lower, tugging at the V-neck of her top.

It was so loose it gave way easily, slipping off her shoulder giving him access to the rounded globe of her breast. Taking her nipple between his teeth, he bit down until she hissed. Then, he laved and sucked the turgid peak to sooth it.

Her heavy breathing and the way she clasped his head conveyed her pleasure far more eloquently than words. Whipping off her shirt and discarding her bra, he reacquainted himself with the twin mounds of pleasure. Alyssa's gasps and moans of enjoyment egged him on, but they weren't enough.

Nudging her hips, he wordlessly encouraged her to lift them. Quickly ridding her of the rest of her clothes, he dropped to his knees placing his face eye level with her pussy. With no preamble, he seized her nether lips in an erotic kiss. Only his hands on her thighs kept her from smothering him with their pillowy softness.

"Oh shit! Carver!"

Galvanized by her exclamation, Carver used his tongue and fingers to bring her to the edge of an orgasm. When he felt her walls tighten around his digits, he pulled them free and stood up. Alyssa's face wore the prettiest pout, but he simply grinned.

"Why did you stop?"

"You didn't think it would be that easy, did you Baby?"

Eyes at half mast, she reached for him. "Don't be like that. I was so close."

"I know."

A lopsided grin stretched across his face as he watched her squirm to get closer to him. Gliding his fingers up her leg, he slipped two digits into her warm sheath. Her sharp inhale at his exploration fed his desire to both please and punish her.

Nimble fingers grasped at his shirt. He didn't stop her as she lifted it higher. When she'd pushed it as far as she could go, he even raised his arms to help in her quest to get him just as naked as she was. He indulged her as she pushed at the waistband of his pants once more.

This time, instead of stopping her, he allowed her to move them down far enough to release his steely shaft. When her palm touched his length, his eyelids slammed shut. Taking a deep breath, he reminded himself of his goal. Tracing his lips down the column of her neck, he worked his fingers in her welcoming channel.

It wasn't long before her grasp on his cock tightened in conjunction with her pussy clamping down on his plundering digits. She was teetering on the edge, so he stopped cold and pulled away.

"No, no, no, no..." Alyssa's eyes misted in frustration.

"I told you it wouldn't be that easy, Baby."

Her face pinched in the cutest little aggravated pout. Kissing the tip of her nose, he plucked her from the countertop. He'd changed his mind about torturing her in the kitchen. It wasn't because of the security team. He didn't fear them walking in on anything. Carver wanted her spread out for him to deliver his punishment effectively.

"Get your ass upstairs."

Leaving their clothes where they landed, Carver followed Alyssa's swaying hips all the way to their bedroom. Once inside, he ushered her onto the bed. The sheets and duvet were still pulled down from earlier, so he didn't have to bother stripping them off.

As Alyssa lie on her back, Carver crawled up her body, placing kisses and touches as he went. Despite her pouting earlier, she didn't complain about him building her desire again. It didn't take much for him to bring her right back to the brink. This time, instead of pulling away, he pushed his entire length inside her velvet walls and held still.

"Why are you doing this to me?" Her moaning words dripped with distress.

"Because, Baby." Bracketing her head with his forearms, Carver pecked her pursed lips. "I'm feelin' some kinda way about you not lettin' me fully take care of you."

When she attempted to wiggle her hips beneath him, he dropped more of his body weight, pinning her beneath him.

"Uh-uh, Bit baby. Stop that. You don't get to fuck me and take your orgasm. You come when I say."

"Carver..."

Alyssa's nails scraped his skin as she held on to his flank. Her thighs were spread to accommodate him in the cradle of her legs. Carver slowly withdrew until only the tip of his shaft remained inside her clinging channel.

"I need you to answer a couple of questions for me baby."

"Why...?" Her fingers gripped his sides as she undulated her hips in an attempt to pull him back inside.

"Cuz, baby. You keep forgettin' and I gotta remind you." With a quick thrust, he embedded his length into her hungry sheath drawing a startled gasp from her lips.

"Now. Open your eyes and look at me."

Dark amber, lust glazed, pools were revealed when she lifted her eyelids. Withdrawing from her depths again, he stopped before leaving her sweet pussy completely.

"Who takes care of you, Baby? Hm? Who protects you, provides for you and gives you what you need? Hm?"

Carver's last question was punctuated with a brutal thrust bringing him balls deep inside Alyssa's honeyed walls. Her slickness coated his shaft. The feel of her pussy pulsing around his cock almost took him over the edge.

"Answer me!" His guttural command was issued as he tilted his pelvis to stimulate her clit.

Alyssa's response came out in a strangled moan. "You do."

"Who?"

"You do, Carver."

Unable to torture her or himself any longer, Carver sat up on his knees and pressed her thighs to her chest. Giving no mercy, he worked his hips until her body quaked beneath him. The suctioning grasp of her canal was his undoing. Releasing his seed, he followed her over the edge into bliss. His harsh breath and groans joined with hers as they climaxed together.

Spent, Carver lowered Alyssa's legs and leaned over her prone body placing soft kisses on her torso all the way up to her closed eyelids. When she graced him with a soft smile, he buried his head in the crook of her neck.

"I love you so fucking much."

"I love you too, Carver."

Alyssa's soft palms stroked over the planes of his back as they came down from their high. Carver knew he needed to come clean. Not only about Ballard. But about some of the other things he'd been up to. Just as he had an intuition regarding Ballard, his gut was telling him he couldn't keep Alyssa in the dark much longer.

Chapter Thirty

GROWN PEOPLE SHIT

"Thank you Ms Munoz."

Alyssa closed the lid on the thermal mug and exited the kitchen. Although she and her staff only came in a few days a week, whenever Xinia Munoz was in the house, she made certain Alyssa had a good breakfast and left with a steaming cup of tea.

She assured Alyssa the blend aided in digestion. Since Alyssa wasn't knowledgeable on that subject, she took Ms Munoz's word for it. Everyone working in any capacity on the property had been thoroughly vetted. So, Alyssa wasn't worried the woman was secretly trying to poison her. Even the thought of it seemed surreal. So, Alyssa didn't dwell on it.

Entering her office, she left the door open and sat at her desk to get her day started. Before the computer screen came completely to life, her cellphone rang. Zaria's smiling face was lit up on the display. Putting an earbud in her right ear, Alyssa answered.

"Good Morning, Zee."

"Gurl!..."

Pausing with the mug half way to her lips, Alyssa waited for Zee to continue. When she didn't, Alyssa prompted her. "What? You can't start a conversation like that and not follow up with the tea!"

"My bad. I had to send this message real quick and get these folks to leave me alone for a hot ten minutes."

Her reply indicated that she was at work. Being the senior partner at her own law firm meant someone was always pulling on her for her time.

"Okay, so gurl! You know I went out with a couple of the ladies from my Black Lady Lawyer group last night right?"

Alyssa didn't bother to correct Zee regarding the way she referenced the chapter of the African American Women Association for Nevada attorneys to which she belonged. Zee was gonna Zee. All day every day.

"Right."

"So, one of the ladies is pregnant and the only thing her baby likes are milkshakes. No biggie. Baby wants a milkshake. Baby gets a milkshake. We're driving past the *Epe* and see the *Steak and Shake*, so we pull in. Guess who I see working the valet stand at the hotel?"

Zaria pauses for what Alyssa is sure is dramatic effect. Knowing she won't be rushed, Alyssa waits for Zaria to continue. It had to be juicy for the theatrics her friend was putting on.

"You're not gonna guess?"

"No. You called to tell me. I have no idea who you saw."

"You're no fun."

"Ma'am. Get to the point."

"I saw your old boo thang."

Alyssa frowned. She didn't have an old boo thang. At least not in Vegas.

"Huh? Who?"

"Damn...you forgot about him already?" Zaria released a cackling laugh. "That's cold, Lyss. That's really cold."

That's when it dawned on Alyssa who Zaria was talking about. "You mean Torrence?"

"Don't be tryin' not to claim your old flame."

"Stop playing, and stay on topic, Zee. You're telling me Torrence was working the valet stand at the *Epe*? Torrence Phillips?"

"One in the same. With his little valet vest, name tag and everything."

"Wow...I guess times got hard and he picked up a second job."

Alyssa heard tapping and knew Zaria was rapping her finger on her desk. "See. That's what I thought. But you know I'm nosey. So, I had a little look see. Nichols, Gardner and Hack released him back in the spring."

Alyssa sat up straight and whisper-screamed, "What?!"

"Yes, ma'am. According to my source, he was let go and he hasn't been able to land or maintain a position with any other firm locally. He tried to go out on his own, but he didn't have the capital to get started."

"Hmph." Thinking of all the times Torrence bragged about his financial status, Alyssa couldn't feel sympathy for his lies catching up to him. "I wonder what happened?"

Zaria huffed. "Girl, I wish I knew. Whatever happened, those bean counters are keeping it close to the vest."

Settling back into her chair, Alyssa began moving her mouse around to open up programs and get started with her work.

"That's wild. I guess some of the values his parents instilled in him stuck though. He has a job—even if it's not in his field."

"That's true. But damn. To go from working at one of the premier accounting firms in the city to parking people's cars at an off the strip casino is a steep decline. I could understand if he was working at Anton's or one of the other luxury spots. Those valets probably bring in close to six figures. Easy."

"You're right there. We had an intern who worked as a valet part time while he was getting his degree. When he got an offer to valet at Anton's he seriously considered not finishing school."

"Completely understandable."

While they moved on to general chit-chat, Alyssa opened programs. When she clicked on the email icon, she remembered she hadn't had a chance to talk to Zaria about the whole Ballard incident.

"Since we're spilling tea, guess what I found out yesterday?"

"What?"

"Ballard got fired from *Secure Pull.*"

"Turtle face Ballard?"

A giggle burst from Alyssa's lips at the highly accurate reference to her former co-worker. Still, she tried to take the high road.

"Girl stop!"

"You stop. You know he looks like a pale-skinned blond topped turtle."

"I do, but that's not nice."

"Nice, smice. Why did they show him the door?"

"Confidentially, clients were refusing to work with him. I didn't get the lowdown on why. He wasn't the greatest, but as far as I was aware, he could write efficient code."

Picking up a pen, Alyssa twirled it between her fingers to keep her hands busy without tapping away at the keyboard.

"And how did you come across this information? You aren't in the office every day for Miss Barbara to keep you up to date on all the gossip."

"I called Harrison to find out what Ballard could possibly need to talk to me about for him to keep sending me emails. When I asked, he told me Ballard was let go two months ago."

"Wait a minute. Back up. Ballard was sending you emails?"

"Yes."

"How many and for how long? Why wouldn't you just respond instead of going to Harrison?"

Alyssa didn't appreciate the whiff of accusation she heard in Zee's voice.

"I don't know how many. It's been on and off since I started working at home."

"What?!"

Alyssa squinted against the volume of Zee's exclamation. "Why are you yelling? We worked at the same place, but never on the same team. Him wanting to speak to me wasn't high on my list of to-do—especially after what happened at the restaurant."

Alyssa heard Zaria mumbling, but couldn't quite make out what she said. Their conversation seemed to be taking a turn. So, she didn't press for her friend to speak up.

"Have you told Carver about this?"

"Yes."

"What did he have to say?" Inhaling deeply, Alyssa released the pent-up breath slowly. "He was pissed that I hadn't mentioned it until after I spoke with Harrison."

"He had every right to be pissed."

While she didn't expect Zaria to co-sign everything she did, Alyssa wasn't prepared for her immediate agreement with Carver's reaction.

"You know what, Alyssa? A hard head makes a soft ass."

Tossing the pen on the desk, Alyssa flopped her hand as if Zaria could see the movement.

"Zee, I don't need a lecture from you too. Carver already lit into me because he didn't think I took it seriously enough. I've known Ballard for years. why would I think that he was a threat to me?"

"I'm gonna need you to stop right there. Don't try to brush this shit off like it's normal. I know you, Alyssa. You have a habit of avoiding things when you think it's going to be uncomfortable.

You could've answered that man's message a long time ago and found out what he wanted. Instead, you let that shit go on for months. **Months.** Now he's going to be big mad, like Super mad. Especially since he lost his damn job."

After a beat of silence, that Alyssa didn't try to fill, Zaria spoke again. "I'd bet five year's salary Carver had something to do with that shit. Ballard and Torrence."

Alyssa frowned at Zaria's assertion. "What? No. How would Carver have anything to do with them? Cursing them out maybe, but come on."

"Oh, so now you're blind too? Listen, even though he's been in the spotlight, I had him investigated just like I did Torrence's scrub ass. Do you have any idea the kind of bank your man is sitting on? If he wants shit to happen it can happen. He didn't just sit on his ass during the off season. He made his money work for him.

That man has his hands in all kinds of shit. Y'all need to talk more. I mean I know his dick may be magical or something. But, have some conversations, because you're missing stuff."

Folding her arms across her chest Alyssa's eyebrows dipped. "I'm not sticking my nose into Carver's finances. It's too soon for all of that.

Not to mention, I haven't told him anything about the money I've made developing apps on the side. I'm not going to be a hypocrite and ask him for something I'm not giving.

"First, you're welcome again for me negotiating that bomb ass contract with *Secure Pull* so you could maintain the rights to your own shit. Second, you **LIVE** with the damn man.

Talking about finances is some grown people shit that you're supposed to do. Girl...I love you, but you're getting on my nerves. You're too smart to be this damn oblivious."

"Oblivious to what? You're accusing my man of purposely causing people to lose their livelihoods. Is Carver protective? Yes. Would he stomp a mudhole in someone who hurt me? Also, yes. But, come on, Zee."

"Me come on? You come on. You just said it yourself. Carver is protective. He's gone out of his way on more than one occasion to show you that he can protect and provide for you.

Do you really think he'd allow Ballard and Torrence to fuck with you or put you in danger with zero consequences? Get your head out of the sand, lady. The more I think about it, the more I'm positive he's behind it."

Alyssa wanted to continue to dispute what Zee was saying, but her friend was right. She was much too smart to be so oblivious. As much as she didn't want to jump to conclusions, she mentally started putting things together.

She'd brushed off the way the guys from that awful group chat tried to talk to her in the following weeks as them just trying to kiss up after Harrison got on their asses. Now, after learning of Torrence's and Ballard's situation, Alyssa had to consider that they were attempting to do the same thing Ballard was probably trying to do.

Whether that was make amends to stop the ruining of their careers or sincerely apologize, she couldn't say. What was clearer was that there was too much for it to simply be a coincidence. A quick search of the company directory showed that two of the guys from the chat group were no longer listed as employees.

She sincerely tried not to read too much into what she'd learned. However, Alyssa knew she wouldn't be able to concentrate on writing code, so she shot off a quick email to Harrison letting him know she was taking the day off. After which she wrapped up her call with Zaria. Seemingly content that Alyssa's eyes were wide open, Zaria said her goodbyes.

Alyssa would never go so far as to dig into Carver's personal things, but she could educate herself with information which was publicly available. So, for the next few hours, she followed the links she'd ignored over the years when she'd come across opportunities to keep up with Carver's life on and off the field.

~

Long after Ms Munoz and her staff had left for the day, Alyssa was on the sofa in the rarely used sitting room staring blankly at the television. If asked, she wouldn't be able to describe one scene of the show she appeared to watch. It was Carver's late day, so the sun was sitting lower in the sky when she heard his footfalls in the foyer.

Ten minutes later, she felt his presence when he entered the room.

"There you are. I was looking for you, Baby."

"I've been sitting right here."

Alyssa didn't look away from the television nor did she lift her face to him as she normally would to accept his kiss. Usually, if she was looking at TV when he came home, Carver would lean over to peck her lips then immediately move out of the way.

Today, he stood directly in front of her completely blocking her view of the sitcom she wasn't really watching. Apparently, her change in behavior was noted.

"Bit, what's going on?"

Carver's face was blanketed with concern. His hands rested on his hips. Her natural inclination to sweep her gaze along his frame, appreciating how he filled out the athletic gear, wasn't present as she stared at him blankly.

"What do you mean?"

"I've been calling out to you, looking for you for the past ten minutes. You didn't answer. You won't even look me in the eye."

At his last statement, Alyssa transferred her stare from his chest to his eyes. At present, they were filled with concern, not hurt or anger. She wondered how long that would last.

"If I ask you a question, will you be honest with me?"

Snagging the ottoman from its position in front of a chair, Carver slid it in front of the sofa and sat down facing her. Reaching out, he clasped her hands in his. She didn't pull away, but she didn't tangle her fingers with his as was her habit.

"I'll always be honest with you, Baby. Ask me whatever you want."

Alyssa silently searched his face for the truth in his words. She really couldn't tell if he meant it. He seemed earnest enough, but she no longer trusted herself when it came to Carver.

"Did you have something to do with Ballard and Torrence losing their jobs?"

Carver blinked, and the earnest expression disappeared. It was replaced by one she couldn't accurately read. It looked like a mix of guilt and resolve.

"Yes."

That was it. One word was his response. While she'd asked a yes or no question, part of her hoped for a denial followed by outrage that she'd ask him such a thing. Instead, he clearly acknowledged it.

"Why, Carver? Why would you do that?"

"Are you seriously asking me why? For you."

Shaking her head, Alyssa drew her hands from his hold. "I didn't ask you to do anything on my behalf."

"Of course not." Him agreeing with her didn't make her feel better, but she didn't think that was his goal. "You'd never ask me to defend you, but I'll *always* do just that."

"Carver, I didn't appreciate the things either of them did, but that didn't warrant them losing their careers."

"The fuck it didn't." Carver immediately shot back. "People get fired and have their futures ruined every day for the things those two did to you."

When Alyssa began shaking her head again, Carver held up a hand. "It's true, Bit. And you know it. What Torrence did, sending you an unsolicited picture of his junk, was sexual harassment. Are you telling me you haven't heard of people losing their job behind a sexual harassment allegation?"

"I have, but I didn't report him for that."

"And you wouldn't have! So I did it." Carver sprang up from the ottoman and began pacing. His movements telegraphed his agitation more clearly than his words. "Just like I dropped a bug in the right ears about Ballard not bein' a person of good character. That he was someone who put himself above the safety of other's around him."

Shooting her a glance before she could say anything about what he revealed, he continued, "and don't tell me that he didn't do that when you lived through that mob at the restaurant. He didn't give two shits about what could happen to you when he went runnin' his mouth tryin' to get laid.

See, your problem is, you think if you just ignore someone they'll get the hint and leave you alone. That's not it works, Baby. Especially not with men like Ballard and Torrence who are more adult-sized boys than they are real men."

"It wasn't your place to do any of that, Carver."

Carver stopped in his tracks. The muscle in his jaw ticked as his eyes pinned her to her seat. His expression was so fierce, she had to remind herself to breath. She had no fear of him physically, but she realized her poor word choice too late.

"Not my place? Did I hear you right? Did you say it wasn't my place?"

Alyssa's heart hammered in her chest and her mouth refused to work after running off, spilling words with reckless disregard. She'd meant what she said, but she could've found a better way to express herself.

"I'm so fucking tired of this shit!" Carver's voice echoed off the high ceilings causing Alyssa to jump. "What do I have to do to get through to you, Alyssa? What will it take for you to understand and value yourself as much as I value you?"

Snapping out of her stupor, Alyssa stood. Standing between the sofa and the ottoman, she began to shake with anger.

"Don't do that, Carver. This isn't about whether I do or don't value myself. This is about you going behind my back and exacting revenge on my behalf. Revenge I didn't want. I *never* would've asked you or anyone else to exact revenge for me."

A mirthless laugh fell from her lips. "Now I know why I would get strange looks when I'd tell people how nice you were. How you helped others and stuck up for the little guy.

I always admired that about you. But, it appeared they knew something I didn't. I had no idea you were the kind of person who could destroy people with zero guilt."

"If you didn't know then that means you weren't listening to me. I might not tell you my every move, but I don't lie to you. I told you there were no limits to what I'd do to protect you. I didn't say that shit to talk big. I meant it."

Hanging her head, Alyssa closed her eyes. The articles she read earlier, while not completely damning, showed a pattern of behavior. People who pissed Carver off or hurt someone he cared about fell on difficult times. It wasn't always immediate, but when it happened, it was to the point it would take them years to recover. That knowledge led her to ask another question.

"What else did you do? My gut tells me you didn't stop with Torrence and Ballard."

For a moment, she thought he wasn't going to answer. He simply stared at her, his face granite hard.

"I've been buying up shares of *Secure Pull* to gain controlling interest in the company. According to the last report from Michelle, I'll have enough to take over very soon."

Alyssa wanted to scream. Like literally throw her head back and shriek. Instead of giving in to her desire, she clenched her fists and held it all inside. *Who was this man?*

His face held zero remorse. Based on what he'd done to Torrence and Ballard, she didn't want to consider his plan once he had the shares and votes he needed to take over *Secure Pull*. She also didn't want to consider what that would mean for her as an employee of said company.

It was too much. All of it. She couldn't do this. Throwing up her hands, Alyssa walked toward the doorway. She didn't say a word to Carver. He didn't try to stop her, nor did he call out to her as she ascended the stairs. Once she reached the bedroom they shared, she picked up the small crossbody purse she'd lain on the dresser the day before.

When she turned to walk back out of the room, Carver was standing behind her. Saying nothing, she walked around him. When she headed down the back stairs he followed. As she turned the corner leading to the hallway at the back of the house, he broke his silence.

"Where are you going?"

Just as quickly as he wrapped his fingers around her wrist he released it. "Bit...Baby. Talk to me. Yell. Throw some shit. I don't care. But don't just walk away from me like this."

She tried with everything in her to ignore the pleading in Carver's eyes. She wasn't able to do it. However, Alyssa didn't allow it to dissuade her. She walked a little farther down the hallway before she stopped and turned back to him.

When she spoke, her voice was thick with the emotions crushing her heart. "Today, I realized I don't know you. I know a fairytale I dreamed up, but I have no idea who you are."

Carver's eyebrows shot up in disbelief. "What? That's not true. You probably know me better than anyone."

Carver tried to close the distance between them but she walked backwards keeping them apart.

"Carver, all that means is that no one **really** knows you. They know pieces of you."

Turning away from him, she opened the door to the security office. Relieved to see Samira still there, her eyes scanned the room seeing Remi and Blake as well. Remi was seated at the conference table while Blake was in front of the monitors mounted on the wall.

"Is there something we can do for you, ma'am?" Samira stood from the chair behind the desk.

Clearing her throat, Alyssa ignored the heat from Carver's body at her back.

"Yes. Samira, could you take me home?"

Confusion wrinkled Samira's brow as she responded, "Ma'am...you are home."

Shaking her head, Alyssa swiped at the tears that spilled from her eyes. "No. I'm not. I want to go to my house please."

Looking to Remi, Samira tapped a couple of keys on the keyboard in front of her and moved from behind the desk. Remi stood and walked around the conference table.

Alyssa rotated only to encounter Carver's broad chest as he blocked her exit. Leaning over, speaking barely above a whisper, he only said four words. "Please don't do this."

Closing her eyes against the pain coursing through every fiber of her being, Alyssa searched for the strength to follow through with what she needed to do.

"Carver, I can't. I have to go. Let me pass...Please." Clogged with emotions, her vocal cords strained to get those few sentences out.

Just as she thought he'd ignore her plea, Carver stepped aside. Not daring to look at him, Alyssa left the room. Without speaking she, Remi, and Samira went to the garage. Remi grabbed the keys to the larger SUV while Samira opened the back door for Alyssa.

As they pulled away, Alyssa saw Carver framed in the doorway of the garage. He hadn't tried to stop her again, but his eyes were trained on the back windows as if he could see through the dark tented glass. She was unable to turn away until she could no longer see him. Burying her face in her hands, Alyssa spent the thirty-minute car ride quietly bawling. *What the hell had she just done?*

Chapter Thirty-One

ACTIONS HAVE CONSEQUENCES

Carver watched the darkened windows of the SUV as Alyssa got farther and farther away from him. When she'd asked Samira to take her home, his heart dropped into his stomach. *This* was her home. Not because he bought it for them, but because *they* were here. *Together*.

Only, she wasn't here. Did that now mean this place couldn't be their home? The vehicle taking his love away turned the corner and he could no longer see it, but he stood there in the garage opening. The sun, which was setting when he got home, completely disappeared behind the mountains dropping him into shadow.

Finally, he turned to go inside. As he moved through the house, he replayed everything in his head. Not just their argument, but their relationship, past and present. Although he'd worked out with the team earlier, his feet took him to the exercise room. If he didn't find something to do with himself, he was going to follow her. Carver had no doubt of it.

In the months since they'd reconnected, they'd never spent more than three nights apart. Even then, they hadn't been at odds. Knowing they'd be apart, she was hurting, and he was the cause of it, had his gut churning.

Internally, he warred with feelings of regret and rebellion. Externally, he pulled on a pair of gloves and started mindlessly punching the freestanding heavy bag. Trying to conjure his hurt into something he could physically battle with, he took his frustrations out on the equipment.

The electronic strains of music from his cellphone pulled him out of the fog. Using his teeth to lift the Velcro from one glove, he hurriedly removed his right hand. Not paying attention to the display, he swiped the screen to answer.

"Hello?!"

"Hey, son!"

"Hey, Pops..." Carver's shoulders dropped. He'd hoped it was Alyssa, but hadn't checked to be certain before he answered. His father's cheerful voice wasn't the one he wanted to hear and he couldn't hide his disappointment.

"Whoa...What's wrong?" His father switched gears in the space of a heartbeat. In the background, Carver heard his mother asking if everything was okay. "I don't know, Carol. He doesn't sound right, so I just asked. He hasn't told me nothin' yet."

After a bit of fumbling, Carver heard his mother's dulcet southern drawl. His father had obviously switched the call to speaker.

"Carver, baby, what's wrong?"

Unlike some of his peers, Carver had always been close with his parents. They were his greatest supporters in all aspects of his life. He was always able to talk to them about anything. Even the uncomfortable stuff.

Slightly older than most of his friend's parents, many didn't understand their relationship. But those people didn't know their story. Although they'd met and married young, his parents were ten years into their marriage before Carver was born. By that time, they thought they wouldn't be able to have children and had resigned themselves to that fate.

He was their miracle baby. They weren't rich by any stretch, so fertility treatments weren't an option. The pregnancy was extremely hard on his mother and his birth was accompanied by the doctor's recommendation that she not get pregnant again. In an unprecedented move, his dad got a vasectomy.

"Carver?"

Carver struggled with telling his parents and keeping his and Alyssa's business between the two of them. However, he knew he'd fucked up and aside from begging, he had no idea how to fix it.

"It's nothing, Ma. I'll be okay."

"Boy, don't you lie to your mother. I heard the way you sounded when you answered the phone versus when you realized it was me. You sounded like you lost your best friend."

Hell, he had. **Nope.** Giving himself a mental shake, he dismissed the defeated voice in his head. No matter how they'd left things, Carver couldn't allow himself to think of Alyssa as lost to him. Couples argued. It was normal in any relationship.

"I'm not lying, Pop. I will be okay."

"Being okay in the future and being okay right now aren't the same." His mother's words skated over him chipping at his resolve. "You know, no matter what it is, you can talk to us about it, son."

"I know, Ma."

Dropping onto the wooden bench situated to the side of the room, Carver leaned back and rested his head against the wall. His eyelids closed as he gave in. He needed to talk. Left to his own devices, he'd be on the doorstep at the townhouse before the night was done.

"Alyssa and I had an argument."

"Okay...Couples have disagreements. You two just need to talk it out. *Talk.* Not yell. And listen. Listen to understand, not just to respond. I'm sure you can get through this."

When his mother said not to yell, Carver's mind went to the moment he had done just that. He regretted it instantly, but he was too far gone to pull it back. His silence prompted his father to re-enter the conversation.

"Sweetheart...I'm thinking it might be a little too late for your advice. Am I right, son? Is that really what has you sounding like a kicked puppy? Did you raise your voice in anger?"

The hard edge to his father's question made him sit up straighter as if the man was in the room with him. He was transported to his teens to a time when he rebelled and his mom's best friend said he was *smelling himself.* That was the last time his father had to speak to him about verbally lashing out in anger.

As if he were still that teen, he mumbled his response to his father's question.

"What was that?" Though his father posed it as a question, it wasn't a request.

"Yessir. At one point I did."

"Oh...Carver..." The disappointment from his mother was worse than being chastised for his behavior.

"Now, you know I'm not one to dig into your personal life." Carver heard his father's words and knew he was about to do the exact opposite of what he said.

"Tell us what happened. From the beginning."

Slowly removing the glove from his left hand, Carver flexed his fingers. Exhaling deeply, he told his parents everything he'd done. They didn't interrupt, they simply listened. Carver didn't know what unnerved him more, them not interrupting to ask for clarification or their silence once he stopped speaking.

"Boy...What the fuck is wrong with you?!"

"Lance!"

"Don't Lance me, Carol. Did you hear your son?"

"Yes, but let's not judge. He's being honest with us. The least we can do is not judge him. Maybe he has a good explanation."

"Ok. Let's ask." His father didn't sound as though he held out hope for Carver to have a good reason for the things he'd done. "Son, I get you wanting to protect your woman. Hell, I applaud that. But, why on this green earth did you think you needed to stick your fingers into those people's lives the way you did?"

Scrubbing a hand down his face, Carver dreaded answering, but knew he had to. "I didn't like them thinking it was okay to hurt her or put her in danger. Actions have consequences, Pop. You and Ma taught me that."

"Don't you put that shit on us. We taught you that so you'd understand how something you did could end in unpleasant results for you. Not so you can go out and make sure other people experienced those results when they pissed you off."

"So, this is a case of do as you say and not as you do?"

"What the hell is that supposed to mean?" His father growled into the phone.

"I can't be the only one who remembers the scandal that brought down the superintendent when he blocked Ma from being a principal to put his empty-headed son-in-law in the position. We both know how that information got to the school board and the local papers."

It was below the belt. Carver didn't even recognize himself in that moment. He'd never spoken to his father in such a snide tone. Nor had he ever even hinted to his mother that his father took down the cheating, embezzling, superintendent after seeing how hurt she was at being passed over again.

"Carver Wyatt Jamieson. That is enough!" His mother got as close as he'd ever heard to yelling at him. "You're hurting. I get that. But you don't get to talk to your father that way because you got your ass in a sling and don't know how to get it out."

Shit... He'd really stepped in it this time. His mama was cussing. She **never** used profanity.

"I'm sorry, Ma." Carver apologized, but he had little hope it would save him from what was to come.

"Son...Do you know one of the things I love about you? I love how hard and completely you love. For the longest time we only got to see it when it came to us and your closest friends.

But, when we came up that first game weekend your junior year, and we saw how your eyes lit up and danced whenever you looked at Alyssa, we knew she was your one. Even though you were with that other girl, Alyssa was your love."

Carver wasn't sure where she was going, but he was surprised to hear once again how transparent he was in his feelings for Alyssa. At least to those who knew him best.

"But, son. By your own account, you made it your mission to punish people on her behalf—without telling her anything. Did you ever think your actions could actually make things worse for her?

People aren't wound too tight these days—especially some of these men. They aren't used to hardships and hearing the word no. They snap and lash out."

With the team Jasper put together, Alyssa was well protected, but Carver didn't like hearing that his activities could put her in peril. He didn't like that. At all. However, he continued to listen as his mother handed him his ass.

With his father randomly chiming in, she shined the light on just how much of a hypocrite he'd been, by demanding Alyssa tell him every-thing, in the name of her safety, while he withheld things because he knew she wouldn't approve.

"Son, healthy relationships don't work that way. If you want her to trust you, you have to extend her trust as well."

"I do trust her, Ma."

"Then you have a piss poor way of communicating. I don't know Alyssa's mind, but it seems to me that her not being forthcoming wasn't just about her being independent. It was because she feared what you might do if she did tell you something."

At his mother's revelation, Carver blinked. Hard. How had that never occurred to him? Had he been walking through their relationship with blinders on?

His mother continued dropping her truth bombs. "Carver, Alyssa can't trust you not to fly off the handle—even if it's aimed at someone else instead of her.

What I remember of Alyssa aside from her outer beauty is that she's kind, loyal and has a gentle spirit. She's not a person who seeks revenge or wants anyone to do such on her behalf. You on the other hand think you're supposed to swoop in to save people and right wrongs, in what-ever way you see fit."

Carver couldn't dispute her words and his father wasn't chiming in to save him or add to anything his mother said. So, the line went quiet for a few moments.

"Now...I've said my piece. Do with that what you will, but I'm done. Lance, let me know when my son is back. I don't know this person who goes around manipulating people's lives without care of consequences."

Carver dropped his head into his hands. He heard the click of his mother's heels against the hardwood floor as she appeared to leave the room.

"Woo, boy. You done done it now." His father said once his mother's footsteps faded. If Carver wasn't mistaken, he detected a hint of a chuckle behind the man's words.

"I don't find this funny, Pops."

"Hell, that's cause it ain't. This is sad bordering on pitiful."

Leaning back, Carver pressed his shoulders into the cool wall dropping his head against the hard surface. His breath came out in deep gusts. The argument with Alyssa along with the things his mother said swirled in his mind. *Bit didn't trust him.* That little nugget was on a loop in his head.

"What am I gonna do, Pop?" Carver was beyond caring how pathetic he looked. He needed help.

"Hell...If it were me, I'd be over there begging my woman to forgive me." His father's guileless response was quick. "But if you're gonna do that, you have to be willing to listen to her.

Don't do that shit where you only hear enough to answer with what you think she wants you to say. ***Really*** fuckin' listen and do the work to be a better man for her. Be the man your mother and I raised you to be. Not whoever this is that you're becoming."

"I can do that, but Pops...The thing is, I know I'm not wrong about that Ballard guy."

"Whether your instincts are right or wrong about the guy, ***your*** actions got you here. Not his."

That was another gut punch. Neither of his parents were holding back tonight. As lovingly as they reared him, they didn't shy away from bald honesty when the situation called for it.

"Now...I'm gonna go in there and take care of ***my wife***. I suggest you do the same. That is if marrying Alyssa is your goal. Don't let the sun come up without the two of you working this out and you making it right."

"Thanks, Pops."

"Thank me when you get my daughter-in-law back home."

With that, his father disconnected the call. Despite them only knowing Alyssa from brief phone calls and the limited time they were around her while the two were in college, his parents adored her. It's no wonder his mom lit his ass on fire.

Honestly, Carver was surprised his father didn't do worse. However, considering he and his pops both knew where Carver got his vengeance streak, his old man had cut him some slack. At least that's the only thing Carver could figure kept him from taking up where his wife left off.

Standing, Carver paced the room looking at his phone. He wanted to simply go to the townhouse and do whatever he needed to mend the rift between he and his Bit. But, he knew he couldn't just show up. It felt like he stood staring at the device in his hand for hours, but in reality it was less than five minutes.

Unlocking the screen, he looked at the picture of he and Alyssa standing on the balcony of the suite he rented when he first moved to Las Vegas. He had his arm wrapped around her as he kissed her bare shoulder. Her head was tipped to the side and her eyes were closed. The slightest of smiles graced her lips.

Tapping the icon, Carver lifted the phone to his ear. Instead of ringing or her voice floating over the line, he heard an automated response sending him straight to voicemail.

"Fuck!"

Carver vented his frustration. Putting the phone in his pocket before he did something stupid, he stalked toward the door. As he passed the heavy bag, he lashed out with a sloppy punch. He knew before the pain registered that he'd just compounded an already fucked up situation.

By the time the throbbing radiated up his arm, he was already cursing himself for being so careless. Cradling his hand to his chest, he opened the door. Blake stood on the other side holding up a set of car keys.

"Don't be a smartass. Take me to the hospital. I broke my fuckin' hand."

"Yes, sir."

Turning on his heel, Blake led the way to the garage. Following behind him, Carver considered trying to one hand a text message to Alyssa but thought better of it. The optics of it slammed into him. Although she knew him better than anyone aside from his parents, it could come off as him trying to manipulate her by saying he hurt himself.

So, instead of calling the woman he loved, he called the team doctor. He'd need someone trustworthy to meet him at the hospital to treat his hand. He preferred to do this as quietly as possible.

Three hours and one pain prescription later, Carver was watching the lights of the city from the front passenger seat as Blake drove. He only rode in the back when Alyssa was with him.

They had just left the private hospital Frank recommended. Although Carver hadn't asked him, Frank had even met them there. Carver's original suspicion about his hand was confirmed by the X-Rays. His sloppy punch had resulted in a 'boxer's fracture'.

Luckily, the bones were still aligned and Frank was able to put him in a cast to keep his fingers immobile. Compliments of the shot of morphine Frank gave him, he felt no pain.

Carver's stomach grumbled reminding him that he'd skipped dinner. The crackers they'd forced on him when they gave him the meds didn't count. It was late, but Vegas was a city that didn't sleep. So, he asked Blake to pull in somewhere for some grub.

Carver wasn't picky. So, it didn't matter to him where they stopped —just about anything would do. Blake pulled into a burger place and they both got greasy combo meals.

As they were leaving the restaurant, Carver noticed the vehicle waiting at the light at the intersection. Normally, it wouldn't have caught his attention, but the license plate was the same as the SUV Jasper supplied for Alyssa's security team.

His heart rate picked up and he sat up taller in the seat. "Blake, is it the happy juice Frank gave me, or is that who I think it is over there?"

"They gave you the good shit, but you're not mistaken. Looks like Remi is driving and Samira is in the passenger seat."

"Alyssa?"

"In the back."

The muscle in his chest pounded so loudly, Carver barely heard Blake's reply. He hadn't called or texted her from the hospital. There was zero expectation of seeing her in his mind after his call went to voicemail and he hurt his hand.

Based on the direction the vehicle was pointed it was possible she was going home. To their home. A tsunami of relief washed over him.

He might yet be able to follow his father's advice and make things right between them before the sun came up.

The traffic signal changed and the big body SUV rolled past them. Blake smoothly pulled in behind it. Staying far enough back as to not ride their bumper, but close enough to discourage anyone from getting in between them, Blake kept pace. Although the glass was tinted to just shy of the legal limit, Carver was able to somewhat make out Alyssa's head through the back window.

While Frank and the nurses worked on his hand, Carver had been going over what he'd say to Alyssa. Whether any of it would make a difference was still to be seen, but it looked like he'd get a chance to try sooner rather than later. The next few seconds moved in slow motion for Carver.

Having the right of way, the SUV carrying Alyssa, Remi and Samira rolled through the next intersection. When they made it to the halfway point, a big grey pickup truck barreled into the side. As his seat belt jerked him to the seat, Carver shouted in disbelief.

The impact of the collision locked the two vehicles together and they spun in an arc which clipped the front of the SUV with Carver and Blake inside. A cacophony of sounds rang out around him. From his peripheral, Carver saw his arm extended as if he were reaching out to stop the crash, but it was useless.

When all three vehicles came to a stop, Carver wrestled with his seatbelt trying to get out. Blake had barely pressed the park button before Carver was flinging his door open and running full tilt toward the meshed together automobiles. He didn't look back to see if Blake was behind him. He had to get to Alyssa.

So intent on getting to her, he didn't realize he was yelling her name as he ran. When he reached the back door on the undamaged side, he yanked at the handle trying to open it. Through the driver's side glass, he saw that the airbags had deployed. Both Remi and Samira were fighting against the inflated fabric, but the back airbags blocked him from seeing Alyssa.

"You got time to talk to me now, Bitch?! Huh?!"

Carver didn't recognize the voice, but he heard the words clearly. The body of the SUV was heavily reinforced, so the windows didn't shatter on impact. He had to step to the rear to see who it was.

To say that he was standing was an overstatement. It was more like a sloping lean against the door of the pickup which now had a crumpled front end. Ballard Grimes. Bloody, with one arm dangling at his side, Ballard held onto the perilously attached door yelling for Alyssa to get out and face him.

Chapter Thirty-Two

HOW ABOUT NEVER

When Remi turned onto the street leading to the gated community of the townhouse she'd purchased, Alyssa wasn't ready to leave the car. So, she asked him to drive around for a while. After a couple of hours, she thought she was prepared.

She wasn't. The minute Remi swung the SUV into the driveway, she knew. That place wasn't her home anymore. And, no matter how much she wanted to escape the pain, she had to go back. She and Carver needed to really talk and try to find common ground.

"Remi...I'm sorry to keep doing this, but can you just take me back please?"

"It's no problem. If that's what you want. That's what we'll do."

"Thank you. Thank you both."

Alyssa wanted to further apologize for putting the two of them in the middle of she and Carver's mess, but she held back. Things were awkward enough for her, she didn't want to make them uncomfortable as well.

As he drove, Alyssa looked down at her phone again. Initially, she'd turned it off, but during their ride around the outskirts of Las Vegas, she'd turned it back on. She wasn't one for playing mind games in relationships. Having no idea what she'd say, she didn't call Carver, but she fully expected the device to light up at any moment with at least a text message.

She hadn't left their home with the purpose of having Carver chase her. However, she was surprised he hadn't reached out. It wasn't like him. He didn't like for things to fester. His determination to face situations head on was one of the many things she loved about him.

And she did love him. So deeply, even the thought of spending one night away from him hurt too much to consider. Despite her pain and disappointment in the moment. Alyssa now knew she shouldn't have left. She should've stood up to Carver, let him know how she felt about him raising his voice, and actually talked to him to work through their issues. Instead, she'd run.

Alyssa pulled away from her thoughts when she checked the phone again and noticed the time. It had been more than twenty minutes since they'd left the townhouse, but a quick glance out of the window confirmed they weren't anywhere near home.

As a matter of fact, they were a few streets over from the Vegas Strip. Looking at the passing landmarks, Alyssa frowned. She trusted her team, but something was off.

"Remi, what's going on?"

There was a moment of uncomfortable silence as she saw Remi quickly glance at Samira before turning his attention back to the road. He avoided making eye contact with her in the mirror.

"Hopefully, nothing, ma'am." Samira supplied. "I thought we might've picked up a tail, so Remi is simply varying our route just in case."

Sitting up straighter, Alyssa stretched her neck looking through the side windows. They prohibited people from seeing in, but her view of the outside was relatively clear. Turning, she tried to see something through the window over the hatch.

"Someone's following us? Where? What does the car look like?"

Twisting in her seat, Samira sent her a look of reassurance. "We're being cautious ma'am. I don't want you to worry about it. We've got it under control."

Alyssa wanted to heed Samira's words, but the thought of being followed dropped her right back into all of the warnings from Carver about her taking her safety more seriously. What if it wasn't just him being overprotective?

They drove for another five minutes before reaching the strip. When Remi turned the vehicle in a direction which indicated they were now on track to go back to the house, Alyssa released some of her tension. Resting her shoulders against the soft leather seats, she scanned the businesses lining either side of the street.

She was calm, but still alert. So, when the dark SUV pulled out of the burger place and fell in behind them, she turned to look over her shoulder.

"You can relax, ma'am. That's Blake driving the SUV behind us."

"Blake?" Alyssa sat up straighter. "Is Carver with him?" Her desire to keep her bodyguards out of she and Carver's business flew out of the window.

"Yes, ma'am. He is."

Alyssa's eyebrows dipped. "Was it them following us? Why wouldn't they just call?"

"No. It wasn't them." Remi supplied. "Them being behind us is simply a coincidence."

Alyssa watched too many crime dramas and sci-fi mysteries to believe in coincidences. However, Remi had never given her reason not to trust him. So, she spun back around in the seat. Resting her elbow on the cushioned door handle, she propped her chin on her fist.

As they rolled through the next intersection, Alyssa looked to her right. There was absolutely nothing she could do as she saw headlights barreling toward them. Her scream was snatched from her throat as she was thrust away from the window by the force of the vehicle slamming into the passenger side of the SUV. The sound of her voice was swallowed in the deafening squall of tires skidding across asphalt and metal scrapping against metal.

Stars exploded behind her eyes when the side airbags deployed striking her cheek and knocking her toward the other side of the bench seat. Only her seatbelt keeping her firmly pinned prevented her from being flung about the backseat. Alyssa felt as if she were on a carnival ride that had gone haywire.

After an eternity that lasted less than a minute, the SUV came to a stop. The blare of a horn brought Alyssa back to herself. Stunned, she looked down at her body running her hands along her limbs mechanically checking her faculties.

Vaguely, she heard a strange woman's voice, but she didn't listen as Remi and Samira responded to the woman's questions. Had she been more alert, she would've understood that it was the vehicle emergency service.

Carver's voice jerked her into full consciousness. The fear and desperation in the way he bellowed her name shot adrenaline through her system. Frantically, she tugged at the seatbelt trying to get it to release. Although it was deflated, the airbag blocked her from seeing out of the window.

Her heart raced. She wasn't certain if the pounding noise in her head was the organ loudly beating or something else. When she hazarded a glance at the front seat, she saw Samira and Remi in similar situations as herself. If they'd been stunned by the airbags, they'd recovered enough to fight through the material trying to move the deflated bags out of the way.

"Alyssa! Bit! Baby say something!"

"Carver!"

Alyssa finally got the safety belt to release. It didn't retract as usual, so it thumped against the bag covered window dully when she tossed it aside. Deformed by the crash, the door pressed into her hip. So, Alyssa knew opening it wasn't an option.

Thankfully, the window didn't shatter leaving glass for her to crawl over as she scrambled across the seat. Carver's yelling of her name had ceased, but what she heard next made Alyssa's hand freeze on the door handle.

"You got time to talk to me now, Bitch?! Huh?!"

Ballard. Even though he screamed and his voice held a maniacal edge, she recognized it. It didn't take much for Alyssa to put two and two together and deduce that it was Ballard who'd been following them and who'd rammed into the side of their vehicle. *What the fuck?*

Samira's hand on her shoulder startled Alyssa shifting her focus from opening the door.

"Do not open the door."

"What?"

Alyssa's brain had to still be in a fog, because she thought she'd heard Samira tell her to stay in the car. Samira didn't raise her voice, but the steel undercurrent made Alyssa reluctantly withdraw her fingers from the handle. Remi had already flung his door open and stepped out.

"Ma'am. Stay inside and let us do our jobs."

Samira climbed over the center console to follow Remi. The open door didn't provide her with a view of what was happening, but she could hear everything clearly.

Every part of her wanted to ignore Samira and get out of the SUV. Carver was out there, and judging from Ballard's shouting, he'd gone over the edge. The things he said wouldn't have made any sense if she hadn't confronted Carver earlier.

Ballard thought she was the reason he'd been fired. He screeched about her running his name in the mud with clients and cursed her for ruining his life.

In the distance, she heard the howl of sirens. A thump against the back passenger side door, next to where she was previously seated, drew her attention. Following the noise, Ballard's yelling ceased and Samira, Remi and Blake's voices took his place. They were all shouting Carver's name.

Ignoring Samira's instructions, Alyssa pushed open the door and scrambled out of the back seat. She still couldn't see anything, but she heard her security team along with screams of pain. With her heart in her throat Alyssa rounded the back of the vehicle.

When she cleared the bumper, she saw Blake and Remi pulling Carver away from Ballard. The other man had one hand thrown across his chest. His large blue eyes seemed to bulge in his head. Something told Alyssa that his disheveled appearance wasn't completely due to the accident.

As the two bodyguards pulled Carver away, Samira stood between them with her weapon trained on Ballard. Some part of Alyssa knew her security team was armed, but knowing and seeing were two different things. Samira being in a recognizable shooting stance gave Alyssa pause.

However, she spent less than a minute on Samira before turning her attention fully to Carver. He continued to strain against Remi and Blake, who had to use all of their considerable bulk to hold him back.

Not sparing Ballard another glance, Alyssa rushed to Carver. She had just enough presence of mind to not touch him. Instead, she tried to capture his gaze as she called out his name.

"Carver?..."

"Alyssa! Stay back!"

Alyssa wasn't sure which thing made her stop, Remi calling her by her first name or the way he ordered her away. He only ever called her ma'am or Ms Ripley—no matter how often she told him it was okay to drop the formality.

Alyssa didn't have to move any closer. Apparently, hearing Remi say her name snapped Carver out of his haze. His eyes cleared as they raked over her from head to toe.

"Bit?..."

Frowning, he looked from Remi to Blake who each had both arms wrapped around one of his up to the shoulder. The wails of the sirens drew closer as Carver assured the guys he wouldn't go after Ballard.

"I just wanna see about my woman. I promise, I won't touch that sack of shit."

Blake and Remi seemed to have a silent conversation before they released him. When they did, he immediately closed the distance between he and Alyssa sweeping her into his embrace. Her arms went around his waist, her fingers twisted in the fabric of his shirt.

"Are you okay, Baby? Why did you get out of the car?"

"Are you serious? I was worried about you."

"Worried about me?" Carver's expression and voice held surprise at her confession. "I'm okay, Bit-baby. No need to worry."

Cupping the sides of her face, he leaned his forehead to hers, then placed a gentle peck on her lips. His voice was gritty with emotion as he spoke.

"I'm so sorry, Baby."

Alyssa shook her head. "No. I'm sorry."

Her movement caused her cheek to rub uncomfortably against his right hand. Most quarterbacks develop calluses, but Carver was retired and no longer had them. So, the roughness she felt was foreign. Pulling back, she saw that two of his fingers were immobilized in a cast.

"Carver? What happened to your hand?"

Carver was saved from answering her question by the arrival of two police cars and an ambulance. Alyssa watched as Blake immediately walked over to the officers to show them his credentials. With the cops on scene, Samira put away her weapon. She also presented her identification and permits for inspection.

Once the police showed up, Ballard started again with his accusations, but they were quickly shutdown by the responding officers.

"Ma'am, sir, are you injured?"

Alyssa was pulled from her detached observation of the ranting Ballard and the group surrounding him. A paramedic, carrying a satchel, stood in front of her with a concerned expression.

"Um. I think I'm okay."

"Are you sure, ma'am? Were you in either of the vehicles?"

"Bit, baby, let him check you out." Switching his gaze to the paramedic, he gestured to Alyssa's face. "Her cheek is a little red. She might have hit her head in the accident."

Guiding them to the open rear door of the ambulance, the medic encouraged her to sit on the bumper. "What about you sir? Do you have any injuries? There's blood on your shirt."

Alyssa scrutinized Carver's chest, arms and hands. How had she missed the blood splattered on his shirt?

"It's not mine." Carver responded flatly. "Our vehicle barely got grazed."

"Are you sure, sir?"

Carver tipped his head at the group next to Ballard's crumpled pickup. "Positive. It's his."

Understanding painted the young man's face and he returned to asking Alyssa questions. He went through a routine where he shined a light into her eyes, checked her responsiveness and examined her extremities for any signs of injury.

Despite Carver's assurances that he was okay, the paramedic went through the same routine with him with the addition of checking the cast which covered two of Carver's fingers and reached just past his wrist.

"This looks fresh."

"I just got it. I was on my way home from the hospital when..." Carver waved his other hand at the vehicles blocking the intersection, "all of this happened."

More patrol units showed up and began directing traffic. A minute later, a second ambulance joined the first. Although she seemed okay, the paramedics suggested Alyssa go to the hospital for a full work up. They were concerned about a concussion and strongly recommended she get checked out.

One look at Carver's face and she knew it was pointless to argue. Not that she would've. When she stood from the ambulance, she felt a twinge on her thigh. The adrenaline rush she'd experienced had worn off leaving her body with the reminder of what she'd gone through less than a half hour earlier.

The second ambulance took Ballard away under police escort. The medics attending to Alyssa and Carver offered to take them to an ER, but they declined. The SUV Blake and Carver arrived in was still drivable. With Blake driving and Samira in the front passenger seat, Alyssa and Carver were transported to a private hospital. Remi stayed behind to secure the other vehicle.

On the drive, Alyssa and Carver didn't have a chance to talk because his phone rang almost as soon as they were in motion. She listened to his end of conversations with first Jasper then Michael. By the time they arrived at the hospital, Michael was waiting at the entrance to the Emergency Room.

It wasn't until much later as Alyssa lay semi-reclined, on a bed in a posh suite that didn't belong in a hospital, that she had a moment alone with Carver. As it turned out, the paramedic was correct. She had a mild concussion and was admitted for observation. The doctors assured her that it was likely she'd be able to go home in the morning.

In the meantime, Carver pulled an armchair as close as he could get it to the bedside. The fingers of his left hand were entwined with hers resting on the soft comforter covering her from the waist down.

"So...are you going to tell me what happened to your hand?'

Carver lifted his forearm with a grimace. "It was a stupid mistake."

"Okay..."

"After you left, I went to the workout room to blow off some steam. I threw a sloppy punch on the heavy bag. Fractured a couple of fingers."

She squeezed the fingers of his other hand in silent apology. His only acknowledgement was a kiss to the back of hers.

"Frank met me here to set them. He said I should only be in this thing for a few weeks."

Silence fell between them as she absorbed the words he spoke along with what he didn't say. He didn't have to tell her the reason he was blowing off steam was because of their argument. Which made her stomach twist with guilt. If she hadn't left, maybe he wouldn't have hurt himself.

Or even if he had, they would've been at the hospital together. Then, they would've gone home together and maybe Ballard wouldn't have had the opportunity to use his truck as a battering ram. But...the past was the past. It couldn't be changed.

"Carver..."

Alyssa searched for the words to convey her feelings without triggering another argument. She didn't want a repeat of what they'd done earlier. A slight press and release of her digits was given in encouragement from him.

"Carver, I love you. And, I don't see that changing any time soon."

"How about never? Because that's exactly when I'll stop loving you. Never."

He seared her with his stare, almost causing her to forget what she intended to say next.

"Right. Never." After his curt nod of acceptance, she tried again.

"Carver, we need to set some boundaries. Number one, tonight needs to be the last time you raise your voice to me in anger. I expect that we'll disagree on many things in the future, but I won't stand for you yelling at me."

Bringing her hand to his lips again, he pressed more kisses to the back. "Fuck, Bit-baby. I'm so sorry. It won't happen again."

His eyes were filled with regret. "I let frustration get the best of me. That's no excuse. But, I promise, going forward, I'll get my shit together before I speak. I never want you to think I don't respect you enough to talk to you like I've got good home training'."

Touching the side of his face with her free hand, she dipped her head in acknowledgement.

"Number two. I love that you want to protect me, but I can't support you meting out punishment to people for hurting my feelings. I'm an adult who's fully in touch with my emotions. I know how to process and move on. You don't have to beat up bullies for me—figuratively or literally."

Clearing his throat, Carver looked away for a few seconds before recapturing her gaze. "Can we compromise on that?"

Alyssa furrowed her brow. "Compromise? I think that's a reasonable request."

"It probably is perfectly reasonable to you. But, I'm not built to let *anyone* hurt you and just walk away."

"Carver..." His name came out in a weary sigh.

"Bit...Baby, do you trust me?"

"Of course, I do."

Her response was immediate, but Carver shook his head just as quickly. "I think you trust me about many things, but not *all* things."

Alyssa shifted in the bed. Absently, she picked at the comforter with her free hand. "Why would you say that?"

"Because, if you trusted me completely, you wouldn't avoid telling me things out of fear that it'll set me off. That's why you didn't say anything about Ballard. You don't have to confirm it, but I'm guessing if I hadn't seen the text message from Torrence, you would've just blocked him without saying a word to me."

As much as she wanted to object and say he was wrong, she couldn't. Alyssa hated to admit it. She would've chalked Torrence's behavior up as a Fuck Boy tantrum and blocked his number. Telling Carver that he sent her a picture of his dick wouldn't have been a consideration.

Her reasoning was similar when it came to Ballard. As much as she avoided him because she didn't want to deal with him, she didn't mention it to Carver because she was sure he'd go into protective mode to get Ballard to back off.

Who knows how things would've played out if they'd simply communicated better. With the memory so fresh of the way they went wrong, Alyssa opted to see what Carver considered a compromise.

"So, how do you suggest we meet in the middle? Please keep in mind that I'm team keep Carver out of jail, and don't ruin people's careers without serious cause."

"Our definitions of serious cause aren't the same." Alyssa narrowed her eyes and Carver held up a conciliatory hand.

"Okay. Fine... To answer your question. First rule is, don't keep things from me. If something seems odd or off, tell me about it. When something happens, if it causes you discomfort or pain, I want to know about it. Then, we'll talk and decide what—if anything—we'll do about it."

"No sneaky, behind the scenes maneuvering?" A single eyebrow lifted as Alyssa pressed him for specific concessions.

"No maneuvering. But..."

"But what?" Alyssa folded her free arm under her bosom. Carver still held her other hand firmly in his.

"But, if some idiot has the audacity to pull some bullshit right in front of me, I reserve the right to correct them immediately."

"I won't visit you in jail, or put money on your books."

"Yes you will, Bit-baby. You love me. Besides, who says they'll be able to prove I did anything?"

"Carver! You just promised no sneaky maneuvering not ten seconds ago!"

"And I intend to keep my promise, but the pyramids weren't built in a day, Baby."

Closing the gap between them, Carver captured her lips in a gentle kiss filled with potential. Alyssa allowed herself to be swept up in the moment. They had a ways to go, but they'd taken steps in the right direction. Since walking away wasn't an option, she'd take it.

Chapter Thirty-Three

DON'T BE A CREEPER

Carver looked out the window as they soared above the clouds. His fingers tangled in Alyssa's coily strands as she lay asleep, curled on her side, with her head on his lap. As soon as they were given the all clear, they moved from the upright seats to the sofa in the sitting area on the plane. He'd tried to talk her into going to the bedroom, but she shut that down.

Saying she knew no resting would happen if they were within three feet of a bed, she grabbed a blanket from the built-in chest and wrapped it around herself. Carver couldn't dispute her, because she was absolutely correct. They had more than four hours in the air before they touched down at the small south Georgia airport.

The last couple of months had brought about some changes in their relationship, but it was all for the better. After the Ballard Grimes incident, he and Alyssa had some serious conversations. As expected, the news of the accident was all over social media before the sun came up the next morning.

Urena and her team were all over it controlling the spin. They made sure neither he nor Alyssa were dragged through the mud because of Ballard's unstable behavior. They didn't have a chance to get ahead of it with their families though. Both of their phones rang almost constantly once the sun came up.

After reassuring their parents and friends, they had to contend with giving police statements. At least for that part they were safely at home and not at the private hospital. Since Ballard was caught on several CCTV cameras, he was being charged. They assured Carver no charges would be filed against him for the dust up between he and Ballard.

Carver hadn't given it a second thought. When he'd heard Ballard ranting and saw him moving toward the SUV as if he planned to get to Alyssa, Carver was on him within the space of a heartbeat. It had taken Blake and Remi to pull him away.

Alyssa shifted on his lap drawing Carver back into the present for a moment. Carver lightly dragged a couple of fingers down the side of her face. He didn't want to think about the rift in their relationship and how much hurt it caused both of them.

Wanting to save their relationship, they both agreed to therapy—individually and as a couple. To maintain their privacy, they found someone who was willing to meet with them via video conference on a schedule that worked for the both of them.

There was no doubt he loved Bit with everything in him and she loved him just as deeply. However, they both had to recognize the things they did which weren't good for them as a couple. Carver could admit, to himself at least, that there were times he felt like he wasn't emotionally mature enough to give her what she deserved in a partner.

But, since he had no intention of ever giving her up, he resolved to learn new tools and do what it took to be the best version of himself. For Bit and for their future. It helped that she was willing to do the same. Although he thought she was perfect, she assured him she had stuff she needed to work on as well.

Staring down at her, he drank in how serene she looked. Naturally long eyelashes rested low adding to her angelic look.

"Don't be a creeper." Alyssa murmured without opening her eyes.

"How exactly am I creeping, Bit? It's not my fault you're so beautiful. Blame your parents."

Rolling to her back, she quirked one eyebrow as she looked at him. "You're incorrigible."

"You love it." Grinning, he leaned over and pecked her lips, appreciating their plushness.

"I love *you*. Your cheeky attitude is an unfortunate part of the package."

"So your little nap made you sassy, huh?"

Carver skated his fingers down her rib cage eliciting the exact response he wanted. Squirming under his touch, Alyssa burst into giggles. Wiggling under his touch, she made a show of trying to get away, but didn't actually ask him to stop until she declared her need to pee.

Freeing herself from the blanket wrapped around her legs, she hopped up from the couch sprinting to the bedroom to use the bathroom there. Picking the blanket up from the floor, Carver dropped it on the couch and prepared to follow her.

"Sir?" The flight attendant called out to him.

"Yes?"

Carver looked at the woman hired through the service Anton recommended when Carver told him he was in the market for a new jet. So far, he'd had no issues with any of the attendants provided. They didn't hit on him or Alyssa. They were pleasant and efficient.

"The captain says we'll be landing in the next half hour. He's asked that everyone return to their seats for final approach."

"Ok. Thank you."

Continuing to the bedroom, Carver didn't bother knocking. He entered, closing the door behind him and leaned against it to wait. A moment later, he heard flushing then running water. When Alyssa opened the door, her eyes landed on him immediately. She stopped in the doorway as if she were considering going back inside.

"If we had the time, I'd make you pay for thinking about trying to hide from me."

"I don't know what you're talking about." Biting the corner of her bottom lip, she stared at him.

Stalking toward her, he watched as her eyes rounded taking in his every move. Tells, she didn't realize she had, let him know he could do any number of the things in his mind and she'd be ready for all of it. However, they really didn't have time. Stopping with the tips of his soft leather sneakers just shy of her feet, with her toenails sporting pretty, pink polish, he cupped the side of her face.

"I really wish our schedule allowed for me enlighten you, but we have to get back to our seats. We'll be landing soon."

Taking her lips, he tasted the slight minty flavor of the toothpaste she loved. He grinned at her fastidiousness. She wasn't keen on kisses first thing in the morning or when she first awakened—even from a nap.

Alyssa's fingers latched on to the sides of his shirt as she opened under his silent request for entry. Carver felt himself thickening in his jeans. Groaning, he pulled away from her lips with a few parting pecks. Desire wafted off her in waves as her lashes lifted to reveal her dark amber eyes.

"Let's go sit down, Baby. I'm sure you'd never forgive me if you smelled like sex when you saw my parents for the first time in years."

His statement snapped Alyssa out of her haze in half a second. Pushing at his chest, she tried to create space between them.

"Oh my God! That would be awful! Your mother would think I'm some kind of trollop!"

Turning back to the lavatory, she stood in the mirror tugging at her coily curls.

"What are doing, Bit? I told you. We gotta go get buckled in for landing."

"This won't take but a minute. When this thing lands, I won't have time to make myself presentable. I can't have your parents seeing me looking like you just sexed me up."

Leaning against the doorframe, he chuckled at her harried movements. "You and I both know that's not how you look after I've had a good one on one session with my best girl."

Grinning in response to her scowl, he grabbed her hand, tugging her out of the bedroom and back to their seats. Bending low, he slipped her sandals back onto her feet before sitting beside her and buckling his safety belt.

Alyssa's fingers sought out his and laced them together. In spite of his assurances that his parents loved her, she was nervous about seeing them again in person. Carver thought this trip was the perfect opportunity.

As Denzel and predicted, Carver had received the call from the university. He was being inducted into the T-Club and the University Hall of Fame. Just as she'd promised, his Bit had cleared her schedule so she could accompany him. He'd wrangled some additional days off with the team as well.

They were going to visit his family first, then flying up to spend some time with hers before going to campus to participate in the pre-game and other activities. Carver's heart filled just thinking about the next nine days. This wasn't their first time out together publicly, but it would be the first time around people who'd known them all of their lives—in addition to those who knew them under very different circumstances.

He knew Alyssa was only mildly apprehensive about being around people they hadn't seen since college. She was more concerned with their families. Carver wasn't worried about any of it. He was simply happy to have the woman he loved at his side. The rest would work itself out.

When the wheels of the plane touched down on the private airstrip, Alyssa's eyes were glued to the landscape—Carver's were on her. Although she told him she'd gone home for Christmas the previous year, her family was farther north and she rarely came to the southern part of the state. Carver surmised her time in the desert made the lush green of south Georgia look even more vibrant.

Alyssa had been in a tizzy about not having time to get herself together before they met up with his parents, she'd forgotten they had the drive to the farm. A sleek black SUV waited for them when they stepped off the plane. Michael stood next to it waiting as Remi, Samira and Blake preceded Carver and Alyssa down the stairs.

Michael had flown in ahead of them as a de facto advance team of one. He'd arrived in Atlanta earlier in the week and driven to each location before coming to meet them in Albany.

His parent's farm was actually in Coralee, Georgia. The town was north of Albany, not big enough to be classified as a city, but big enough for a high school,. Even if the average size of the graduating class was less than one hundred students each year.

The limo style SUV was large enough to easily accommodate everyone, so they settled in as Michael drove them the thirty miles north to his parent's farm. As if she was a kid on a field trip, Alyssa's gaze was glued to the passing scenery. Their fingers were intwined and resting on Carver's lap.

"I think the only time I've been down this way was when I let one of my cousins talk me into driving to some concert in Tallahassee when we were fresh out of college."

"Oh yeah?"

This was a story he hadn't heard. She didn't talk much about her life immediately following graduation. Most likely trying to avoid mention of Mary Beth. They'd remained friends up until Mary Beth revealed her true colors right before her own wedding. Alyssa told him realizing Mary Beth never really considered her a friend in the same way she did was enough for their relationship to unravel completely. Knowing your best friend didn't want you to take part in their big day because of such a superficial reason as your weight, wasn't something anyone would want to rehash.

"Yeah. It was me, my cousins Virginia, Candy, and Cherry. We almost didn't bring Cherry because she wasn't even twenty-one yet. But, since it was just an overnight trip, we figured it couldn't hurt."

"I vaguely remember Virginia, but I don't recall you mentioning Candy and Cherry."

"I haven't?" Her faced scrunched in concentration for a second. "I'm related to them through my Grandma Patricia. She and their Grandma Hortense were sisters.

I usually see them if I'm able to get home on the holidays in the summer. There's usually a big cookout at my cousin McKenna's parents' house. It ends up being like a mini family reunion."

"Sounds like fun."

"It is." Her face lit up with a smile displaying her pleasure in the memories. "Maybe we can make one of the cookouts next year."

Bringing their joined hands to his lips, Carver kissed the back of hers. "If that's what you want, we'll work it out."

Houses and businesses were fewer and farther between the closer they got to the farm. When Carver was a child, his parents had a small farm that his father ran while his mother was a teacher turned administrator. Once Carver was drafted, one of the first promises he kept to them was purchasing the land and equipment his dad needed to run a larger farm operation and retiring his mother.

Initially, they didn't want to accept it, but they eventually came around to seeing things his way. As they rode up the slightly winding road separating the main house from the city street, Carver joined Alyssa in her window gazing. In the distance, he saw cows in one field while the opposite side of the road contained rows of soybeans almost ready to be harvested.

As they rolled to a stop in front of the large two-story ranch style home, the front door opened and his parents stepped out. From the quickness of the action, he had no doubt they were watching them drive up the road. Carver was barely able to get Alyssa from the car before his mother swooped in engulfing Alyssa into a hug. Due to their height difference, Alyssa had to stoop slightly to return the gesture.

"Hey there, sweetheart! It's so good to see you again. How was the trip?"

Looking at Carver with wide eyes over his mother's shoulder, Alyssa offered a soft reply. "It was good, ma'am. It's good to see you as well."

"Carol, don't monopolize her. I wanna say 'hey' too." His father groused tapping his mother on the shoulder.

Carver stood back watching as his parents fawned over Alyssa, essentially treating him as if he didn't exist. It was an interesting turn of events. Although it was a well-established fact that they adored her, he didn't quite expect their welcome.

With a guiding arm around Alyssa's shoulders, his father started walking toward the house. Carver's mother had her arm looped in Alyssa's on the other side.

"Don't just stand there with your mouth open, son. Get the bags." His father tossed the order out as they continued up the short walkway.

"Glad you remembered your only son." Carver called out to his father's retreating back. Alyssa looked over her shoulder at him with questioning eyes. She was so not ready for Lance and Carol Jamieson. At least not this version of them.

Barely stifled laughter brought Carver's gaze to the back end of the SUV where Blake and Michael stood next to the cluster of luggage belonging to Carver and Alyssa. The security team would drive around to the other side of the property and set up in the pool house—similar to the arrangement they had in Vegas.

Grumbling about smartasses working as bodyguards, Carver stacked the smaller pieces on top of the larger ones, grabbed the handles, and rolled the luggage up the walkway. It's a good thing his hand was healed because the cheeky bastards didn't help him get anything up the stairs.

Although if they'd asked, he would've turned them down. They were there to protect, not play valet. It was something he'd established pretty early on. If their hands were full, it decreased their response time when they were needed.

He entered the house in time to hear his mother ask Alyssa if she was looking forward to visiting campus. As he walked past the doorway, he saw them gathered around the kitchen island. His mother was pouring tea into a glass of ice.

Instead of joining them, Carver continued up the stairs to the bedroom he used whenever he visited. His parents had their main suite on the first floor. It was on the opposite side of the house from his room —which he hoped helped create something of a noise barrier.

By the time he deposited their things in the room and returned to the kitchen, Alyssa was seated in one of the high back chairs next to his father while his mother moved around the kitchen. Standing beside the empty seat on the other side of her, he leaned in to kiss her cheek.

Starting from the sudden touch, Alyssa turned wide eyes on him. "Carver!"

"What?" Carver was genuinely confused. Bit never rejected his kiss.

"You don't have to be shy on our account, dear. We're an affectionate family." His mother assured Alyssa as she came around the island to give Carver a hug.

"Oh, so I'm not invisible anymore?" Carver joked as he scooped her off the floor and turned them in a circle.

"Don't be a brat and put me down!" His mother swatted at his chest. Her peals of laughter belied her admonishment.

Setting her on her feet, he accepted her kiss to his cheek before moving to greet his father. Almost matching him in height, his father had more of a rangy build in comparison to Carver's muscular frame.

Both of his parents had gone completely gray or really white haired and embraced it.

Sliding into the chair next to Alyssa, Carver watched and listened as she continued in conversation with his parents as if it were an everyday occurrence. Her shyness at him showing her affection aside, his Bit fit easily into their family dynamic.

Carver's chest swelled with pride while observing her wrapping his parents around her little finger just as surely as she'd done to him. There were only a few things he could think of that would make the moment even more perfect. All things in their own time though. All things in their own time.

Chapter Thirty-Four
WHAT? NO!

Looking down at her phone, Alyssa giggled at Carver's antics. He was trying to get her to join him as he was supposedly helping his dad check on the animals in the smaller barn closer to the house. She'd gone with him the previous day, but she'd been overwhelmed by the smell. It was pungent.

Her visit with the smaller animals, and the horses they kept there, was cut short along with Carver's plan. He wasn't the least bit slick with his intentions to pull her into the tack room. Just now, he'd sent her a picture of himself holding one of the new kids.

The baby goat was black with a patch of white on its forehead and around the front hooves. Bright silver eyes, with a black horizontal slant at the center, stared into the camera as if the little rascal was in on Carver's plan to woo her with cuteness. Her phone pinged with an incoming message.

> Carver: Come on, Bit. I'm not actually in the barn today. I'm outside mostly.

> Carver: You don't wanna cuddle with Rosie?

Alyssa grinned at the newest picture he'd sent. In it, Rosie was snuggled into the crook of his neck. She could swear the kid wore an expression which said, '*Don't you wish you were here?*'

> It's highly unfair to tempt me with baby cuddles.

> Carver: Is it working?

> I'm considering it.

So engrossed in the back and forth with Carver, Alyssa didn't hear his mother enter the room. A polite clearing of a throat garnered her attention.

"Oh. Hey, Ms Carol." Alyssa didn't miss the older woman's slight grimace at the way she was addressed. It wasn't that Alyssa was trying to be disrespectful, but she wasn't comfortable calling Carver's mother by her first name. Nor was she at the point where she could use Mom, Mama Carol, or Ma as had been suggested by both Carver and his mother. His family was affectionate. *Very affectionate.*

Alyssa's parents weren't slouches in the area of dispensing hugs and kisses while she and her brothers were growing up, and they hadn't slacked off as adults. However, the Jamieson's took it up a notch. In some ways it was understandable. Especially since Carver was an only child.

"What has you grinning and blushing?"

Carver's mother settled onto the sofa one cushion over, with an angular cushion/tabletop separating them. The little console had a flat top that covered a storage compartment. At the end of it, were two cup holders.

"Why am I even bothering to ask? I'm sure that son of mine is up to something."

Nodding in agreement, Alyssa put the phone face down on the flat surface between them. "He's trying to get me to come outside and play."

As soon as she said it, she slapped her hand over her mouth thinking of the way it could be taken instead of the way she meant it. Her intent was for it to sound like they were children—playmates. Carol simply patted her on the shoulder and smiled.

"I know you meant it innocently enough." She chuckled as the heat of embarrassment crawled up Alyssa's neck and settled in her cheeks.

Alyssa's phone pinged again and was immediately followed by ringing. Flipping it over, she wasn't surprised to see Carver's face on the display. Swiping the screen, she answered.

"Yes, Carver."

"Are you coming out to play or not?"

"I'm gonna say, not. I'm talking to your mother."

"You don't have to make up excuses, Baby. I can take a hint."

"I'm not! I really am. I'm sitting right next to her."

Carol tapped the console to get Alyssa's attention. When Alyssa looked her way she held out her hand. Yielding to the unspoken request, Alyssa passed her the phone.

"Carver, Alyssa and I are talking. You have her all the time. This is y'all's last full day here."

Although Alyssa could faintly hear Carver's response, she couldn't make out the words. As soon as there was silence on the other end, Carol spoke again.

"Yes, I know we'll be with you both again on Friday. But, you'll be going all over campus doing whatever P.R. stuff they have lined up for you. If I know you. And I do. You'll want Alyssa with you during all of that. So, why don't you enjoy your time with your father and leave us be?"

Apparently done with the conversation, whether Carver had a reply or not, she tapped the screen to end the call. Placing the device on the console, she smiled warmly at Alyssa.

"Now...It looks like you're feeling better. You were looking a little green this morning."

Nodding, Alyssa picked up the travel tumbler from the cup holder. Taking a sip, she then gently swirled the remaining liquid.

"Much better. This tea really helped. I guess I've gotten so used to it, it didn't feel right not having it. Ms Munoz has me hooked on her digestive tea blends."

"Mhmm. Well, that's good." Carol responded.

Crossing her legs, she propped her chin on her hand as she leaned against the cushion divider. While Carver looked more like his father, he got his sparkling emerald green eyes from his mother. If anyone were to peek into the room, she and Alyssa would look like two girlfriends dishing on the latest gossip.

Alyssa was happy Carver's parents were so accepting of her. Considering the circumstances under which they first met, they could've easily assumed the worst about her. Fortunately, they didn't. Mary Beth had only come up once in conversation. At which point, both parents volunteered that they'd never been fond of her and were happy when it ended.

"So, are you looking forward to being back on campus?"

"Yes, ma'am...Well kind of."

"Why, kind of?" The woman latched on to those two words.

"I mean... It's been a while since I've been there, so it'll be nice to see what's changed and what's still the same."

Alyssa looked down at her fingers wrapped around the steel mug bearing the Ravagers logo.

"But?..."

Carol leaned over to recapture Alyssa's wandering gaze. Alyssa scrunched her face and lifted one shoulder.

"It's homecoming. The crowd will be larger than a normal football game. I'll be with Carver. Which means far more attention than I'm used to being on me.

It'll be an adjustment, but I wouldn't miss the chance to support him. Being inducted into the T-Club and the University Hall of Fame is a great honor."

"It is." Pride poured off of Carver's mother with those small words. "It took them long enough to recognize my boy's contributions to that school and that football program."

"That's what I said!" Alyssa placed the mug back into the cup holder. "Carver thought I was being biased, but he was eligible for consideration five years ago. They took their sweet time putting his name on the list. It's not like they have a boatload of Super Bowl MVPs and Pro Bowlers coming out of Tech. I know they have a few, but, it's not enough for them not to have come calling sooner."

Alyssa folded her arms over her chest. She'd worked herself up thinking about the university dragging their feet. Carol's laughter snapped her out of her mini-snit bringing a smile back to her face.

"Sorry. I guess I got a little carried away."

Carol gave her bicep a reassuring pat. "Don't apologize. You didn't say a word that wasn't true. Besides, it's nice to know someone else is in my son's corner ready to do battle alongside him if necessary."

Relaxing her pose, Alyssa returned Carol's smile. After that, they slipped into easy conversation about a variety of things. They discussed Carol's hobbies, life on the farm, Alyssa's career and life in Las Vegas. By the time Carver and his father came in, they'd moved from the family room to the kitchen.

Alyssa was helping his mother prepare a light lunch. Since they were planning to leave around mid-day the next day, they'd made plans to have dinner at a restaurant in Albany with a few members of his extended family. They'd pretty much stayed at his parents' house—which suited Alyssa just fine.

Carver reached around Alyssa attempting to grab a piece of the celery she'd just sliced from the stalk. Before he could make contact, she swatted the back of his hand.

"Aht!" Alyssa heard her grandmother's voice fly from her lips.

"Ouch!" Drawing his hand back, Carver held it against his chest. "Ma did you see that?"

Alyssa mouthed, "Tattle-tail"

"Yes, I did. And it's no more than you deserve. You know I don't allow anybody touching stuff in my kitchen with dirty hands. Go wash up."

Adding her own swat with the oven mitt in her hand, she shooed both men from the kitchen. As Carver followed his chuckling father from the room, he grumbled while the older man echoed what his wife said—with his own special commentary, of course.

Carol looped her arm with Alyssa's at the elbow and tried to bump shoulders with her. With the three-inch height difference, it was more of a shoulder to bicep bump. Alyssa looked into her face a few seconds before the two erupted into giggles.

~

Alyssa sat in the chair next to the window admiring the view of the Atlanta skyline. She didn't think she'd ever seen it from this angle. Living on the outskirts of the city for almost half of her life, there hadn't been much cause for her to stay in a hotel. There wouldn't be now, except her parents' home wasn't large enough for her, Carver and their entourage.

*Entourage...*She was now a person who traveled with a group of people. Alyssa had grown accustomed to the personal security and knew it was a necessary part of her life now.

They could've possibly made it work, but Alyssa knew her old fashioned father was going to try to put she and Carver into separate rooms, which would mean two of the guys would have to bunk together. She couldn't ask them to do that. As it was, they were basically on duty twenty-four-seven during this trip.

"Bit-baby, I couldn't find the exact thing Ms Munoz said, but the lady at the herbal shop said this was a close substitute."

Carver entered the room and walked toward her holding out one of those fancy paper bags with a logo embossed on the front. Once she took it from his hands, he dropped a kiss on her lips and walked away.

"I'll put some water on."

"Thank you. I didn't want you to scour the city looking for tea, Carver."

"Ain't no problem. I was already out running anyway. I just looked it up on the internet. Michael was following us in the car, so he drove us to pick it up."

While he talked, Carver filled a kettle with water and placed it on the stove. After pressing a few buttons, he grabbed the bottom of his shirt as he walked toward the bedroom.

"I'm gonna grab a shower."

Alyssa's eyes tracked his movements and the play of muscles as he unashamedly disrobed on his way out of the room. Although she was still feeling a little *blah*, Alyssa had showered and dressed while Carver, Blake and Michael were out. She didn't even consider touching the breakfast she'd ordered from room service.

When she rifled through her bag of snacks earlier, she realized she was out of the tea she'd packed for the trip. Room service was a bust, so she broke down and called Carver while he was out. The kettle whistled calling her from the chair. The suite had two bedrooms and a full kitchen—which had come in handy since they planned to have her family over for dinner later.

Since her parents were only partially retired, Alyssa and Carver decided to spend evenings with them and do their own thing around the city during the day. It worked out well, since it gave them some alone time without pressure to be anywhere or do anything. Today was the exception. Carver had an appointment and Alyssa was meeting her mom for a little mother-daughter time.

Alyssa had managed to score them appointments for the works at Murphy's Salon and Spa. She had to put in a call to her cousin Kari to smooth the way with her sorority sister Stephanie, who owned the salon. Alyssa hated calling in favors, but even with a two-week notice, there was a chance she couldn't get both she and her mother in—at either location.

By the time Carver strolled back into the room, Alyssa was seated on the sofa, blowing on her mug of tea. He'd drank some type of shake mix before he'd left for his run, but she asked him if he wanted breakfast anyway. He declined saying he'd get something while he was out.

"So, you and your mom are doing the whole spa day thing today, right?" Sitting next to her on the couch, he slid his arm along the back, lightly running his fingertips across the tops of her shoulders.

"Yes. She should be here any minute. I told her we could come and get her, but she said Daddy would drop her off on his way to his meeting."

"Okay. Sounds good."

Reaching into the breast pocket of the suit draped deliciously on his body, Carver pulled out his wallet. Alyssa cocked one eyebrow.

"Carver, tell me you aren't about to give me money."

"I'm not about to give you money." He quipped, then proceeded to produce a matte black credit card. Holding it between two fingers, he held it out to her.

"You just said you weren't giving me money."

"I'm not. This is your card."

"Carver...Don't play with me."

Pressing the card into her free hand, he cupped the side of her face. "Bit, you understand that it's my responsibility to provide for you right?"

"Yes."

"And, you also know that I take my responsibilities very seriously."

"Yes."

"Then, stop balking and take the card." Tilting her face to his, he pressed a kiss to her lips. "Now, I want you and your mama to have a great time, and I'll see you back here later."

"Okay."

Receiving another quick peck from Carver, Alyssa swallowed any objections her inner Miss Independent had. Zaria was right, she deserved to have someone pamper and care for her. Carver wanted to do it, and she needed to simply appreciate his efforts.

Ten minutes after Carver left, the door to the suite opened and Samira stood to the side to allow Alyssa's mother to enter. Detouring from her trip to the kitchen, Alyssa went to greet her.

"Hey, Mama."

"Hey, Baby Girl."

Accepting a hug, Alyssa smiled at the sparkle in her mother's eyes. "What has your eyes shining like a new penny?"

"I can't be happy I get to spend the day with my only daughter?"

"Of course you can, Mama." Giving her another quick squeeze Alyssa turned back toward the kitchen. Tossing away the tea bags, she placed the mug in the sink.

"What's with this?" Her mother held up the pretty container which held the fancy organic tea Carver brought her earlier.

"Oh, it's something Carver found for me a tea shop. I ran out of the tea Ms Munoz normally makes for me. I've gotten so used to it my stomach feels queasy when I start a day without it."

"Mhmm." Her mother murmured distractedly as she scanned the box.

"I'll send you some when I get back home. Apparently, she gets it from a local place because we couldn't find any here. That stuff is supposed to be a good replacement."

"Supposed to be?" Her mother placed the box back on the counter. Her brow dipped in question.

"Well, that's what the lady in the herbal shop said. So far, it's doing okay. My stomach is settled enough for me to eat something and we have time to grab a quick bite on the way to our first appointment. Just let me get my purse."

Alyssa walked into the bedroom to get her handbag. When she came out, her mother was in the exact same place holding the same pose. Slowing to a stop, Alyssa studied the expression on her mother's face.

"Mama?"

"Are you pregnant?"

"What? No! Why would you ask me that?"

"Because you're talking about having an upset stomach in the morning, not being able to eat and needing special tea to settle it down. On top of that you're glowing brighter than the north star on a clear night."

"Mama, don't they say people in love have a glow? That's all it is. And, besides, one upset stomach does *not* equal pregnancy. I get my shot religiously."

Alyssa didn't allow herself to think about how many mornings she'd awakened with the same queasy feeling. She never actually threw up, she simply felt like she was on the verge of it until she'd finished her first cup of tea. After that, the rest of the day was normal.

Holding up a finger, her mother wagged it at her. "Number one, the only one hundred percent birth control method is abstinence. Which brings me to number two. We both know you and Carver aren't living in the same house and *not* rolling around in the sheets. So, pregnancy is a possibility."

"Mama!"

Alyssa averted her eyes as heat crawled up her neck. Yes, she was a full-grown woman, but her sex life wasn't something she discussed with her mother.

"Don't, mama, me. I'm just stating facts, and you'd do well to consider them."

"Okay, Mama." Alyssa's tone was conciliatory since she had no desire to continue this conversation.

"Uh-huh. I know you just want me to stop talking about it. So, I'll leave it alone for now."

Alyssa's mind swirled with uncertainty. As much as she protested to her mother, the thought had occurred to her. However, it had been quickly dismissed since the only so-called symptom she had was the hour or so of queasiness in the morning.

Exiting the suite, she pasted a smile on her face and launched into their itinerary for the day. Her mother squealed her excitement when Alyssa rattled off the list of services they'd enjoy at the spa before heading over to the salon side for their manicure, pedicure, and hair appointments.

As the elevator doors closed and the car started to move, it took a concerted effort for Alyssa to remain focused on the moment. *What if her mother was right?* If she was, what would that mean for her and Carver?

Chapter Thirty-Five

USE YOUR WORDS

Carver held Alyssa's hand in his with their fingers entwined. They walked along a tree-lined campus street. The sun setting behind them put a picturesque tint on the buildings. Although it was technically fall, the leaves hadn't begun to turn colors yet and it was warm. When a narrow path intersected the wider sidewalk, he tugged her hand to veer them off from their current direction.

"What is it?" Alyssa's eyes searched his turning from her appraisal of the condition of the buildings on this side of campus.

"I wanna walk down this way." Her head tilt of suspicion made him quickly add, "for old time sake. Come on, Bit."

They'd spent the day hobnobbing, as his dad would say. This was the first time they'd been relatively alone—security team notwithstanding. Carver had suggested a walk after they attended a reception. To sweeten the deal, he had a change of shoes for her that were more comfortable than the pretty strappy heels she'd worn. Carver's stomach performed a nervous flip when she yielded to his request.

"Being here brings back a lot of memories." Carver panned his gaze at the new stonework on the buildings as they walked along the path.

"It does." Alyssa's response was more of a wistful sigh.

"Being here with you kinda makes me wish things had been

different the first time around. That we'd found each other sooner." Lifting their joined hands, he pressed a kiss to the back of hers.

"Aww, Carver...That's sweet, but I think things happened exactly like they were supposed to. I don't know about you, but I wasn't ready for a serious relationship.

I thought I was. Especially, since I seemed to be full of sage advice to others at the time. But now... I understand that there was so much about life that I was oblivious to."

"I don't know about all of that, Bit. You've always seemed like you had a pretty good head on your shoulders to me."

They came to a wye in the path and Carver took them to the left. The sidewalk intersected with a wider brick pathway which led to a well-lit entry of a building. His eyes were glued to her face as he watched the realization dawn on her.

"Oh wow...They've really done a lot of work on campus. I had no idea they'd changed the library so much."

"Let's go in." Carver's lips stretched into a wide smile at her awe filled stare. It didn't take much convincing for her to go inside with him. She was so enthralled she probably didn't even notice Michael was already there.

It was after seven p.m. on a Thursday, so there were students moving throughout the building, but not many. Those there, spared them barely a glance as they walked through. Carver listened with half an ear as Alyssa talked about the upgrades and improvements.

He managed to nod at the appropriate times, but his mind was already two flights up from where they stood. As he knew it would, the grand staircase leading to the upper floors finally drew her attention. The staircase was the reason he'd chosen to enter the building from this side. If they'd continued on their previous path, they could've entered from the back, but he wouldn't have had the grandeur of the entry to pull her in.

"That's fancy." Alyssa gushed tugging on his hand to take them to the stairs.

"It is. I heard it took them a few years to get this completed once they got started. I'm kind of glad we were gone by then. It was probably a nightmare to find anything."

Shooting him a glance, she quirked an eyebrow. "You talk like you spent a lot of time here."

"Are you sayin' I didn't?" Stopping on the landing between the second and third floor staircases, Carver released her hand and slid his arms around her waist pulling her body flush with his.

Patting his chest Alyssa peeked at him through her lashes. "I'm not saying you didn't study, but didn't the athletes have a place they used?"

"Yes, but they cut that out by junior year. NCAA said athletes couldn't be treated differently than other students. If the campus library was good enough for the other students, the athletes could have study hall here as well."

"I remember that now. I guess I didn't think about it, because I hardly ever saw athletes when I was using the study rooms here. Other than when I saw you every so often."

"Speaking of study rooms...Let's go up and see if our room is still there or if they changed it."

"Our room?" Alyssa looked at him with raised eyebrows.

Dipping his head sheepishly, Carver smiled. "Well...That's what I called it."

The softness of Alyssa's palm rested on his cheek. "You are being really sweet and nostalgic tonight."

Kissing her palm, he enclosed her hand in his once more. "So, will you indulge me a little longer before we call leave for dinner?"

The apples of her cheeks lifted in a smile. "I think I can do that."

With a quick peck to her lips, he led her to the stairs and up to the third floor—home of the study room in question. The third level of the library was essentially empty. When they reached the top of the stairs, even the lounging areas were barren. On the previous floors, there had been at least one or two students wearing headphones with books spread out around them on the sofa and coffee table.

Carver's heartrate picked up as they veered to the right walking past the open tables and stacks of reference books that couldn't be removed from the library. They finally reached the end of the row where the glass enclosed study rooms were located.

Other than a face lift to the doors, new furniture and whiteboards, the rooms were exactly the same. Going directly to the second door from the left, Carver ushered Alyssa through the doorway. Walking farther into the room, she stood at the window.

Outside, the sun's final descent was seen through the branches of the trees. The last few rays landed on her cheek giving her face the appearance of glowing. Carver's palms started sweating like he was seconds away from the biggest game of his life. In a way he was.

When Alyssa turned from the window, he was down on one knee in front of her. His hand was clasped around the muted gold box. The lid was still closed.

Alyssa's jaw dropped and her hands flew to her face, covering her mouth. "Carver..." Her hushed whisper of disbelief matched the wideness of her eyes.

"Bit...The first time I saw you, I knew there was something special about you. It wasn't just your outer beauty. You seemed to emit a kind of light. You didn't even seem to realize the way some people were drawn to you—to that indescribable goodness that seeped from every pore of your being."

The tears welling in her eyes, caused his throat to tighten with emotion. But Carver didn't stop. He was doing his damndest to stick to his plan when all he really wanted to do was wrap Alyssa in his arms.

"The night I saw you in this room working on extra credit, of all things, it changed everything for me. I tried to fight it and keep things friendly, because I knew you weren't *that* kind of girl." He didn't expound on what he meant. They both knew. Clearing his throat, he continued.

"Do you know why I call you 'Bit'?"

Swiping at the tears streaming down her cheeks, Alyssa lowered her hands from her face. "Because I'm a computer nerd and that night when I explained binary numbers, the bits, bytes and words?"

Shaking his head, Carver gave her a soft smile. "That's part of it, but not all of it." Opening the box, he turned it so she could see what lay inside on a black velvet pillow.

"That night, when I sat at a table, much like this one, watching you at that whiteboard, you taught me about the foundation, the beginning of computer language. About how bits make up bytes which become words and how every piece of computer-based technology can be broken down to the bit. The beginning."

Taking her left hand in his, he kissed the back. "Bit, you are my beginning, my foundation. Everything I love can always be traced back to you. Your touch. Your influence. It's in every part of me."

Setting the box on the table, he pulled out the ring placing it at the tip of the appropriate finger on her left hand. The steadiness of his fingers defied the quaking of his insides. Carver's heart pounded so loudly, he feared he wouldn't be able to hear her over the noise.

"Alyssa Renee Ripley, will you do me the honor of being my wife?"

"Yes." Alyssa's voice was a whisper to Carver's ears, so he searched her eyes for confirmation.

"Yes?"

"Yes, Carver Wyatt Jamieson. I'll be your wife."

Sliding the ring fully onto her finger, Carver stood lifting her in his arms on the way up. Hungry, grateful lips sought hers in a searing kiss. His heart was full to bursting with uncontainable joy.

When he finally released her from the kiss, he pressed his forehead to hers. He made silent and audible promises to himself and Alyssa regarding his commitment to her and their future. They remained locked in their bubble for a while, before the need to be truly alone with her drove him to get them back to the hotel.

As they exited the room, they passed Michael standing sentinel outside the door. Grinning broadly, Carver looked at him.

"She said 'yes'!"

"I see. Congratulations to you both."

"Thanks!"

With his arm around Alyssa's shoulders, Carver grinned. Alyssa Ripley was going to be his wife. Life couldn't get much better.

Now that subterfuge was no longer necessary, they took the elevator down and left the building through the back. The vehicle was waiting at the curb to transport them to the hotel. Carver had booked suites for them, the security team and his parents.

He'd offered to do the same for her parents, but they'd decided not to stay overnight. Since Tech was only an hour away from Logan City, they were going to drive down Saturday morning and drive back after the game.

Entering the suite, Alyssa's steps faltered prompting Carver to reach out to steady her.

"What's wrong?" His sole focus was on his new fiancée. *Fiancée.* He liked the sound of that, but he'd enjoy *wife* much more.

"I'm okay. I was just surprised."

Following her gaze, Carver realized why she almost tripped over her own feet. Momentarily, he'd forgotten about the celebration dinner he'd planned for them. While there was always the chance she wouldn't accept his proposal, he anticipated a 'yes'. So, he had a candlelight meal prepared for them.

Everything was exactly as he'd specified. The doors to the balcony were open revealing a small dining table. It was covered with a long white tablecloth. Tall, tapered red candles emitted a soft glow against the backdrop of the night sky. The table settings were a mixture of red and gold.

Stepping fully into the room, Carver placed his hands on Alyssa's shoulders and turned her to face him. "Would you have dinner with me?"

Tapping his chest, she grinned shyly. "Of course I will." Raising on her toes, she pecked his lips.

With a quick detour to the bedroom to deposit their things and wash their hands, they were soon seated at the table overlooking the college town they'd called home for part of their young adult lives. Attendants appeared with covered dishes to serve them.

Alyssa's face appeared radiant in the candlelight. Carver's gaze was transfixed on her every movement and expression. The large center diamond of the engagement ring, he'd had designed to look like a computer chip, sparkled in the low light.

In those moments, over their celebratory meal, he fell even more deeply in love with her. He didn't think it was even possible. But there was something about knowing the woman you loved was committed to joining her life with yours.

It was a heady feeling. Such a heady feeling he momentarily had the insane notion of flying them back to Vegas to make it official as soon as possible. The idea was dismissed as soon as it flitted across his mind. Besides knowing both of their parents would be disappointed, he didn't want her to feel rushed. Although, he planned to make it clear that he preferred they do the deed sooner rather than later. In his opinion, they'd lost enough time.

"What are you thinking about?" Alyssa's head was tipped slightly to one side as she swirled the water in her glass as if it was the wine she'd declined.

"I'm thinking about how I can't wait for you to be my wife." Carver grinned wolfishly at the way she blushed prettily under his blunt reply.

"Oh." Clearing her throat, she took a sip of her water.

"You know what they say, Baby. Don't ask questions you don't really wanna know the answer to."

Setting her glass on the table, she met his gaze. "I wanted to know. I guess I thought you were thinking the same thing I was."

"What's that?" Reaching across the table, he tangled their fingers together.

"That you're happy we're here together and maybe that you're looking forward to spending the next fifty years or so with me."

Leaning forward, he captured her gaze with what he knew was a blazingly intense stare. Carver pressed a hand against his heart as if making a pledge.

"I *am* happy we're here together and I'm *abso-fucking-lutely* ecstatic about spending the rest of my life with you. But if you think for one second you're only going to be my wife for fifty more years, you've got another think coming.

I plan to be loving on you well past the century mark. Hell, even if I have to follow you in my hover-chair, I'm gonna be with you woman."

Alyssa's giggles cut into the intensity of his declaration. "A hover-chair?"

"Hey, a man's gotta do what a man's gotta do."

"If you say so."

"I do."

Finished with their meal, they moved inside. Closing the doors behind them, Carver was grateful they'd dismissed the waitstaff once the meal was served. He didn't have to worry about getting them out in order to get to what he wanted next.

The dress she wore hugged her figure perfectly, making him want to take it off the minute she put it on. He'd made himself a promise to remove it later. His fingers were itching to do just that. As soon as they'd come in from the balcony, she kicked off her shoes.

He followed suit as he reached for his phone and opened the streaming music app. Carver was certain there was a way to link it to the speakers in the suite, but he didn't have the patience to figure it out. At present, he wanted his soon-to-be wife in his arms.

When the first strains of the guitar floated into the room and Ed Sheeran's voice sang the first words about her legs not working like they used to, Alyssa turned to him with smile. With his arms stretched toward her, he invited her into his embrace.

Holding her close, with his cheek resting against the top of her head, they swayed to the music. It was likely too slow for the melody, but he didn't care. His Bit was in his arms while the red-headed crooner sang about how his love for his lady would never grow old. The song encapsulated his feelings about their relationship.

By the time Ed sang his last la-la and the song reached its final note, they were standing at the door to the bedroom. The next tune started up, but Carver was focused on Alyssa. Tilting her head to his, he took her lips in a kiss which started gentle before quickly shifting to a far more carnal caress.

Fulfilling his promise to himself, his fingers sought out the zipper he'd help close earlier. Tugging on the pull, he dragged it down. The smooth release was an inaudible whisper against the backdrop of the sensual music. Sliding the dress from her shoulders, he made quick work of her bra and panties.

Alyssa uttered not a word of protest. Carver knew she was just as stimulated as he was when he undressed her. She stood before him in all of her voluptuous glory. Her puckered nipples drew his eyes. *Were they larger?* It was if they were swollen and begging for his attention. Not wanting to deny them, Carver took one of the turgid peaks between his teeth worrying it gently before releasing it with a suckling pop.

His groans combined with Alyssa's moans, as the blunt tips of her fingernails scraped across his scalp. She held on to him as he transferred his attention between her breasts.

"Damn, Baby. You're so fucking beautiful." Standing to his full height, he pulled her body flush to his. "Do you have any idea what you do to me? Hm?"

Taking one of her hands, he placed it on the bulge tenting his slacks. Feeling her soft digits close around as much of his length as possible, through the barrier of his clothing, he almost came. Reluctantly stepping away from her touch, he yanked the upper layers of cover from the bed.

"Get on the bed, Baby. We gotta practice consummatin'."

Chuckling, Alyssa climbed onto the bed. "You're nut. I never know what you're gonna say."

Leaning against the mountain of pillows, she watched as he rushed through his own disrobing. The way she stared at him had him struggling to get his boxer briefs off over the stiffness of his erection. The heat of her gaze, as she raked her eyes across his body zeroing in on his thickness jutting from between his hips, made him even harder.

Carver would bet money he could literally pound nails with his cock right now. But, nails weren't his target. Currently, his goal lay between Alyssa's thick thighs at the end of the low landing strip giving directions on where to find his best girl.

With his clothing in a pile at his feet, Carver crawled onto the bed—stalking Alyssa. The lust in her stare matched his own. Spreading her legs, he wrapped his arms around her thighs. A sharp tug pulled her from her pillowy resting place to flat on her back.

Her squeak transformed into a keening wail as Carver latched on to her pearl and began worshiping at her temple. Her pleasure was his pleasure as he fed on her enjoyment, fueling his own. Alyssa's nectar coated his chin, but he continued using his tongue and fingers to bring her to completion. Her vocal appreciation drowned out the music still playing somewhere from the floor where he'd dropped his pants.

When Carver couldn't take not being inside her a moment longer, he quickly rose to his knees. Holding her legs to his chest, he aimed his stiffness with his hips. Unerringly finding her slick channel, he slid into paradise.

Throwing his head back, his voice joined hers in expressing their mutual appreciation. Her velvet walls clamped onto his shaft almost wringing his seed from him with the first stroke.

"Fuck, Baby. You feel so good."

"Mmm, Carver."

Alyssa moaning his name took his desire to another level. Working his hips, Carver sought out that special place inside her guaranteed to bring her the most pleasure. He wanted her as crazy for him as he was for her.

When he discovered the right angle and hit it, his Bit's cries reached a level they'd never attained before. It motivated him. He wanted to hear it again. So, he ruthlessly stroked that spot until she became a babbling mess, begging him for relief.

Lowering her legs from his shoulders, Carver leaned over her kissing the tears streaking down her temples into her hair. Their bodies were slick with sweat and his shaft remained buried inside her channel to the hilt.

Bracing himself on his elbows, he stared at her face as he resumed stroking her pussy. He worked his hips rhythmically keeping them both on the edge of orgasm without tipping over. He'd already seen to it that Alyssa found her release. She'd cum on his cock twice already, but he wanted one more.

He wanted her to soak his shaft and take his cum. Carver had thought many times of creating life with Alyssa. Now that she'd agreed to be his wife, it was more than a thought. It was a mantra. Pressing his forehead to hers, he narrowed his field of vision to her dark amber pools.

"Do you know what I want, Bit-baby? Hm?"

Alyssa's nails dug into his flank and her chest arched as she worked her hips in time with his. Her eyes fluttered closed on a moan. The action resulted in a twisting thrust from Carver.

"Open your eyes!" Her lashes snapped apart at his harsh command. Once he had her eyes on him again, he returned to rolling his hips massaging her walls with his cock.

"Now...Do you know what I want?"

When she attempted to shake her head no, he stopped her. "Use your words, Bit-baby."

Her "no" came out in a strained whisper. Grinning, Carver added a pelvic tilt to his thrust, grazing her clit on the downstroke.

"I wanna plant my seed in you." Her eyes widened. Carver captured her lips in a soft kiss which defied the cruel twist of his hips.

"You heard me right, Baby. I wanna plant my seed and make a baby with you."

Alyssa's legs came up, bracketing his waist and her fingertips dug into his sides. Her eyelids drooped until barely a sliver of her eyes were visible.

"Is that a yes, Bit-baby. Do you want that too? Hm? Answer me, Baby. Do you want me to paint your womb with my cum?"

When Alyssa's only response was a moan, Carver halted. "What did I tell you, Baby use your words."

"Mmm! Yes. Yes, Carver!" Alyssa cried as she bucked her hips trying to restart his movements.

Part of Carver wanted him to demand she tell him exactly what she craved, but he didn't have the patience. Her agreement unleashed the demon riding him and he lost it. His thrusts became wild and uncoordinated. Reaching between them, he worried the little bundle of nerves sending her crashing into her orgasm pulling him along with her.

Once the jerking aftershocks passed. Carver rolled to the side and tugged Alyssa into his embrace.

"Don't think I'm not gonna hold you to your word. When we get back, we'll talk more about it and figure out how we're gonna move forward."

Alyssa shifted in his arms. When he realized she was attempting to sit up, he loosened his embrace. Carver noticed the tremble in her fingers as she pushed her hair from her face. She bit her bottom lip as she finally met his stare.

"Carver, I need to tell you something."

Chapter Thirty-Six

MARY FUCKING BETH

Alyssa looked down at Carver as he lay reclined with a pillow under his head. Concern creased his brow beneath his short, tousled hair. She knew her words sounded ominous. Although it wasn't her intention, there was no other way to start the conversation.

They'd been on the go since they left Atlanta. At least that was the excuse she used to put it off. However, her therapist's voice was in her ear reminding her of the promise she made to herself and to Carver about her avoidance issues.

Sitting up, Carver cupped the side of her face with his large hand. "Hey...What's going on, Bit? Talk to me."

"I'm pregnant."

Alyssa blurted it out in a rush, fearing that if she didn't she would come up with another lame excuse. Which was absolutely ridiculous. They'd just had explosive sex in which he'd voiced his desire to father a child with her. Telling him he'd already performed that task effectively was good news. *Right?*

A slow grin spread across Carver's face. Laughter laced his words as he slipped his fingers into the hair at her nape and kissed the tip of her nose.

"I know I put it down just now, but I don't think you can say you're pregnant just yet, Baby."

Shaking her head, Alyssa looked into his eyes. Detangling his fingers from her hair, she climbed off the bed.

"Where are you going?" Carver rose to follow her.

Holding up one finger she continued to the bathroom where she'd left her cosmetic bag. By the time she'd located what she was looking for, Carver was standing in the doorway. *Of course,* he hadn't heeded her silent request. Holding the oblong object in her hand, she offered it to him.

"Here."

"What's this?" Taking it, Carver stared at it for a solid minute in silence. "Is this? I mean...does this?"

Clearing his throat, Carver looked from his hand to her face and back to his hand. Under different circumstances, Alyssa would've found his confusion utterly adorable.

"You're for real? Like. For real-for real? You're pregnant?"

"That's what the test results say—along with the three others I took because I didn't believe the first one."

"We're gonna have a baby?" The words came out in a shaky awe filled whisper as he stared at the pregnancy test he still held.

"Holy shit... I'm gonna be a dad!" Carver's gaze returned to hers, the tears glistening in his eyes triggered her own vision to cloud with watery joy.

Strong arms wrapped around her and warmth blanketed her front as Carver swept her into his embrace. Kisses were rained on her face, neck, and shoulder before finally being placed on her stomach. Carver was before her on his knees, his eyes locked onto her midsection.

His fingers were splayed across her abdomen in reverence and protection. Stroking his hair, Alyssa tangled her digits in the short tresses drawing his gaze to hers.

"I'm gonna be a dad."

"Yep. You're gonna be a dad."

"We're havin' a baby."

"I still need to see a doctor to know how soon. But yeah...We're having a baby."

"Thank you, Bit." A new round of kisses to her stomach ensued between murmurs of thanks.

It took some doing, but she finally got him off the floor. The return to his feet sparked his desire to spread their good news.

"I gotta call my parents!" Before he could go in search of his phone, Alyssa stopped him.

"Wait, Carver! We can't tell people yet."

Frowning, he turned around to face her. "What? Why not?"

"I don't know how far along I am, but they say the best practice is to not tell people until you're out of the first trimester."

"Why?"

"Because, if there's a miscarriage, it usually happens in the first trimester. So, we need to wait until after I can see a doctor."

Giving her a probing stare, he pointed his finger between the two of them. "So, we're the only ones who know?"

"Yes..." Alyssa knew her reply didn't sound convincing; so, she continued.

"My mother suspects, but I didn't tell her. She's actually the reason I took the test. When she came over for our spa day, she said I looked different. She came right out and asked me if I was pregnant. I told her no, but I couldn't get the thought out of my mind. So, I bought some tests. You know the rest."

Carver slid his arms around her once again holding her in his embrace. "So, I can't tell *anyone*?"

"Not yet."

Lifting on her toes, she pressed a kiss to his lips. The man was outright pouting.

"I know. It sucks. But, as soon as we get the all clear, we'll set up a video call with our parents and tell them first. Okay?"

A few silent beats passed before Carver nodded in agreement. Next, she had to contend with him treating her as if she was suddenly made of glass and the slightest touch might cause her to shatter. He insisted on bathing her in the shower, drying her off and rubbing cream on her body.

Him rubbing her body in any way usually led to sex, so she wasn't surprised when his erection tented the towel still wrapped around his waist. What did surprise her was that he didn't act on his obvious arousal.

"Are you just gonna waste that?" Alyssa finally asked about the stiffness jutting from his hips.

"Waste what?" Carver's face was a mask of concentration as he rubbed cocoa butter on her legs.

Reaching under the towel, she wrapped her fingers around his girth. "This. My boyfriend wants to play again."

Moving his hips, he pulled himself from her eager digits. "First of all, there is nothing boyish about my dick. Second, don't you think we should hold off on the sex? You know, until we see a doctor?"

Alyssa stared at him, dumbfounded. "Less than an hour ago, you had my ankles beside my ears, and now you're worried about hurting me?"

"In my defense, I didn't know then what I know now."

Placing her hand on his, halting his diligent moisturizing of her calf Alyssa responded, "Carver, it's sweet that you're worried about hurting me, but it's fine."

Holding on to her leg, he turned her as he sat on the bed draping her lower limbs across his lap. His hand migrated to her rounded tummy as if drawn by a magnet.

"I don't mean this ugly, but how do you know? It's your first time being a mama, right? Just like it's my first time bein' a daddy. I don't wanna do anything that hurts you or the little bun in your oven."

Resting her hand atop his, Alyssa squeezed his fingers. "I understand, and you're right. This is my first time, but I've been a woman for quite a while. Which means I've had chance to interact with more than my fair share of expectant mothers who were more than happy to enlighten me about their pregnancy highs and lows. As long as we don't get rough, we can do whatever we want. Just like always. I promise. It's perfectly safe."

"Oh yeah?"

"Yeah."

"You're not just sayin' that because you're horny and want my body?"

Lifting an eyebrow, Alyssa leaned away from him. "Excuse you, sir.

But, no matter how gorgeous it is, I'm perfectly capable of resisting your body."

"You don't say?" Carver's southern drawl deepened in challenge. His movements were so quick, Alyssa couldn't tell anyone how she suddenly found herself straddling his, now uncovered, lap.

His thickness stood tall between them; the side of his shaft pressed between her folds. Moisture gathered at her apex as she gave herself over to the desire that seemed to always ride so close to the surface. Tilting her hips, she began what became their second celebratory round of love-making for the night.

Neither of them marked time, and post-coital bliss came after they finally sated themselves for the third time. Mumbling about having a long two days ahead of them, they drifted off into slumber.

Alyssa looked around the posh lounge filled with people in various stages of conversation as they stood in small groups or sat on the luxury furnishings. It was clear to her where many of the athletic donor's coins were spent. The T-Club lived up to its reputation.

Caterers were set up in a dining section serving everything from game day hotdogs to steak and potatoes. Alyssa was simply happy none of the scents restarted the queasiness she'd awakened with. The relief she felt at being able to tell Carver about her pregnancy dissipated when his parents arrived Friday morning.

His mother remained as friendly and loving as usual. However, the expression she gave Alyssa was eerily similar to the one her own mother had given her right before she bluntly asked Alyssa if she was pregnant. Mother's intuition was a helluva thing to try to deny. Especially when they were right.

Carver's fingers squeezed hers drawing her back into the conversation. Alyssa had no clue who the others in the group were. Their parents had momentarily abandoned them for each other's company. So, she stood at Carver's side trying to smile at the appropriate moments, but not really keyed into the discussion he was having.

"My fiancée is a Tech graduate as well. Class of 2006."

"Oh really? And what was your degree in?" The older man replied turning his gaze to Alyssa. He had a shock of silver and white hair; his face and neck wore his devotion to the sun in a deeply tanned coloring.

"Computer Engineering."

"Don't be modest, Bit." Carver gripped her fingers again. "She earned both her Bachelor of Science and Master's degrees in the time it takes most students to get just one."

"What is that you called her? Bit? How cute. I thought you said her name was Allyson. You young people and your nicknames. I can't keep up." The woman standing next to the overly tan man piped up, laughter brimming in every word.

Hoping to head off a Carver comeback, Alyssa corrected the woman. "Actually, it's Alyssa."

He had a thing about anyone else calling her *'Bit'* other than him. When she glanced at her, Alyssa remembered why her mind wandered in the first place. She was trying not to stare at the excessively botoxed faces of the two women and the leathery, appearance of the sun worshipping men. As soon as Carver entered the club, there had been one variation or another of this group looking to press palms with him.

"Right, Alyssa. Now tell me, dear. What does one *do* with a degree in Computer Engineering? It seems like something men do. I can barely work my remote control. I can't imagine fixing computers."

Alyssa was certain the woman had no idea how insulting she was being. She was from a different era where men did certain jobs, and women, if they went to college, were only there to find a husband. Drawing on her stores of politeness, she managed something of a smile when she replied.

"I actually don't *'fix'* computers. I write the code that's used to keep gaming machines secure from hackers. While you're correct in the field being male dominated, I know quite a few women who work in the engineering profession. And, they don't just do well, they tend to outperform their male counterparts."

"Oh! Well, I had no idea." Frosted tipped fingernails adorned the hand the woman placed on her chest inches away from clutching actual pearls—although Alyssa had said nothing worthy of the action.

Alyssa looked at Carver, who graced her with a wide, reassuring smile. He had her back and that's all that mattered. After a few more minutes of dreaded small-talk, Carver was able to extricate them from the conversation. As they walked away, Alyssa spied their parents. They appeared to be in an animated discussion. The sofa and chairs they used were arranged in a conversational grouping, similar to others spread around the room.

The two of them immediately moved to join the group. At that moment, Alyssa's bladder decided to protest. Tugging on Carver's hand, she got his attention.

"I need to go to the restroom."

"Okay. I'll show you where it is."

"That's okay. I remember." Alyssa pointed to the hallway leading to the ladies bathroom.

"It's not a problem, Bit. I can take you."

Stopping, Alyssa managed to not put her hands on her hips. "Carver, I'm certain I can make it to the bathroom. Besides, you and I both know Samira is coming with me. Are you saying you don't trust her to do her job?"

Carver stopped walking as if he'd just remembered the other woman was there. Looking over her head, she was certain he saw Samira standing far enough away not to crowd them, but close enough to step in if things didn't look right. His normal overprotectiveness was on steroids since she'd told him about her pregnancy.

Patting his arm, she released his hand. Samira fell in step with her as Alyssa walked to the hallway leading to the restrooms. The ladies room was more of a lounge. Leather sofas, and chairs lined the walls. Side and coffee tables laden with fresh flowers were interspersed, injecting color into the cream and brown of the walls and furnishings.

Continuing through the lounge, Samira pushed through the door leading to the actual bathroom. Giving Alyssa a nod, Samira held the door for her to step inside. Proceeding to the first available stall, Alyssa didn't give thought to Samira stepping back into the lounge. She simply relieved her bladder and went to the sink to wash her hands.

As she was drying them, she heard another voice. Thinking someone else needed to use the facilities, Alyssa finished quickly and tossed the paper towel into the trash bin. Opening the door, she met the bun

Samira secured at the back of her head. On the other side of the body-guard, Alyssa heard a familiar voice.

"I don't see why I can't go in. We're friends."

Mary Fucking Beth. Alyssa hadn't seen her ex-best friend in more than ten years. That she would stand there and blatantly lie to Samira, knowing she'd been on the internet telling anyone who would listen that Alyssa was a boyfriend stealing tramp, made Alyssa's blood boil.

"Samira, could you step aside please?"

"Are you sure, ma'am?" Samira kept her attention on Mary Beth and didn't turn her head towards Alyssa.

"Positive." Alyssa's voice was sure and firm.

She knew there was a possibility she'd run into her old friend. It was homecoming. Mary Beth was popular when they were in school. If she stayed true to form, she wouldn't miss an opportunity to revel in her glory days.

When Samira stepped to the side, Alyssa was hard pressed to keep her shock from showing. Mary Beth had changed. *A lot.* In the videos she'd posted online, she'd only shown herself from the shoulders up. Alyssa now understood why.

Mary Beth had gained weight and it hadn't landed in the best of places. Sponge Bob immediately came to mind—if he had big boobs. She had to literally stifle a laugh. Not because of Mary Beth's weight gain, but because Alyssa knew how vain the other woman was. It was probably horrible for her that she no longer lived in a thin body.

"Hey Alyssa!" The plastic smile and forced enthusiasm in Mary Beth's tone did nothing to move Alyssa.

"Mary Beth." Alyssa made no attempt to pretend she was happy to see her former friend.

"I was just telling her," she pointed to Samira, "that it was okay if I came in, since we were friends. I just wanted to say 'hey'."

"Why?"

"Huh?"

"Why did you want to say hello to me?"

The smile on Mary Beth's face faltered. Alyssa knew she wasn't the same person Mary Beth remembered. She wasn't the quiet nerd who went along to get along. The veil had been irrevocably ripped from

Alyssa's eyes in those months prior to Mary Beth's wedding. There was no coming back from finding out your best friend essentially considered you a hanger-on that had over stayed her usefulness.

"Because…" She took a hesitant step in Alyssa's direction but stopped when Samira matched her movements.

Was Mary Beth dumb enough to try something with Samira right there? Probably not, but Alyssa was certain the bodyguard had picked up on what was really happening and wouldn't take any chances.

"You think I'm gonna hurt her?"

Mary Beth had the nerve to look offended at Samira's protectiveness toward Alyssa. *Cue the tears*, Alyssa thought, as her former friend's face reddened and sure enough, water welled in her eyes.

"Mary Beth, she's doing her job. She doesn't know you, but I do."

"So, you can tell her I wouldn't hurt you." Swiping at the tears that had yet to fall, she looked between the two of them.

"Why would I lie?"

"Excuse me?" Yet another woman in Alyssa's presence reached for her pearls. But, in Mary Beth's case, the pearls were imaginary.

"I'm certain I spoke clearly. Why would I lie about whether you'd hurt me? Considering you've done it before and as of a few months ago you were still trying to do so by attacking my character online. What part of your brain made you think I'd want to chuckle it up with you like nothing happened?"

"Alyssa…Lyssie… You know me. You know I get mad and say stuff, but I really don't mean it." Mary Beth's attempt to look contrite fell way short of the mark.

Alyssa tipped her head to one side. Raking her gaze over Mary Beth's unfortunately square torso, thin arms and legs, Alyssa took her in from the top of her, bleach damaged, frizzy hair to the outfit that screamed *'trying too hard'*.

It was obvious that she thought the blousy tank top would camouflage the lack of a dip where her waistline should've been. The denim miniskirt she wore was fringed with atrocious leopard print ruffles. No matter whose body that outfit was on, it would've been terrible.

"Here's the thing Mary Beth. I *do* know you. You showed me exactly who you were and in case I had a memory lapse, you reinforced it by trying to ruin my reputation. We both know I never, not once, made a play for Carver in college. Ever."

Mary Beth's face morphed into a snarl at the mention of Carver's name. Apparently, she was done trying to fake friendship.

"If you say so. I just find it funny that you two happened to get together when he moved to Las Vegas. You can say you didn't have anything going on, but I don't believe you."

"That's because you don't know what it means to be a real friend. *Real* friends don't make passes, flirt with or do anything that can be considered stepping out of bounds with her friend's boyfriend. But, I know you don't know anything about that."

Folding her arms across her middle, Mary Beth glared at her. "I don't know what you're implying, but I *was* a real friend to you. Just because I suggested you lose some weight, doesn't make me a bad friend."

Chuckling, Alyssa actually smiled at Mary Beth. She was completely self-absorbed to the point she couldn't see anything beyond her wants and desires.

"Of course, you'd think I was only talking about the shitty way you let me know you didn't want me in your wedding. When instead, I was talking about the fact that the guy you married was the boyfriend of your sorority sister—someone you'd previously called one of your closest friends. You stole that man from her and tricked him into marriage."

"How dare you!"

"How dare I what? Tell the truth? Did we forget which one of us has the reputation for being honest?"

Turning on her low-heeled, ankle boots, Mary Beth made to leave. When she reached the door, she whipped back around pointing her finger at Alyssa.

"You think you're so good and so smart. You were just a charity case for me. I felt sorry for you because you were such a big nerd you couldn't make friends. Now, you're trying to act like you're somebody because Carver defended you on the internet. Big whoop! It doesn't matter. None of it matters, because you'll end up just like me. Tossed aside when he moves on to the next big thing."

Folding her arms, Mary Beth smiled triumphantly—certain she dealt Alyssa a death blow.

"You know, Mary Beth, I told my mama she was wrong when she said you were jealous of me. I couldn't see how. You were popular, pretty, you weren't socially awkward, and had your pick of guys on campus.

But, I've come to realize she was right. *As usual*. It ate you up that he even noticed I existed didn't it? That's why you kept doing things to try to make sure I knew he was wrapped around your finger. Except it backfired. And he kicked your ass to the curb.

Now, what are you doing? You're divorced and broke. You lost custody of your kids; so, you don't have any child support coming in to keep you in the lifestyle you think you deserve. Since you only came to college to find a husband, you have a degree that's worth about as much as the paper it's printed on.

I'd almost feel sorry for you, except you bought and paid for the ass whooping life is giving you. I could offer you the same advice you gave me and tell you if you dropped a few pounds, maybe you could find a new sugar daddy to put you back into the lifestyle you crave...But something tells me you already tried that.

And as for what will happen between me and Carver, that's not really your concern. However, if you must know..."

Alyssa took a step forward and lifted her left hand clearly displaying the big ass ring Carver placed on her finger two nights ago. Mary Beth's eyes locked on to the sparkling jewels and her jaw dropped.

"I do believe he has stated his intentions towards me very clearly. But, you're welcome to keep thinking whatever you'd like. I'm going to go on living my amazing life with a man who loves me like crazy and wants to spend the rest of his days on earth with me."

Alyssa smirked as Mary Beth let out a squeaking huff before hightailing it out of the bathroom. It wasn't her nature to gloat, but Mary Beth had it coming. Alyssa had no intention of mentioning her marital situation or the loss of her children. Except, Mary Beth went low, so Alyssa went to hell.

"You tore out her ass, then scooped it up and smacked it in her face." Samira's assessment was delivered in what sounded like awe.

Alyssa looked at the other woman and burst into laughter. She laughed so hard, tears streamed from her eyes. When she finally got herself together, she went back into the bathroom to clean up her face.

As they reached the top of the hallway to enter the main area of the club, a commotion drew their attention to the door. Mary Beth was being escorted out by security. Escorted was actually too generous a description. The two men, dressed in campus security uniforms, held her arms as they bodily carried her out into the foyer.

Even after the glass doors closed behind them, she could still be heard screeching about being invited and saying she belonged there. Samira and Alyssa exchanged glances, neither of them could contain their amusement at the spectacle.

Chapter Thirty-Seven

BAG OF CRAY-CRAY

Carver watched Alyssa walk away with Samira at her side. No matter what Alyssa said, he didn't think he was being overprotective. He was simply offering to help her find her way. This was her first time in the T-Club lounge. He'd been many times as a player and a guest. This was simply his first time as an inductee.

In the future, he'd have access and privileges to bring his own guests as he did today. Carver delayed too long in his trek across the lounge to join their parents and was pulled into a conversation with another group of older Alumni—big donors. His and Alyssa's time on campus had been the same way since they arrived on Thursday.

It took more than a few minutes, but he was finally able to get away. Before he was dragged into another discussion he didn't particularly want to have, Carver redirected himself toward his and Alyssa's parents. From the corner of his eye, he saw a blond woman threading through the crowd.

Instinct made him turn to fully look. *Well, ain't this some shit?* It was Mary Beth. Something appeared to have gotten under her skin. The redness of her face and her pinched expression told a story, but he didn't really care to know what it was. Somehow, he didn't think he'd be spared the details though.

He didn't approach her, but he didn't have to. Mary Beth stopped and scanned the room. When she zeroed in on him, he cursed internally, then made eye contact with Michael. He didn't need security to protect him from her, but he'd damn sure have her removed before he let her drag him into any bullshit—especially today.

Once Michael was within earshot, he instructed him to get the campus security officers that were posted outside. As Michael walked away, Mary Beth stalked in his direction. Deciding it was best not to take the impending conversation anywhere near the parents, he folded his arms and waited. A few seconds later she stood in front of him.

"I guess congratulations are in order." Mary Beth bit out.

Instead of responding Carver simply stared at her. He didn't know if she was talking about his induction into the T-Club or his engagement to Alyssa. He and Alyssa hadn't made an official announcement regarding their engagement—although she wore his ring. So, it's possible Mary Beth was only talking about the T-Club and University Hall of Fame. He really didn't care either way. Carver just wanted her to get to the point and get out of his face.

"What do you want Mary Beth?"

"I just said it. I guess congratulations are in order. You finally have everything you wanted."

"Not everything," Carver responded.

A smile crept into her expression letting Carver know she'd completely misunderstood his statement.

"If you don't have everything. What's missing?" She tipped her head to the side and began twirling a lock of her long ash blonde hair.

If Carver didn't know better, he'd think she was trying to flirt. She couldn't possibly be that stupid or arrogant. She'd literally tried to blow up his life and relationship. There's no way she thought there was a snowball's chance in hell that he'd want to be with her.

"It's not what's missing. It what's here. Standing in front of me." Carver did a quick up-down of her frame, but passed no judgement other than to think her outfit choice was lacking in the style department.

"If I truly had everything I wanted, you wouldn't be standing here in front of me. In fact, I would never have to see your face nor hear your voice again. Ever." It was harsh, but Carver gave zero fucks.

Mary Beth's eyes widened. Her breaths came in deep huffs as the redness that had receded from her face, crept into her cheeks again. It might've been fifteen years, but Carver recognized the warm up to a tantrum.

"How dare you!" She didn't scream, but her volume increased.

"How dare I what Mary Beth?" Carver worked to keep his voice even. "How dare I tell the person who tried to blow up my life that I don't want to be around them? That's called setting healthy boundaries. I don't have to subject myself to people who don't mean me well. And, it's in both of our best interests that this conversation ends right here."

Carver's intent was to give Mary Beth no more than a parting glare, but she had other thoughts.

"What did you expect me to do? I put years into you and you just dropped me after you got drafted. Then I had to watch for years as you dated models and movie stars, while I was stuck in a no-name town in Georgia with three kids."

"So, you're blaming me for your life? I *never* promised you anything. You *assumed*."

"You **knew** what I wanted!"

"Yeah...but you also knew what I wanted." Carver didn't feel the need to rehash an old discussion. In his opinion, she didn't deserve a breakdown on why he wasn't ready for marriage immediately following graduation. Even if he had been, it wouldn't have been to her.

"You led me on!"

"Is that the lie you tell yourself? Is it the one that made you feel justified in getting on the internet spewing lies about me and the woman you'd said was your friend?"

Carver really didn't care what she'd had to say about him. It was her attack on Alyssa's character that set him off. Alyssa had never done anything to Mary Beth but be kind and supportive. Hell, even when Mary Beth was a complete asshole to Alyssa, she didn't make it her business to ruin the other woman's reputation. No matter how warranted it would've been.

He was so done with this conversation. His eyes roamed to the glass doors leading to the elevators, searching for Michael and the campus police. In his periphery, he noticed the clusters of people that were previously engrossed in their own conversations, had gotten moderately closer. The noise level in his direct vicinity had quieted as well.

"You know what Carver? I knew. I always knew she had a crush on you." Flipping her hair over her shoulder, the meanness she'd kept well-hidden all those years ago coated her face.

"It was fun for me to watch her give you moon eyes and know that at the end of the night, it was *my* bed that you were in. She tried to pretend it wasn't like that, but I saw it. It didn't bother me, because I knew she didn't stand a chance with a guy like you. So what if you gave her a little nickname to go along with her nerdy love of computers. It didn't matter."

The tears Mary Beth had worked up earlier, came back and actually fell onto her cheeks this time. "But then one day, I'm killing time on the internet and I see a video. It's Alyssa with some guy, then you were there. And, you were defending her. You looked at her and you held her in a way you **never** looked at me, or held me."

The tears dripped from Mary Beth's eyes unchecked. "All that time. All that time, I just knew her little crush was one sided, but I was wrong. The way you shielded her was different. That's when I knew. You wanted **her** that entire time."

Swiping at the tears on her face, she continued stating her grievances. "I read the comments on that video and people talked about how great it was and some crap about protecting black women. So, yeah. I made a few videos. Because they needed to know how the two of you stabbed me in the back."

"You're fucking delusional. No one stabbed you in the back. You're the one who does that shit. By the time Bit and I got together, you were so far in my rear view you weren't even a thought."

"Don't you stand there and lie! You did stab me in the back! And you're doing it again. Giving her the ring and the life that should've been mine!" Mary Beth slapped her hand to her chest for emphasis. "I can't wait for you to make your little announcement. I'm gonna get a lot of content out of that."

Carver's vision tinted red. He ignored the malevolent smirk on

Mary Beth's face as he leaned forward slightly. Although anger was licking up his neck, he kept his voice calm.

"Mary Beth. Listen and hear me good. If you allow Alyssa's name to drop from your filthy mouth again to say anything that ain't praise, you'll wish you didn't know the internet existed. You think your life is bad now—with you losing your alimony, not havin' your kids and havin' to move out of that big house. You ain't seen shit. If you don't keep my woman's name out of your mouth, your loss of status will be the least of your worries."

Had he not been so angry, Carver would've smiled at the look of surprise on her face. He didn't have to see the videos to know she was probably on social media pretending her life was still perfect. Carver knew of her issues because her former sister-in-law had reached out to him through social media channels.

Mary Beth's unhinged response to him and Alyssa going public with their relationship was the fuel her brother needed to get his kids away from Mary Beth. Carver was more than happy to provide any assistance and information to aid the other man's case. In the interest of transparency, he'd told Alyssa all about it.

In a hushed whisper, Mary Beth responded. "You? You helped Chad take my babies from me?"

"Happily. Those children deserve a mother who doesn't use them for leverage and a paycheck."

The hand Mary Beth lifted never made it to his face. Michael picked that moment to arrive with campus security. And, since Mary Beth had been in the process of actively trying to assault him, Carver didn't have to explain anything. They removed her. Uncaring of making a spectacle of herself, she kicked and screamed the entire time.

As she was being led out, Denzel walked in. The expression on his face as he watched the scene was a mix of confusion and suppressed amusement. When they locked eyes, Carver knew his friend was about to be on his bullshit. It wouldn't matter that all of their parents were there. He'd make time to give Carver shit about Mary Beth's very public outburst.

By the time Denzel reached Carver, his face was stretched into his signature wide smile. As much he wasn't looking forward to the potential ribbing, Carver was happy to see his friend. They hadn't hung out since before he'd moved to Vegas. Although Los Angeles and San Diego weren't super close, the years Carver was there before moving to New York, they'd hung out more frequently.

Despite good-natured jabs, Denzel was the closest thing Carver had to a brother and vice-versa. As only children, they'd bonded during Carver's sophomore year when he took the cocky freshman under his wing.

"Do I need to ask why your ex-girlfriend was being dragged out of here like an unwanted groupie who snuck into the after party at the penthouse?"

"Denzel!" Denzel's mother admonished him, but he continued to grin and watch Carver expectantly.

"Let's just say she got a little surprise and leave it at that."

Ignoring his friend's knowing stare, Carver greeted Denzel's parents. He hadn't seen them since Denzel's final game in the NFL.

"Mr. and Mrs. Reyes. It's good to see you again."

Shaking Mr. Reyes' hand, Carver gave Mrs. Reyes a hug leaning down to accept a kiss on his cheek. A nudge to his shoulder made him grin.

"You're holding on to my mama too long. It's disrespectful."

"Aw hush!" Mrs. Reyes swatted at Denzel and gave Carver another hug for good measure. "You are in rare form today. I'll be glad when whatever has you snarky and hyper wears off."

"Men aren't snarky, Mama." Denzel frowned at his mother.

"Just let it go. I was trying to be nice. It's your big day." Although her words were delivered with warmth, her expression was apparently all it took to get Denzel on the page.

As much as Carver wanted to laugh, he stifled it. Denzel's mother had a wicked side eye game. Instead, Carver invited them to join him and the rest of his group. By the time they made it over to where Carver and Alyssa's parents were seated, she and Samira arrived from her trip to the restroom.

Although he picked up on a slight difference in Alyssa's demeanor, he didn't dwell on it. Making a mental note to speak to her about it later, he introduced Denzel and his parents to Alyssa's parents. In their long-standing friendship, Carver and Denzel's parents had long since been acquainted. As often as Carver's parents came up to see him play while he was at Tech, it was amazing that they hadn't run into Alyssa's parents in all of that time.

Most of the morning, Carver had managed to contain his desire to share his and Alyssa's news. However, both of their parents were aware of their engagement. He'd told his father during their trip to the farm that he planned to propose. Then, while Alyssa and her mother had their spa date, Carver met with Alyssa's dad to officially ask him for his daughter's hand in marriage.

For the briefest of moments, the man had Carver thinking he was going to say no. He just stared at Carver for what felt like an eternity. Not normally one to fidget, Carver had to make a concerted effort to keep his hands still and not fill the silence with any words. Finally, Mr. Ripley's face split with a big smile.

Remembering the relief he felt in that moment, Carver curled an arm around Alyssa's waist resting one hand on the curve of her stomach. Alyssa gently glided her fingers over his and tangled their digits together. She tried to be casual, but he knew what she was doing. Moving his hand without drawing attention to what he'd done. The joke was on her though, because when he looked at his parents, his mother's eyes were glued to where their hands lay. But, she didn't say a word.

When the game got underway, everyone turned to face the tempered glass windows that gave the T-Club the best view of the field. The middle windows were situated on the fifty-yard line directly above the President's box. They only got to enjoy part of the first half before he, Denzel and their families were escorted to the sidelines in preparation for their introduction as the newest inductees into the T-Club and University Hall of Fame. Since they were limited on the people who could accompany them on the field, Alyssa's parents stayed behind.

Their class consisted of Carver, Denzel and two others. While they milled around under the tent to the rear of the endzone, Carver stepped away to get Alyssa a bottle of water. Denzel joined him under the guise of getting something for his parents.

"So...what was up with old girl getting thrown out earlier?"

Carver knew Denzel wouldn't be able to wait to find out what happened. Chuckling, he gave him the short version. Now that it was over, he wasn't angry. Although he'd make good on his promise to Mary Beth if she didn't find some business of her own and keep Alyssa's name out of her mouth.

Keeping his voice low, Denzel leaned into him. "CJ, go on and tell me the truth. That chick is a head doctor isn't she? I can't see any other reason to put up with that kind of crazy."

Shaking his head, Carver looked at his friend. "I can't believe you asked me that. Wait...Yes I can." Thanking the person passing out beverages, Carver turned to make his way back to their little group.

"So are you gonna own it or what? That was a straight up bag of cray-cray. I'm gonna say head doctor supreme."

Shaking his head, Carver knew Denzel wouldn't let it go. "Fine...at the time...as far as my twenty-one-year-old self had experienced, she performed that task well above average. Now..." Carver shrugged. "I can't say that was anything to write home about."

"Damn man...that's cold."

"It's amazing what some years and the love of a good woman will do for your perspective. Besides, she didn't act like that when we were in college. She went off the deep end today."

"Did you push her?"

Carver smirked in response.

"Yeah...your ass pushed her. What did you do?"

"Nothing but tell the truth. She didn't like hearing it."

"Mhm..." Denzel gave him a twisted grin shoving his shoulder. "I still wanna know if Alyssa knows how crazy you are. I need to let her know my offer still stands to help her hide from your wild ass."

"The fuck you will. She doesn't know about the first offer and I'll be damned if she hears the second. She doesn't need to be hidden from me."

Carver got so riled up he almost let it slip to Denzel about the baby. Despite knowing Denzel was kidding, he couldn't help his knee jerk reaction at even the thought of her being somewhere that he couldn't get to her. Now that she was carrying his child, his obsession had grown ten-fold.

"Aw man. Don't be like that. She deserves to know she agreed to marry a demon."

"If I'm a demon, what does that make you?"

"I'm an angel sent straight from heaven."

Carver stopped and stared at Denzel for a moment. Then, he burst into laughter. "If angels do the shit I've seen you do they need to revise all of those stories they told us in church."

Ribbing each other good naturedly, they returned to the group. Carver was happy he and Denzel were a part of the same induction class and that their loved ones were able to be present to share in the moment with them. When the horn blew announcing the start of halftime, his heart rate kicked up. Emotions he hadn't expected well up in him.

It was surreal to take the field he'd played on for four years as the newest member of the University Hall of Fame. Doing it with the woman he loved by his side put a lump in his throat. As their names were called, the announcer listed their accomplishments during their time at Tech, but also in the years that followed.

Carver listened as the unseen man chronicled almost twenty years of his life. He raised his right hand, waving to the crowd. His left hand firmly clasped Alyssa's. It was something about being on that field that evoked strong feelings in him. Combine that with being accompanied by the people who loved him best and it was damn near a magical moment.

"Coach Jamieson is currently the quarterback coach for the Las Vegas Ravagers. He is joined on the field by his fiancée Alyssa Ripley— who is also a Tech graduate, as well as his parents Lance and Carol Jamieson."

Alyssa's fingers gripped his a little more tightly when the announcer said her name. Looking at her upturned face, he couldn't resist dropping a quick kiss on her lips. She had no idea he'd given them her information. He stood up straighter and his chest filled with pride. Although it was his moment, he wanted the world to know the beautiful woman at his side had agreed to be his wife.

The rest of the day was much calmer than it began. After the game, Alyssa's parents got on the road back to Logan City while his parents opted to retire early to their room. When he and Alyssa were finally alone again, they were cuddled together on the sofa in their suite discussing the events of the day.

"So...would you happen to know why Mary Beth was dragged out of the T-Club like a criminal?"

Carver squeezed her a little closer with the arm he had wrapped around her shoulders and rubbed her bicep.

"She got in my face talking shit about us, when I didn't tell her what she wanted to hear, and I told her what would happen if she didn't keep your name out of her mouth, she thought it was a good idea to try to slap me."

Alyssa bolted upright. "She did what?!"

Gliding his hands along her arms, Carver tried to calm her. "She didn't get a chance, Bit-baby. Campus police pulled her away before she could lay a hand on me."

Poking out her bottom lip, Alyssa frowned. "I knew I should've let Samira rough her up when she tried to talk shit in the bathroom."

Now, it was Carver's turn to frown. "She tried something with you today too?"

Switching their roles, Alyssa cuddled into his side and stroked his chest. "She didn't try anything physically. I'm not sure what her original goal was, but she felt the need to tell me that you wouldn't stay with me. When she got a gander at this big ass ring you laid on me, she got a little upset and stormed out. I had no idea she would seek you out. I don't even know how she got in. Don't you have to be a member or the guest of a member?"

"Yeah. Actually, I spoke to the couple who allowed her to come in with them. They are friends with her former in-laws. They apologized for bringing her in. I accepted their apology, but its's not their fault Mary Beth is unhinged."

Alyssa's shoulders gave a shuddering shake. "How did we ever get tangled up with that kind of cracked human being?"

Her question made him remember his conversation with Denzel earlier. He definitely wouldn't be recounting those reasons to Alyssa. Instead, he hugged her closer.

"I don't know, Baby. I think we have to chalk that up to the ignorance of youth."

"Hmm." She murmured and burrowed closer to him. He knew that move. It wouldn't be long before she drifted off to sleep.

"Bit?"

"Hm?"

"I was hoping to wait until the end of the season, but now I'm thinking we should get married sooner rather than later."

"Excuse me, what?" Alyssa sat upright staring at him in disbelief.

Chapter Thirty-Eight

MY THOUGHTS AND A CUP OF TEA

Alyssa sat looking at her reflection in the oval shaped glass on the vanity. For the first time in months, she'd awakened without Carver beside her. But, according to tradition, it was bad luck for the groom to see the bride before the wedding. Them adhering to tradition was hilarious considering all the ways they'd thumbed their noses at societal norms. Her mother and the rest of her small bridal party hadn't descended upon her yet, so she had a few moments of quiet to herself.

The past few weeks had been a whirlwind of activities. When Carver brought up them getting married sooner rather than later, Alyssa thought he'd lost his mind. Where, in either of their busy schedules, would they have the time to do more than go to one of the chapels in Las Vegas? Besides, there was no rule saying they *had* to be married to have a baby. They weren't living in the eighteen hundreds. There was no longer a stigma attached to having a child out of wedlock.

But...she should've known Carver wouldn't bring it up without a plan. Proving he knew her better than she thought he did, he'd already researched wedding planners and locations. Due to the rigor of the season, they only had one window of opportunity between October and February—the bye week. It gave the team thirteen days between games.

It was the only time available, and it meant they'd have to do things quickly.

Alyssa wasn't one of those women who'd been planning her wedding since she was old enough to know what marriage was. She didn't have a wish book with her dream dress, wedding location and colors. Being a typical introvert, she simply knew she wouldn't want anything big and ostentatious.

The moment she and Carver met with the wedding planner, Cindy, Alyssa knew they had the person who could meld both of their visions together. A soft-spoken woman, she was flexible but firm and she had excellent contacts. She was able to find a property for them to rent in Bali that could house their guests and had a place on site for them to hold their small wedding.

She further endeared herself to Alyssa at the dress fitting. The owner of the shop had curated dresses based on Cindy's instructions; however, she was running late to the appointment. The woman who stepped in decided to show Alyssa a different set of dresses. At the first awful ball of fluff presented, Cindy halted the entire process.

"Pardon me, may I speak with you a moment?" Excusing herself from Alyssa and her mother, Cindy walked out of the fitting area with the salesperson.

"I hope she's about to set her straight. Because, if she doesn't I certainly will." Alyssa's mother watched them leave with narrowed eyes. "The nerve of that toothpick heifah to bring that ugly ass dress in here. Why do they even have that for sale? It's a shapeless mass of hideous material."

"I don't know mama. But, I have no intention of wearing anything like that."

They were only gone a few moments, but when Cindy returned, the sales lady was nowhere to be found. Instead, there was a tall woman with dark brown skin accompanying the wedding planner.

"My apologies for being tardy. I'm Hallie Blackwell." Her warm smile immediately set Alyssa at ease.

"Also, please accept my apologies for Taylor going off script. That shouldn't have happened and I'm truly sorry. It's my desire for each bride to walk out of my shop with a gown that makes her feel her most beautiful and special.

With that in mind, allow me to show you the designs I've pulled for you. Based on your schedule, I picked items that I think would require the least alterations while still showing off your assets to the fullest."

At her mother's drawn out, "Mmhmm." Alyssa nudged her. Returning Hallie's smile, Alyssa stood to look at the selections the shop owner presented.

Alyssa noticed Cindy remained alert and focused on her. She didn't relax until she saw that Alyssa had sincerely accepted Hallie's apology and was happy with the wedding gowns offered.

Looking over her shoulder, Alyssa looked at the flowing creation draped on the headless mannequin on the other side of the room. The butterflies fluttering in her stomach were due solely to her anticipation of donning said dress and joining her life with the man she loved.

It was too soon in her pregnancy for the gentle flapping to be caused by the life growing inside her. That wouldn't happen for at least another two weeks. As had become habit, her hand dropped to her stomach. Although she couldn't tell the difference other than how firm her abdomen felt now, Carver swore he could see the changes. Considering the time he spent studying her body, Alyssa conceded to him. Smiling, she thought back to their first visit to the OBGYN the Wednesday after their return from Georgia.

Dr. Zora Kent had been Alyssa's OB since she relocated to the Las Vegas area. Alyssa loved their relationship and had no intention of changing to some 'doctor to the stars' simply because she was with Carver. Thankfully, Dr. Kent was able to accommodate them to maintain their confidentiality beyond the normal measures.

Her staff was aware of the stiff penalties involved if they were to sell information to the tabloids. To further ensure their privacy, she also arranged Alyssa's appointment as the last in the day, after all other patients had been seen and cleared the building.

While it may seem a little over the top, Alyssa was gun shy when it came to having her business put online for public consumption. Carver respected her decision to stay with the doctor she knew. Alyssa was certain his protective nature meant that he'd run background checks on more than a few people—just to be safe. That aspect of his personality had taken an adjustment simply because Alyssa wasn't accustomed to men outside of her family protecting her and even they didn't do it with the same vigor as Carver.

However, the moment Dr. Kent turned the monitor in his direction showing the little bean shaped image on the screen, Carver melted into a gooey puddle. His fingers gripped hers and tears misted in his eyes.

With a few clicks, Dr. Kent started explaining what they were seeing. "Just based on the size of the fetus and the information from your blood-work, I'd put you at the eleven weeks. So, you are coming up on the completion of your first trimester."

Carver perked up more at that morsel of information. He'd been having the hardest time not at least telling his parents their little secret. "So, are we at the beginning of eleven weeks or the end?"

Smiling at his question as if she were privy to the many conversations the two of them had on the subject, Dr. Kent answered him. "You can start telling people in a week."

"Thanks, Doc."

"No problem. Most couples are anxious to share their big news with their loved ones. It's completely understandable."

Carver's face lit up. Alyssa was happy, but seeing his joy took hers up a notch. It filled her to the brim to witness how all-in he was on every aspect of their relationship. She resolved to show him that same level of enthusiasm and commitment.

A knock pulled Alyssa her from her memories. Placing the brush she'd yet to use, back on the vanity she rose to answer it. On the other side of the door was Zaria looking refreshed and ready to get the day started.

"Good morning, Bride-to-be! Are you ready to become Mrs. Carver Jamieson?"

"Hey Zee. I guess so." Alyssa smiled and extended her arm inviting her friend inside.

"You guess? Girl, you are about to say 'I do' to a man who loves the stank off your dirty draws. You need to do more than guess at being ready. Do I need to go tell him it's a no go?"

"What!? Absolutely not! I love Carver and I want to be his wife." Alyssa stared at her friend in disbelief.

"If that's the case, I'm gonna need you to show more umph about yourself."

Sweeping past Alyssa with a garment bag in her hands and a tote over her shoulder, Zaria strode into the lounge area of the suite. Alyssa had no idea how she was supposed to add more 'umph', but she'd give it the old college try. Smiling at her friend's back, she followed her across the expanse of the suite.

Walking in a circle around Alyssa's dress, Zaria ghosted her hand over the fabric. Not quite touching it—she air stroked it in reverence.

"I love this dress. It's so you. Simple but elegant with a touch of risqué."

Hanging the garment bag on the clothing rack, which resembled the ones from a department store, Zaria clapped her hands. Looking around the suite, she asked Alyssa, "Where is everyone else? I thought we were meeting here for a light breakfast at nine, then getting ready together so we could help you."

"We are. You're just a little early."

"I am? It's..." flipping her wrist up, Zee looked at her watch, "oh... Seven a.m. My bad." Grinning sheepishly, she made to leave. "I'll come back in a couple of hours."

Halting her, Alyssa placed a hand on her shoulder. "You don't have to go. I was awake and trying to figure out what to do with myself for the next few hours anyway."

"Oh ok. If you're sure."

"I am. All I have is my thoughts and a cup of tea to keep me company."

Zaria lifted an eyebrow and chuckled. "That damn tea is what got your ass in trouble."

Swatting at her friend playfully, Alyssa shushed her. "Stop it! How was I supposed to know that some natural herbal teas could interfere with medications and render my birth control useless?"

"All that's telling me is that you and Carver had plenty of love without the glove." Laughing at her own turn of phrase, Zee skipped away from another playful swat from Alyssa.

"Whatever. You could've kept that thought in your head." Walking toward the vanity, she gestured to her friend.

"Come over here and help me with my hair. I'm regretting not taking the offer for to have a hair stylist onsite. I'm not feeling like tangling with this stuff." Alyssa fluffed the curly coils framing her face.

"Mhm. Being cheap." Zee twisted her lips, sucking her teeth at Alyssa.

"I wasn't being cheap. I just didn't see the need to spend thousands of dollars to fly someone here simply to have them pin my hair up for me. Between the two of us, we've pinned up my hair in the past better than some of those paid hair stylists."

"You didn't get a hair stylist, but you have a make-up artist?"

"I have my cousin, who I invited to the wedding. She volunteered to do my make-up as a gift."

"So, you're going to look me in my face and act like your *cousin* isn't an award-winning make-up artist?"

"I didn't say that."

"Oh, because I was gonna tell Candy you're over here talking about her like she's Shay-Shay beating faces in her mama's basement bathroom or something."

Giggling, Alyssa bumped her hip against Zaria. "You will not. Besides the fact that it's not true. I already have some of the family giving me side eye because I kept the invite list so tight. I don't need one of the few people who made the cut turning on me."

"I'm just amazed she said yes when she has a new husband and a five-month-old."

"Well, even though we aren't as tight as her and Kari, Candy and I have always been good friends as well as family. You know I don't have many that I call friend."

Sitting once again on the chair in front of the vanity, Alyssa looked at Zee in the mirror's reflection. Stepping behind her, Zaria leaned over and wrapped her arms around Alyssa's shoulders hugging her.

"I know. I'm just picking with you." Reaching past Alyssa, she grabbed the water misting spray bottle and began lightly wetting Alyssa's tresses. "It would've been nice to have a hair stylist, but for what they'd do, you can save that ten grand and just send me a nice spa day gift certificate as a thank you."

"Ma'am!"

Throwing her hands up, Zaria giggled. "I'm kidding. I'm kidding."

The two continued their good-natured bantering while Zaria sectioned Alyssa's hair and started twisting it. They finally settled on a style which left part of Alyssa's curls free with twists leading up to the curls at the crown of her head. A cascade of coily locks fell across the right side of Alyssa's forehead half framing her face. Just as Zaria was securing the wrap to hold the style in place, there was a knock on the door.

Since she was already standing, Zee went to answer it. Alyssa's and Carver's mothers swept into the room immediately followed by an attendant pushing a wheeled food cart. Hugs were dispensed as the two women directed the attendant to the terrace where they'd share the meal.Their arrival signaled the start of the day's activities. Soon after, the wedding planner arrived as well as Candy. Having appointed herself official greeter, Zaria opened the door and stared at Candy for a moment before allowing her in. Once Candy stepped over the threshold, Zee poked her head out of the doorway and looked from left to right.

Staring at her with a confused expression, Candy asked, "What's going on? Am I being followed? Did I miss something?"

"Yes ma'am you did miss something." Zaria closed the door and turned to Candy with her arms folded. "How dare you show up without that bundle of cuteness I only got a glimpse of yesterday before y'all whisked her away. You're keeping me from smelling her baby smell and giving her cuddles."

Smiling, Candy laughed at Zaria's antics. "Oh no ma'am. I'm not keeping you from her. I'm saving you. She's in a mood right now. The time difference has been a beast and she's not happy about it. So, when Kenneth said he had it covered, I hightailed it out of there."

The mothers re-entered the suite just in time to hear Candy's explanation. They looked at one another, then at Candy and burst into laughter.

Carol walked over to Candy. "Let me guess. She's a daddy's girl."

Nodding Candy affirmed her statement. "One thousand percent. I'm not saying she doesn't love her mama, but she just watched me leave with no additional tears. On the other hand, when her daddy walks out of the room, you'd think he left her forever."

"Oh, that's gonna get real interesting when you have baby number two." The two older women slapped hands as though Alyssa's mother had told the best joke ever.

Candy looked at her as if the other woman had slapped her across the face. "Auntie...with all due respect. I need you to take that back, right now. Ain't nobody said nothing about another baby around here. You're not gonna put that on me."

Although Alyssa's mother was technically Candy's cousin, they tended to call all of the older women in their families Auntie. Smirking, Alyssa's mother simply patted Candy's arm.

"Baby, I can't do that. I've seen your husband and the way he looks at you. That second baby is coming, so you might as well get ready."

In an attempt to save Candy from her mother's prophesying, Alyssa suggested they go out on the terrace and have breakfast. Smiling at Cindy, Alyssa hoped the wedding planner wasn't uncomfortable with the unfiltered banter. Lord knew Carver didn't completely inherit his irreverent way of talking from his father alone. Miss Carol could hold her own with Anna Ripley.

Once they were seated for breakfast, Alyssa allowed her gaze to wander to the women around the table. Due to time, location and their personal wishes, Carver's and Alyssa's wedding would be small and intimate. Zaria was the only bridesmaid and her maid of honor. Candy was there as one of the few invited guests.

Alyssa completely understood some of the others who couldn't make it because of the short notice and scheduling conflicts. She got lucky with Candy and her husband being able to work it out. Alyssa's mother informed her that her brothers finally made it in late last night which eased her mind.

In total, their wedding would be attended by less than twenty people which included their security detail. Although Alyssa wasn't surprised, Carver asked Denzel to be his best man. Neither Jasper nor Andrei gave him grief about it even though Andrei had closed down the bar across from *The Rooftop* to host their joint Bachelor and Bachelorette party before they left Las Vegas a few night ago.

Considering the small amount of people she'd even invite to such a gathering, Alyssa was more inclined to not have one, but Zaria wasn't having it. She roped in a few ladies from her, as she called it, *Black Lady Lawyer* group. Alyssa smiled at the memory. Those ladies knew how to party.

One of them was engaged to a friend of Andrei's who crashed the party when he learned Ensley was attending a co-ed event at Anton's. The big cowboy made quite an impression. Thankfully, Carver didn't make a big deal out of it. He knew Ryker as the CEO of the custom boot company *Cordwainer*. In fact, he'd personally gifted Carver a pair of boots after he won his first Superbowl. According to what Alyssa learned, the man had an uncanny ability to look at a person and the way they moved, then fit them with the perfect boot to match their gait.

Thinking of the party brought Alyssa's mind back to Zaria and Andrei's conspicuous disappearance as the night drew to an end. Alyssa had been patiently waiting for her friend to bring it up. But so far, nothing. She wasn't worried though. Alyssa knew she'd eventually get it out of her.

Following breakfast, Cindy whipped out her clipboard and got them on task for the day. All of the ladies' attire was in the suite so they could dress together and be ready for the photographer. Alyssa's nerves had calmed during the meal, but as time crept closer to the hour for them to begin, the butterflies returned.

It didn't help that her mother burst into tears once the cape covering Alyssa's dress was removed revealing her completed look. Quickly turning away before she joined in causing the moment to devolve into a cry-fest, Alyssa looked at herself in the standing mirror. Her hair and make-up were flawless and her skin appeared sun-kissed.

The only jewelry she wore was a necklace from Carver's mother. It filled the category of old and borrowed as it belonged to Carver's maternal grandmother and was being loaned to Alyssa for the day. The lavender hues in the silver backed pendant caught the colors in her dress perfectly.

Opting for comfort combined with cute, Alyssa wore flat strappy sandals instead of heels. Other than comfort, she wanted to avoid an argument with her new husband on their wedding day. He was *team no heels* while she was pregnant—wary of her falling.

Alyssa picked up the beaded pouch from the vanity. Her something new. It only held a handkerchief, but she looped it around her wrist thinking about her Grandma Patricia. Her only living grandparent. She wasn't able to make the wedding because of the flight, but wouldn't hear of Alyssa and Carver changing their plans to accommodate her. A gifted seamstress, her grandmother sewed the pouch and hand stitched each bead onto it.

By the time the entire group was dressed and ready, the hour had arrived for everyone to take their positions. Giving her one last hug, Candy and the mothers left her and Zaria alone. They stood together in a small room right off the double doors leading out to where the archway was set up. Neither spoke, but words weren't necessary at that point.

Soon, Alyssa was alone as the sound of instrumental music drifted in from the outside. When her father appeared in the doorway, Alyssa had to fan her face to stem the possible flow of tears. *This was really happening. She and Carver were minutes away from being husband and wife.*

Chapter Thirty-Nine

MR. AND MRS. CARVER WYATT JAMIESON

Carver rolled to his stomach, grunting in complaint of being awake after the trouble he'd had falling asleep in the first place. Wrapping his arms around the pillow beneath his head, he wished he was holding Alyssa. But no...they had to adhere to some archaic tradition. So instead of cuddling next to her plush curves, he had a cold pillow in his hands.

"Ugh!"

Tossing the covers off, he left the bed. With one hand holding back the gauzy curtains covering the floor to ceiling window, he stared at the beautiful view. When Alyssa agreed to marry him in less than a month following his proposal, Carver knew he'd have to present her with a plan she couldn't resist.

Bali was on her travel bucket list, and it also offered them the opportunity to preserve their privacy. They had very little worry of there being paparazzi or jealous exes showing up to ruin the festivities. Which was a good thing, because Carver had no problem cracking heads to keep a smile on Alyssa's face.

Stress wasn't allowed anywhere near her. That's why he took care of hiring a wedding planner and any of the small details. Did it add to his level of stress? Yes. Would he have it any other way? No. He worked it out with team management to allow him the consecutive days off to get it done, but it meant they'd have to put off a formal honeymoon.

That didn't necessarily bother Carver, since every day felt like a honeymoon to him. He was marrying the woman he'd been in love with for more than a decade. Nothing could put a damper on that.

Pounding on his door pulled Carver's attention from the magnificent view.

"Hey! Wake your ass up!" Denzel's yells made Carver speed up in his trek to the door.

Swinging it open, he reached out, snagged his so-called friend by the arm and yanked him into the room.

"Why the hell are you yelling so early in the morning? There are other people here you know. Some of them might be sleeping."

"Excuse you." Pulling his arm from Carver's grip, Denzel straightened his t-shirt, like it was fine linen instead of worn cotton sporting their college logo.

"First of all, I have sense. Everyone else is up and moving around, so there's no one to wake up. You're the only adult lazing around in the bed. Hell, even that little baby is up and about." Denzel looked at Carver accusingly.

"What?"

Carver strode into the other room to get his phone. Waking the screen, he looked at the time. It was already nine a.m. *Wow. Was it the time difference?* They'd been there for two days to allow them to acclimate.

As much as he wanted to blame his late rising on the time zone difference, he knew he only slept so late because of the issues he had getting to sleep in the first place. He was addicted to his Bit and sleeping without her, for even one night, messed with him.

He left the bedroom to encounter a smirking Denzel standing next to the sofa. Giving him the finger, Carver leaned against the door jamb.

"Okay. You've confirmed that I'm awake. What's next?"

"You take your ass in there and wash it. While you do that, I'll take pity on you and have the kitchen staff send up some breakfast." Checking the watch on his wrist, he continued. "The concierge has arranged for someone to come in to get you spit shined and ready to tie the knot."

Stopping mid-turn, Carver looked at his friend. "I'm sorry what?"

Raising an eyebrow, Denzel shot him a haughty look. "I take my best man duties seriously. I'm not gonna have the future Mrs. Jamieson on my case about letting her man go out looking any kind of way. Now go on. Git!"

Shaking his head, Carver followed directions. A hot shower may be just what the doctor ordered. He had some time to fill before he'd see his Bit and whatever Denzel had planned may be just the distraction he needed.

Goodness knows the other man felt robbed of giving Carver a proper bachelor party. The least Carver could do was let his friend fulfill the tasks of his best man role. It was actually a relief. One less thing on his plate.

Honestly, had Denzel not arranged it, Carver would've simply shaved himself, put a little product in his hair, slapped on some cologne and called it done. He'd visited the barber the day before they left, so Carver wouldn't have considered doing anything more.

After he showered and dressed in loose shorts and a t-shirt, he exited the bedroom to find that Denzel had been joined by Jasper and Andrei. Stopping in the doorway, he held up his hands.

"Is this some kind of intervention?"

"What?" Denzel waved a hand at him. "Man, quit playin'. This isn't an intervention. I heard through the grapevine that the ladies were having a breakfast/brunch for Alyssa and I thought we could do something similar—without the froo-froo drinks though."

"Speak for yourself. I like a good mimosa." Jasper chimed in.

Andrei remained mute as he sipped from a coffee mug that Carver was certain hadn't been in his suite earlier. Their group dropped into an easy conversation no one really discussing the wedding or any nuptial related topics. Of course, Jasper and Denzel were happy talking about football.

While Andrei could hold his own in a discussion about the game, his sport was hockey. So, he was only interested enough in football to discuss odds when it came to placing bets at his casino. They didn't handle much in the way of sports book, but he allowed it for clients at certain levels. It couldn't be said that Andrei left money on the table by sending his clients to another casino or an app to get their fix.

Carver tried to steer clear of too much in-depth discussion about football. Denzel was his friend, but he was also a sports journalist. A real one, not a talking head. It bordered on giving inside information, so Carver had to choose his words carefully. Because of that, he only allowed the conversation to linger there for a few minutes before moving on to another topic.

Before he knew it, an hour had passed and the butler was there to start getting them ready. Actually, it was more like a team. Denzel wasn't playing around. Men entered the suite carrying or pushing all the implements necessary to turn the outer area of Carver's room into a mobile barbershop.

While Carver was first in line, the other guys took advantage of one service or another. Even Carver's dad, and Alyssa's father, Melvin, showed up to have their hair and beards trimmed. The room was bustling with activity that didn't allow him much time to linger on thoughts of the upcoming ceremony. Which was good.

Carver wasn't nervous in the least. If anything, he was excited. Before the sun rose on them again, Alyssa would be his wife. He couldn't be happier if he tried. At one point, he opened the door leading to the terrace which wrapped around the villa. The sound of Alyssa's giggles drew him to the outside like a moth to the flame.

Before he reached the edge of the stone railing, his father was there turning him back into the suite.

"Where do you think you're going?"

"I just—"

"You just thought you'd get a quick peek. I know. I've been there." Tapping Carver between the shoulder blades, his father gave him a little push. "Come on back inside. You can venture out again when the temptation is gone."

His dad was so right. Carver had been on his way to look over the railing hoping to catch a glimpse of Alyssa. Grinning ruefully, he appreciated at least getting to hear her laughter. It let him know she was in good spirits and hopefully looking forward to the time for them to meet under the arch and be joined together as husband and wife.

Wife. In less than eight hours, Alyssa would be his wife. That fleeting thought had him stumbling. Reaching out, he tried to grab ahold of something to steady himself. Instead of the wall, he wrapped his fingers around Andrei's forearm.

In his normal stoic fashion, the Russian simply looked at him. He didn't even adjust himself to accommodate for the additional weight Carver placed on him. *Big fucker.* Not Jasper or Bama Boy big, but taller and broader than Carver. Which was saying something, since Carver was six foot four inches tall, and well over two hundred pounds.

"Whoa there, son." Carver's dad caught his other arm to help steady him. The activity in the room came to a halt and a sudden silence dropped over the space.

Melvin's brow furrowed in concern as he approached Carver. "Is everything okay?"

Carver's father led him to the couch where he dropped heavily into one corner. "It's fine. A proverbial anvil just dropped on my boy's head." His hand squeezed Carver's left shoulder.

Although Carver didn't immediately understand, Melvin Ripley's face stretched into a wide smile.

"Oh... Reality finally hit him huh? He's about to be a husband *and* a father." Slapping Carver's other shoulder, he offered his own comforting squeeze. "Yep. That'll knock a man on his ass every time."

Carver stood under the floral archway with Denzel on his left and the minister on his right. The small grouping of seats on either side of the rose petal covered aisle were filled with his and Alyssa's loved ones. Zaria had just entered to music Carver would be hard pressed to name, as his entire focus was on the French doors. Behind those doors was the woman to which he was to pledge his life.

He'd essentially already done that, but this would be his public declaration of that pledge. Carver couldn't see Alyssa, but he knew she was there. After escorting Alyssa's mother to her seat, her father had gone through the doors just moments before. Carver knew, the next time they swung open, his bride would step over the threshold.

The day was balmy without being oppressively hot. The light breeze allowed the tuxedo he sported to breathe, keeping Carver from sweating bullets. Behind him, he heard the gentle lapping of the infinity pool. It was a good thing they had a tiny wedding party.

Past the seats, the aisle narrowed, extending just above the edge of the infinity pool. It widened at a platform only large enough to house the arch, a short podium and the five people set to occupy the space. Carver inhaled the scent of the fresh flowers adorning the podium and arch.

The smell seemed to calm his anxious energy. He was ready for Alyssa to stand next to him. He wanted to feel her hands in his to make this moment even more real for him. Seeing the pretty decorations adorning the backs of the chairs, the floral bounty or even the faces of their family and friends couldn't do that. Only having Alyssa at his side could solidify the moment.

The music faded and the first chord of the *Chill Babies* version of the Shania Twain hit, *From This Moment*, floated into the air. The French doors opened into the villa drawing Carver's eyes. His rapt attention triggered the guests as everyone turned to see Alyssa and her father framed in the doorway.

Carver's breath caught in his throat as his eyes devoured every inch of his love. Her skin seemed to glow against the colors of her dress. The flowing material started as white at the waist, but had an ombré effect going from white to lavender, ending in a darker purple at the hem. Lighter shades of flowers were embroidered at the bottom giving it the appearance that she was walking through a field of the lovely blooms. The bodice was sheer across the shoulders and at the very center. While more embroidered flowers concealed her breasts, the see-through effect between them, yielded a very nice view of her cleavage.

For once, lascivious thoughts weren't at the forefront of his mind. They were there. They simply weren't first. When he finally remembered to breathe, the exhale which followed the deep inhale was accompanied by a sheen of tears welling in his eyes. His complete and total focus was on his future slowly coming closer to him. Once the wetness fell onto his cheeks, it fell unchecked.

His gaze locked on hers as she seemed to float down the aisle. Her dark amber eyes were glossy with moisture as well. Once she stood before him, he couldn't stop himself from reaching out to touch her. The minister loudly cleared his throat.

"We're not quite there yet, son."

Gliding his fingers along Alyssa's silky soft skin, Carver reluctantly broke contact. Looking at the man with what was assuredly not a polite expression, Carver silently urged him to get on with the ceremony. Taking the unspoken cue, the minister delivered his opening lines.

Carver listened just enough to respond when necessary. He keyed in on the words, "Who gives this woman to be joined with this man?"

The moment Alyssa's father said, "I do" Carver had Alyssa's hand in his pulling her closer while her father went to sit next to her mother. With a strength he didn't know he possessed, he managed to not kiss her —despite how delectable her lips looked with the glossy lip color. He didn't kiss her, but that was where he drew the line.

Cupping one side of her face, he devoured her with his gaze. "You look so beautiful, Bit-baby."

Alyssa blushed prettily under his compliment. Pulling a handkerchief from the beaded pouch dangling from her wrist, she dabbed at the wetness on his face.

"Thank you." Her naturally long lashes framed her eyes. Staring at him, she returned the compliment. "I knew this tux would look amazing on you."

"I know something else that looks amazing on me." Carver smirked.

Alyssa's jaw dropped and she whisper-hissed. "Carver! Behave."

Gifting her with a broad grin, Carver stroked her nape with his fingertips. "I am behavin', Baby."

Coughing into his fist, the minister got their attention to continue the ceremony. While they'd opted for the exchange of rings to be done with traditional vows, they also chose to have a moment where they each spoke their own vows to one another. As Carver stared into Alyssa's face, the words he'd practiced flew from his mind. Instead, he clasped Alyssa's hands in his and allowed his heart to speak in the moment.

"Alyssa Renee Ripley. Bit. My Bit. From the moment we met, I knew that you would be important in my life. With each interaction, that feeling grew. The night I proposed to you, I told you that you're my beginning, my foundation and that remains true. There isn't a time that I don't want you beside me. As my partner. My forever teammate.

I love you beyond measure. I look forward to spending my life loving you and being loved by you. Being blessed with the opportunity to be your husband, I promise to protect you and our children to my last breath. There will never be a time when you will question my love and devotion to you and our marriage. You have entrusted me with the gift of your love and I will not squander it."

Squeezing his fingers, Alyssa gave him a watery smile. "Carver Wyatt Jamieson...you are *a lot*. And I love that about you. You love fiercely and protect ferociously. I have never felt more loved and cherished than I do when I'm with you. Even when I was young and naïve, I knew you were a safe place for me.

With you, my heart is protected and I'm free to be myself completely. It is my hope and promise that I can and will be all of those same things for you. *You* have entrusted *me* with your heart and I pledge to shelter and nurture your gift until my last breath."

When the last word left her lips, Carver couldn't hold himself back any longer. The minister hadn't extended his final blessing, but Carver gathered Alyssa close, capturing her lips in a searing kiss. Eventually the clapping, whoops and whistles from their small assembly of guests, penetrated their bubble.

Pulling away from Alyssa delivering parting pecks, Carver finally turned back to the minister. The older man simply shook his head and smiled indulgently before finishing the ceremony with his blessing.

"And *now* you may kiss your bride."

Ignoring the sarcasm from the clergyman, Carver cupped Alyssa's face in both hands and brought their lips together again—officially sealing their bond as husband and wife. Her fingers latched onto the lapels of his suit holding him and showing her desire to continue matched his own. Reluctantly, they separated. Standing side by side with their hands joined, they faced their family and friends.

With his arms raised the minister announced, "I present to you Mr. and Mrs. Carver Wyatt Jamieson."

Carver's cheeks hurt from the wide smile he couldn't wipe off of his face. His gaze sought out his parents. His father had one arm wrapped around his mother's shoulders hugging her close to his side. His mother dabbed at tears. Both wore identical expressions of pride.

Shifting his attention to the other side of the aisle, Carver looked at Alyssa's parents. Similarly, her father had his arm around Alyssa's mother and her mother was patting at tears. Locking eyes with Melvin Ripley, his new father-in-law, Carver received the message in the other man's nod.

He was now fully entrusting Carver with his daughter and Carver accepted it wholeheartedly. Slipping an arm around Alyssa's waist, he guided her back down the aisle.

The metaphor, of the end of the aisle being the beginning of their life as husband and wife, wasn't lost on him. He fully embraced it. This moment eclipsed all other important moments in his life. Even the night he was selected as the number one draft pick couldn't compare to knowing he'd get to spend the rest of his life with Alyssa.

Sneak Peek

DRAFT PICK SEASON II: ANDREI

Beeping brought Andrei Antonov out of dreamland. It was one helluva dream, but the compact plush body of the women in the dream was better in reality. Blindly reaching out with one arm, he picked up the cellphone making the offensive noise, robotically swiping the screen to end it.

Once the noise was silenced, he put the phone down and rolled to his left. Empty space greeted him. Where there should've been a bronze-skinned beauty, there was nothing but the stark white of his sheets. *Where the fuck was she?*

"Svet!" He called out hoping she was simply in the other room. "Zoyra!" His Russian accent thicker than usual as he tried again.

Sitting up in the bed, he listened for sounds in the suite. *Nothing.* The previous night, he'd been too eager to make the drive to his home. So, he'd brought her to his private suite above his casino. The floor was littered with the evidence of the multiple rounds of mind-blowing sex the two had engaged in.

For Andrei to admit, even to himself, that a sexual experience blew his mind, was a feat within itself. His years as a star hockey player, from his time as an Olympic athlete to his time as a professional, he'd had too many partners to count. But none of them had anywhere close to the level of impact that Zaria Coleman had on him. Not one.

He'd planned to start his day between her thick thighs. Andrei needed another taste of her honey before he wrapped up his business to allow him to hop a plane to fly halfway around the world to attend his friend's wedding.

But, Zaria ruined that plan by not being where she was supposed to be. Only the faint scent of her perfume remained. *Who did she think she was?* No one ghosts Andrei Artyom Antonov. Whipping the sheet away from his body, he got out of bed and stalked into the bathroom. Just wait until he saw the little escape artist again.

Fuming, he turned on the shower and set about getting his day going. Not starting it balls deep in Zaria's pussy wasn't something he let go of easily. He was gonna spank her ass for her disappearing act. A sinister smile stretched his lips as he thought of how great the rounded globes were going to look with his handprint on them.

His shaft hardened between his thighs drawing another curse. Adding this to her list of infractions, Andrei took his length in his hand. Closing his eyes he pictured Zaria's plump lips, imagining them stretched wide to accommodate his girth. She was definitely going to pay for him having to relieve himself.

Acknowledgments

The journey involved in bringing Carver and Alyssa to the page involved spontaneous inspiration coupled with a hefty nudge from Author Cereza. She encouraged me to try the serial platform for publishing. I released the first five episodes of Draft Pick in July of 2022, and the rest is history. I eternally grateful for that nudge and to all of the readers and authors who supported me throughout the process. My loyal Draft Pick readers gave, and continue to give, me life with their feedback and analysis of each episode. Thank you ladies.

About the Author

Darie McCoy is an independent author of contemporary, interracial, romantic suspense, and paranormal/shifter romance books. A reader first, she enjoys reading books across many genres although romance holds a special place in her heart. Her experience working in a STEM field offers her a unique perspective which she uses in each story she pens.

When she doesn't have her nose in a book or her fingers on the keyboard, Darie enjoys working in her vegetable garden. A serial hobbyist, she also enjoys knitting, sewing, baking and canning. One of her favorite treats to make is salted caramel popcorn. Amongst her friends, she's known to transport the sweet treat in large quantities to share whenever they get together.

Born and raised in the south, Darie stands by the staunchly held southern sentiments that the best tea is sweet tea and college football is life.

Also by Darie McCoy

Central Valley Pack Series

Chosen

Healed

Frost Family Series

For Real

Sano's Queen (A Novella)

Christmas Candy

Other books/stories

Involuntary

Draft Pick Season II: Andrei

Just Kiss Me (Part of Cupid's Kiss Anthology)